I0690617

THE COLLECTED WORKS OF SID GERSHGOREN

Sid Gershgoren

The Twenty-fifth Catalog of Past Rentals:

A Selection of Historical Journeys
from the Paleolithic to the Year 2000

THE COLLECTED WORKS OF SID GERSHGOREN:
VOLUME ONE

Red Dragonfly Press

ISBN 978-1-945063-26-8 paper

Library of Congress Control Number: 2018963930

Second Edition

Designed and typeset at by Scott King at Red Dragonfly Press
using Warnock Pro digital type and Quadraat Sans OT

Printed in the United States of America

Published by Red Dragonfly Press
P. O. Box 98
Northfield, MN 55057

For more information and additional titles visit our website
www.reddragonflypress.org

Introduction

¶ Past Rentals is an organization devoted to bringing to its customers the largest and most insightful selection of historical journeys available today. To that aim our staff has spent the last twenty-five years developing a comprehensive list of representative historical life events, which are unmatched by any other company in the historical travel field.

Historians, anthropologists, sociologists, botanists, poets, musicologists, electricians, numismatists, philosophers, epidemiologists, and others from disparate fields of endeavor (the list is, indeed, immense) have come together to make history more than statistical exercise, an account of kings and battles, or a ground for argument. For us, history is a living, biological endeavor, an action and an event which puts our customers more than in the middle of things; through their own identification with history, they, themselves, become both observers and participants.

We believe that history exists at the intersection of the personal and the transcendental, the immediate moment of time and the infinite space surrounding events. We want our clients to know history from the inside, not to create grand theories (projections only of desire) but to make existence a fact. Without the lighthouse beacon of these journeys, history remains a dark sea on which we are traveling. Without that experience of our "being history," our lives of people inside us remain an abstraction, looked at only through the ivory tower lens built into the eyes of the ivory tower historian. We believe in a participational history. We believe that what our customers experience in their journeys echoes in their lives today. The experience of the past and its moment of departure, the present, both produce the reverberation of historical reality, never distorting, but enlarging the present into the future.

Therefore, our compilations have been planned as explorations. We know that the sum of all our catalogs and the sum of all possible catalogs will never complete us. But in each journey, in each event among infinities of events, the traveler glimpses the shifting shape of the whole, which, through his entrance, becomes a decipherable message imminent with meaning. Signs, suggestions, values, indications, continuities, prefigurations, shapings and siftings, textures, tendencies, trepidations, ambiguities, geologic upheavals and sedimentary deposits, and more—all are found in the event itself, for each journey partakes of the nature of everything.

We offer, then, historical journeys, not only tourist events of a high order, but also revelations. Our clients may enter the life of an infant in 9th century BC Burma (somewhere near Rangoon), a peasant in southern Afghanistan in the 13th century, a shoemaker in 8th century BC Egypt, a spy in 16th century France. We offer trips as specific individuals in specific situations for specific lengths of time. And we offer them at prices which most can afford. And, finally, we offer a special youth program for those below the age of eighteen.

We shun the historically famous. No, we do not want our customers to appear as Napoleon or Isaac Newton or Albert Einstein. We leave these journeys to lesser catalogs. Rather, we have always chosen ordinary, representative people who reflect those universal feelings, attitudes, desires, thoughts, manipulations, ambiguities, etc. which flow into the river of humanity. In short, we do not extract humanity from the mass, but immerse our customers in the mass movements of humanity in order that they may be melted down, to merge with the universal waters of the human. As Eugene Debs, the socialist candidate for President, once said, "I do not want to rise from the lower classes, I want to rise with them."

Our staff has looked everywhere for this representative material. Like dictionary makers, they have tirelessly catalogued the known events, the particulars of speech and action of whole populations, the reverberations of thought, the psychological underpinnings of action and inaction, the projections of desire, the migrations of peoples and their thoughts and artifacts, the speed at which history is transmitted, as virus or antibody within the river of time. They have recorded, analyzed, integrated, coordinated, synthesized, re-figured and prefigured all possible definitions, parameters, overtones, scenarios, permutations, repercussions, game plans, projections and/or resultants of possible actions (and/or inactions), mutations, time management studies, newspaper accounts, rumors, and other analyses too numerous to mention. And among the multitudinous mountains of information available to them, they have placed the client in a truly representative situation in both space and time.

Because our staff has had enormous help beyond its limited capabilities during these past twenty-five years of our existence and because our clientele has increased a hundred-fold (perhaps by an even greater magnitude), the level of the definition of our projects, the scales of possibilities within them, and their resonances, both within each catalog and within the total of all catalogs and also within the larger world in which our products have meaning have reached levels of insight which the original compilers could not even dream of, let alone present to their public.

We have had help, yes, and especially from our clients, for they have suggested far more avenues of exploration than our staff has produced. Each journey presents opportunities to expand the limits of possibility for us all. Since it is guided by specific goals—by the net of the human, that is—we are not surprised to find reactions which hit the mark. Our compilers, after they have established the personal nature of an entry, return to the data, where these personal possibilities can then be merged with the information banks.

Fortunately, the incentives come from within. Our clients

are not paid for their suggestions, but neither is Past Rentals an organization created to make a profit. Only through an absence of profit incentives can we hope to maintain a fruitful relationship between staff and clients.

This, the twenty-fifth edition of our catalog, provides us with an opportunity to open up for our readers and customers selections from previous catalogs, items long called for but which we had neither time nor space to re-offer, the demands of other entries having taken precedence over these older items. Here we have also introduced a hitherto neglected area of history, the paleolithic, which, we have always felt, deserved far more attention than it has received. We intend, in future catalogs, to continue our explorations of this vast subject.

Our offer to our clients comes with the following guarantee, one unmatched by any other business and yet one which has seldom been taken advantage of, proof, we find, that our customers have, in some way, known or unknown to us, been truly, historically, and personally fulfilled. We say this: That if you are not satisfied in any way, you may apply for a refund with no questions asked.

We also guarantee the safety of each journey. This sounds more difficult to provide than it seems. The client, appearing at one of our many way stations, is given a mild hypocanthus penetrator as a psychic relaxant. The one we are presently using is similar to, but more effective than, the Reynolds Hypodrive, which, although it functioned well in most instances, still left a few travelers with a slight afterimage of amnesia. Also, we have improved on the clarity of breakdown of the subconscious membrane, a dissolution necessary to actively propel the client into the period of history and situation which he has chosen.

The participant then enters the body of the historical personage, only as a guest, of course, being removed by his own will from any pain he does not wish to feel. Yet for the time allotted him, he is capable of entering into and experiencing any feelings of the person whose body he is inhabiting. (We draw the line at death itself, however.) In short, clients may or may not experience the pain or joy or ambiguity or helplessness or any other feeling of the person they become—it is their choice, their responsibility how far they enter. The responsibility firmly shifts to the client.

We give our clients material to read before their transportation as well as expose them to brief psychic playbacks, which serve to orient them to the period and situation they are to encounter. Their entry, at all costs, must not be sudden or harsh. They must know what they are getting into (perhaps in the root meaning of that phrase). For example, if a client chooses the North African entry from 1403, he must learn what possibilities exist in North Africa at that point in history. Of course, we cannot teach him everything, but in our twenty-five years of preparing customers for their journeys, few clients have complained of being shocked. At present, we are experimenting with several new chemical substances, which will allow the previewing to proceed even more smoothly.

History, as we now conceive of it, can have no beginning and no end. It is lost in what the German novelist Thomas Mann called "the deep well of the past," how deep we will never know. Our attempts to scan it beyond those dim moments of the early Paleolithic have not been successful. Except for certain archeological artifacts, we have been left with nothing, as it should be, in fact, because there must be a place somewhere at which all material representations of humans vanish and from which all artifacts from that moment on begin to appear, more and more. That is the nature of history.

If history fades out at some point in the past, Past Rentals Incorporated, however, does have a history and a moment of origin, one which has clearly colored the world around it and sounded itself within the historical record. And it is important to understand that its genesis and development are themselves a product of history, for context expands both perception and identity, even in so successful an enterprise as this one has become.

On May 1, 1966 at 11:49 p.m. exactly, the insertion of two historical articles appeared suddenly in the evening edition of the New York Times. The articles were similar but not identical. They had as their basis an account of two unseemly yet unavoidable events—one, the landing of Polynesians on what is now the island of Hawaii in 902 AD and the other, the uncovering and subsequent deification of the skull of Ulysses in the southern part of Bulgaria (also called Thrace). Both articles used almost the same language and phraseology, identical assumptions and historical guidelines, personages, and time projections. The reader, glancing at either, might read both as one historical event rather than as two separate accounts, a kind of "cross-eyed déjá vu," as one historian called it.

Struck by the similarities and differences between the two articles, commentators called up Heisenberg's Principle of Indeterminacy, which states that an object observed in space and time may only be completely and accurately placed in either space or time but not in both, or may be partially placed in both. These two articles, printed side by side, had within them a meaning which could only be seen through one or the other but not through both, for one completed the other (it was demonstrated the following week) and, like Siamese twins could not exist without the other.

Never had this happened before, but it was to happen again and again in the pages of Past Rentals, founded fourteen weeks, two days and ten hours after the articles appeared.

Although we may argue over whether history (as some have suggested) has within it any sense of progress, either moving toward greater or lesser integration, toward or away from more satisfied perceptions of the world as part of each individual perceiver or in any other way; there can be no doubt that the history of Past Rentals as a contained and unified and self-conscious movement has progressed, but not as many would imagine such a progression. We have moved forward through deepening the understanding of us all, as we fall into one another's lives, through echoing the real, unspoken needs of our customers (and especially those who are not).

From the beginning, we have had no intention of becoming a travel agency or anything resembling that nefarious, low order of activity. We do not advertise, except through our catalogs themselves, and almost all of our business has come through word of mouth, that singularly and collectively personal communication that grounds society in the immediate. In fact, an immense number of our catalog entries have, as we have already stated, been suggested by others outside our organization.

By progress, we mean providing a deepening sense of what our existence as a human being actually and tangibly means. Our catalog, from its first issue in fact, has had as its aim the presentation of a montage of humanity—its perceptions, joys, disgusts, tragedies, meldings, whimsical moments, hard work, fevers, fanaticisms, fears, dramatic gestures, long and short term journeys, pride, larceny, doubts, cupidity, transcendent insights, emergences from communities or mergings into them, discoveries, conspiracies, moments of reflection, temper tantrums, logical progressions, temporary explosions of awe or tenderness, rhapsodies, dark nights of the soul, compensations, manageable and unmanageable joys and fallings out, confrontations with the unknown, clashes of personalities, loves, and hates. The list goes on, as it must. But it is a list of our qualities, the things that make us human and which provide a texture of our history against a background of changing situations, climates, psychologies, etc.

We have asked ourselves with regard to history what we as an organized resource provide for everyone and what we can suggest we are at every instant as grounded perceivers. How can we answer the questions, What are we, where are we, who are we, when are we, and why are we? We are, first of all, lost. And in that condition we must reach out to complete ourselves, to place our lives within greater and greater circles of identity. Walt Whitman, the great, expansive, bearded bard of America (and bard beyond America), relating the "noiseless, patient spider" to his soul (and our souls, as well) in his and our abilities to reach out and grasp the world in order to achieve a sense of identity beyond the impersonal and yet include it, says to himself and to us,

> And you, O my Soul, where you stand,
> Surrounded, detached, in measureless oceans of space

And concludes this expansion and attachment:

> Till the gossamer thread catch somewhere,
> O, my soul.

This is the reach for identity which all our customers, all who have entered the journeys we provide, have yearned for, whether or not they are consciously aware of their desires.

This reaching out for identity also occurs in a far larger and more fundamental context, one which all the journeys we have offered have as their permanent landscape. One important example from biology should focus our attention, providing history with its larger context. The simple prokaryotic cells, which had existed for two-thirds of the history of all life on our planet, may have merged to form the first eukaryotic cells, cells from which we and other multicellular animals have descended. And we, in our social groupings, ideas, nations, and societies, have also gone beyond the individual self to find the others, to reach out into deeper mergings. For it is so small an existence to remain painted into a corner of the self for fear of journeying beyond the family, the neighborhood, the world. We expand through recognition by journeying toward our past and, perhaps, even toward what we call our future. We reach not just toward our own kind, though we indeed start from there. We also extend ourselves into the animal and vegetable and mineral kingdoms and beyond them to areas of existence we can only imagine, points of identity that will, when we find them, truly surprise us.

And, as some have seen, our progress is really no progress. We have reached out to those who have called us over the unmeasurable ages and shaken hands with history, with our former selves, for our bodies extend not only in space but also in time. Events of the past, with their tones and overtones, ring through space, to sound within us, calling us all to listen with more than only our ears. That is our progress if there is progress, a greater and greater listening, on all levels, to what we have been and to what we are, intensifying the rainbow of possible phenomena. It can be said that toward this aim and this aim only we have "progressed".

We have learned a great deal from our explorations and much more from our clients and others, who have contributed themselves to these entries. And we have learned much (how much we are still discovering) from the 1978 Consortium of Historical Evaluations, which at that time so generously and completely reviewed the first ten issues of our catalog. This loose grouping of organizations provided us with our first long distance glimpse of ourselves—our productions, our successes and our failures. The Association for the Abolition of Power (AAP), Growth Anonymous, United Meditators of North America (UMNA), Builders Beyond Infinity, Mathematicians for Unlimited Insight, Marginal Knowledge For the Millions, Inc., The Society for the Preservation of Everything (SOPE), Help Unwanted, Spoilers without Guilt, The Magnificent Aunts and Uncles of Greater America (MAUGA), The Society for the Abolishment of Language, The Society for the Creation of Water and Air, Clear Sight, Friends of the Dead—all came together for this truly monumental task.

Also, among and within this amalgam of organizations, a few historical testifiers, forced to join some organization, formed one among themselves, one which included only those whose principles denied them membership to any group. They called themselves UNGROU and were a great help in commenting on the powerful role of the marginal in history, a force not easy to reckon with but one which has played an overwhelming part in that overwhelmingly odd integration of the unknown.

Fortunately, the delegates from each organization numbered no more than six. Each participant selected twenty-five items and proceeded to investigate them thoroughly. Entries were selected at random, and each entry was entered into by more than one person. Investigators could compare journeys, reach conclusions, extend the scope of encounters, and notice gaps and pitfalls when and if they occurred.

The reviewing process lasted eighteen months, not much time, considering how much had to be accomplished. But when the process was completed, the participants quickly presented their findings.

We at Past Rentals did not sit patiently waiting for what would be the extensive conclusions of the Consortium. We had work to do, another catalog to prepare. We were hard at work on the many suggestions we had received, programming, investigating, gathering materials, questioning everything within and outside of the data banks, projecting the inputs and outcomes, balancing entries, reacting to specific and even unspecific ideas and suggestions, coordinating, consolidating, and deepening our own goals.

Therefore, when the findings (ten volumes of them) were first made known to the public (several copies were sent to our offices on publication), we were caught by surprise. We knew that release of the document was indeed imminent, but we did not expect the results to be thrust on us without warning. But they were and, of course, we accepted them as such.

We could not stop our work on the new catalog, but we did manage to find time to read at least a summary of the report, and a lengthy one at that. Each member of the Past Rentals committee read it three times. It was necessary to absorb not only the ideas, the recommendations, and the criticisms, but also to look beneath our own assumptions, clear away unwanted mental matter, organize ourselves in other directions and reduce our work-a-day worlds to the inertia of leisure in order to allow that analytical and critical world to enter. It took us six months to do this, and, we must say, we were up to the task.

Most important for us, the writers of the report were extremely excited by the whole experience; they were, they did not hesitate to state, favorably impressed. But, reading through "the pores of the world," as they began their preface, they felt that "true, deep, significant, immediately perceived comment" would be more than necessary, would be, in fact, imperative.

The report began by criticizing some of the catalog items, though the ones the writers felt should have been eliminated were few and those which should have been improved were less than we had expected. (Specifics as to how to improve questionable entries were appended to each entry.) Items 4, 58, 92, 137, and 188 were considered unworkable because they partook too much of pure journeys and had no overlying human value. Items 6, 14, 42, and 197 had "inconsistencies, which might tend to produce minor mental and emotional vibrations of an unknown sort". Entries 17, 99, 102, and 208 were limited because they did not contain "a deep core of universal, physical force". They did not, as the report asserted, "arrive at the core of meaning as it is manifested in the here and now".

But the consortium singled out many entries which, they felt, they were constrained to praise and praise thoughtfully. Entries 2, 93, 111, and 212 were among those chosen to receive detailed comments. We present only one of these, number 93. Anyone may consult the rest of the above by reading the analyses. The entry is as follows:

No. 93: Krems, Austria, March 3, 1164. [8 months; $950] You are a fanatic priest leading others to revolt against the established order of things in ninth century Austria. Your sexual and intellectual powers have outgrown the container in which they have been forced by the world of your time. You see and feel too much, and your compulsion to lead a revolt against what you consider iniquities is as much a part of your frustration as it is a measure of actual conditions.

You construct an elaborate theory of the coming of the Messiah and spread it throughout your parish and beyond. It kindles the discontent of the peasants, who have suffered enough, and spreads quickly over the whole region, making you, as you know, a dangerous outlaw, a heretic who will, when caught (you have no doubt you will be caught), undergo the most dire punishment. But you proceed anyway, knowing it is your fate.

You are driven. Yet in the force that compels you there is great truth, and you cherish that truth and the friendships you have made. For the first time in your life you find compassion of cosmic proportions in the people who surround you, and yet you refrain from allowing them to prostrate themselves before you, to obtain relics of your life, or to call you their savior. Rather, you exhort them to call themselves saviors, to find salvation in themselves and dignity in their labor.

COMMENTARY: This entry contains both a spiritual and a psychological dimension, a yearning on the part of the principle entrant and a resultant surprise which is, happily, known from the beginning. There is also opportunity for growth through time, as well as a latent but still unconscious dissatisfaction in the nature of the social reality of mid-twelfth century life in Austria, as well as in many other places at that time and at other times, which provides a more universal dimension to the entry. On the personal level, the entrant has the potentiality to grow within and beyond himself as a representative entity, transcending the conditions under which he was raised and, as a representative of his and our times, reach out to all of us who find dissatisfaction with both the social and the personal worlds, a factor which propels us into a knowledge of ourselves. Thus, with the aims and philosophy of this organization, the personal merges with the historical and enters the universal. The entry also has a clearly potential esthetic line, reminiscent of the Shakespearean tragic flaw. (See Shakespeare's Hamlet: . . .Blessed are they/ whose blood and judgment are so well commingled/That they are not a pipe for fortune's fingers/To play what stops she pleases.) There is, indeed, esthetic tension between the personal and the social worlds and at the same time a universal setting, which allows the entry to be applied everywhere. The letter which follows (we have read it, also) extends the implications, though we feel it might have gone much further in its exploration. All in all, this is a most satisfactory example of the purposes toward which Past Rentals, Inc. has moved. We recommend it highly.

We were pleased with this response—no doubt of it. It had validated more than ten years of work; it had awakened a touchstone which, we felt, had been there from the beginning. The singling out of this entry had roused us again to purpose and direction. It had shown us, moreover, that the merging of the personal and the historical provided the key to everything.

We have, of course, made errors, and sometimes serious ones. But we have kept to our purpose, failing only, at times, in insight.

Our last three catalogs and the present one, our 25th, have moved further into the spectrum of human desire while maintaining the universal within the particular. We have included more material from the Paleolithic era, and we intend to include more in future catalogs; its overall importance is so great we cannot ignore it. We feel that it is here, in this vast and open period, that our species had come closer to its sense of self and seen most deeply its integration with the world. It is the most "hopeful" period of all, if we can accept the idea that the best ratio of happiness is one which comes closest to maximizing the relation of what can be had to what one wants. We refer the reader to the various catalog entries of this period.

We at Past Rentals have always wished our clients more than a pleasant journey, for we know that journeys, to be significant, must be more than a release or an escape. They must both contain and integrate the basic elements of our existence, within the present and throughout all time. Our clients have achieved something when they have learned how it is to be human (within the context of an even wider history) and how it feels to identify those experiences with their contemporary lives at this moment in time. We hope to bring our clients as many significant historical entries as possible.

Before wishing everyone a significant journey, we announce a new and, we hope, important publication, an anthology of what we consider the best of Past Rentals. We caution our clients to consider that this publication is only our idea of what is best, since it may not be theirs. However, as always, we await your responses.

ENTRIES

No. 1: Ardabil, Persia. March 3, 1558. [9 years; $8,500] You were a young man in northern Persia, on the verge of marriage, who had been a witness to the abduction of your young fiancé by a roving band of Persian soldiers, who had periodically made incursions into your lands but until now had avoided your mountain homestead. Then, eleven years after that wrenching event, you began your wanderings, first as an itinerant scribe with an acquired knowledge of several languages and then as an apprenticed toolmaker. Finally, after several years of acquiring the skills necessary in various departments of knowledge, including such matters as poetry, music, hunting, boat building and a scattering of biological science, you pushed on, wandering erratically, looking for something on the edge of your mind's touch, and vaguely, sometimes familiarly noticing a warm echo as if you had begun to find what you were looking for, and then losing the scent, but still persisting, settling down for a while in city after city, and sometimes in the small villages, for a deliberately short while, briefly making friends, observing the ways of the people and only adopting them sparingly and sometimes for only a short time, always moving, in circles in your mind, around and around some unknown center, and in a crazy, lazy fashion in your body, dreaming through the streets and over the mountain trails, collecting what never was yours though you had known you had dreamed it somewhere sometime, through your wandering, which felt to you like an unraveling of your life, leaving only a thin thread behind, and then, suddenly, one day, noticing the scent grow distinctly warmer, feeling it glow in your bones, the bones of a hunter too long after his prey, and settling down there, in that middle-sized city of a roving, destitute commerce, to wait, to feel your way through the motions and turnings of the population, sensing it stronger, as if you had been in this city in another lifetime, under another body, knocking at the doors that other people held out in their faces toward you and reading what they spoke out of their bodies, as if the key to all your turnings were there, invisible, in the air between you; and in the morning, one morning when the sun stuck fast to the white walls of a small house built into an unguarded corner of the city, hearing a singing voice which warmed you and yet left a shiver, like a cold ghost inside all of your filled yet empty body, a voice singing a melody you did not understand, in a language you had only vaguely remembered, but not in another lifetime, in this one, in time which stretched back before you, the notes growing fuller and purer, as the sun fastened itself to the house, pulling you toward its walls to listen, in a suspended curiosity of loss, to the voice which plaintively sang on and on, as if to the distant sunset, which would remove the light and reveal her, voice and all, for the time called night, day after day returning to that voice which made even the light shiver in its spineless body, and finally seeing her one day, a clear day in fall when the light was at its purest but had not fallen away from itself, the woman singing there alone in the courtyard as you watched her through the half-opened door, rapt in amazement, with tears streaming through your eyes, your whole body repeating to itself in all its wanderings, "My love, my love, my love!"

No. 2: Alexandria, Egypt. November 28, 125 B.C. [1 week; $500] You are a librarian at the great library before it was finally destroyed by fire in the 4th century, being surrounded by walls, words, books, pages, languages of all kinds, in your cramped spaces, where you huddle, reading, entombed by manuscripts of mostly vellum and papyrus from Lower Egypt, Mesopotamia, the Indus Valley, Ethiopia, and regions whose languages you nor your colleagues can understand, reading through rich, powerful shafts of sunlight through the hours of the day, and in the evening, wandering the narrow streets of the city attached to your institution, watching the shadows flicker in the lamps, the people prepare their breads, their meats, and their heavy wines, and stopping to talk to one person or another with the glad chance of breathing again, being outside of the compressed thought you had followed so laboriously all day, and then wandering to the river, the river of rivers, whom all knew as the river of their blood and breath, to watch in remembrance the already fallen sun and the stars emerge from the growing darkness, one by one, leading you back again, each evening, to immensity.

No. 3: Paris, France. May 18, 1819. [13 hours; $150] As a concierge, you are a woman in charge of the large apartment building where you live. Though you know the great city of Paris, even in your dreams, you spend all your time in this one part of the compressed bundle of humanity, going back and forth to the market, cooking, imagining adventures which you will never have, listening to the complaints of the renters, the butcher, the street sweeper, falling asleep in your chair looking out the window at the street and the automatic acceptance of its noises, feeding the fire, and barely raising your three children, who spend their time roaming the neighborhood and other neighborhoods as far afield as possible, touching everything in order to know it intimately, peeling back mystery after mystery and returning home, bedraggled, night after night, to eat, sit at the fire silently while all their day falls into them like an immense, collapsing whirlpool, and then go to bed, to repeat the same thing for years, and you being neither center nor periphery of this thing which passes in front of you like a parade you watch from your room, a kind of amazed, half-asleep being let loose in a universe it did not completely absorb, drifting with the partially understood, partially chaotic events in the great soup of life, which you see often from the chair in front of the window which looks out at the moving wallpaper of the busy street.

No. 4: Limerick, Ireland. December 4, 1610. [6 years. $2,900] You were a soldier who had been sent with the Spanish Armada to invade England. In that foolish venture, almost all of your ships went down in the battle; but yours, escaping, sailed north, rounding the tip of Scotland and making fast, finally, in Ireland, where, impossible to return to Spain, you settled in that wild, green, Catholic country, married an Irish woman, and raised your sons and daughters to know that you (and they) were of both countries and cultures, carrying your fading accent with you as you carried the memories of your youth in Saragosa. Little by little, your children forgot your story and origin, merging into the Irish landscape, because Spain was never in sight and could hardly be kept in both mind and spirit under such conditions. You, only, retain the memory and bodily feelings which make you a Spaniard, a creature of that dry, barren flatland sliding into Africa.

No 5: Somewhere in the Kalahari Desert, Botswana. September, 14, 994. [2 months; $450] A young Bushman girl, slender, short, with powerful legs from walking through your whole life and "a smile that opens everyone it falls upon"—you wander through this desert you know so well, as do all the members of your little group, people who have, beyond love, bound themselves to each other and, as a result, bring back, without thinking of "yours" and "mine" (words you do not understand), everything they find and experience, songs, the footprints of animals, their hunger and fear as well, and the roots and edible plants and grains which you know so well how to find, walking continually ten or fifteen miles a day, lean, muscular, the other women as well, who are adaptive, all of you, intelligent in the broad way; and when you joke there is always someone beyond you, or some thing in which you live and have your being and thank it as you thank yourself for being a part of this world which is really indistinguishable from what you sometimes call the beyond. You are moving now through this now wet season, where game and edible plants are abundant, but another thought is in your mind, what your father said last night about the movement of the sky that pulls the stars along with it. At night in your dreams you felt you had heard the sky moving, listened to its music, like the sound of the earth rumbling, which you heard once as you woke. What is happening now, during the day? Has the night disappeared like the water in the dry season and along with it the animals, or has it remained, in your dreams, where you protect it, night and day?

You will talk to your father about these things that have come to you in your dreams and in your waking.

No. 6: Budapest, Hungary. February 5, 1699. [3 months; $300]
Though you are a printer who loves to read, you cannot afford to buy the books you print. But with other printers you know, you have worked out a system of barter and exchange among all of you in Budapest: You borrow each other's books, only for a week— that is the limit. You read late into the night, the books your only responsibility. There is no wife and no children. You live with an aunt in an extra small room for which you pay almost no rent. She also cooks for you, though you pay her for the food. You devour in a few days all the books you bring home, and sometimes your aunt, the Lady Kertesz she likes to call herself, will read them herself, and you will talk, late into the night, exploring one thing or another that is brought up in the course of your reading.

"But," she said one night, all the things you have told me, that we have talked about, have come from your books. And you, you, what do you think, how do you feel, where is your own heart?"

How her words later the next day jogged you. Your whole body, your heart and mind, felt as if they had been displaced, moved over only a few inches and were now not together. In this new arrangement of your life, the parts did not work in the same way. You now needed to bring them together, remember her words about your own heart, your own thoughts. You accumulated paper, scraps around the print shop, and began writing a diary, explaining what you had discovered in your own life, then deeply and feelingly pulling back, carefully at first, the cobwebs which you had been born with and which had protected you through all these years and the blended learning you had acquired along the way through your careful reading. This book, you know, will never be printed; it is only for you, for your own "flowering angel," the Lady Kertesz says. It is your "patient forest of words," the explanation of your own life.

No. 7: 1888. South Bend, Indiana, U.S.A. January 31, 1888. [One week; $200] You are a pig slaughterer. Each day, after a hard twelve hours of work, you smuggle home a bit of meat to feed your four-member family. All of you live in a small apartment, which leaks and which is owned by somebody who charges exorbitant rent and will not fix even the front door or the windows. But loving your wife and children so much, you heroically risk something important each day. Your wife stays at home gossiping with the neighbor women and discussing the times, the weather and politics, and cooks and cares for the children, who are happy to see you.

Having said hello for a short while to your son and daughter, who have been desperately expecting you all day, you wash and crawl into bed with your wife for a few moments of intimate, necessary bliss.

Dear Past Rentals,
  Do you know what a pig slaughterer does each day? I

was there with him, in him, for a week, and it was a hard, hard week of work in this hard, hard existence. And that's almost all I did work. Six hours would pass, and I'd still be cutting up pigs. The knife did the work; I didn't think. My body wasn't there, only the knife and the hand. It would go into a kind of trance. I'd be sleeping, and my arm, my hand, my knife would be awake. I could have done it in my sleep, except that one day I saw a guy ten feet from me cut off his left thumb because he dozed off. It took him a while to realize what he'd done. The thumb lay in the pig fat, bleeding, and his hand was bleeding all over the pork, all over even the blood of the pig. And this guy didn't even notice it for a while; he was asleep and still working. And this poor sucker just went back to work again, after he'd tied up his hand (minus the thumb) and stopped the bleeding. He couldn't help it. He knew he just had to keep on working. I knew then that I had to stay awake. I knew the whole thing was going to end, something these guys didn't know, couldn't know. I was the lucky one, thanks to Past Rentals, and I would like to thank you, even for this horrible experience, which has taught me a lot about how people suffered in the past and some people still suffer today.

I want to say one more thing about my journey. My wife and my children out here in South Bend, Indiana were incredible. Oh, it was a great joy to see them, even for that short time between when I got home and when I fell asleep. You couldn't believe how much life there was in my children when they saw me at night, how they'd stayed up just to see me. They couldn't let go. I had to pull them from me, really, pull them from me. Back home where I come from, in Portland, Oregon, my kids (the same ages, in fact), hardly want to talk to me when I'm home, except to ask me for something. God, what a difference! I'm shocked. Why should the kids of a pig slaughterer, who works twelve hours a day, feel such joy? And my wife, for those few minutes—we were hardly together half an hour each night—devoured me and I her. And then I sank into exhaustion, into a sleep farther and deeper than I've ever known before. I've never been that tired, and, to tell the truth, I've never felt what it is to have a body before, that is, to know how much the body means, how important it is. (I know now that I've taken it for granted.) Now, when I go to sleep (at least for the last few months), I feel that I'm going to something really foreign, and this trip, thanks to you, has been my passport to that world. Thanks again.

> Robert Williams,
> Age 28, bookkeeper.
> Portland Oregon

No. 8: Monterrey Coast, Northern California. February 5, 63. [3 hours; $75] You are a young girl, eight years old, a Chumash Indian living on the coast of Northern California. You have gone down to the sea today with your mother and several other women, a cold, foggy day it is, to gather mussels, baskets of them this February morning. Seals out on the rocks bark at themselves a long way off, and birds wander in and out of the surf, hunting and occasionally flying off in small flocks, only to return to another place on the shore to hunt and wander. You hear the gulls and the powerful sounds of waves echoing against the cliffs above you. You notice the small, twig-like footprints of the gulls and occasionally the tracks of deer that came down early to drink from the small stream before its water disappeared into the sea. Shells in abundance, and seaweed, great mounds of it, are dragged up on shore by the waves, then washed and cleaned and washed again, and over them you hear the buzz of enormous clouds of flies. Far out, the water is striking the high rocks where seals are calling to one another.

No. 9: Bolzano, Italy. May 16, 364. [3 weeks; $575] Here in the mountains of northern Italy you await the return of your blessed savior, Jesus Christ. He will come soon, amid light and joy and great sorrow and distress for the unfortunate, for has not the great book of John said that the 144,000 will be saved, that the four horsemen will appear to spread their sorrow over the earth, and that Rome, that mighty city, the citadel of the Anti-Christ, will fall under the weight of the sword of Jesus Christ? You look everywhere for the signs. Has not the emperor himself, Constantine the Christian, become one of you, and has he not made the religion of Jesus Christ the religion of the Empire? And have not earthquakes and great storms and even astounding visions appeared to many, and have they not foretold the final days? You find these signs everywhere, in a pigsty, in the sudden dropping of leaves, in the weather, in the crops from year to year, the rumbling of the crowds in Rome and in the other cities of the empire. Have you not, in seeing them, become a prophet yourself, an Isaiah of the times before the final days when all time shall vanish? More and more you see yourself as a visionary predictor of the coming Apocalypse. You preach to others wherever you can, telling them to repent, to open their hearts to Jesus Christ. And though they may laugh and spit in your face or even just walk away, you are daily more confirmed, yes, in the knowledge that He will come, and come soon, very soon. The signs are spread upon the world.

Dear Past Rentals,
   I must say that I've always wanted to become an early Christian martyr, but your catalog has not as yet offered such a choice. I was surprised to find your entry No. 9 which

is as close as you've yet come. Therefore, I took it and have come as close as I think I will come to being one until your catalog produces a genuine Christian martyr, a Saint Sebastian for example, which I hope you will soon offer; for, even after this trip, which I must admit was ecstatic, this coming entry, which I will await with great anticipation, will fulfill my deepest desires.

A Christian martyr is someone who suffers for the soul and spirit of Jesus Christ, who suffered for us all. In every Christian there is a deep desire to become the Christ, who suffered as we want to suffer to show that this earthly life is only a small journey to the eternal palace of our Lord, who showed us the way to His kingdom.

It was for lack of a Christian martyr entry that I became the man Paulerius Christus in Bolzano in northern Italy and took on me for three weeks the conversion of the heathen sinners, who were everywhere. The triumphant life of our savior, the conversion of the emperor Constantine himself, the many portents, signs, presaging his coming—all these made that era a time of wonders. It is not important that our Lord did not return, has not returned—yet. The wonders were there, the soul of the times was there. His spirit remained vibrating in the air around us, and we drank it, as we would drink our wine and eat our bread, his body and his blood. And therefore what did it matter we were spit on, kicked and reviled for our attempts to present the blessed miracle of his birth and death and his ascension to heaven? They, the others, the heathens, were the sufferers. And though we tasted the pains of the flesh, placing our bodies into the torments of this world, denying the flesh so the spirit might rise, we also placed ourselves in an ecstasy impossible for the heathens among whom we lived to understand. This brief life, this transitory existence, was nothing compared to the promise. And what importance was it to us who had felt the new dispensation and ourselves growing, to build his church, his world, his kingdom, his resurrection?

Therefore, your catalog is my miracle, for God has sent you for our salvation. He has created your great lists of journeys into the heart of our lives so He might show us what it really meant to swim in this terror of living in all the spectrum of our quivering spirit and flesh.

My great, deep prayers go with you and all the companions of your journeys, for to be one is to be all.

John Ralphius
Age 28. Floor refinisher.
Nottingham, England.

Dear Past Rentals,

What an asshole this guy is! He really believes that Jesus Christ will come any minute, come knocking at his door in this little town, Bolzano, in northern Italy. Some guys will believe anything! But I want to describe something peculiar that happened to me, and I guess it's happened to a lot of people who've gone on your trips.

And right here I want to say right off that I'm no believer. I can't stand that Jesus Christ stuff. I was brought up a Presbyterian, but I couldn't stand those people either. The Presbyterians are, on the whole, cold and rigid people, and I can't stand cold and rigid people. This guy, on the other hand, was certainly not cold. He was just the opposite, hot as hell (if you can pardon the expression). He was a good sort of guy, but his goodness, it seemed to me, came from a desire to please someone else, not himself. He was always looking over his shoulder to see who was watching. That meant to him *some supernatural somebody, not people. They would spit in his face, even kick him, and throw things on him, pig's blood, for example, that's what they threw at me.*

But the guy couldn't help it. He kept on coming on to people, telling them the whole bit about the signs and where to look for them, the emperor, the misery in the cities (and there was, God knows, a lot of misery there), and the earthquakes and the storms. Every earthquake and every storm was some sort of sign. The lightning was god's wrath, his great judgment (and there was a lot to judge, believe me), and the clouds during a storm were just about to split apart and a godlike figure was going to come down on a Roman chariot, almost like that Greek god Zeus with his thunderbolts, splitting open everybody's head and house, which I'm sure wouldn't have pleased all those people one bit.

God knows they were simple people, full of their own gods and ways of doing things. And this guy comes along and tells them, "You fools, you blind beggars (these are the real words he used), get yourself down on your knees, look up, and tell Jesus Christ that you've sinned." And they didn't even know what sinning meant. Most of them just laughed and walked away, though a few kicked the shit out of him.

You know, I've suffered a lot because of this poor religious zealot, but what I wanted to say at the beginning of this letter was that even though I'm opposed to this religious pig shit, though the guy still stinks in me like I'd eaten a pound of garlic for dinner or stepped on a box of Limburger cheese, there's something in him, some craziness that wants to set things right and won't stop until he does. And the kindness and gentleness this guy had toward animals was amazing. Every animal he saw he practically cried over, got down on his knees and prayed for the poor critter, and believe me, they were poor critters, full of fleas, one quarter fed, and kicked around from one place to another, and, by the way, a lot of them were rabid, too. He'd get down there and wallow in the pig shit to show, he said, his contempt for the flesh, and his friends would do the same, and every new convert they made, and there were a few of them even in the three weeks I was there, they all did it. That was part of the initiation, the price you had to pay for accepting Jesus Christ, showing contempt for your body.

Well, you asked in your questionnaire, what did you get out of your trip. Strangely enough, I got to like the guy, I got to see someone I'm opposed to and feel what it's like to be someone else. That would be hard as hell if it weren't for you folks and the good work you're doing. Even if I got shit dumped on me, or I got kicked and spit on for a while, I now know how someone who's that different from me feels, and that's made me someone I can't quite explain.

Leonard Franchi
Age 46. Meter reader
San Diego, California

No. 10: Kaifeng, China. September 4, 1120. [2 days; $250] A bow maker in the capital city, you have learned a great deal about your trade from your father and from other craftsmen. Your brother is a small merchant, specializing in the shipping of pottery from Chengu to the area around the capital. Every month he disappears on his journeys, and when you meet again there is a big dinner and singing and drinking into the night. You and your brother sometimes go hunting together and often return with a few dozen birds to your credit—you are both very good marksmen. Most of your time, however, you spend selling your bows to huntsmen and soldiers. They come from miles around the capital to see your work, which is excellent. But today you are off to hunt. Your brother has brought an extra horse. You will hunt all day and the next.

No. 11: Granada, Spain. October 14, 1582. [7 months; $1200] You have been a craftsman, interested in crafts and mechanics since you were a young boy. Every mechanical device you could find and play with you took apart and learned how to operate. Once you learned about it, you went on to the next challenge. By the time you were twenty-one you could take apart and put together almost anything. You became an engineer, unofficially, because you had not been to the "learned" schools, but you helped people, drew for them diagrams which they could follow, and even aided in the construction of some of the things necessary for the success of a particular project, like irrigation systems or special kinds of waterwheels.

This, too, fell away from you, though you still pursued it, for now your interests had come to include the constructing of what you call "social units" to fulfill certain mechanical projects, the organization of people's minds and energies for the building of a small dam, for example, or a bridge over a river, and then from there an integrated movement on your own, which expanded the possibilities inside you into "a dense dreaming". You did not receive money for those proposals you created for other projects, some of which were possible and some only possible in the imagination, but you received an "inner payment," which satisfied you and enriched you much more.

More and more, things were coming together, first the mechanical assembly of parts into wholes, then the guiding of people through the construction of bridges and dams and devices for boat building. Then, the new projects, which allowed others to see the possibilities in them and make the necessary social connections, streets to fortifications, layouts of houses to take advantage of breezes, quick escape routes, etc.

Now, at fifty-eight your earlier Faustian skills and interests have diminished. There is no more grasping of things for their own sake, though that too was a part of your exploration. After forty years of work, you feel the air of your life thickening and a growing permanence and solidity filling you until finally you realize there is no emptiness in the plenum of existence. There is only the contact and the shaking of hands with the possible. All the plans you have, and they are many, will fall or not fall, it does not matter, and for that reason they will be more than projects with a goal; they will be simply things that happen to you and things to learn by.

Dear Past Rentals,

I didn't conspicuously pick this trip to Granada, in 1582. In fact, I decided on a past rental by "throwing" the I Ching, an ancient divinatory book from China. The book strongly indicated chance, not deliberation. Therefore, I sat down with the catalog and a copy of the financial page of the New York Times, and picked the last three digits of the stocks traded that day, an old numbers game idea. It turned out to be this trip, which I would like to tell you the results of, not because it changed my life significantly but because I realized something, another part of me, that I had overlooked.

That part was the latent constructor in me, the mechanical builder, the hands-on man, who wants to see things to their completion rather than dream of or imagine them. And this was surprising. I had never even dreamt of being an engineer, a mechanic, a designer of bridges, towers, dams or anything, for that matter remotely like it. When I was a child, I had had my usual supplies of model airplanes and, in my day, erector sets. But somehow I was never good at the airplanes. The glue was not put on right or the paper was not stretched very well over the wooden frame. It got wrinkled and ugly, and somehow—I could never figure this out-the models ended up unbalanced. After that I started playing the clarinet (I have never stopped) and writing long articles on the philosophy of magic.

Now the I Ching pointed its finger for me in a direction I hardly thought existed, the world of the mechanical. And where? Strangely enough, in that most unmechanical country, Spain, and in an almost unmechanical year, 1582. At that time Spain was preparing to invade England. It was busy with its "Golden Age". It had been bringing back booty from the New World for decades (with a little disturbance from the English). What did it need? What did it want with the mechanical? In fact, what did anyone at that time want with machines?

And I was right, at least in general. But wrong in the particular, as I have always been, much to my discomfort. In every age, everywhere, there is someone, or a few people who will always want to know how something is put together, and they will go to great lengths to take apart almost every device they can get their hands on, and when they have gotten it apart, try to put it back together, sometimes unsuccessfully.

My man, now in his fifties, has gone beyond the assembly of machines, or the assembly of social units (organizing people to mentally integrate themselves into what they have accomplished), into a philosophical aura of instinctive connection which only someone, like a great musician who has been playing for thirty or forty years can understand, a truly automatic consciousness, like the accuracy of breathing or walking or sleeping. But the getting there is still inside him, and the process of living becomes something far greater than the somehow intellectual encounter with a specific, practical problem. For now it means that the whole of his (in this case my) existence is a working out of a configuration of possible events, which come together almost gratuitously, without any projection on his part and therefore include him in the move-

ments of things as someone who would think of a problem as
a problem would not be included.

This is my partial revelation, a course of action pointed
at by the I Ching, which pulls combinations out of possibility
through the unexplainable sense of "chance"—others have
different words for it. It is all the same. Some will describe to
you the beauty of Granada, the fountains and the gardens of
Spain, all of which are beautiful. But it is the central direc-
tion of a journey we discover when all the unessential ele-
ments are fleshed away and the path is cleared for us through
some revelation into the nature of things.

> *Claus Hennings*
> *Age 31. House painter*
> *Bremen, West Germany*

No. 12: Sighisoara, Rumania. September 4, 1509. [6 months; $1775]
For many years now you have been haunted by a bear you had
narrowly escaped from in the forest but which still has pursued
you in your dreams and sometimes in your waking life. You
imagined him, in dream after dream, malevolently following
you, even in the midst of cities, until you had to face him one
day when you thought you were least prepared. Then, your body
rose up to turn all its energies to this problem, which had been
consuming you for so long. And you won; gradually, through
years of unremitting struggle, your body rose up and won, won
totally, not through denying the bear or the fear it represented,
but through a greater integration, a great acceptance of fear
within the flow of things.

> *Dear Past Rentals,*
> *I want to ask you, What is the value of a life in which all*

the physical and mental events have been easy, not too easy, but easy enough to have triumphed over minor problems, leaving a sense of having miraculously escaped, but somehow also of having cheated the nature of things, and as a result being haunted by a nemesis so vague that it has become over-powering? Nothing here can be defined. When, and if, it is defined or attempted to be defined, it vanishes, appearing in another mental or physical place, like a morning fog that won't quite go away.

I am now a wealthy man, no, rather say that I am fairly well off. I have done everything "right"—married well, had two wonderful, talented children, both themselves doing well, and lived a life of interest and comfort. But one item in your catalog attracted me greatly, in fact, drew me toward it with an almost magnetic intensity. It is item No. 12 about the struggle with a bear who pursues a man even in his dreams until he rises up, totally in his completed person, every mental and physical ounce of him, and wins against the separated beast of body and mind, wins totally.

Somehow, I feel, most people do not have the opportunity to affirm themselves in all their sense of being. Rather, they hide from it, in society, in the world of the mind, in the deep fissures of their fear of death, fear of themselves, fear of the world into which they have been born, not knowing the nature of the thing which sustains and yet pursues them at the same time. It is partly themselves, as the world is partly ourselves, yet it is also foreign. What do we make of it? Our whole lives are spent running as fast as we can away from the mystery, from the total use of our energies, thinking we will gather our strengths for that one last, desperate blast on the trumpet of our beings when we may speak of what we have become.

But the moment does not appear, the crossroads have been effaced, the audience is not the right audience, or the configuration of what we think is reality, in fact, what we hope is reality, does not appear to us, and we vanish, again, into our castles, our caves of fear and doubt, only to pretend that we are brave toward death, toward the ultimate questions. I was this person, like so many others. I took this journey, the only entry in your catalog, which called to me from some sense deeper than I can imagine, inside the deep inside myself. Perhaps it was chance that it appeared; perhaps it was the necessary part of everyone's strongest affirmation. For this, someone should be thanked.

Tuan Saelee
Age 41. Temple manager
Manila, Philippines.

No. 13: Pleven, Bulgaria. March 16, 1762. [3 months; $450] You grew up with parents who abused you, beat you and in many ways, physically and mentally. At the first opportunity you ran away. In Pleven you found someone who taught you to be a violin maker, a trade you learned well and kept at for the rest of your life, living into your 80's, a well-respected man renowned for his musical interests but never, never again visiting your parents, except in memory, alternating in your mind between times of fleeing and times of desired, tender return. But as the years passed, you developed a deepening awareness of your own worth, which had been so terribly neglected by your parents in their frantic pain and misery. There have been chances to return, communications from a sister, a neighbor, who have found you through chance or deliberate investigation. But brooding on the possibility of experiencing once more that nightmare, you have concluded that the pain of the actual confrontation would be worse than the healing which your memory provides. However, you have allowed one visitor, your much younger sister, who has arrived

with her husband to spend a few days with you, and there is in
your life a new, ambiguous ferment which churns up acre on acre
of physical fear and projected memory. But now that only the
memory obtrudes, you feel that reconciliation on some level will
open your life to a greater picture of who you were and who you
have become.

Dear Past Rentals,

*I have been through a lot in these last thirty years of my
Past Rentals journey, actually the last three months, though
it feels like thirty years. And in this terrible childhood I have
had in my "adopted" journey, I have learned much, and as a
result there have been compensations. I now know how hard
it is to judge someone's life as if it were my own, for these last
three months the life I have lived through your catalog entry
has created in me a deep sense of the continuity of existence,
the importance of all its stages, but most important, that of
childhood, where everything is formed, where the basic pieces
of our world are absorbed by our growing selves. We breathe
in when we are children and there is the world, inside us, and
with each breath a bit more of the world sticks. We grow fat
on this breath. We are eating it even when we sleep. And in
childhood it enters, silently, when we are unaware, even
when we have denied it.*

*But each stage leaves unfulfilled the hidden sides of our
natures, holes into which nothing or the unabsorbed has
fallen, connections and responses which we may become
clumsy about later on in our lives. Such was my journey of
three months in that desert of somebody else's life, tragic, yes,
certainly, but also triumphant.*

*As I look back on this journey into the rolling dynamics
of a Bulgarian peasant of the 18th century, I see that one
action will determine another and that, still another, and so*

on until the end, or something we call the end. In this man's life, I ran away from home because my parents abused me, beat me, forced me to work like a horse. Even though other children worked and worked hard, they were not beaten as I was nor were they forced to work even beyond their limits. Of course, I had to run away.

Now it was chance that introduced me to my benefactor, (although I am sure that my upbringing had a hidden talent in it which I, of course, did not understand at the time and only understand dimly now), allowing me to become the apprentice to the greatest violin maker in all of Bulgaria at the time. It was my own talent, which was able to emerge after I had found a real father. I had been a workhorse; now I was a craftsman, and, through the years, a great one. Part of this was chance; part was skill, emerging from an unknown territory inside me, that deep mystery which I hoped to unravel by my journey.

My parents, in my actual life, had never abused me, nor had they worked me hard, although I did work for them. "Why the interest in this catalog item?" I have often asked myself. And it is a difficult question to answer. My answer is not rational, but intuitive. My actual life had a good, though limited, foundation in childhood. Yet now at sixty-five, if I had not taken this journey, I would have felt "ordinary," someone who, though needing a significant and fruitful conflict, had lived so that one smooth period of existence had followed another, until death came and I "smoothly" rolled off the assembly line and into the dust.

It is the brooding, the years of brooding on this journey, brooding (as I was this man) especially about that terrible childhood, about my parents, the guilt I felt having never gone back to visit. And out of the brooding, figures appeared, as through a fog in the landscape, shapes of my boyhood, noises and movements of the farms and the animals and the *fences dimly seen but in time growing clearer in feeling and sight and touch and smell. The last five years of brooding did that. They allowed me to talk with everything there without suffering the misery of going. They allowed me to speak without fear, to listen, to "overhear" the creatures of that life without fear of their fear of me.*

I don't know how else to describe it, except to say that "time heals all wounds" in some way, and maybe not in the way we intended. I am not religious, and I was not religious when I left on my thirty year "journey" to Pleven, Bulgaria. But I feel something, now that I have returned, and I don't know what to call it, and I will not join any organized religious group. But it is there, the muck of the pig yard, the horses steaming in the winter mist, the whip of my father there in his hand, the whip of his horrendous voice, and my mother urging him on. I can feel it all, every bit of it. It has come back, and now without fear, only as a story I tell when my friends ask me for "postcards". It is only to tell my story that I tell you this, "Senza tema d'infamia ti rispondo," as Dante says.

May all your customers' experiences be proof of the stories we tell of our own real journeys, for in the telling there is much healing, even unto the listening and the brooding.

> *Luigi Boccherini*
> *Age 48. Butcher*
> *Aquila, Italy*

No. 14: Huntsville, Alabama. May 2, 1894. [2 years; $2,050] You are a poor white southern tenant farmer, more well off than most, who has employed about twelve black people every year for the last ten years. You work them hard and pay them little, and yet you feel they are shirking their responsibilities and being paid too much for the work they do. "I'm generous to my niggers," you tell them, seriously, although you know that's what you have to say; they expect it of you, you think. You drink a lot with your friends, other poor white tenant farmers, play cards at the local store at the crossroads, and go hunting in the fall. Your life, however, feels miserable.

You have felt that Blacks have to be kept in their place. They don't know anything, and that's how it has to be. If they started getting power and money, they would be after your skin and maybe after your daughter, too. You have already participated in one lynching. The young man you killed said he was never near the girl, but you believed differently, and the sheriff wasn't going to stop you, not for a nigger. But white men having black women is something necessary. It can't be helped. It's a call of nature, and anyway, they like it. Therefore, you have sex with any black woman you can find, even paying her with a little money. Still you go to church every Sunday and sing in the chorus and pray to God, your God, the white God who will save you all. (The niggers will go to their own place.)

Dear Past Rentals,
God, it was horrible. I was no longer black. I was white. I was no longer a stockbroker in San Francisco. I was a poor white southern tenant farmer. At first, that is, the first several weeks, I couldn't get used to it. I knew what I was doing, what I was saying. The words came out of my mouth, but behind them I could still hear my real self, James Robertson Johnson, screaming, "What have you put me into? Let me out! This guy is crazy. I don't want people like this to exist!" Yes, I screamed it, but no one heard me because all that shouting went on inside me, and what came out, in spite of my strongest urges, was the language and action of this hick, honky, miserable, crude, angry, basically helpless excuse for

a human being, and I've seen some pretty hopeless cases in my real life, believe me.

Well, I didn't go back. I got used to it. Something started to jell. I could step back after a few weeks and see that guy without trying to steer him one way or another. (I couldn't, though I tried. The wheel was not in my hand, nor was the car. And the road was different than any road I have ever driven down before.)

First of all, I was wearing overalls. I was smelling of pig shit and horse shit and tobacco and cotton and the good earth of Alabama. And I was swearing and cussing like you wouldn't believe. I'd say, "I'm really generous to my niggers" and watch what I'd said hang there in front of me like a puff of smoke, and gradually dissolve. And even my "politeness" was a thing to behold. And was I polite? Yes, in a southern, Huntsville, Alabama, 1894 way, polite to the big shots, the mayor, the big plantation owners and their families, polite to all the white women I met in town. But I wasn't polite in any real way, only polite on the surface.

And when I was with my friends, people like me who owned small farms near Huntsville, I'd use other language. We'd sit around for hours, smoking and drinking and talking in that slow southern way, especially in the summer, and all the Black people would sit around, too, but not with us. When they did need something, they came, hat in hand, to ask for it, by god, hat in hand and speaking in the meekest voices I'd ever heard, and most of the time they'd get cuffed for their efforts, old or young, it didn't matter.

But when we were drunk (and they knew when we were drunk), they didn't come around. I saw why once. One of my neighbors had put away about a pint and a half of somebody's whiskey and was rolling around in the back of the store with a black gal and some black guy came around and tried to get the woman to come home with him and my neighbor up and shot the guy, killed him on the spot. Nothing happened to that white man, nothing, and I, my stockbroker self, was screaming inside, impotent.

And then I had one of the black girls who worked for me, had her in my own shack and fucked the living daylights out of her. I knew it was only a power game. She wanted anything I could give her—money, clothes, food, anything. And I wanted to see how much she would beg for it. I put her through her paces. And still, my God, I went to church on Sundays, that little white church in town, sat there and sang the hymns and prayed to God, watching all the white women, just in case one caught my eye (and some of them caught more than that).

There were other things also, human things. I remember shitting in the outhouse on my farm and listening to the shit hit the bottom of the hole. I remember taking walks in the woods and hunting for pheasant and deer every year and how beautiful the woods look when they wake up in their fall or spring colors. I remember the slow creak of the wagons in town, and the sound of my own wagon, too, and I remember the days of rain when we'd sit on the porch, the black workers and I, and tell stories, good ones, too. There were a lot of nice things.

But the hardest part was getting used to it. By the time I was ready to come back, I was that guy, that pitiful, hungry man. I knew him in and out, and I knew all the men and women he knew, and I knew that most of them were the same kind of person. But here's something interesting I was able to do, but only after about eighteen months. I was able to be two people at the same time, the man and myself. When I relaxed, I could look at others more carefully, step back and see them, look into their souls as it were. And, you know, I could feel for them, all of them. But that was hard.

James Robertson Johnson
Age 28. Stockbroker
San Francisco, California

No. 15: Clarkesdale, Mississippi. December 27, 1882. [3 weeks; $725] You are an illiterate Black cotton picker in Mississippi. That's all you have known how to do, and you have done it all your life, working hard, even desperately, to keep out of debt, for you sharecrop sixty acres with your son and that is hard work, especially in Mississippi. Lately, you have kept noticing funny things going on in people, strange, erratic things which leave their print on their bodies, on the way they speak, the way they approach each other, both Black and White. You merely observe and say nothing, for there is nothing to say, just people moving through their slow dance. But you wonder if there is any way to get out of it.

You notice how people are afraid with words, how words shake them inside and how they hold in their intestines a tight knot of thorns when they hear words they can't absorb.

You notice that they stand, not facing each other, but a little to the side, and their voices are also a little to the side, as if they were speaking not only to another but also to someone else or partly to themselves.

You notice the fervency with which they pray or plunge themselves into things, well out of proportion to the value of the thing they are doing.

You notice that people wear a walk and a language and a speech and a speed all their own.

You notice that they are competing for the same future, which they believe they own.

You notice that they all need to find some corner in which to be different, even if their difference is ridiculous.

You notice that their children cling so desperately to their mothers and their mothers berate their children with an intensity beyond all proportion to the actions of their offspring.

You notice how someone will hide something of value for years and then squander it in a few hours of gambling.

You notice how there is an almost perfect attempt at order in the house, but there is disorder in the mind, in the feelings.

You notice that if they were offered a chance to escape from this life, offered money, enough to go north and live comfortably, they would hesitate, feeling the pull of their lives here in this miserable delta country where work is hard and the sun is hot, even overwhelming.

And you notice that they do not see much around them. They take most things for granted and look only when it is absolutely necessary, for looking is pain and their whole souls are completely tied up with the goal of pleasure and respite from pain.

You cannot remember how many things you notice, but you notice them, and you don't know what to do with the things you notice.

Dear Past Rentals,

My life changed when I read your catalog entry No. 15. I grabbed it and couldn't wait to get there. It seems strange to want to be a Black sharecropper in Mississippi in 1872. It's strange to pick him and strange to become him. But as any-one can notice, this is not an ordinary person. Very few people really notice things, are able somehow to stand back, look, and still keep themselves intact. And who finds these people anyway? You folk at Past Rentals have, and you've changed my life, or, at least improved it.

I realized one thing when I read that entry, and it hit me square between the eyes and knocked me over, in fact, knocked me just to one side so I could see a bit more, even stand beside myself and see myself, take one good, long swal-

low of what I was. I gasped when it happened, gasped so hard my wife looked a little frightened. She didn't say anything, but she looked a little frightened.

Over the next few days I began to realize more and more that I had never really looked. That moment, when your entry knocked me outside of myself for an instant, was a real eye-opener. But it lasted only a short time, and I could feel myself move back to my old habits. In my mind, I wanted that moment to come back, but I couldn't make myself do it. That's why I couldn't wait to get there, to Mississippi, to be that sharecropper who could see into people. I knew it would help me to see, even after I finished the trip, and I have to report that it has.

It's certainly strange getting used to being someone else. But after a few hours you begin to do it. There's a bit of you in the person you've become, just in case you get lost, but you never really get lost. You've got a safety button, even though you know you won't ever use it.

It didn't take me long. I fitted right in and knew exactly what was going on with this guy. There was a calmness about him which I've never experienced before. All the guys I've known at work or in the neighborhood have a kind of wiry edge to them. They're nervous. They're worried all the time. They have to be doing something. If they're alone doing nothing, they feel lost. They have to be doing something. Most of the time it really doesn't matter. And I have to admit that I've felt that way most of my life. This guy I "entered" wasn't super-bright; I mean he wasn't educated. In fact, he'd never really been to school, didn't even know how to read and could barely write his name. But there's more up there, I tell you, than most professors have going. Someone once said about philosophers that they create a fog and then complain they can't see. Well, that's not what this guy did as he went about living. Everything was clear, not necessarily explainable, but clear. Language didn't get in the way. He saw and heard and sniffed it out.

Now I'm going to talk about what I did, but I want you to think that he's doing it, even though I'm going to tell you that I did it. It's the same thing, but it's confusing telling you that he did it. So I'll use I. Here are some things I saw, and this guy was very careful about what he said and did. He knew that if he said or did the wrong thing in front of a white man, he might either get beat up or killed. He knew how to survive. But so did a lot of people around there at that time.

First, he knew something about the uselessness of saying anything to people about this seeing of his. He'd tried. And, of course, it didn't work. People either didn't understand him, or else they thought he was crazy. He wasn't crazy. Others were crazy. He just knew that life was a matter of seeing things, looking around at almost everything, from buttercups to people getting drunk.

In order to give you an idea of what I saw, I'm going to list things with no explanation. That's important. It gives flavor and variety. And without saying it, it even gives a kind of method.

I saw bird shit falling from the bird to the ground. I followed it down all the way until it plopped into the snow. I tried to hear it, and sometimes I heard the sound it made when it hit the snow. I did this for a whole three hours once in a field in the snow, just watching a bird until it dropped its shit. You had to watch carefully because you didn't know when the bird was going to "let fly," and it took a lot of concentration.

I saw people walking together along the road and walked with them for about a mile or so, noticing whether or not they looked into the woods on both sides. They didn't. I listened to them talk, but I was more interested in listening to the "musical" sound of their talk than to what they were *saying. Then, after a few minutes, I began listening to both what they said and to the music of their words. I never said anything. I just listened.*

I went into town and saw two people, friends of mine, drunk. I liked what they were singing as they made their way home. I even sang along with them a bit. I liked what they were wearing. They wore the same hats everyone in Clarkesdale wore, but they wore them differently. They had never noticed that before.

I saw the way the cracks were forming in the wood in the sign above the local store. I sat across the street for a while and just looked at the sign. Then, I noticed the steam from the horse droppings melting the snow around them.

A young man sat across from me at the local restaurant, and I noticed that when he talked a lot his hands stopped shaking. When he stopped talking, his hands started again, not much, but slightly. Even he didn't notice that they were shaking.

There's no end to these observations. They just go on and on forever until you die. That's what I think life's about, observation. Without it we're just sleepwalkers. That's what we've been put here to do, look. I can't believe that people haven't "seen" this. I can't believe that I missed it all my life, the looking at what's going on. I'm glad I went, and that's an understatement. Life wasn't easy for this man. He had problems. But he gave me some thoughts about why problems are important, too. And thanks to Past Rentals I, too, have begun to see, thanks to my two teachers.

Jack Martinson
Age 45. Plastics factory worker
Minneapolis, Minnesota

No 16: Near Benares, India. 472 B.C. [2 days; $150] You are a poor farmer who has just met the Buddha wandering through your farmland and stopped to talk with him, remembering the few words spoken between you about the willow trees and the river and how the rain had not come and how terrible it was, this drought. You were left with a feeling of an "ordinary immanence" and something that could never be described because it was "seen" at that moment, making you feel human again who had for a long time felt as if your body were somehow following a shadow and was trapped into following it forever. And that was all.

No. 17: North Platte, Nebraska. June 12, 1887. [2 weeks; $350] You were born and grew up in Canton, China. In 1872 there was terrible famine; thousands of people were dying every day. Your family had very little to eat. People asked for workers to go to America, so you signed up and left, knowing only a few words of English. America was a strange land, but you could, you hoped, send money back to your parents. You would be the savior of your family. And so it has been, but not as you expected. Your English is still only passable, perhaps because you do not see or know many white men, except for the bosses, who are always complaining about all of you and threatening you with deportation. Your wages are low, but by Chinese standards they are high, and you are able to send money to your parents, who greatly appreciate your help, your sacrifice. Here you can eat, although you must save, always save, and live as cheaply as possible. The work is hard; twelve hours a day in the hot sun of Nebraska, a country as flat as your hand. And there is nothing here but other Chinese like yourself, who work and save and hardly complain. Your life is a kind of holding action.

Yet if at first you wanted to go back, now you are not so sure. You have been thinking of moving, probably to Salt Lake City, and for that purpose you have been saving money. With another person you have met, you want to open a business there. Maybe you can make it, but the work goes on here twelve hours a day, and you need the money—desperately.

Dear Past Rentals,

How could you do this to me, turn me into a Chinese and send me out to work on the railroad, and in Nebraska, a place I've always disliked?

But first I have to say that some of this was my own fault. I decided this time around to use no judgment in picking my item. I opened the Past Rentals catalog at random and found No. 17, North Platte, Nebraska. Without thinking, without preparation, I sent in my money and my biographical information. When my papers arrived, I traveled to the designated spot in order to be transported.

What a surprise to land in Nebraska! I don't think I even read the catalog entry, and if I did, I didn't remember it at all. To put it simply, I was Chinese and I was in Nebraska, and it was 1876. And it was summer. And I was set to work twelve hours a day at hard labor. Was I in prison? What crime did I commit? After these thoughts passed through my head, I realized what I had done, for how could I not have known? I had been on other trips and had realized immediately the situation I was in. This time it took me a few days to get into the swing of things. I must state that I have been a traveler for ten years and this is the first time I have been totally shocked by my entry. I have only gradually woken up to the "responsibilities" of this immersion.

Hard work was not what I was looking for, nor did I need to sacrifice myself for my family. There was no connection here between my real and my "tourist" life. What purpose was there in this backbreaking work, this heroic sacrifice, the work of desperate men in an alien land? The bosses were mean, sometimes cruel. But the sun was even meaner and sometimes crueler. How many men passed out from heat stroke the first week, I don't know, but a lot. And even in the summer they got sick. The food was expensive and there was not much of it. A man can't live on rice alone. And water. (The Chinese prison diet, rice and water? That's a joke.)

But I made the most of it. I put my shoulder to the wheel, figuratively and literally. I gave of myself to that young Chinese man who had made the sacrifice for his family and who had only his labor to give them and then only a little money to send back. There were fights. There was also a continual gambling game going on, and people lost their shirts to the sharpers and lost their shirts to the company. The Indians, who had not ever seen a Chinese, rode up to our camps and stared at us from their horses, amazed at a new kind of person. Yet they were friendly, friendlier than the whites.

My English got better during the week I was there and I began to get ideas of escape, escape ideas, maybe Salt Lake City, maybe San Francisco, (I had seen San Francisco), maybe even St. Louis. I made plans to run away to these big cities and get lost there among other Chinese.

I learned what I could from this trip. I learned about sacrifice and hard work and desperation. But I don't want to learn about it any more. It is a terrible lesson. Next time I plan to read the catalog entry and think about it for a long time before I go anywhere.

Ronald Hatfield Brownell
Age 42. Hatmaker
Cincinnati, Ohio.

No. 18: Higashiosaka, Japan. December 3, 1913. [2 weeks; $150]
Your husband is an engineer, but for the last five years, when he

brings his planning home with him, you sit down and draw what he, a trained engineer, has difficulty doing, not that he cannot draw, but he cannot draw well. His limited ability gives you an opportunity to do what you like best.

You have learned a great deal about more than drawing these last five years. You have learned much about civil engineering, though they would laugh at you if you went to apply for a job doing what your husband does. "Imagine," they would say, "a woman as an engineer. Stay home, woman, watch those children." You know the possible words well, but still, there is the pleasure of drawing, using all the variables at your command to produce something practical, beautiful and lasting. And your husband, because of you, has prospered in the company. You will also draw the children, your husband, yourself, and your neighbors.

No. 19: Silver City, Nevada. April 17, 1860. [3 months; $450] You have been an itinerant prospector for two years, coming out west with the others to find gold or silver and knowing, at first, nothing about finding it. But information travels fast. You, and thousands of others, learned quickly where to look for it, how to get it, and how to protect yourself once you got it.

But finding gold was harder than hearing about it. Hungry and desperate, you traveled from camp to camp, looking and hoping like all the rest. You found a few dozen ounces, but you spent almost as much as you found. Prices were high because things were not generally available.

Gradually, however, and almost unconsciously, you began settling down in the territory in which you wandered, and more and more it was not the gold you were looking for; it was the people you began to mine, not for money, you were no con man, but for a growing curiosity which has held you in its grip ever since. All kinds of men and women have wandered into your "camp" and have left, too, but left behind in you (and you in them) a meeting of some sort, a tangible connection. So you have stayed, preferring the movement from one town or camp to another, picking up a living in more ways than prospecting, and finding more "gold" than you could carry away.

Dear Past Rentals,

He was really a kind of silly, old man. I first thought, after reading your catalog entry No. 19, that here was a person of great discrimination. Then I read it again. No, there was nothing subtle in him, only a portrait of a camp follower.

But what a camp follower! Here was a man who came with greed, like all the rest, and stayed to mine the other gold—talking, laughing, joking, just being lazy and crude with a crowd of confused, somehow desperately crazed men (and a few women) and introducing himself to anyone and everyone, a quietly recognized person.

He had the same desires they all did. And he dressed the same, too. But the way he developed (it didn't grow on him; he had to work at it), his walk allowed you to know him three hundred yards away. And when he was sitting, talking to you by the fire, chatting away a mile a minute, his wink was a sign of trust, comfort, charity, sly innuendo and positive hilarity all in one. He never went to church, but when a man died from cholera or typhus or some cave-in at one mine or another, he always said something about that man. He was always called upon at the funerals because he knew everyone, and what he said there was generally right, good and bad, a real summing up.

Here's what he said about Jim Henderson, who died in a mine explosion in 1853:

"Well, folks, I see you're wearing the same clothes as I am, proud clothes for these parts. Some of you have your Sunday suits on, but they're covered with dust, too, proud

dust. *Proud dust, that's what we all are. Proud to be seen carrying a little dust on us.*

"*Jim Henderson had this same dust on him as we have on us, dust from the earth which the rain tries to wash away, even out here in the West. Jim Henderson's gone back to the dust. He got married at last. He finally found a hole where he would strike it rich, an eternal mineshaft I'd call it, to put his self in. Jim Henderson's gone home. And I want to say that we're all Jim Henderson, and you know what I mean. We have the same dust on our lives. And soon we'll be all dust. That's to the good, I say, all to the good.*

"*Have you all seen the dust storms? (Everyone says, "Of course, Matt Handcock. You go on".) Well, people go underground to get away from some of those storms. There's always chinks in the cabins and the dust gets through those chinks. Close your eyes and the dust covers the chink, too. It gets in your shoes, in your shirt, in your shit. It's a kind of blanket. Or a cape we wear because we're all covered with dust. A miner's life is like that, one big dust storm, and he can't get out of it. That's Jim Henderson's life, too.*

"*That cave in that killed him, finally killed him because he was dying before that. That cave in brought him back to us. No matter how much he washed and scrubbed, he couldn't get all that dust off his body. That's the dust of life I tell you, and we're in it all the time. There's no escape, except at our final cave in.*

"*So let's remember Jim Henderson the way we remember all of us here gathered by his grave, trying with our tears to wash away that dust. Let's remember that it's hopeless. We can't do it. And we're all together in this. Now let's throw a little of it in the grave with Jim.*"

Well, that was his little sermon or speech. He said it quietly, and everyone knew that what he said was right. Sometimes he told little stories about someone, and they made everyone feel that the people he was talking about were the people they knew, even themselves. Sometimes he just told jokes and everyone laughed.

But in the end, somehow, he still felt like a silly, old man. Crude and drinking and joking with everyone. Loved to talk. Loved to listen. Loved to go on wild goose chases with a couple of guys in search of gold or silver. Never found anything, at least nothing to strike it rich. But he did bring back some interesting looking rocks and a few arrowheads and some animal skulls—mountain lions, deer, coyote. If he found a kid who would listen to him (few and far between out there), he'd make him a present of them, and the kid would light up and hurry off to show his dad, and his dad, more than likely, would throw the whole show out the window. (The kid would sneak out at night and get them.)

Those gold camps were wild places where people got shot every day, or at least once a week. But nobody would bother to shoot Matt Handcock. He had nothing to rob. You could turn his pockets inside out and find holes and a lot of dust, and not gold dust either. But there was always someone with a meal for him, beans or venison or cornbread or anything. He ate it up like it was his last supper, hungry as a bear in the spring. I think he went on eating and talking and drinking and telling stories and jokes long after I left him. I guess there are a lot of silly, old men like him around, even today, just ready to sit down with people and do what Matt Handcock did, and good at it, too.

Ralph Gleason
Age 58. Leather worker
Fort Wayne, Indiana

No. 20: Near Fukuoka, Japan. September 15, 1284. [3 days; $205]

The Chinese Mongols had come before, a year earlier, and you had not been ready for them, but with unconquerable courage and determination, and with great losses in men, the Mongols carrying off many of your women, you managed to turn them back as did that "divine wind," the great typhoon which destroyed many of their men and ships.

This time you are prepared. Stupidly, they have landed on the same beaches. You are a young bowman of considerable skill, ready for the invaders. They are now on the beach, by the thousands, and other bowmen have begun to shoot. There is noise and confusion everywhere as the swordsmen begin their battles with the enemy.

No. 21: Marseilles, France. August 21, 1671. [5 days; $380] You are a travelling musician, but your real profession is to listen, report, and note carefully the mode and manners of the people through which you move, to engage them in conversations about political and social matters, and from these conversations to draw conclusions about the state of your region. In short, you are a spy.

Good at what you do, you have taken advantage of your abilities to accept money from both factions. But there is a price, as you know there always is. You are the price. Through years of eliciting information and opinions from all kinds of people, you have become disillusioned with everyone—they are all no good. They have been reduced in your heart to counters in a game of chess, to be moved and positioned for no one's benefit, except your own pecuniary one. You take a certain pleasure now in setting up situations and conversations, which you know will drive fear into both sides.

In doing this, you feel the power which is yours. But if you remain a musician and a spy, you may not remain one long. There is a future for people like you, people who have all but given up their human traits, using them only as trappings for other, more dangerous, activities. You know there is no hope for you if you do not stop "rising" in this little world of yours. Habit is a hard current to go against, but you must oppose it now or you never will. It will grow, destroy you, and doom you to one level of hell or to another.

Dear Past Rentals,

Contrary to what everybody says about a spy's life, anybody who's been one will tell you that it's very routine. I guess James Bond and other movie types will keep you going for an hour or two, but a real spy, especially one who lived two or three centuries ago, probably yawned more than he ran.

Well, this guy was a careful one, meticulous. Kept notes all the time, first in his head and then on paper. Remembered everything, down to the heels on a man's shoes. He was a real operator, a manipulator. He kept them all going and they, of course, fools that they were, thinking they could pay someone to give them good information, didn't know anything about his work. They didn't even care. They knew even less about the man himself. They thought he was happy making a good living, putting it away so he could retire in five or ten years. And he kept them thinking that. But they didn't know my man.

The funny thing is that I didn't even know him until three days into my trip. Then it hit me what he was, what was knawing away at his guts, eating up his soul. It was the goddamn profession, what it does to you to live that kind of life. Better a shoemaker than a spy; better a dung collector. Better anything than a spy. There is a kind of syrup of emptiness that creeps into you because you have to be someone else all the time. You can't escape to yourself, but you must escape from yourself. That's the real problem with being a spy, a kind of occupational disease.

Our man was so good at it that he could probably have juggled the world and all the people in it. He had managed to live with poverty so long it didn't effect him. The drinking he wallowed in from time to time and the whores he took or the mistresses he secretly had over the years were only local palliatives to keep those shadows of his unexplored, real self at bay. He felt Armageddon was chasing him all the time, even in his dreams. And it wasn't the other side, knowing he was a spy and people were out to get him, that was in any way a worry. He could get out of anything like that. It was what he had become that made his life hopeless, more hopeless than the poorest beggar in France.

Where does a man like this go if he somehow lives with those terrible shadows of emptiness because of an absence of personality, a lack of true self? I did not realize how universal the answer to this question was until I spent those five days as this professional spy. He goes into the political world. He becomes the politician's helper and then his indispensable right hand man, and then the man himself, just walks into his body and starts speaking, not as in Past Rentals, but naturally, as if he were always this person and there was no other. But the real man always speaks, aware of the terrible fall into the pit of nothingness. The real man remembers childhood. He remembers the words of the poet:

> *Delve deeper back in years to your first youth,*
> *Passionate, clean, untarnished by small fears.*
> *And if your conscience truly bears my memory,*
> *Rekindle if you can, the dying candlelight....*

This is the voice of his essential being, which habit has eroded until it is a small voice coming from farther and farther inside him. This, then, is the beginning of the real struggle, begun during those five days I was with him, a struggle of gigantic proportions. It was not something that most people go through because they are themselves and would be frightened to enter someone else's body, a kind of mortal sin of the spirit. But my man (our man) knew the disease he had contracted and knew that this was his last chance.

One day, just before I left him, he stopped a child walking near the sea where the boats were stacked up tier on tier, acres of masts and seagulls everywhere. The boy (he was about eight) was returning with some fish he had bought for his mother and whistling some children's song and unconscious, as children will be, of everything around him.

The boy looked up into his eyes, straight into them, and saw his reflection, doubled. The boy began to laugh, and our spy began to cry. He cried for ten minutes, silently, in front of that small boy. He didn't know what to do. He just stood there, looking at himself in his eyes, doubled. Then, he reached out and offered him one of his fish. He thought he was hungry. My spy pushed the fish back into the pail and held the boy's hand as long as he could, even though he struggled to take it away and even though the boy finally let him hold it. There was something cold and from the sea about him, but his face was like a bright, full moon that you suddenly notice one night. It was all red and shining with the great blood of life. His smile was right there in front of him, growing bigger and bigger.

The boy began to laugh. He couldn't stop laughing, and the man began to laugh, also, infected by the boy's own laughter. And then he began to cry and then to laugh and then to cry and again to laugh. The boy didn't know what to do. He got frightened and ran away. The man sat down and looked out at the forest of masts, and beyond them, to the sea, and stared and stared for hours at everything that surrounded him, afraid and alone, shivering and hopeless.

Jean Francois de Ronsard
Age 23. Toolmaker
Bordeaux, France

No. 22: Near present day Al Jizah, Egypt. November 4, 2105 B.C. [2 hours; $55] You are an agricultural laborer on a medium sized farm owned by a man of moderate means. You are sitting down to your midday meal. You will have bread with a stew of leeks, onions, garlic, chickpeas, beans and some figs. You eat carefully, looking out at the fields and beyond them, at the Nile, and quietly bless the gods for your food and the small amount of barley wine you will drink with your supper.

No. 23: Lancashire, England. November 5, 1889. [2 months; $395] You work in the mills, twelve hours a day, six days a week, and on Sundays you sleep and drink and sometimes talk to your wife and children, who are also tired from working. Everyone you work with is tired and angry—it is hard to know which is more important, fatigue or resentment. But your small group at work has been talking, whenever it can, constantly, for six months—lost hands, lost fingers, the total lack of control and the powerlessness under which you live, almost worse than slaves, lied to, and preached at (and many believe the church desires to maintain the status quo).

It is time to shut things down, destroy the machine and demand, not ask for, a fifty hour week, a ten hour day, and a five day work week. You know there is no reason why this should not be. Many other factories in England have this workweek. You will begin on Monday. Everyone knows what he is going to do; and even if you do not succeed, you will have done what you feel in your souls is necessary, indeed vital for your salvation as human beings, who are, as it is, being slowly turned into animals.

Dear Past Rentals,

I want you to know that we made it. Two months of revolt, and the most miserable two months of my life. And they relented. We got our fifty-hour week. We beat back those miserable mill owners. Our lungs improved, and we stayed together. We were hungry; we ate anything we could, but even in our weakness we beat back the scabs. When we could, we talked to them for hours, convinced them that we were right. And often, when they left, they told others, and those others stayed away. We had help, mostly people who sent us food and clothing and some coal to keep us warm through the rest of the winter. My wife worked and brought home some money. My children begged and brought home a little more. My uncle sent us twenty pounds, which we managed to use only for food and shared it with some of the others.

Of course, the church came out against us. But after a while nobody listened to them, the clean-washed and prissy. We simply ignored them, and those who thought we were right helped us as they could, and those who were against us talked on about us as if we were the destroyers of order and not the bosses, who were the real destroyers. It's always been that way, and only the struggling gets you what you need and want.

Now we are not animals. Though we still work hard, we have gotten our dignity back and also our momentum. We are together, and the terrible conditions will be ended, not by the owners, but by us—we have no doubts of that. And fifty hours a week is only the beginning. We're going to start working toward forty, and not just here in Lancashire, but all over England, where working men are oppressed and treated like animals. All over England, and nobody is going to stop us, nobody.

I hope this has convinced you how much this journey has effected me. I feel like a mill worker, and, as you can see, I speak like one and feel that many today among your broad audience could use this experience to teach them something about love and solidarity.

Charles Blaine
Age 41. Metal plater
Bournmouth, England.

No. 24: Bombay, India. October 3, 1889. [4 hours; $45] You are a seven-year-old girl of the lowest Hindu cast, the untouchables, who works with her family, whose job it is to carry garbage to the dump. Often there is enough food for all of you, but at other times you must go hungry for days, begging when you can for food and for the meager clothing you wear. You have hardly time to look around you at the city. You almost always stay in your own district, for it is forbidden to speak to the other castes—even your shadow should not touch the bodies or shadows of others.

It is cool this morning as you get up from the earth, on which you sleep, wash yourself, and eat the little rice, left from yesterday; in fact, it is all you will eat today. There is no more. You will work with your family, carrying refuse to the dump and while you are there, hunt through the garbage to find something of value which you can sell to buy more food.

No. 25: Bourges, France. April 13, 952. [10 hours; $75] Having come as the youngest of acolytes at the age of fifteen to this monastery in Bourges, you have, in effect, "buried" yourself here, and you have lain in this "grave" for about sixteen years.

Because of your ability with languages and your six years of careful copying of texts, you are in charge of the manuscripts collection, which has some prize items, among which are some in languages which you (who are conversant in five) cannot read.

You spend your days praying, singing in the chapel, copying manuscripts and working in the garden. It is a peaceful life. There is food and music and books and even the brotherhood of your small community, but though you do not want to acknowledge it, there are no women here. Effects of what you call "the dire demons of the flesh" attack you at odd hours, working in the garden or copying manuscripts or even when you're singing the most beautiful hymns to the virgin or the psalms set to music by your fellow monk Jean de Chamonix. To escape from them you spend your time arguing with other monks on the fine points of legal scripture. "Where will it go?" you ask yourself somewhere inside your body, which is forcibly raising itself up to the mind, which preys on your body a little at a time. Today, too, it has come again.

Dear Past Rentals,

It's fun to tinker around with the body and the mind, to see where you will go, for you're no different than anyone else. Take me. I'm a well-to-do businessman earning upwards of $290,000 a year out here in East Texas, where I have a few oil wells and raise a lot of beef and a lot of hell. You'd expect me to have a Cadillac (most people think that way about rich Texans), but I don't. I have a Mercedes, and I like to drive it myself.

Now here was a project I'd never thought of before, a monk in charge of a manuscript collection in the Middle Ages. "Well, why not?" I said to myself. "I can spare a little time." So off I went. Bourges has a wonderful monastery, and being thirty-one again is a real treat. (I'm sixty-two.) First of all, I like the singing, always have liked to sing, and here was a chance to hear it first hand. And gardening. That's some-

thing, and for monks, too, and the soil's better in Bourges. (Soil in East Texas ain't too bad, but when you go further west, the soil peters out; you have to go all the way to the Panhandle to find decent soil, and it's better "here" in France.)

You know, I also liked the books. It was nice to read five languages, but it was just as nice to look at the ones in languages I couldn't read. And the monks there! If you just stood back and listened, let the conversation drift along, you started getting the feeling of a deep piety mixed with, well, hypocrisy—I can spot that bullshit a mile away. It wasn't that they didn't believe. They believed the hell out of the religion—worshipped, prayed, flagellated themselves, even cried for mercy, and would have done penance forever if they had eternity to do it in. But there was that other, human side, which wanted to throw everything over, turn them into their opposites, even (lurking way down deep) become the devil himself. (Well, they had all the images of the devil in them. They were brought up with the guy since childhood, maybe even from birth, so why not?)

And the itch for women, the temptresses, hidden within their own flesh! Some of them just made it together out of need, but most were pretty straight and wanted the right sex (in both meanings of the word). And whenever they saw a woman, they looked, Oh, not directly, but looked anyway, and the women looked back, of course, because they knew what was going on under those robes. That was often enough to push them into full flight with a shower of words and pious exclamations, just a measure of their excitement, if you took it that way.

And how do I know this? I was one of them. I did the same thing, and yet, because I am Richard Dixon from east Texas and a rich man to boot (who doesn't think about getting through any eye of a needle, only through the door with

*my whole body), I could see this monk who, at the age of fif-
teen, buried himself in this place. And why? Well, just to get
away from the wave of sex that was invading his body at that
time. That was the pious thing to do. But now (as I left him
at thirty-one) he's not so sure. There are temptations that will
suck him right out of that monastery into some woman's
arms, and she'll make an honest sucker out of him yet. He's
too good for a place like that, even if it has great music and
a bountiful garden and wonderful manuscripts. He'll get out,
and he'll probably go over the wall, too, not through the gate,
and certainly not through the eye of the needle. (He's too desperate to go through the gate.)*

*Well, it's fun to tinker around with the body, but I
wouldn't go too far. It can get you in a lot of trouble. Don't
hold it in. But don't let it out too much either. Somewhere in
between's a good place. That's why I went for ten hours. Years
in a prison like that, even a decent prison with good food and
talk and work, even with hot and cold running water, will
drive any man crazy, especially a Texan.*

Richard Dixon
Age 62. Investor and cattle rancher
East Texas

No. 26: Near Manisa, Turkey. June 26, 35,363 B.C. [3 days; $415] You
are thirty-six, old enough to be a grandmother, and you will be
one soon, but besides your children and, up to four years ago,
your husband (who died while hunting), you have been occupied
in collecting plants (something that started when you were a
small child), all kinds of plants, "Playing with them" as you say,
but mostly looking for the edible or medicinal ones. Fifteen times
you have barely escaped dying from them.

You have developed the ability to smell a plant and tell if it will be useful. A brief taste will often indicate if the plant is good or can be made good through leeching or mixing it with other plants. You have also developed your own ideas about why some plants can be eaten by humans and why some can be eaten by other animals, only deer, for example. You make forays into the mountains to collect plants, being gone sometimes for days, once for two weeks.

Today, at thirty-six, very old by comparison with others, you will be gone for another three days, this time into the mountains. You will take food, but not enough, by itself, to last you for the three days. That, however, is no problem, since you can always find something to eat. Again you are taking your daughter with you. She will learn, as she has for the past ten years, what the plants are doing. She will learn more away from the others, who do not believe everything you say or

Dear Past Rentals,

I've always loved poking around in history. I used to love 9th century China, the Tang dynasty and all that. Therefore, I was tempted by your China entry. But there's one period I have in my bones. It seems to have been in me for a long time, longer than I can remember. That's the Paleolithic, anywhere back from about 10,000 years ago, a period of our history not too many people are curious about. And if they are curious, they know almost nothing about it. But I do. I've made it a point to learn something, not much, but something.

I live a pretty active life and use my body a lot. I'm a plumber in Krakow, Poland. Every day I get down in the muck and filth of people's "important parts" as I call them. I clean out their sinks and toilets and drains, and I put in new pipes when they get too clogged or too decayed. We're now using plastic, but I don't like working with it. It's cheaper, but in the long run (and no one thinks that way now) copper is more economical. But there are people, and there were people who never heard of plumbing. A pipe wouldn't mean a thing to them, even a pipe to smoke. People that far back didn't need what we think we need now, with our 6 billion people on earth in comparison with their few hundred thousand then.

I'm impressed most by the absence of people. Animals and people were more in balance. People were also the prey of animals. Today, that's impossible. I like the idea of living with animals. I don't know if I like the idea more than I like the reality, but I definitely like both.

I imagined these people spread out over vast territories, wandering, and every season finding others only at prearranged, traditional, long established meeting places where they could talk, exchange information, choose a mate and fertilize themselves in all kinds of ways—mentally, intellectually, socially, bodily.

And what I like most—and this is all from my imagination, I guess—is that they were direct; there was no separation between their words and their actions, no time to maneuver around others. When their bodies stuck, they stuck for as long as they were going to and then became unstuck. There were good reasons why they should have stuck and not fought and killed each other. For one, there were too few of them. Mysterious ailments killed or crippled them without warning. And they didn't live very long, as we do today. (But what is quantity in comparison with quality?) In those days forty years was a long life, and I guess if you lived to fifty or fifty-five, you were remembered and revered. In those days "old age" was a sign of great power.

Paleolithic people had to study nature in a very special way. They looked at everything and passed on each discovery and observation carefully, with great tenderness, yet with great excitement. Where we would wander through a large *meadow filled with all kinds of flowers and only take it in generally, they would look around them for many things. Was this a vulnerable place? What edible plants were there? When would they become useful? What parts of the plants were edible? Why could the animals eat them and they could not? Where should they look for these plants, by rivers, in meadows like this, inside the forests, by swamps? What happened when you ate one that made you sick? Did you have visions with some and not with others? Did the colors make a difference? Why were there so many plants on the earth? Did the stars and the sun and the seasons have any-thing to do with them? Why did plants need rain? Why were certain places almost absent of plants?*

Many questions had many answers, and some knew a great deal more than others. Some, though few and far between, had spent their whole, short lives studying plants, and to these people one went to ask and be made wise or return with more ignorance. Such was the old(?) woman I became, a woman living, with others, on a dry plateau near Manisa, Turkey, a woman with a daughter, and a husband who had died four years before in a hunting accident.

But this woman was special, perhaps because she had been allowed to be special, perhaps because of her intelli-gence or some force of nature she possessed, some moral character or personal power. It is the passing on of informa-tion, which interests me, what is lost and what is gained. The connection of the generations makes me morally and intel-lectually alive. I also didn't know how human beings are with each other in a real wilderness, and I wanted to know. For all these reasons, I became that woman of 35,363BC. And the three days were worth everything I paid.

First, she went out alone with her daughter, a knowl-edgeable woman in her own right (twenty-one years old). She knew the country. Both knew how and where to get food.

(Others did, too, but both of them knew it better, and they weren't looking only for food. She had other things on her mind, namely plants.) Her sense of smell told her a lot of things, not only where the animals were lurking. She could smell water, put her nose down to the ground and smell animal droppings, crumble them in her hands and smell them again, tell what they had eaten, where they ate, and how long ago they had been there. She crushed leaves, tasted them, then spat them out, knowing whether or not they could be used. Some she picked, putting them in her pouch, and some she and her daughter consumed on the spot, even picking berries and digging for tubers.

The wandering was slow, and often they just stopped and sat for a few hours, seeming to do nothing, but in their inaction the world was coming to them, always. That's how they knew it. They had to wait, as the world had to wait. There was nowhere to go. There was only the whole earth and sky and waters moving around them, slowly. Their "then" was a time to move and a time to sit, and having people around you was often a distraction when you were hunting for the right things. You believed these things would come to you because you didn't often have the power to come to them.

No one has impressed me as much as this "old" woman and her daughter. (She was not old, in our reckoning. But she looked old, wrinkled and bent over. But there was life there, like a hearth on a stormy December night, a hearth blazing in its container. And there was a knowledge in her that we have lost today, a feeling for things, a feeling of just being here, not of goals, of fixing something or pleasing someone, just being in it all. I know that sounds mystical. Well, so what? Let it. The experience counts, not the words, unless the words are the experience, and sometimes they are, but these days they aren't very much.

If I had to do it again, I would go back and be the

daughter. She listened with everything in her. She had deep brown eyes, dried out brown hair, legs that knew how to walk over rough terrain, and a kind of swinging gait, and ears that stopped her, suddenly, to listen, there in that dry, semi-barren country near Manisa in what is now called Turkey but was then the wide-open earth of the world.

> *Maria Paderewski*
> *Age 46. Bus driver*
> *Krakow, Poland*

No. 27: Isfahan, Iran. February 16, 351. [3 years; $5,750] At eighteen you are a young man who has a passionate interest in mathematics. But beyond the actual normal properties of the number system or the progressions of absolute or relative values for the movement of primes or the problems of the sub-divisions within the real or imaginary number systems, you have faded into a new interest these last three weeks, the geometric properties of landscapes, which seem, in your mind, to have practical applications to road building, irrigation projects and architecture. You "imagine" the mathematical and geometrical relations of whole sets of social and agricultural configurations, pulling them together through several "threads" which contain "radial energy" within themselves, like the "spokes" on some flowers. Or else they have "a positive value of suggestion" which forms "the field of linkage" and allows the mathematical and biological worlds to coalesce.

Surprisingly, when you present your ideas to your teacher, who is known for his mathematical subtlety, he does not laugh, and proceeds to tell you that you must study the "geometry of seeing". Music, also, would help, he thinks. And you must "fast at least one day a week," for that will "open the pores of sight". You must study these subjects deeply for three years. He is serious. You will not laugh at him; you cannot. He is your teacher and is now fifty-three years old, a man who has lived and seen much. And so you begin the three-year training, expecting nothing.

Dear Past Rentals,

What do I know about mathematics? If there is a cause, it must be floating beyond the territorial waters of my daily life, because there is no practical reason I can think of for choosing the life of an eighteen-year-old mathematician from Isfahan, Iran, and a kind of mathematical mystic for that matter.

There is no reason, of course. Perhaps I'll have to invent it or else pull it up with the fishing line of my conscious mind. Strange things happen when something is picked "almost" at random. Threads are attached to the event. Figures start to form in the hazy half-light of experience, in a suggestive chiaroscuro. And thoughts, events, and feelings begin to cluster around tangible reasons, seemingly solid directions, in effect, what turn out to be rationalizations for action. There is a reason or there are reasons somewhere, but they are slightly beyond us, like voices in a dream. Like shadowy fish anchored a mile deep in the pelagic seas, we need a very powerful antenna to listen, and the message is often, at best, garbled.

But an attempt should be made to find some meaning within the seemingly meaningless. If not, our personalities will, in time, fall apart and we will fail to recognize that we have created anything. We will end up the victims of some incredible emptiness.

First, there are levels of belief. Without them, we would not be able to feel we are approaching anything. The levels are, at first, arbitrary, then more specifically related to a growing hierarchy of needs. Then, there is a compulsion to impose one's needs on the world in the form of beliefs. Finally, an ambiguous, floating consciousness exists beyond belief or the need to impose belief.

Now, to the journey to Isfahan and the eighteen-year-old mathematician. I will project three sets of reasons why I chose this entry, and you may, if you will, regard them as being some sort of outgrowth or expression of my own situation and personality. But in order to see them in some larger context, it will be necessary to expand from there into the third level of existence in which there is no imposition of need in the form of belief. I chose this item because I am somehow attached to Iran or to what I imagine Iran to be or to have been. It is, in my mind, that big land, old as the ancient transmission of texts, the pathway of others in their migrations, a land without natural defenses (unlike China), and containing a music and style toward which I am drawn without completely knowing why.

It is both a cold and a warm land. (I am referring to climate, not to personality or culture.) But the mixture of its cold north and its warm south, its fertile flatlands, its villages built up from bricks as from the earth itself, its sensuous, intellectual people, its sophisticated music and art—all these mean that Iran has had to assimilate much and yet maintain some central core of personality. Assimilation produces a corresponding movement toward the creation of a core of selfhood. Yet, also, there is the diversity of its people, the Kurds, the Baluchis, the Fars, the Afshars, and others, many of them nomadic and yet having certain fixed frames of reference, in fact large, traditional ones. There are the cities—Shiraz, Isfahan, Yazd, Ardabil, Meshed, Tabriz—some of whose architecture is enough to make your esthetic mouth water. No bells but the call to prayer. And in the ancient cities no sounds, but the call to prayer (that is, after the Islamic invasion). And beyond the cities, a vast silence, flat and solid as the air which blows up from the Gulf of Oman or the colder wind out of the Caspian Sea.

If the aura of the land were not enough to attract me (why do I like that music, that art, those rugs, the ones of the nomadic peoples), there is also my waxing and waning interest in "the imagination of social projects". Whole utopias have been created in my head for the purpose of solving real problems. And here my mathematician friend has fallen, in his desire for some thread of connection with the real world through the imagination and abstraction.

Can this not have been (and still may be) a common response in the face of an incredible weakness of power? Those who could not defend themselves originally found another useful level of strategy, slipped like a spy into the mind, walked along with others, pretending to be their shadows, their gestures, their lives. They became the projection of the outwardly unlived lives of others, even of the whole people, a shadow thrown out like a cape of breath onto the landscape. And here our mathematician has fallen (if up or down have any relevance in that world).

The interest in the movement of primes or the problems of the sub-division within the real or imaginary number systems have been lost in the sexual urges of the body to connect the real world of desire with the salvaged world of the mind by throwing it out onto the screen of life, but still with a certain hesitancy, an imagined relief (in both senses), a positive yet invented direction. And thus it is his master who must guide him, for the young man must return to childhood, undergo a deliberate neoteny. The advice is great, greater than we would expect, for this man asks him to fast, to "open the pores of sight" not to abandon his projects but to exist with and within them, and the response of the young man is also, somehow, unconsciously profound—he expects nothing. For how else can he be filled, except by emptying himself?

Then, there is a third reason, more obscure and yet more

practical than the first two, a personal one. It is necessary to relive someone else's life in order to understand one's own. Thus, the value of children, or the value of establishing within oneself a relation with the earlier world, either through association or generation, preferably through both. We review our histories at certain ages, and as we get older we either more frequently dwell on each particular, call up whole landscapes of sound, of touch, or speech, or else we deny that past, either forgetting it altogether or turning it into some fairyland beyond us. This is the problem set by the master, for he sees the division, natural ones for a young man of that age into which his student has put himself. He knows that in order to avoid the "fairyland" of the past or to see the movement into that imaginary escape as only one solution among many, there is only the large, the larger solution.

I say to you that these three "reasons" can be defined to dust, turned into a raft to which we cling, a raft of dust slowly deteriorating in the sea of impossible solutions. There is always the ocean, but it is good to come out onto dry land, as our ancestors did so many years ago.

Eric Thorvalston
Age 57. Travelling salesman
Linkoping, Sweden

No. 28: Near what is now Port Harcourt, Nigeria. 974 A.D. [6 days; $425] As a nine-year-old girl, you spend your time with your mother, milking the goats, grinding the millet, and watching the men go off to tend the cattle, while you work at the pace of the land, the movement in the sky and the ocean, but with laughter and many hilarious verbal games you play with everything you see and even with the things you don't. Such is life, surprising "entrances" of ordinary things, which require the surrender of digestion to make you more open in your growing, accepting to everything from ants to ocean, to the day and night dreams that come to you, to the cries of the goats, to the urine of cattle—as everything opens.

You watch, as the men go off fishing in the mouth of the river, an enormously wide mouth of an enormously long river—no one has ever followed it to its source. They stand on platforms in the water and spear the fish with long jabs, calling out to each other, aware of the young women who are watching them. Later, you will smell the fish they have caught, cooking over the fires the women have prepared, and all will come to eat.

The fish and the birds that settle near you, when they are caught, are eaten; but the cattle, the spoiled and pampered cattle, are not. Sometimes a cow will die and all of you will eat it, down to the bones. That is the only way you have tasted the flesh of cattle, for you do not slaughter them. They are the sign of wealth for all of you, and therefore they are milked and bled, and the milk and blood mixed with millet and other foods, and eaten. How nourishing the blood and milk of cattle can be and the smell of fish roasted on the fires. You are all thankful for their lives.

You listen to the men singing their cattle songs and sometimes, though it is greatly forbidden, listen to the other songs they also sing, never telling anyone about them, as the other girls you know also listen, a bit afraid but full of the transport of that singing.

Sometimes a trader will come from far down the coast, bringing things you have never seen before, and you will watch, straining on the edge of the crowd of adults and children, watch with wide eyes, your mind saying nothing, only watching, as they are unfolded in all their mysterious glory. Thus, there is news from the others along the coastline, whose lives are sewn to the ocean.

As you grow, you watch your mother and the other women around you, listening to their stories, watching them laugh with their husbands, seeing them dance, sometimes for hours at night when the full moon has risen over the ocean. Though you're nine years old, you know where you will be going when you reach "the age of the first bleeding". You will be ready.

For the last few weeks, you have been playing with sand, at first feeling it fall through your fingers, warm and comforting, unconscious of anything, lost as you are, floating in a warm, dreamy breath. Then you started smoothing out the waves of sand, drawing patterns in the sand, old designs and then new ones, feeling your fingers, your hands, your arms moving beyond you as if they were another person, while your whole body still floated on in your dreamy breath.

One day, some extra dye you had brought with you accidentally spilled on the sand. As you began to smooth it out, you noticed the colored patterns the dye had made. Your hands played with the single color as it was absorbed, and you began to see that coloring small handfuls of sand would allow you to make up larger patterns. You would bring the sand back to the village, to your home there and dye each handful, and when they were dry, you would use the now colored sand to create designs, patterns.

But you have worried about what others would think. Would your mother give you enough of the barks and roots to make dye? You would start with small patterns and use only a little dye. What would people think? You had never seen, and you imagined they also had never seen, anything like that. But you wanted to continue, and it was a dreamy sort of painting, letting the sand run out of your fingers, something fallen out of your life as you smelled the cattle and watched the young men fishing at the mouth of the enormous river.

Dear Past Rentals,
I liked the smell of the cattle. I liked the sounds of the

goats. I liked the feel of the millet mortars, and I liked the rhythm of the work and the songs we sang. I liked the quietness and the voices singing and talking after dark. And I liked getting up early in the morning to watch the men fishing at the mouth of the river on their platforms. I liked being a very young girl and remembering how I, too, was a very young girl, and I like comparing my childhood with hers. I liked doing important things and having a sense that what I did was appreciated, was needed. I liked walking, always walking, everywhere. I liked milking the goats and feeling the wind from the sea. I liked my bare feet on that earth, now soft with mud, now sandy, now hard and dry. I liked not having a difference between indoors and outdoors. I like really being outdoors all the time, even when I slept. I liked sleeping on the ground with only a mat under me. I liked watching the birds come in to their nesting places. I liked the way the sun slipped up and down the sky in the evening. I liked every part of the day, and I liked the feeling of being in every part of the day. I liked the cradlesongs I heard, and I liked holding the babies while the mothers continued with their work or their talk. I liked being nine years old, and I like what that meant. It meant having responsibilities and yet being a young girl, wandering and looking, playing small games with the other girls and just talking near our favorite place near the sea. I liked eating the fish the men caught and I liked cooking it, which I did sometimes. I liked everything I touched in the morning when I got up, usually while there was still just a little light and there were large pieces of shadows everywhere. It is hard to say, exactly, how a young girl feels, how her mind works, how sometimes she is totally concentrating on something she is doing, like sewing, or sometimes she is just unconsciously looking and everything is automatic. But it doesn't matter. The things I like are still wonderful, still so much a part of me I wouldn't know them for myself. I am now two *young girls, even though I am now fifty-one years old.*

There is one more thing I need to tell you, and it is about my "sand painting". For a while it was the most talked about thing in the village. The children loved it. For weeks they begged their mothers for some dye or gathered the plants themselves and made their own dyes. They were all busy with dyeing. Some of their patterns were wonderful, and in the dry season they remained for weeks. Even the adults began to paint with the sand and there was much looking and much talk about the paintings. I don't know how long it lasted, whether it was a fad or something that continued and grew and became part of people's lives. But I do remember that there was a dreaminess about that painting that came from some other world, and that first feeling on the beach watching my hands and fingers and arms moving as something apart from me. In fact, since I have returned, I have spent much time learning to make natural dyes and have done several sand paintings myself, preserving them on a board covered with glue. I recommend this activity to all my friends, especially the young ones.

Marie Cristos
Age 51. Housewife
Volos, Greece

No. 29: Tunis, Tunisia. February 26, 94A.D. [6 weeks; $1975] You have been a Roman sea trader for twenty-five years and have made incursions into North African markets, where you have loaded spices coming through the Red Sea from the Indies and silks from China, stopping in Leptis Magnus to take on a shipload of grain and in Gaul to load a cargo of live pigs for the tables in Rome.

You often accompany the ships to some of their destinations, staying a while to negotiate, at other times remaining to visit friends made over the years, but most of all seeping yourself in the foreignness of the landscape, which you always marvel at. What is it about the Empire and the regions beyond it which tempt you to linger, to feel the play of difference, the aroma of another sense of time and history? Perhaps a feeling of a partially erased self, which had, in one way or another, allowed other influences to enter your creation and truly be lost among those whom others call "your kind". You have never been "a Roman" in your flesh and bones, but rather some other, more vague, less immediate entity, less than a god but more than a provincial.

You are in Tunis arranging for a shipload of grain for Rome, which you will unload at the port of Ostia. From there it will be sent to the capital. They may do with it what they will, but you will return to Sardinia, or Accra, or Tunis. You are only yourself, one person in this vague empire, yet you are the thread which continues to weave together the whole net of this vast sea.

Dear Past Rentals,

A man's world is hard to enter, even though I am sixteen years old and am from Santiago, Chile and the daughter of a tanner of hides (not mine, fortunately). My mother goes about her business, shopping, cooking, talking with the neighbors in the suburbs where we live. Sometimes she likes to sit and sew a dress for me or create some embroidery for herself (although she often doesn't like what she's done and throws it away). My father works near our house. He comes home for lunch, rests, talks to my mother, visits with his friends for a while, drinks tea and talks, and then goes back to work, five days a week. On the weekends we often go to the sea a little way from Santiago.

A man's world is hard to enter, but I wanted to try to enter it in order to know it better. After all, I am going to have to know it if I am going to have a husband, and I want to

*please him more than by cooking and shopping as my moth-
er does. I want to know what he really wants. Therefore, I
wanted to be a man, just for a while.*

*But I chose a long trip, six weeks, one a long way from
home. I guess I'm just an ambitious young lady! I hope you
don't suppose that I really want to be a man. No, of course
not. I like being what I am. But you have to know the other
side a bit, too. And I admire men greatly!*

*I also wanted a life of adventure. I haven't been many
places, and my friends and parents haven't either, though we
all read and look at the pictures in travel books and magazines. They've always seemed to me too pretty. I once saw
pictures of my native land, Chile, and especially of Santiago
and a few places in Chile I've visited. They didn't look like
that. In a way, they looked better and worse. The photogra-
pher didn't see the shacks near the sea. He didn't see the roses
some poor people plant by their back fences. He didn't see
how people belch at the dinner table, how they smile when
they've done something bad, how they wake up at night from
a bad dream, and it's only the moon.*

*So I wanted adventure, but the right kind, not the kind
in the stories we read—that's more make believe than you
can imagine. Not the movie adventures either. Not even the
kind I imagine when I think of adventure. But real adventure, far away and long ago as they say.*

*I'm glad I chose being a Roman sea trader. I got to visit
many cities around the Mediterranean Sea in the first century. I got to speak with many people this man knew well and
many he didn't know. But most of all I got to see things I'd
never seen, the grain in the holds of the ships, the silks from
China, the Roman city of Leptis Magnus, which is all made
of stone.*

*After a while I actually began to believe that under my
new self (maybe under my old self, too) there was another*

person waiting. He was seeping in, telling me to visit places I had never been to. He was always excited by how people looked, how they dressed, impressed by what they ate and how they smelled, and he didn't feel bad if they stank! Now, there's a real adventurer. All those stuffed shirts in Rome! They didn't know what they were missing. They could only eat and get fatter and fatter and finally die. They didn't know about Egyptians and Nubians, Gauls coming down to talk to us by the sea, Carthaginians who knew the people inland in the desert where I wanted to go but couldn't because I needed to stay by the sea. All kinds of people.

I didn't give my sailors anything but a good time when we got to a port. But they busted their backs for me before they got there, and I think they felt better for it. "Grumble at sea and praise in the port," they would say as if that was the most natural thing in the world. A fresh wind and they put their backs to the work, but a storm made them shake, and (to confess something to you) it made me shake, too. The ocean is a dangerous place even now, and you have to give it respect. That's one thing I learned. That's why I like men; they're courageous, most of the time, and this man in particular. He may have smelled like the oil and grain he carried in his ships, but he knew when to move and when to stay in port. "Any port in a storm," he used to say, but when the sea calmed down, he'd be off as fast as he could. He didn't like sitting around after he'd unloaded his cargo, but despite his desire to be off, he liked to talk with his friends in the port.

So what did I learn about being a man? I can't say exactly, but for me it means being courageous, wanting to explore, to see new things and to know how to talk to people, all kinds of people. And it means being a friend and not forgetting your friends and remembering your enemies, too. Actually, six weeks wasn't much time at all; maybe six years would have been better, but I'm not complaining. I got to be a man for six weeks and that was worth it.

> *Rosa Valdez*
> *Age 16. Schoolgirl*
> *Valparaiso, Chile*

No. 30: Loyang, China. December 16, 492 BC. [6 months; $1650] You have been a gourmet cook in Loyang for twenty years and have worked for some of the highest princes in the land. But for the past few years you have been on your own, owing to your great reputation. Now you are called upon to cook, and supervise the cooking of, great meals, for those same principalities.

But, now in your fifties, your great delight is the observation of all levels of humanity, from the kitchen help you employ to the most exalted princes and princesses. You are meticulous in noting down your observations with regard to the relations between food eaten, the manner in which it is eaten, and the personality of the eater.

> *Dear Past Rentals,*
> *I don't like going to a foreign country unless I can try the food in a great many places, and under a large variety of conditions. Also, I don't like "Travelling" through your entries unless there is food in it. The better the food, the more inter-esting the journey. Some travelers enter a landscape with their eyes. I enter it with my tongue, my nose, and my stom-ach. I try to smell out the best situations. When I first arrive into one of your "items of historical delectation," I make a bee line for the nearest cafe and there find out what is going on in the world I've come to. People open up when they're eating; they're more vulnerable and their heart is in front of their mind. Because they are then unguarded, it is possible to*

enter into their souls.

A gourmet cook in Loyang in 492 BC—I couldn't pass it up. Many know how legendary these Chinese cooks became. The great poet Su Tung Po was a gourmet cook, did you know that? And the Chinese have much to choose from in their foods. There was a philosophy of eating as there was of living, one, which went beyond Taoism and invaded both Confucianism and Legalism, the other two great ways of thought in ancient China. Even the "ordinary" cooks looked with envy on the great ones.

Although you do not give the early life history of this great cook (his name is Liu Chen Li), a little bit of history is in order, for it throws an important light on the interests of our artist. He was born near Kaifeng on the Hwang Ho River, of "boat merchant" parents. His childhood was not idyllic, for he had to work hard from an early age, helping with the loading and unloading and later, when he was ten or twelve, with the reckoning of "bills of lading" and other bureaucratic matters.

Of course, his mother and father both cooked, mostly fish, which they caught from the river. Mixed with vegetables and rice, it made a good, plain, healthy food for a son who had a healthy appetite (and often caught the fish himself, being taught how to cook it). By an early age he had developed a fairly wide repertoire of fish dishes, mixed with vegetables. Some of them, he remembers, were fairly hot, but most were occasionally flavored with a sauce of one kind or another, though his father preferred the plain fish and felt the sauce "colored" the taste of the food rather than "exposed" it.

The father and mother, as did their son, both liked food, and when they stopped at Kaifeng or some village along the river, they usually found the best place to eat (they had tried them all over the years) and as a result had many friends among the cooks of that region. One day when Liu Chen Li was eleven, they came to eat at a "restaurant" (that is our word today) whose cook was a friend. Unfortunately, the cook had become sick and the shop was closed. Their friend, the cook, had come down was a nasty case of dysentery and had taken to his bed. They knew he was not wealthy and asked if they might do something for him. "If only you could open my shop for me, I might be able to make a living until I was better," he replied. Spontaneously, but half-jokingly, they mentioned their son, Liu Chen Li, who was, they said, "a fairly good cook." Laughing slightly, their friend replied, "A cook?," looking at the fat belly and broad arms of the eleven year old boy. "Looks more like an eater to me than a cook". At this Liu Chen Li began to get angry. (He was always quick to anger.) His answer was more than a joke. He said, "I eat what I cook and I cook what I eat, and I can make, even you, who are sick with dysentery, hungry. I'll make your mouth water even while you're lying in bed groaning with pain."

"If you can do this," said the cook, still not rising from the pallet on which he slept, I'll put you to work." Then, Liu Chen Li disappeared into the kitchen, and there placed, forty-five minutes later, before the astounded cook, a meal of fish and rice, simple in its preparation but elegantly cooked, and this meal did make the cook's mouth water.

And what were the parents of Liu Chen Li doing all this time while their son was preparing this feast for the sick man? They must have known of their son's talents; in fact, they had tasted them for years. But a wink between them was all that was needed. The act itself was the proof of the boasting. "We cannot spare our son for more than three weeks, dear friend, but if he is willing to cook such a meal for you, you must be willing to let him cook for your customers."

"Of course," groaned the cook, tasting only a small part of the food and dying to eat more.

Liu Chen Li stayed with the cook for three months, not

three weeks, and from there his reputation grew. The cook became greedy and wanted Liu Chen Li to stay permanently, but the parents refused. However, they did see something to be gained by their son's abilities, and it was not long before they had another opportunity for their son to show off his talents, this time to a much more famous cook, a chef, in fact, who had cooked for more than the common merchant or peasant. Liu Chen Li, by this time, had had an opportunity to improve on his already great gifts, and when the chef tasted the food, he took him under his wing for five years, and it was here that Liu Chen Li rose greatly in the eyes of the true gourmets.

That is the early story of Liu Chen Li, whom I became for four years and six months. But I entered the story of his life much after he had become famous, and it is better that way, although at first I didn't believe it. I so much wanted to be Liu Chen Li, the boy. But the wisdom of a great man grows beyond himself until it cannot be measured, except through its incorporation of the lives of others into his own, until he has lived those other lives, if only vicariously.

But despite his temper and ambition, Liu Chen Li changed. He eventually "fell"(opened?) into a life of quiet observations, wanting to know the men who brought the vegetables, the farmers who grew them, the fishermen who caught the day's catch he used to prepare his masterpieces, and even the talents of the vegetable choppers and the cleaning boys.

His delight in haggling was almost as great as his skills in cooking. He would spend half an hour or more arguing over a few mushrooms, with a sly wink in his eye and a wide, histrionic air about him which made the peasant enter into the style of discourse himself and bargain as hard as Liu Chen Li did, always knowing that the harder they bargained the more this famous cook would pay for the vegetables.

"Friends should part as friends, my friend," he always remarked as the peasant or the fisherman or the seller of knives was about to leave him. There was never a greater complement to him than that shown by an argument over a pound of cabbage or a few carp, an argument which made the sweat stand out on both their bodies as they parried and thrusted with words of great subtlety. And at the end they embraced each other with laughter and smiles. Often, they would end by going to the local tea house and talking about one thing or another for a few hours, even if the summer would be late, even if the helpers would be left with nothing to do, and even if the guests would be kept waiting.

Liu Chen Li always knew his men. The women he was not so good with, except when he plied them with his delicacies. They could coax him out of his sulky boastings, even get him to dance a bit until he laid down his tired body in a great sweat and said, "No more, please, no more for me now," and laughed until it hurt him.

I talk about him, using the word "he" because I do not think that I was ever a great part of this man. I looked only through a small window in a corner of his soul, and that window was dusty and warped by too much of myself, my age, and my expectations. The meals colored my mind as well as my stomach, and toward the end of my "stay" I was troubled by persistent gout, which pained me greatly. But I learned a kind of great humility from this man who had come far and remained so "low" in the world of a common, widely profound crudity, and yet with a deep culinary sophistication. His laughter shook the stoves, but his warmth was more than he put in the pots.

Misha Rabinowitz Castenberg Klein
Age 43. Shoemaker
Lvov, Poland

No. 31: Krems, Austria. March 3, 1164. [8 months; $1,150]. You are a fanatic priest leading others to revolt against the established order of things in ninth century Austria. Your sexual and intellectual powers have outgrown the container in which they have been forced by the world of your time. You see and feel too much, and your compulsion to lead a revolt against what you consider iniquities is as much a part of your frustration as it is a measure of actual conditions.

You construct an elaborate theory of the coming of the Messiah and spread it throughout your parish and beyond. It kindles the discontent of the peasants, who have suffered enough, and spreads quickly over the whole region, making you, as you know, a dangerous outlaw, a heretic who will, when caught (you have no doubt you will be caught), undergo the most dire punishment. But you proceed anyway, knowing it is your fate.

You are driven. Yet in the force that compels you there is great truth, and you cherish that truth and the friendships you have made. For the first time in your life you find compassion of cosmic proportions in the people who surround you, and yet you refrain from allowing them to prostrate themselves before you to obtain relics of your life or to call you their savior. Rather, you exhort them to call themselves saviors, to find salvation in themselves and dignity in their labor.

Dear Past Rentals,

Did I have to go in the direction of my anger again? Yes, I did. For anger is a great force for good as well as evil. You would think that a man of my age (26) would not have these strong feelings, or, at least, many would think that. That is not the case. When we become angry, really angry, we forget about the world. All that exists is our anger; there's nothing else. Only from the periphery come flying the disconnected pieces of our ambiguous surroundings, like objects thrown by a poltergeist—out of nowhere. There's no reason here, except when we settle down with our anger and let it have its own life. Then, we find that it is about ourselves, how some part or parts of us have been dislocated, especially in our childhood, at least in mine, which was indeed a very dislocated one.

I don't want to carry the virtues of anger too far because getting too angry becomes a way of building a wall where none should exist. I have seen people who are angry all the time, angry at everything. A child makes them angry; a stone makes them angry; a shadow makes them angry; even a word, a single word, makes them angry. First, there was the looseness, the letting loose of the anger. But then there was the fear of that looseness, and the anger became the protection. When we are angry, we are vulnerable. We have shown ourselves, our needs, if only to an empty landscape, a release that is echoed in our fear of reprisals. Like Midas hiding his ears, they come back to us.

But there is another kind of anger, which is a path some have followed, successfully and unsuccessfully. It is the path of social anger, anger at injustice, social injustice or even "cosmic" injustice. I think of Padre Hidalgo of Mexico in the Orozco mural, waving his fist at evil. I think of Captain Ahab going down in a tremendous whirlpool of anger, as if the very fact of evil in the universe offended him. These are, perhaps, examples of "good anger".

But the opposite lurks in the shadows, waiting to speak its mind (or mindlessness). It is the anger of the inquisition, of a revolutionary-like Stalin rising on the waves of just anger and turning, inside himself, toward the evil shadows, another Ivan the Terrible, allowing himself to become the plaything of the physical world which he denied.

I chose the fanatic priest of Krems, Austria because I wanted to see how far a man of true compassion and powerful bodily feelings would go, how much he might be corrupted by the shadows lurking around him, how much the "saint" might overcome the "devil". I wanted to feel what he felt and suffer what he suffered, not for any masochism inherent in my nature (and we all have it in us) but for a chance at balancing the two forces and growing out of both, for they are both unstable.

There is also the matter of real suffering, which must effect others, and there is the matter of how we deal with it. Do we deny it? Do we collude with the forces, which cause the suffering? Or do we push it down into our daily lives, living on the edge of things, fearing the choice, wanting no part of the decision? There are innumerable ways of finding nothing, of wandering into a "prepared" landscape. Nowadays, the landscape has already been created for this purpose, far more subtle a landscape than we could have painted, ourselves, even in our imaginations.

The paradox of Rabbi Hillel so many centuries ago still remains inside our lives, unable to be exorcised: "If I am not for myself, who will be for me? If I am for myself only, what am I? If not now, when?" It is the last question which brings us to the moment of decision. Every moment is that moment. But if we think about it at every moment, we will be unable to decide. Meanwhile, the righteous (truly righteous) man will have eaten the apple in the garden, enjoyed the woman, and gone on to proclaim his divinity.

This priest was not a strong man. He had been tormented by many things in his own childhood—the sufferings of his mother (who was slightly hunchbacked) the drinking bouts of his father, a kind man most of the time but with a self-abasement astounding even to others in an age which glorified it, and a poor village existence which had no room for tolerance or wider applications of feelings and thoughts. He was not an extraordinarily intelligent man, but neither was he an intellectual dolt. He lived within the confines of the church, a proper and upstanding representative, or (as he thought of himself) "Christ's vicar on earth".

But his emotional powers were immense. They must have come from his father, whose self-abasement was probably an emotional release from a body which could not be contained by work alone. It assumed, in his father, the self-abasement of a Dostoevsky or of a martyred saint.

But the son could at some point no longer tolerate the wild acceptance of his father and turned against him. This was the beginning of his anger, his denial of the father in him and perhaps, secretly, the denial of God the father and the acceptance of his son, who abased himself for the salvation of mankind, to his way of thinking, at least, and to the thinking of most of his generation.

But, as with most actors on the stage of history, he did not realize this deep revolt until a late hour in his life. For a long time, when it rose up inside him, he countered his reaction with more anger, more action, and, oddly, more love. Yet there was in him a desire not to be thought of as the savior of the people he had attracted in his revolt against the church and the nobility. They, his followers themselves, were the saviors, he told them. They deserved the inheritance of their labors. But here again was the same self-denial, the revolt on the one hand from the authority of the father and the denial of self on the other. Was it the influence of the mother as well that kept him repeating the parental balance? The mother remained in him a shadowy figure, quiet and hard working, resting in the shade of the father and his afflictions.

At this point I had to leave him. Eight months was enough of suffering, deprivation, and a strange and negative assertion, the great truths of our fate, and our living anguish.

I do not consider myself a tourist in the twelfth century; yet I do not consider myself a full participant. I am in the middle distance, listening to myself listening to others, always on the borderland between the assertive anger and the self-pitying, destructive shadows.

> Nedeljiko Prica
> Age 26
> Zagreb, Yugoslavia

No. 32: Fez, Morocco. February 11, 1658. [One day; $100]. You are a small farmer living not far from Fez, who comes every week to sell his vegetables in the market. Because you have made this journey for twenty-eight years, you know everybody. You often sit in a cafe, drinking tea and smoking hashish with the local merchants and your farmer friends. It is your weekly enjoyment. Here, you talk about everything, gossip and laugh and at times even mourn the death of a friend or companion. Life is quiet and relaxed. You spend the day, sell what you can, talk, drink, pray at the appropriate times, eat, and then return to your farm and your family.

Your wife usually comes to the marketplace with you, but this week your son, eleven years old, has come. Though he has come many times before, he will today sit with the men, drinking tea and be looked upon and questioned. You hope, in fact you expect him, to acquit himself well, for he is a jewel among boys, quick in body and mind and devoted to his friends and his elders. You are, of course proud of him.

No. 33: Near Tuscallusa, Alabama. June 24, 1836. [2 years; $2,050]
You are twenty-six years old, a slave woman living in Alabama. Brilliant and courageous, you have devised stratagems which have

made you almost invisible, in all your lifetime rescuing hundreds of people, infants and elderly, even cripples and the insane. You knew the routes and the people along the way, friends who would help you hide your people, then pass them on to the next person until they reached the North, where the horror was less.

You never married, but were welcomed by all men. You are committed to something more than a game, something that involves a grand process in which you almost enjoy the movement, dangers, personalities, and stratagems.

Dear Past Rentals,

The rental, even of a small part of a life (though the shadow of that short time may be immense) requires in us an obligation of our own, a responsibility for our own life. Some things ring the right bells, strange bells that have their own illusive harmonies, their own movements toward something we want to discover about ourselves. And so it is with this catalog entry, along with the others I have requested.

In short, there was a slavery in me that I needed to escape from, the slavery of my boring, actual suburban life. I was not told that everything would erupt from its settled mass. I followed the deep and unstated assumptions of my class, white and middle, and its horizons. But somehow—perhaps it's age only that brings about change—life has a way of teaching, which is not found in the stating of problems alone but in the transformations of our sets of intuitions into situations we would never have dreamed of entering.

I am a thirty-six year old woman, in good health, with a "good" family, two children, twelve and sixteen, and a husband who brings home lots of "bacon". I see my women friends regularly and in the last five years have taken many classes at the local college, classes which I have loved, indeed, have been fascinated by. I have eaten well and slept well and even made love well. My children go to a good school, eat good lunches, and are involved in many activities, which they seem to like. There are no "problems" in our family.

Well, that's true. At least until you run into something like a transparent wall. I'm sure you want to know what a "transparent wall" should be. It's a barrier you can see through but can't completely get through. That's what I saw in the period of a few months last year. First, I saw one wall, and then the others started appearing. If you can walk through one of them, you can walk through many others—not all of them, however.

That's when I started seriously looking at your catalog. Why I took the first trip to 19th century Paris right after the fall of the Paris Commune I can't figure out and really don't want to. It really isn't a question of why I did it but one of what it did to me. It knocked me right through that transparent wall. Something opened up. And something also stopped in me. It was a kind of death and at the same time also a kind of birth. Once you walk through a transparent wall, the landscape changes, the children look different, your husband becomes a different person to you—not that you don't love him, but that you want to love him in a different way.

Then, I took one more trip, this time to North Africa in 1872 BC. This was a quiet, walking trip, filled with occasional people and long periods of moving along the Mediterranean coast, a whole, different feeling. People lived in a different world, neither better nor worse than my own, but different. One thing is important about these trips. At first you think that the world you have entered is really better than the one you've left. But soon you begin to find out that they are all equal, and the more worlds you enter the more you realize this.

But a trip must require of us, as I said earlier, an obligation on our part, an obligation to our own life, which is the center of our experience. At first I regretted my life, denigrated it, thought it was demeaning in comparison with all the other "lives" I was offered through your catalog. But all lives are equal, equally important because they all return to our own. Yet, I further realized, these journeys are ways of working out the conditions of our own existences, breaking through the transparent walls and increasing the possibilities of our selves, clarifying and broadening the overlays of feelings and the tones of action. We are like a bell which must be rung in order to be heard, a bell of many timbres.

The last catalog gave me clues. Just reading it opened the pores of my life. I was still searching. And this time I found it. It was your Tuscallusa, Alabama entry for two years as a twenty-six-year-old slave woman who was a transporter on the Underground Railroad in 1846. The action to me was truly symbolic. As I said at the beginning of my letter, I needed to act out through this trip the break with the slavery of my past, my suburban past, and find some resolution, some accommodation with it as well. Here was a heroic woman, a brilliant and courageous one, who used her intelligence and courage to rescue herself and others whose lives were a part of her own—children, old people, cripples, the foolish, it didn't matter to her. Each life was a part of her own, and she wished her own to be a part of theirs. And they were; they truly were.

Cynthia Miller
Age 36. Housewife
Los Angeles, California

No. 34: Near Maknassy, Tunisia. January 3, 816. [6 hours; $45] You are now ten, a young, and sometimes serious Tuareg girl, and tonight, after weeks of work, there will be an ahal. You will gather at night, in a tent, forming a circle with the other young people, joking and singing for most of the evening, rubbing noses with the boys, and generally having a good time. Then, you will walk back to your own tents and go to sleep. That is all. But you are looking forward to the singing tonight and especially to the boys.

No. 35: Near Santa Barbara, California. March 20, 1384. [10 days; $150] You are a California Indian, forty-six years old, who has never left this area between the mountains and the ocean. The silence of the landscape is immense. The ocean is a few hours journey away. You spend your days visiting friends, going on hunting trips, gossiping, discussing religious questions of great speculation. But in all this life of yours you are immersed in something you cannot describe yet accept totally, a world and a landscape, a fruitful desert, the hills filled with bear, deer and cougar, the rivers with fish, the ocean, and the round sun rising and falling into the sea and rising again from the mountains.

Dear Past Rentals,

In school last year we studied the California Indians. I did a report on the Indians near my home, Santa Barbara. It was five pages. I drew pictures of their homes and pictures of their boats and pots and tools. But I didn't say much because I didn't know much.

My father was looking through your catalog. He showed me No. 35, "Near Santa Barbara, California," about a forty-six year old Indian. I wanted to go, but my parents were worried about me. They wrote to you, asking if I would be in any danger. You said no, it was safe. I could also go, you said, on the young people's plan, especially for kids my age. Therefore, I went. It was a ten-day trip. I now feel like a California Indian. Every time I look at the mountains or hike there with my father and my friends, I know something almost nobody else knows.

I can only say a few things about these people. They hunted deer, of course. They fished in the ocean and in the streams that came down from the mountains. They gathered acorns and ground them up to make food. I didn't really like the acorns. The man I became was forty-six years old and he didn't know any other food, so he liked acorn mush. Acorns are a lot of work to prepare.

They spent a lot of time telling stories, all kinds. That's what I liked the best. There were stories about all kinds of animals. There were stories about people who turned into animals. The stories told how they became people again. I liked the women's stories a lot. The men's stories were good, too. When I came back, I told a lot of these stories to my class. (I'm in the fifth grade.) Everybody liked most of the stories.

There were lots of stories about Coyote. He could change himself into anything he wanted. I like hearing those stories. Some of them were funny. When I got home, my teacher asked us to write a story, and I wrote one about Coyote. It was not one of the stories the Indians told me. I made it up myself. I'm going to tell it to you now. Remember, it's only my story:

Once Coyote wanted to show the humpbacked whale Hamphump that a whale couldn't sing any way he wanted. So coyote turned himself into a very small fish so he could swim right into Hamphump's mouth, so now Coyote was inside the whale. The whale started hearing music from inside himself, but it was only Coyote singing. Hamphump started singing, too, because he thought there might be another whale nearby and he wanted to show that he could sing better. But Coyote started to sing with three voices. Hamphump couldn't do that but he still continued to sing.

Coyote then started to sing with ten voices. All of them were very beautiful. Because the voices sounded like they were all around him, Hamphump had to stop singing and listen. He listened for a long time, and when he was tired he swam along the shore of the ocean to leave the voices behind him. But wherever he went, the singing was still all around him, on the top and on the bottom and on the front and back and on the sides. "How could this be?" said Hamphump. A voice inside him answered, "It can be because I can do this." It was coyote speaking. Hamphump recognized the voices of Coyote and said, "Oh, Coyote, can you teach me to sing like that? I have a beautiful voice, but I can't break it up into ten voices like you can." Coyote said that he hoped that Hamphump had learned that he couldn't do everything, even though he was very big, and Hamphump said yes, but he still wanted the voice that Coyote had created. Coyote said, "I will give you one wonderful voice, but I can not give you ten wonderful voices because that would make all the fish in the ocean very unhappy, and they need to be happy, too." So coyote gave Hamphump an even more beautiful voice and he was very happy. And that is why the humpbacked whales have such beautiful voices.

I'm glad I went. There were a few problems, but mostly it was pretty quiet, not like Santa Barbara today. No cars. No busses. No tractors. No factories. No rock and roll.

Carla Margolis
Age 10
Santa Barbara, California

No. 36: Near present day Ft. Lauderdale, Florida. April 2, 1546. [5 hours; $75] You are an Indian who has been fishing in the estuary of a small river in southern Florida. You see a ship you have never seen before out to sea about 250 yards from shore. It has three masts and its sails are down. Smaller boats are being lowered and some men are on board. You see them row closer to shore. You stare at them for a long time, then quickly paddle back to your village to warn your people about a vision you had seen, one which, you think, presages evil and destruction.

Dear Past Rentals,

Thank God for the short time of this trip because I really didn't want to see that ship offshore, even though, within my actual, present day self, I knew what it was. (I still received a shock from the newness of the experience as an Indian and also from the recognition of what I, Maurice Clouse of Nantes, France, have known since my American history class when I was nine years old.)

Still, the shock works both ways, "forwards" and "backwards". I liked being out in the estuary alone, quietly fishing, watching the birds overhead and feeling the quietness and gentleness of the waters, half salty and half fresh, mixing below me. Were the fish I had caught fresh water or salt water fish? I still don't know, and I should know.

But somehow the arrival of those people from across the sea frightened me so much I fled to the safety of the shore (watching them enter their small boats and row toward me, metal covering their bodies and shining in the sunlight). A kind of cold lightning ran through me. I felt as if I had been struck by an invisible thread of something, like a long sword of sunlight rushing through the water or a spear I could see through, quickly, bending and twisting through me from my fingers through my torso and down to my feet, dispersing through the ground and, as I saw it, shaking the earth.

I saw a cape full of snakes come hissing toward me. The cape was made of light, like the dawn without its red or the thunder without its sound. I saw the head of each snake speaking in a language I did not understand. They were all speaking together and moving slowly toward me. They knew I was there and I knew they wanted to destroy me. I shook again. I winked, but the cape of snakes was still there and kept advancing. I even threw my net at them, as if I could have captured them in mid-air and rendered them harmless. I laughed at them at first, but they showed no sign of human response. I ran toward the village. What else could I do but warn the others that these strange men were coming, and their weapon was a cape of light full of snakes.

> *Maurice Clouse*
> *Age 9*
> *Nantes, France*

No. 37: Lyons, France. November 1, 1499. [2 days; $250] You are now in Lyons, but you have traveled all over France with your performing bears. Some have died, being baited by the crowds, who are anxious to let out their anger on two not quite defenseless animals, in this case not very aggressive because of the iron collars around their necks.

You have twice been mauled by bears. But you love the sweat and excitement, the cursing and encouragement of the crowd, and you like the performing as well as the drinking and carousing afterwards. For the last five years you have been in your "little palace" in Lyons. You like the neighborhood and the people who come to see you and your show, all kinds, from peasants in town for a day to merchants passing through on their way to Paris or Bruges. You like watching both their animal intelligence and their stupidity. They get excited, as you imagine the primitive wild man of the forest would get excited (except that he is endowed with virtues beyond all civilized men).

Then, you watch the bears, how at first they are confused by the crowd and the noise and the people moving around them. Then, people start throwing things at them in order to provoke their anger, getting bolder as they sense the helplessness of the terrible beast in front of them (and possibly within them). You know the bears will become angry, but you are always amazed at how patient they are, how long it takes them to become aggressive. Either they are stupid or there is a great intelligence inside them.

You pity the crowd as you pity all humans, their sad arrogance, their excuses for living in this vile, miserable world in which love and compassion so seldom exist. But, curious creature that you are, you sympathize with them in a very deep way; in fact, you are one of them, you are all of them, and therefore you understand everything they do. Every bit of their anger, their stupidity, and their intelligence is also a part of you.

These angry, stupid, crazed, animal-people, rich and poor alike are animals, still animals with all the beauty of beasts, the wild abandon of beasts. Therefore, you drink and shout and curse in a kind of exultation of all humans on this earth and imagine your origins, which are still obscure and yet full of great promise because of the deep animal world you all possess.

Dear Past Rentals,

How much of an aristocrat I have become, though I was not born one. I was born in Bohemia, the son of a translator father and a bookworm mother. But I inherited pretensions, pretensions which have seeped inevitably into my character. They did make me learn, read, absorb everything I could find, from the history of genetics to Belgian 16th century polyphonic music. What happens when you begin on this road? You quietly follow the unsaid assumptions of your parents, good people with unfinished business, as we all have. I will pass on this unfinished business to my son, hope-

*fully with an incompleteness, which will be his, and my, sal-
vation. What we do not know, what is incomplete within us,
we bring along in our journeys, infecting our offspring with its
unrealized potential, this shadow, constant only in its ability
to cling to our lives, even in the noon of our consciousness.*

*I became an aristocrat of taste, or so I thought. My job
as the music and literature critic for Le Bricoleur, as well as
my interest in publishing articles on aesthetics and psychology, has made me much admired in certain intellectual circles and even in wider ones. People have commented on my
ability to "see clearly and intuitively into the finer and finer
essences of a work" (as one writer put it) or to merge the musical and the verbal worlds "like overlapping waves in the
sounds of two voices" (as another writer says of me). These
echoed in me like wonderful attributes, and they still do, I
think. But the real shadow, the mystery of my origins, our
origins, where was it? I was truly, deeply aware of this overwhelming condition that exists in all of us, and I tried groping around for it randomly, as a man in a dark room looks
for the light switch, which will end his awkward movements.*

*No, this was only faith raising random explorations, a
kind of panic of experience, to the level of sophisticated heu-
ristics. All of it was again reduced to an elegant statement,
with great insight but one lacking a fundamental, experien-
tial core (and cure). This I felt. And because I felt it more than
I intellectually recognized it, I shook with terror. I was somehow five feet (or fifty feet) off the ground. The earth had vanished below me. It was dark. There was nothing there. I felt I
was falling a long way and would inevitably hit the bottom
without any warning of impact. Who would not be frightened
at this prospect?*

*I had been searching, and it finally came like a clear
blast of a trumpet inside an uncertain word, your catalog
entry No. 37 from Lyons, France, the man with the bears with*

the iron collars round their necks, the man who understood the inevitable calling and merging of the animal and human worlds.

I had known this, at least in my recognition of the "animal faces" people had commented on for centuries. There were faces, which appeared to be those of wolves, or of raccoons or of bears, faces of wild animals, which people saw in others and acted accordingly towards. I knew this history, this psychology of faces, but I did not see it in myself and therefore did not see it in others. When I was groping in the darkness, I did not grab that face and hold it in my hands, feeling its power, its origins, or its potential.

Now inside your catalog entry, I was back where I belonged, back in my shadow, watching myself from another distance, and watching others through my identification with their brawling, inchoate urgings, which howled all over the planet. Now I saw our human fear of wolves, the nightmares in the caves of sleep, the suspicions of others, and yet the solidarity of all humans with one another in their struggles to pull themselves out of their shadows, out of their deep, animal past, a struggle, fortunately, still going on around me. (I mean in 1499, the year of my trip to Lyons, and today as well, though it is now much more disguised and perhaps much more dangerous.)

And I do mean fortunately, for what would we be without this primitive (atavistic?) force which represents the overwhelming image of our ties to the three billion-year history of all living things? This is what has powered us, what makes us escape from it, trailing, not "clouds of glory" as William Wordsworth supposed, but dark tears centuries long, fatal ambiguities which must inevitably turn upon us. There, we must fight to the death to integrate these meanings which appear out of nowhere like levitated sphinxes, urges from the bowels and the pancreas, from the isles of langer-

ham, from the hunger of the cells of the mind and the cells of the body, pasting us, bleeding us, merging us into a landscape into which we must disappear in order to find ourselves.

And so delight and order is restored, but at a cost, a deep one. This struggle with our animal past is the price we must pay for trying to remain "civilized" and still human. The sweat of the crowd is a part of the love we share with the animals and from which our totemistic societies have emerged. No escape velocity will set us free from our past, only a continual integration of the whole of our history.

Roger Christian
Age 33. Critic and walker
France

No. 38: Akron, Ohio. August 13, 1881. [One day; $95] You play baseball on Sunday afternoons in the park with others from your factory, the one that makes shoes for all of Ohio. It's not just the baseball; it's the summer afternoons and the picnics near the river, the songs you sing, the beer you drink, the women you watch, and the general enjoyment of all of you being together, feeling washed in exuberant clarity after those six days of work, let out for a while as if you had been in a cage for those six, long days, time to feel your body moving with other bodies, the sunlight soaking into you deeply after the dim light in the factory, and see your friends' children running and playing and laughing in the open spaces near the river, and, of course, to connect with a good pitch and watch it sail out almost into the trees. That's what life is all about, these Sundays in the park.

Dear Past Rentals,

What strikes me is this whole world of spectator sports. I have never liked it. I have always avoided it. I grew up playing. When school ended, I went home and quickly grabbed something to eat, anxious to get out with my friends. And, of course, somebody always called me out into the street or into the vacant lots nearby or down to the park to play, football, baseball, and other games, all kinds of them. Sometimes we played for a while, totally lost in the game, and then as suddenly sat down and talked for a while.

We didn't just decide to end the game. Something happened in us and there was a general agreement, set off by some sign or signs, to sit down, talk, do something else, wander off or just take in whatever was there in the day. A young boy does this. He doesn't have built into him (or at least I didn't) a desire to win, a sense of great, focused strategy, a need to glorify himself in the presence of others. (At least as far as I can remember, I was totally immersed in the world; the game was just a part of that world, inseparable from it.)

But now the game has been developed into an object we watch through time and space. It absorbs the lives of millions as they have removed themselves from being participants, with the experience and love and growth of participants. And for this reason they grow uglier and uglier, feeding off a removal from the great, wide joy of childhood, for childhood has no knowledge of fear or joy, only the growth in the world, the lack of separation from the world.

Baseball was that way when it first began. It was a game played in a larger social context, before it became refined. It was Sunday afternoons in the park, beer and picnics, a working man's holiday from the factory, a day to be with family and friends, to feel the connections, connections which had been taken away from you during those six days of work, which were a kind of debased existence. I see this debasement of the game in a worker fallen to drinking beer alone in the supposed fortress of his home, focusing his empty anger on a small screen, but without screaming at the world to become a part of it. There is no god in baseball any more. There is no beauty either. There is only the abstraction that the distancing of television produces.

Your Akron, Ohio entry brought together all these feelings, the good ones of my childhood. It put me back into the real world, and for that I am thankful.

> *Ralph Glauster*
> *Age 28. Steelworker*
> *South Bend, Indiana*

No. 39: Salisbury, England. October 2, 1439. [10 hours; $85] You are a cobbler, now thirty eight, who sits in the dim light of his shop, making shoes six days a week, knowing the lasts of your clientele as do all the shoemakers in England, nailing and cutting and stitching without end, old shoes repaired, new shoes to make, boots, sandals, slippers, from goatskin, deerskin, but mostly from cowhides, which you get from the tanner or sometimes cure yourself if a good hide comes your way.

The light of the shop this October day is bright in the late afternoon. In the distance the trees are lined up at the edge of the fields. When you look back inside, you see the reverse outlines of the houses across the street, and then your eyes again become accustomed to the light inside. You continue working, listening at times to the birds in the trees and the matin bells sounding from the church, your hands warmed sometimes from the small fire you keep going.

> *Dear Past Rentals,*
> *Yes, you're right. It was the feel of the hammer, the cut-*

ting of the shears through the leather, the smell of the metal and the smell of old shoes worn out by people you know and see every day and whose history of work is in them, and the pressure in the stitching and the feel of the needle going through leather, and the smell of the newly tanned cowhide. It was all this, all the tangible things, like the darkness of the workshop and the light outside and the sounds of people passing with voices you recognized and feelings you could attach to them and time to attach the people to the feelings. Boots, sandals, slippers and the boxes of lasts, which you kept in the back with the names of people in them. And the smell of the small fire on an autumn day. There is nothing like these particulars. You are right. They are everything.

Benjamin Reshevsky
Age 41. Boxmaker
Saratov, U.S.S.R

No. 40: Nottinghamshire, England. August 28, 1349. [3 months; $675]
Though you are forty-five years old, a woman who has worked hard all her life as a weaver of fine lace, squat and portly and with a fine, deep smile that opens your whole body till it glows, you have seen—may they indeed rest in peace—whole families of friends and neighbors dying in front of you every day from the plague. They are here today, and the next morning they are gone, melted away and carried up to God, into whose judgment you hope to be delivered and to whom you pray as you have never prayed before, with a fervor bereft of uncertainty, with a transcendent faith to balance the horror of this great disaster which has befallen your people and others in the known world and perhaps beyond it.

Though you cannot believe much in the rituals meant to ward off the disease, you participate, beyond your fears, in the general response to this dire calamity, through poultices and incantations and the ritual phrases you recite when you turn your back on a victim. Often you are seized with the horror and firmness of prayer, each day sending your voice upwards to the only god you know, secretly hating everything around you, the stench of the dead, the brutality of officials, the meaninglessness of life and even the choral grandeur of the church, watching your husband and children go down to their graves and yourself shaking each night in your small straw bed, a pile of straw in the corner of the cottage, wondering if you will be next and when it will all end.

Yet you still go on working in the fields, as the smell of the dead accumulates and the masses for them, out of sheer number, grind slowly to a halt. All life, all hope is paralyzed in a single vision of horror and emptiness, you, almost alone in your village in Nottinghamshire, surviving.

Dear Past Rentals,

People turn away from some experiences, suddenly, for example, stepping into a room in which a bottle of ammonia had been spilled or stepping back from a suddenly opened, garbage can full of its cloud of flies. The body and the mind turn away. The burden of the body's dissolutions falls to the side, and we are saved for a moment, through a natural response to living, a denial of death or suffering or chaos.

Another side to this encounter with death is curiosity. But the curiosity, which helps us live, is also a curiosity, which leads toward death. It is for this reason that a natural masochism lies like a spark of life inside us. To go on a journey to a terrible time, the time of the plague, should be understood in this context. It makes the desire to know the worst a natural desire of our living.

Because I have been a doctor for fifteen years, I am naturally drawn to the social and psychological etiology of diseases and their often attendant mass delusions, the social and psychological delirium tremens of the people involved. The plague disrupts everything. But more than that, it creates a terrible, fictional world, which attempts, through exaggeration of the problems people face, to come to terms with the real problem. There is also the escape into "the cosmic" world, into religion. There are no solutions. Everybody knows there can be no solutions. It is an impossible situation. I am interested in knowing the reactions of people to an impossible situation. Therefore, the plague.

Dr. Samuel Ransom, M.D.
Age 43. Clinical psychiatrist
Bethesda, Maryland Naval Hospital

No. 41: At the junctions of the Itapi and the Mapuera Rivers, Brazil. July 24, 447. [3 days; $225] Like all of the young women in your temporary village, though you are only seventeen, you rise at daybreak to take advantage of the light and the coolness of the air, bathe in the river, and bring back on your head the large jars of water which will be needed for cooking, cleaning, and other tasks. The men have just cleared a piece of jungle, and today the women will begin planting the food you will grow there—yams, peas, sweet potatoes, manioc, and other things, but mostly these. You will all work hard for the next few days, using your small wooden digging stick to make a hole for the seeds. The water will do the rest. Such is the way of the women among you, to raise the food for everyone.

No. 42: Near Tiahuanaco, Peru. December 14, 1273. [10 hours; $90] You are twenty-seven, a quiet and yet "visionary" herder of vicunas near Tiahuanaco. You spend weeks alone in the high plain, the Altiplano, wrapped in your alpaca shawl, and at night, sleeping on the ground in the warm summer night. Here there is little sound to interrupt your peaceful meditations and your viewings of the stars, which seem only to be in your eyes, so close they appear to be. The silences and your expansive thoughts wander in and out of you, guests of the mind and the spirit. To the few solitary herders and to yourself, you may talk at great length, or you may sit silently for hours, reciting the poems of your memory.

Words come and go in the great absences. The stars, the wind and the earth—you have them, they are within you, and the gods, or the rumors of the gods. Women spin fine alpaca and llama wool into warm shawls and beautiful blankets and give birth in small, clay huts on the edge of these immense valleys in the midst of their fear of earthquakes, of which there are many.

Tonight you are sitting, as usual, with your herd in the great silence on a warm summer night, watching from an almost minute distance the thoughts and feelings come and go softly, almost imperceptibly through your spirit as you look out over the shadows of the mountains whose shapes play with the shapes of the sky abutting them. The forces of the world are moving. They are alive.

Dear Past Rentals,

I am a young man from Kolhapur, a town just north of Goa. Your catalog reached me last year via a friend returning from Southampton, England. We enjoyed ourselves a great deal reading the entries, but for some time it did not occur to us to apply for any of the items in your offerings.

One evening several friends were talking about travel. We had all traveled a little, some more than others. One of us had even gone on an expedition to Siberia. Somehow, and suddenly, the novels of H.G. Wells were mentioned with reference to time travel, and I soon brought out the by now well-

worn copy of your catalog. My friends were amazed that such a thing was possible, for they could not at all believe there was any foundation to real time travel. My friend, who had just returned from England, stated very positively that people he had known and trusted had indeed traveled through these catalog entries.

We spent the night and even some of the next week reading and discussing many of the catalog items. All of us had different opinions about where we would like to go and who we would like to be. History for us had always been a matter of dry facts and dates to be learned and repeated on examinations, but here were the day to day lives of people from the past, not famous people either, but "ordinary" ones, like us. We are not rich, though we are better off than most Indians. We therefore decided that one of us would go, all of us pooling our resources, and that person would choose his own catalog entry. I must say that I was surprised that I won. I have never won anything in my life.

The decision was more than difficult. It actually made me grow. It made me look deeply into myself. Many entries made my "historical mouth" water. I sat imagining myself being born in a hut in Burma. I spent hours thinking about becoming a porter in Rennes, France. I thought that being a man let ashore by Cabral in 1504 in Brazil would be exciting. I even felt that being an Italian avenger of insults, in fact, a murderer, would be something I could learn from.

But the more I looked (and I had two months to decide), the more I began to think about myself and my own needs. This entry into myself grew deeper and deeper until when the day of decision came, I had to beg for an extension, which I got. Finally, two months later I realized that sound and quietness opened the heart and the mind. I needed to go somewhere, to some land with very few people, a land of vast extent, quiet and slow. I have always been a "noisy" person, always rushing into a crowd, creating confusion wherever I went. Others have always looked at me with a mixture of condescension and ambivalence, though with a certain tolerance. I knew that I had often crept away from these centers of confusion where everyone was trying to be recognized by everyone at once. I knew, with each passing day, that my desire for solitude had moved me toward your catalog entry No. 42, "near Tiahuanaco, Peru".

The price was good. It would not embarrass my friends. And, even better, everything was compressed into ten hours. That was also good since this first trip would be unmixed with complications and easily translated when I returned.

However, this was not to be. There was no way I could explain to my friends what the silences were like. They were large—indeed immense—as I sat on that enormous plain, a herder of vicunas, wrapped in my shawl in the warm summer nights, and looked up at the vast river of stars above me. I felt that I needed more time, I wanted more time, to fill myself with everything that passed, wave on wave, slowly, through a land that spoke in decades, not hours. What was time here? It did not exist for a herder of those animals. The stars did not change, the mountains remained eternally the same, and the earth, dry beneath my feet, continued to support me and my animals like the enormous, gentle hand of a giant whose palm I had come to live upon.

There is no way to explain these things, even to the smell of the vicunas, the shadows of the surrounding mountains, who are patient and do not wait for the people of this earth but for something longer and quieter. They wait in the center of quiet, in a pool whose absence of noise is drawn into itself like a blanket around a sleeping child. The stars do not speak. They look out in all directions. They grow from some other movement of soul or history or process.

My friends were disappointed. I was not. But I agreed to

contribute my share to the pool of the next traveler. And per-
haps he, also, will find his journey as unexplainable as I did
mine.

> *Amal Ramakrishna*
> *Age 19. Potter*
> *Kolhapur, India*

No. 43: Leipzig, Germany. November 14, 1737. [7 hours; $95] You
have been invited, through a violinist friend, to one of the parties
of the Bach family, whose paterfamilias is the renowned composer
Johann Sebastian. You have heard much of these festivities,
and though you are a good Lutheran, you can not imagine that
anything approaching almost riotous good humor and fun went
on anywhere in the world of music as it is reported to have gone
on at the Bach home on these occasions.

A whole family composing, improvising on the spot, the
games with musical themes, the quodlibbets, the singing of parts
backwards and forwards, the mocking of popular melodies as
well as the great performances by the whole family have raised
your expectations so high that you doubt they will be fulfilled.
And though you are a significant performer on the viola, you are
actually thinking of declining to perform if called upon (though
you have a feeling you will be dragged into the fray at a certain
point and forced to participate, as will all the guests, so you have
heard). You are at present getting into a coach with your friend
and will be arriving at the Bach home in about fifteen or twenty
minutes.

> *Dear Past Rentals,*
> *Oh, I have always dreamed of it! Now it has happened.*
> *And what I had imagined was surpassed by the reality of my*

journey. God is a Lutheran, and he is not a trinity but a twelve-toned family whose name is Bach, which means brook in German. When I imagined this happening (and I often did), I felt honored, greatly honored. But when it did happen, the honor disappeared and there was no pride, only the experience itself, which, oddly enough, was over almost before it began. That's how things go when we are lost in something overwhelming.

The lingering desires to return come over me wave after wave as I remember more and more details of that night. I am a considerable musician myself, a performer on the cello, and have always greatly admired the grandfather of that family, the great Johann Sebastian. (I cannot convey to you how much because it is beyond my power with words or even with music.) But I now do not think that returning to that night of music and true, brilliant revelry would add anything to what has already happened. And to say that I have been changed would be a misconception. Rather, it would be better to say that I have been "opened," have shaken hands with the world and the vibrations which attend it.

When we arrived, my friend (a close friend of the Bach's) and I were practically dragged into the house. The password seemed to be the invention of a part of the harmonic whole to go along with what someone would throw out spontaneously as a challenge, a phrase often as crazy and strange as the sounds we hear around us every day but do not translate into music. Here, it was so translated.

At first, we played a game, which could be called "pass the musical phrase" if anybody had bothered to give it a name. One person would offer a series of notes, usually sung, and the next person would transform them into his own music, keeping something of the original intention. Then, the next would continue the process, until everything returned to the original author who would, if he could remember it, sing his own phrase. I found this a wonderful challenge, and I must confess that I was fairly good at it, at least, after a while, when I had gotten into the spirit of the game and had downed several other kinds of spirits, which were continually being offered me with the most pleasant and happy of intentions.

Everything was a game, except that at times the mood changed. There were solemn moments in which the music had to be kept to a depth of harmonic intention, which only the Bach family could maintain, a severity of pious exclamation. First, there were the "monodic" exercises, like the one I have just described, and then things got more complex. We divided ourselves into two's, and I fortunately received Johan Christian Bach as my partner. He looked at me with a deep air of twinkling mystery, a look which eventually egged me on to compete with him and thence with the other partners.

First, a couple would decide on a two part harmonic line, sing only about a dozen or so notes, and stop. The next couple would begin, almost immediately, to imitate it, and when they had come to the end of the original line, change it into their own, but, mind you, neither partner knew what the other was going to do. It was a miracle to see how skillfully each couple manipulated their parts. The Bach daughters were especially skillful. The next time around a different "tone" was set, and after that, other tones and moods. At one time someone even suggested that there be a dramatic change in the midst of each example. Round and round we went with these, and I began, almost deliberately, although with the help of my able partner, to create, no, choose, the most extravagant harmonic combinations, ones I would never have imagined using. And they worked, somehow they worked! God has indeed changed his name to Bach!

Then there was dancing, but the dancing had to become

a parody of the music, the music being supplied by anyone who cared to play an instrument. I choose to dance for a while, just so that I would be able to be in a position to listen, rather than perform. But that changed, too. Though I danced, I was indeed performing. The music allowed me to say things through my movements, to comment, sometimes gravely, on the sounds I heard, often on familiar pieces played in outlandish ways.

It was after my fifth glass of beer that I excused myself and sat down to rest. But no sooner had I reached a chair by the side of the room, than another Bach, Wilhelm Frederich, handed me a cello. He smiled and winked and said, "It is time for us to make fun of what you will play us." I could not refuse. In fact, I did not want to refuse. I played for just ten minutes, creating what I thought were the most inventive and outlandish figures I had ever attempted, sometimes dead serious, almost melancholy, and sometimes crazy with angularity or ribald with rough German humor. I knew I was being egged on and wanted even more to be encouraged in this way.

Then, there was a moment of astounding silence. Everyone was silent. No one moved. No one coughed or sneezed. You could hear the sounds of the winter night outside, dogs barking and a coach passing in the night. That silence was as amazing as the music we had been making. It seemed, itself, to be covered with frost and to sparkle, like a tree of silence. This was, as I saw it later, a kind of prayer, a bowing down or remembrance of a great beginning before the word, as St. John has so eloquently said it, began. And the word was also filled with an infinite silence, and out of that silence came this music.

From a corner of the room, the master had sat down and was playing a piece I had heard only once before. It was a series of variations (thirty of them) on a theme written down by his wife Anna Magdelena, a piece whose amazing inventiveness and yet absolute truth of line and expression was an expansive word spoken after the prayer of the silence. There was silence afterwards as well, for at least a few minutes, a kind of awe-filled silence that one experiences in the Book of Revelation.

Then we ate. But the food was, hungry as we were, forgotten in the after tones of these variations. The applause of our modern audiences I have always felt as a denial of the expanding of the sounds within us, a cutting off of emotional development in a desire to deny the feelings evoked by the music and to sublimate those feelings into an increasingly hostile social environment of our own making. This was not the case here. There was always silence after a performance, or there was another round of invention, as the occasion demanded, according to the mood and elevation and tempo of the room's "vibrations".

I somehow stumbled out late at night with my friend. As we left (not the last ones to leave, I remember), we were so caught up in the timelessness of this celebration that we were silent all the way home, only to be "awakened" by the voice of the coachman, who had suddenly asked us if we were going to get down. At this point we both looked at each other and burst into uncontrollable laughter. The coachman was annoyed, but we didn't care. This was not some laughter of embarrassment, not at all. It was laughter of great power, of recognition, as if we had met a god along the way and conversed with him in the most normal manner imaginable. And when we had finished our "conversation," he had vanished, at least in our visual sense. But the laughter was part of the realization that he had not vanished but had left the greater part of himself behind. And that is my journey to the party of the Bach family.

Reginald Eddington
Age 45, Wood stripper and cellist
Reading, England

No. 44: Palembang, Indonesia (Sumatra). April 17, 428. [One hour; $50] You are a thirty-three year old woman, the wife of a farmer outside Palembang. You have had four children, two of whom have died. Your fifth child is now arriving and you are in labor, serious, desperate labor, from which you know you will not survive, nor will your present child. She has been removed, dead, and you are so weak you can hardly speak to the midwife, who is beside you while your son and daughter remain outside the hut.

An hour of life left in you, you gaze around the hut, your eyes desperately trying to fix on something important to you to remember, an anchor for everything you have been in this existence. You listen to the sounds of the birds, the people passing and the low voices of your children, who do not yet know that you will die. And you remember, as you have never remembered before, all that you have been in this existence.

No. 45: Madrid, Spain. August 6, 1820. [Six hours; $60] You are a twenty-four old woman, from a poor family in a village about sixty kilometers from the capital. Life in your village is difficult. The land is dry and hard, barely able to be farmed. Your three sisters are having a hard time. You are the oldest, so you have left first. There is not much in the city, but there is more there. So you came looking for work, and found it, a kitchen maid in an upper middle class house in a small, pretentious section of the city.

You can hardly stand it, all day in the kitchen, scrubbing the pots, the windows, the floors, scrubbing everywhere. Sometimes you sit, staring out the barely clear glass of the many paned and leaded windows into the lush garden, and dream—only of a good meal, that's all, the one you cannot eat, the one you see the cook serving every evening on the plates you have scrubbed immaculately until they are shining (and if they are not, you will hear about it and be threatened with expulsion).

Though young, you are not a virgin. You do not care about your virginity, as you did before you left. Now, the men may have you, almost any time they want, as long as they give you something, preferably money, or something to eat. (You are half-starved most of the time, and you steal whatever you can.) You feel like a cast off dishrag, lying over the barrel where the pickled meats are kept. You wear the same thin dress month after month, and the soap you get, somehow through charity, is a blessing, which you are afraid may be taken away from you. A bath once a month. A visit to your village once a year to bring gifts, whatever you have stolen or accumulated or been given for your favors. Thank God you are not pregnant! The church is nearby, as it is in your village, and you go often, especially when it is hot in Madrid, as it often is in the summer. There, it is cool, and you can kneel and pray to your patron saint, the saint of the poor, St. Nicholas of Myra, and wait, and wait for an answer, which you know, in your weary body, will never come. But still you go on asking, if only for the relief in the asking.

Madrid is hot, hotter than usual today. But you have taken a bath and your dress is clean, as it has not been for a long time. For weeks you have been talking to a young man, poor like yourself, who visits you when he can, bringing a piece of bread, a meat pie (luxury!), a comb he has probably stolen, and who hardly looks at you, but who is growing tired too early and needs you, if only to relax in your presence, to say what has accumulated throughout a week of hard work, to show a little love (also accumulated), to bask in your eyes and feel some importance in a life of sweat and heat and filth and the chaos of odors which surrounds you both.

Dear Past Rentals,

I, who had always been wealthy, have had everything in abundance, so great an abundance I didn't know how to measure it, have always taken my wealth for granted, and yet at moments, often frequently, felt the maids looking at me in a peculiar way I could not understand, could not even begin to understand.

Now I am not a stupid woman, nor am I entirely unsympathetic to others—I have given where and when I felt it was necessary to give, and often lavishly—but when I caught myself glancing, out of the corner of my eyes (and my mind) at the poor maids and the other servants we employed in our master estate outside Copenhagen, or when I saw them at the houses of my friends, and attempted quite futile-ly to engage them in conversation, to open myself to them so that they might do the same with me—an absolutely useless act I found out—we erected, quite naturally, that rigid wall in front of us, like a shade suddenly pulled down in front of a peeping Tom.

For a long time now I have had a growing "curiosity" (I can't think of a better word for it) about these people, how they think, what they do, what they want, or the kinds of people they associate with. I try to imagine them in different circumstances, at home, at the movies, at dinner (either at home or at a restaurant), but the novels in which they are depicted or the movies in which they are displayed are as illusionary as a smile of compassion at a cocktail party toward the wives of corporate vice-presidents.

Therefore, being an avid reader of your catalog, I was surprised (and somewhat frightened) by your entry about the servant girl from Madrid. I must admit there were two sides of me speaking, arguing with each other when I finished read-ing the entry. One side said, "Go, be that woman, suffer what she suffered, feel what she felt, sit in the kitchen where she sat

*and wear yourself out for six hours in the work of her life."
The other voice said, "This is not for you. You will do yourself
great harm. Your personality will be wrenched from its stable
frame. Be careful. This journey can make you lose your own
voice, make you come back unable to recognize the self you
left behind. No, it is too difficult. The fear alone would make
you recoil to the psychiatrist's couch."*

*Of course the battle went on for some time, and the
voices I have described here are only samples of the extremes
of both positions, feelings given voices, not necessarily voices
with feelings. For three months I went back over and over the
entry, unable to decide, drawing myself into a frightful state
of indecision. I had several dreams about what I would find
if I had gone. I avoided seeing my therapist. I knew he would
do me no good.*

*It was in May that my personal maid developed the
measles and could not go home. She was placed in an empty
room in the back of the house, and I personally attended her
there, bringing her food and liquids, books and newspapers.
She was a young girl in her mid-twenties, from El Salvador,
slightly plump and with a sallow and somewhat downcast
and abasing look about her. Her hands were very clean,
except for her fingernails, which always contained some dirt,
no matter how much she cleaned them. Her hair was crinkly,
barely down to her shoulders but was usually, when she was
working, tied in a tight bun at the back, sometimes in two
bunches on either side and only occasionally allowed to hang
freely.*

*She lay in bed with a high fever, as is often the case with
adults who contract the measles, and there was some real
danger that she could have died from the disease. My doctor
saw her twice, told me what to do and how to do it, and left.
I visited her about five times a day, changing the bedclothes
myself and placing cold compresses on her face and forehead*

to help bring the fever down. There was no danger that I would contract the illness; I had had the measles when I was a child.

I did not, except at first, ask myself why I was doing this for someone in my employ. I knew the reason at first but forgot it as I came more and more into contact with her. It was my curiosity. I didn't want to miss the opportunity of finding a way into her life. As it turned out, I did and I didn't. There were moments when I could sense something, but I still had to read between the lines, though the lines were a little bit more open now. She was truly grateful. She had not expected this. She thanked me deeply. But (looking back now a year beyond my trip) I knew that, once well, she would settle back (as she did) into that respectful distance which servants keep from their employer.

But the days of caring for her moved me, all of me, toward making up my mind. On June 9th I left. I have felt, since returning, that the trip was good for me, but I have had my doubts. The other voice continues, though not as often. There are real fears in that journey, fears I was not prepared to face, terrors which I had no idea existed in me and in others. Though as in all trips there is a core of self which remains looking from its slightly detached posture, the desire to enter more fully pushed me at times over the edge, to the point where I "lost myself" in this nineteenth century maid from the villages.

It must be said that before I left I felt I knew everything about the nineteenth century Spanish maid. I had read and read. I knew the conditions of servants at the time. I knew they were subject to being taken advantage of and were taken advantage of. I knew they subsisted on scraps from the tables of the rich and that their employers had tremendous control over their lives. I knew they were hardly paid and worked long hours. They had little time for leisure or romance or *education. Their duties and the fear of losing their employment circumscribed their lives. Some of them became prostitutes out of sheer desperation.*

I knew and yet I did not know. Those were ideas, the outward embodiments of something which must be experienced to be known. The books could almost be seen as attempts to cover up the condition of the poor in the past. They allowed the suggestion of this poverty of spirit and body but left the reader with the option of rationalizing the experience itself.

But this dish rag of a person, this cast off scrap of clothing lying in the kitchen, this ignorant human removed from her family, isolated from anyone, forced to steal and not want to steal, half-starved most of the time and semi-prostituting herself to keep from going hungry, and desiring the most petty things, a comb, a piece of soap, a small meat pie— this person was the misery I felt.

It was not something that I could talk of, and who would understand? At least here she had a bed, some food, a home of sorts. Often she wandered around in the streets after church on Sunday in a daze, too tired for longing, wanting to sleep, unable to laugh, let alone sing. And when she heard someone singing, she could only stop, stare in the direction from which the voice was coming, and wait until the music finished, then continue on her way. She was a ghost, made so by the terrible poverty in which she lived.

If she had gotten employment from a wealthier family, she might have done better, eaten better, even slept better, or had no need to allow men to make love to her. Her pride would have been intact. But that did not happen. There was no pride, only the desperation of a zombie, a disembodied spirit, a wraith whose existence was labor. Yes, she prayed, but even the prayer was disconnected because food makes for compassion and there was no food in her body. She could have eaten a thousand wafers and still not had the necessary energy to understand what she was doing. The church, though she did not think this way, was a cool place to be on a hot summer day. That was the comfort of God.

These things are still with me today as I write this letter. They will never leave me. The voice which counseled me to stay was right, at least in some ways. There are miseries too great for my body and soul. For some, inured to the pain of a poor existence, the life of this servant girl would have been understandable, both physically and mentally, and perhaps, morally. But the shock to my life has been great.

However, I, too, must take courage from this visit to the darker sides of the Spanish nineteenth century. I must tell myself, as I have, that I, too, have been courageous. And now I have, at least, been able to see my own servants with a sympathy which, though mixed with pain and fear on my part, is still a real one, not an imagined, fictional sympathy gleaned from hours of reading. For this I am grateful.

There is no moral in what I have written you. There is only this one story of a woman whose wealth could not make the bridge across the deep canyons which separate us from the poor. I am sorry that is the case, but I must recognize it as such.

Helen Moustard D'Orleans
Age 31
Cleremont Ferrand, France

No. 46: Rome, Italy. January 4, 52. [14 hours; $60] You started out as the daughter of a small farmer somewhere between Ostia and Rome, selling your father's vegetables and grains every week in the market place. But twelve years ago your father died and there was nothing else for you to do but to register at the aedile's office as a prostitute. The public official, as you had expected, had to urge you to reconsider your action. You had come to your decision months earlier. And you were not going to change your mind now.

You installed yourself, not in a brothel, but in your own small room, and proceeded to wander the streets in search of customers. Your life continued for some time in this way, and little by little your reputation grew. You were known in the districts you frequented and you began to have more and more money. The annual tax was not much and it was duly paid. What you had left over after you subtracted your rent, your clothing, and your various "expenses" began to become considerable because you had placed your money in small pockets of investment.

Now, ten years later, you have bought a small farm north of the capital and have begun making preparations for moving. But during these last few months you have been flooded with remembrances, people you have known here, customers and friends, and you have doubts about leaving for the countryside. You sit in your, now larger, rooms and memories pour into you.

No. 47: Bese, Eastern Congo. May 16, 1793. [8 hours; $375] You are a seventeen-year-old woman of the Nyanga people living in what will become known as the "Congo" and later "Zaire," the Congo being later made a separate territory as a result of western manipulation of the rich resources of the interior. The village you live in has eighty-four huts and nine outlying hamlets, a village famous for its hunters, trappers and fisherman and the art of its blacksmiths.

One night, last February, something happened, stranger than anything that had ever happened before. You had been secretly admiring a tall, muscular man, Candi Rureke, whom you had heard tell the stories of Mwindo, your people's great hero, singing and dancing with his friends and clan brothers. However, you saw him urinating on the earth, a short distance outside of the village. This was a sight very few young girls were given to seeing, though you felt he had known you were close, might see him, and had done it deliberately to seduce you.

For weeks afterward you would not go near Candi Rureke. You told yourself all kinds of stories about why it would be dangerous to approach him, even at some distance, and invented the horrors it would bring upon him and you both if this were to happen. The end of this rash of frantic fears was just beginning to taper off, and you were planning, now, even to speak to this young man, whom for all you knew, perhaps did not realize you had seen him urinating in the forest and was innocent of all your dreams and fears, which you told to nobody. About two or three weeks after this incident had "ended" for you, you had a dream which was both a shock and a revelation and on which you pondered for nearly a year. The dream, as you told it to the tribal male elders, was as follows:

A man and a dog came down the "Road of the Nineteen Animals" singing to each other. The mountain rose up on each of seven hills and spoke to them. It said, "Why do you go along this piece of dirt waking up the Birds of Fourteen Colors? You can't find birds like that anywhere and they need their sleep."

The man and his dog became quiet as they continued along the Road of the Nineteen Animals. An enormous anteater came by and asked them if they had eaten. The anteater invited them to dinner. It was a long way to the anteater's house because he lived at the far end of the forest. The man and his dog had to crawl through millions of crickets for several miles, and this was annoying, if only because the crickets' noise hurt their ears.

During the journey, the anteater began to change. First, he became a glass snake. When they entered water, he could not be seen. Sometimes he opened the lid of a rock. There they could see hundreds of jade insects making a music that sounded like bread being eaten under the earth. "These are my ears," said the anteater. He kept changing all the time. He even became the road itself, or a tongue licking up all the colors of the rocks, so that they actually disappeared. Even the leaves of the Trees With Eyes were frightened. But the man and his dog could always tell the anteater from other things he became by the low hum he gave out when he became something else.

When they entered his home, the anteater's daughter looked straight across at them. She was a thin sheet of water laid upright against the wall on which all their ancestors were reflected. They were speaking all at once so that the man and his dog could understand nothing. The anteater said, "This is the place for you," and the daughter crept back into a beautiful girl and offered them water poured from all the fingers of her hands. When they laughed at her large breasts, she calmly and matter-of-factly replied, "O, they were once a part of the sky, that's all." When they laughed again, she began to shrink, and when they looked at her deep eyes, she grew larger and larger, until there was hardly any room left in the hut.

Soon everything disappeared, except a large mound of plantains which rose up and walked away as if ashamed. The forest was beginning to fall away, little by little, and the man and the dog began pouring water from the spouts of their fingers to bring back the trees, which were gradually fading into the earth with a deep rumble as of continuous thunder. A scream ripped the sky open and blood began to fall from the blackness outside it onto the earth. Then the trees began to grow upward again, stiffer and larger than before. "I'm still part of the earth," the young girl whispered to them, a little shyly.

What was this dream of the man and his dog, the anteater, and the young girl and the sinking and growing forest? You told the men. They listened, and then they talked about it for days.

One of them came to you later and said you would now be a spirit wife, and the man whom you had seen urinating in the forest could be freely chosen as your lover, if you wanted him, though none of the offspring of your union would be claimed as his own. You had spoken, he said, with Kabutwa-kenda ("the little one just born he walked"), and it was your duty to yourself and to your people, to wait, listen and open yourself to the spirits, for they would endow you with great power. You would become a seer who might bring great strength unto yourself and the men you chose to become your lovers.

Now you are sitting in your hut, listening to the cicadas and waiting for Candi Rureke to come. Tonight he will come, you know that, and you breathe deeply. You will tell him your dream again. And he will listen, as he must.

Dear Past Rentals,

At first I thought that only the dream was important. Everything was speaking—the rocks, the jade insects, the daughter of the anteater. Lots of things flashed off and on in me as I read it. Here was a world in which everyone was modified or gradually faded into something or someone else, a fluid world, a biological world.

But there was an added level. It was the dream of the Nyanga woman in relation to her observation of Candi Rureke's urinating, a taboo which excited her "adolescent yearnings". The dream is both an explanation and an impetus toward movement on her part. It contains the menstrual blood falling from the sky. It presents the daughter of the anteater as a sheet of water, at first merely reflective, distant, and, I think it can be said, cold. But she is soon transformed into herself.

The characters in the dream are powerful in their abilities to become many things. But the dreamer is the "meta-

morphizer". She is the one who pulls the strings of the narrative. And, as was recognized later by the men, she is the powerful one. The forces of creation have soaked into her body, and she must be heard. Her special status is recognized and Candi Rureke may approach her, rather than she approach him, something she could not do at her age. The urination of Candi Rureke is resolved in the fertility of the woman, for the taboo is one of the confrontations of male "fecundity" with the province of women, the earth. At least, this is how I see the story, but it is not why I traveled to Bese, Eastern Congo, to the year 1793.

I went there because I wanted to get as far away as possible from my relatives. You might well ask why I just didn't move to another part of the country or even, for that matter, to another part of the world. No, there was something so all controlling about this family I have adopted through marriage that only an escape into time would clear up a world into which I had immersed myself since my marriage to Franz Schmidt fifteen years ago.

My husband has been an engineer for most of his life. He comes from a family of engineers. Even his great-great-grandfather was an engineer. In this family, extending over many generations, everything has had to pertain to "the plan". Even the making of the bed must have a "plan". This sense of movement through prior thought, this lack of spontaneity, has extended even to love making, to feelings, banishing intuitions, guesses, sudden desires, and impulses; for according to his way of life, they can go nowhere because they do not have a goal. The goals of lovemaking, for example, are the giving of the maximum pleasure to both parties and the making of children. Once defined, it can have no other purposes.

I am the foreign element in this large family. Franz married me, I think, in what he has thought of as a fit of madness, *an "unplanned impulse," and he has tried ever since our marriage ceremony to find a series of reasons for his actions. And find them he has. In fact, he needs them periodically to explain his actions to himself, if not to me or to his very large family. But after a few weeks, he becomes dissatisfied with them and goes on to invent others.*

Franz is not a bad man. Within his own framework he is thoughtful and considerate. (Everything must have a framework for him.) He knows exactly when to go out to dinner, and once at dinner he knows exactly what to order, how it should be prepared, what wines he should drink and at what temperatures, when the waiter should be summoned, how the glasses should be filled, and even, horrendous as it may seem, what kinds of conversations one should have with what food. Franz is not a bad man, but a rigid one, to say the least.

I have lived with Franz (and by extension with his family) for fifteen years. They all have the same reaction to me. They try to find reasons for my existence, purposes for my being the wife of Franz Schmidt. On the other hand, I proceed from opposite assumptions, at least as much as I can. I have tried to follow the "family way," and for many years I have. It is a comfortable way if you do not question the other side of things too much. There is a feeling of security in thinking like an engineer.

But I have discovered the other side; I have stepped over into a world of shadows where nothing is exact, and I have not felt comfortable, at least not at first. I had to battle all that I have adapted myself to with my husband and his family, and changing that approach to life is not easy. But maintaining myself in that family while I have been changing is even more difficult. Little by little I have transformed myself, maintaining a dual identity, outwardly being a perfect machine, even though I may appear somewhat strange to myself, and inwardly (and secretly) wandering in another world, one which my husband and his family could never imagine.

I do not want to leave my husband. I have been with him too long to start a new life with someone else, and I am too old to do this. But I do want to develop what I have found in this new world. Therefore, I decided to become that seventeen-year-old girl in Bese, Eastern Congo in 1793. That was as far away from Franz and his family as I could get. It was good for me. At last I had been able to live in a world so different from the Schmidt's that during those eight hours allotted to me I forgot all about them and reached out to touch something far more "tangible," far more unplanned.

Anna Schmidt-Maler
Age 47. Design consultant
Hamburg, Germany

No. 48: Barbados, West Indies. June 13, 1637. [7 hours; $70] One more year and you will be a bondservant no more. Your indenture will end. You shipped with Charles Wolfenstone and sixty-four persons in 1633, and you have been with a planter in Barbados now for three years. After you leave your bond master, who has worked you hard these three years, you plan to marry a local merchant, who trades on the island. You will be betrothed next January and be married the following year. You have grown fond of your new home, though you miss your family in Plymouth and hope that you may arrange their passage to Barbados; however, you do not, for the immediate future, hold out much hope for this to occur.

You are now cleaning the small house in which your bond master and his three servants live. From time to time you look out the door. In the far distance you see the ocean, blue and clear through the terribly hot, windless day. You sweat until your loose dress is soaked, but you are used to this now and take it as it comes, as a course of nature, like the births and deaths around you. Today you are planning to go down to the town and the market, and there you will speak and gossip with all sorts of people, some you know and some newly arrived in this strange, wonderful and yet terrible land.

Dear Past Rentals,

There are some things in life (and I sometimes think that it's all of life) that I can't get over, can't integrate. They go by me, slowly or quickly it doesn't matter, but they go by me. I attach meanings to them, but the meaning is a kind of slip knot bound to my hand, and most of it along the way to the ship, or whatever object or situation I choose to attach it to, is frayed, not only from age, but also from constant wear from the things I don't know, don't see, things from the invisible world. That's why I feel that people, all people, even those who sense they have some social or intellectual, or even religious power, are on the edge of this enormous float, a kind of dock moving just beyond our reach and which we call to in the things we have invented for the purpose of attachment, the wishes which always fail. And, strangely enough, that's what makes it all interesting, this living.

Now to the entry I chose from your catalog: "Barbados 1637, a bond servant". When I came upon it in your present catalog, I felt a sense of the particulars, the exact physical things this woman dealt with each day. These are easier to grasp (so I supposed) than the feelings, which involve a sense of a larger area, a level of dissociation from (and attachment to) the things themselves. Perhaps, I felt, I could sense more fully a connection with the objects of her daily life and in the quietness and simplicity of 1637 Barbados establish some *partial communion with this woman and the things which surrounded her.*

I now know this is impossible. It is all an illusion brought on by our desire to maintain ourselves in this life, to stop everything and hold it in a kind of fossilized amber of desire. That is a natural part of living, and everyone has it, whether they be a factory worker from Canton like me, or a bond servant in Barbados in 1637. All of it is such a mystery that I often think we are allowed before we die one vision of the whole of life, and that vision is the only thing we have. It is what we call our life.

In her very small room, in which she did not spend very much time (one window but no glass), she had a comb for her hair, a pair of shoes which she hardly wore (shoes were almost unnecessary), soap (given to her by her employer), two sheets (which she paid great attention to, for they were precious), one towel (which by her third year was almost falling apart), a plate, a spoon (metal), a hat, and, in her mind, a promised umbrella, not for the rain, but to keep off the sun during the very hot summer days. She had two dresses—there was no need for more—and wore no undergarments (what need of them did she have?), and kept a small, darkened fragment of glass in her room to use as a mirror. Her room was clean (there was hardly anything to clean there), but she could not keep out the mosquitoes. (I imagine in all those years she just got used to them; she put up with the bites, though she had bouts of malaria the second year out.)

When she went to town to shop, she walked with a slow, deliberate pace, like one who knows the way only too well, a familiar walk, almost without looking, having seen everything so many times that looking was not necessary. She liked to sit in the market and watch, just watch. Even when she was engaged in conversation with someone, her head turned away from time to time and she still continued talking.

When the fishermen would come in, she would haggle with them, her head turned toward the sea at times and then toward the marketplace. The bargaining was not much. It was both bargaining and looking, both necessary and both limited. It served as a focal point for the looking, for she seemed to need a fixed point from which to exist.

Often she sat with the other bondwomen who came to visit each other and sewed and talked for hours. Sometimes they would sew in silence, interrupted by flurries of talk, not conversation, and then remove themselves. All of the bondwomen had retreated into silence, as if waiting for their terms to expire. But what they would do when they were set free of their bonds they did not know.

She herself did not know, except, for her, the usual relation of a future marriage to a local merchant was a good match, yet one taken quietly, for the future, not now; now was the waiting. Life was like a very dense, slowly moving wind through which you never struggled but allowed it to carry you along. In the process you could see something coming toward you, or rather something toward which you were being drawn, like a tree passing you while you were standing still, resulting in a lack of will, only the will to remain waiting, holding on to the small things you possessed, a comb for your hair, shoes which you seldom wore, two precious sheets, a worn towel, one plate and one spoon, a hat, and a promised umbrella.

Perhaps this is my life, too, maybe all our lives, being blown past the world, as if on a ship, or an island, watching or waiting for something we know nothing about, feeling, at times, the tension of the wind which holds us, the sail of our tiny ship, rudderless, looking around in the midst of seemingly familiar situations and wondering how, why, and finally, when.

Chen Zhou
Age 39. Factory worker
Canton, China

No. 49: Bandar Abbas, India. January 4, 1759. [8 hours; $85] You are an eleven-year-old girl whose parents are at work almost every day, selling the things they manage to buy from the ships that stop on their way to Europe or further east to the islands.

But you had an accident a year ago and cannot walk. You must stay home alone, moving slowly around the empty house and losing yourself in everything around you. You spend most of your time talking to and stroking your cat, who is your best friend, though your friends come to visit you when they can.

Dear Past Rentals,
Do you know how many cripples exist today or have ever existed? Many died because they couldn't get enough to eat or couldn't defend themselves. And many survived because they used what they had, some other trait which bulged while the body shrank, a cripple's strategy, sometimes a beggar's, sometimes the strategy of an infant, containing within it the drawing power of the very young. Archeologists recently found the bones of someone who lived 11,000 years ago, a man crippled with a rare kind of dwarfism—acrome-somelic dysplasia, it's called—who had survived to around seventeen. From what they deduced, he was taken care of, perhaps indicating that people then had compassion for those who were not physically as able as themselves.

So cripples have always been with us. We have always had the problems of those who have been unable to walk, to see, or to talk, even those who have gone crazy, or perhaps been subject to intermittent bouts of epilepsy.

They interest me, those who are not as capable as we think we are. Two factors operate here. One is our compassion, which may also be our attempts to show others our compassion so they may shower on us, in however limited a way, the attention we require. The other is the frustration we feel and the vulnerability we possess when we must take care of those who are less able.

How many serious cripples were left to die? How many were even murdered to spare others the need to take care of them? We don't know, but the situation is the same today as it was throughout our history. Think of the elderly in "convalescent" homes. But think also how it was in the past within the family, the power of those fathers and mothers over their children, over their children's children. Or consider the struggle between the crippled and the well. And consider also the fear of the son or daughter that they, too, might follow the path of the cripple.

So it was necessary for me, a woman of twenty-eight, in perfect health I should add, beautiful and intelligent as well (so I have found out) to follow the life of this five-year-old girl from Bandar Abbas, India (1759). To enlarge the scope of my sympathy, though with some pain to myself. To look with other eyes. And to see the advantages of that life and therefore see my own, so successful by all physical, moral and social standards, from the eyes of a person I had thought of as deficient.

She had been a cripple for a year. She stayed at home while her parents worked. At first she cried, out of loneliness. Then, she spent hours, and later, days looking out the window at the people and animals going by. Then, she waited for her friends to come. Most of the time they were busy working with their parents, something she longed to be doing, but couldn't. When the friends came, they wanted to get away, though they spent hours talking and playing games she also could play.

The other times were spent, finally, within herself, becoming, as she did, a "collapsed experience," falling inward, to be roused out of her inwardness by the visits of others, the return of her parents, the occasional trip to the market, having to be carried on an improvised litter three miles down the road. During this time, she learned to write and read. Her parents built her a small loom on which she began to "invent" carpets. She sewed. And as much as she could move from place to place, she kept the house clean, washed the few dishes they possessed, and prepared, young as she was, some of the food.

The life of solitude, the life of a sessile human, has its own time, and as a result, its own strategies. However difficult it is for a child, she learned to wait, to occupy herself with things the "healthy" would never think of doing. She did not deliberately think of these things; she fell into them almost naturally.

For hours, though she was not conscious of it, she found herself watching her body, both inside and out. She brought up, over a period of many months of careful observation, the feelings of the kidneys, the lower bowels, the pulse in the inside of her legs. She followed her breath, imagined the light itself breathing, sang the songs she knew, and listened to the vibrations in her head. In the mornings she often noticed the warmth from the sunlight moving up through her toes, her ankles, her knees, warming her body, all the way to her shoulders. In the evenings she would watch for the first stars to appear, then think of the starlight entering her body at certain points in her hands, her forehead, and her abdomen. She did not do this a great deal, but it was one of the things she did do. So the body of a crippled girl adapted, with great pain at first, and then the momentum of her life began to guide her toward other explorations. Beginnings are always hard.

But though her acceptance of her condition was diffi-cult, even more difficult were the feelings of the strain of her condition on her parents. They were prey to that same ambivalence I mentioned earlier. She could feel their attempts to struggle against their daughter's helplessness. It did not come out in arguments but rather in a desire to be more than helpful, a solicitude which cloyed, and she could feel it. And at other times, a removal. Both were painful but eventually understandable. The child adapted, but the parents were slower. Her friends, who were not as sensitive to her condi-tion, showed, as children will, mixed responses, at times playing for hours, helping her with the weaving or the clean-ing of the house and at other times being forgetful, running off at a moment's notice to do this or that for someone who could as easily have done it for himself. But though that wounds, it is only the natural selfishness of children, frail and depen-dent as they are.

And when I returned to my perfect body, what did I see? What did I feel? You may ask, "When you see a cripple, do you immediately feel compassion for him? If a blind man asks you for money, do you automatically give it to him? Are you drawn to the handicapped?" These questions I have even asked myself. The answer is, I guess, yes, and no. Yes, because, from this experience, I had felt that inability to do with my body what I wanted, and I have always been a willful person by nature. No, because I also understood that people who cannot see or speak or walk have developed strengths in themselves, and if they are offered help too often and at cer-tain inappropriate times, out of a feeling of guilt or pride, they will turn soft and develop excuses for their disabilities.

Therefore, I do neither. I wait for the situation to devel-op. I look back at this young girl in my mind and heart (and body) and then decide, not because this or that person can-not see but because of what this person does see. And always, somewhere on the edge of my careful awareness, I envision the possible fall of my own body and tremble a little. For I imagine that we are all cripples in some way, and it is only out of fear that we tremble over the fall of others.

Eliana Marcello
Age 28. Meteorologist
Buenos Aires, Argentina

No. 50: Prato, Italy (near Florence). June 14, 1428. [5 months; $700]
You are sixteen years old, a young man now who has grown up in your father's business. Your father is a cloth worker and, of course, a member of the guild of cloth workers. And therefore you know everything about the craft, the business, and the guild.

You are expected to enter it yourself soon. But you cannot stand your father. Nor can you stand the guild, or tolerate the work, the l'Arte Della Lana. For the last three years you have worked hard and saved money, intending to make your way to Livorno and then, by ship, to Genoa, where you have friends who will not pass on any information about your whereabouts. You have been to Venice once and Genoa twice and you have learned as much as you can about Genoa, this prosperous city, the grand rival of Venice. With some luck you can enter the shipping business there and show your father what kind of a man you are. You practically know the city by heart now, and what is more, you have several friends who can guide you into your desired career.

Tonight you have packed a few things, having prepared your father for your supposed trip to Florence, where you have many friends. He will see you off, but you mean to move toward Livorno and then to Genoa, where you will begin your life.

Dear Past Rentals,

The beginning of a new life is initiated by a denial of an old one. To be sixteen and to set off on a life adventure was to me a powerful act of courage, though I know, in my mind only, that it is also a sign of foolhardiness, which marks the separation of the self from the parent. But to know is not the same as to experience, and experience is something I lack.

I grew up close to my parents and have remained close to them all my life. Even today, at fifty-three, I live near them, and we meet at least three times a week. We have been doing this for as long as I can remember. This closeness to my father and mother is not something I dislike—it has become habitual, like stretching and yawning in the morning—but there is a shadow in my life which I have always yearned to dissolve, so that real part of me that never grew out and away from them can speak.

I think you understand that I am talking about my inability to leave the parental nest when I was an adolescent or a young man, the loss of my chance to wander out into the much larger world and discover it and thereby develop a character similar to but different from my parents. I watched my friends, one after another, sally forth, and their sons after them, foolishly perhaps, from my point of view, but with an intensity rivaling the knights or the gods of old. But what is foolish is often desirable, for it is a condition of growth. I have remained wise and safe, but incomplete. My friends, on the other hand, started incomplete but have grown wise (some of them, at least).

It was not, I must insist, that my parents held me to them with a complete authority from which I was powerless to escape. No, they were relaxed. They allowed me to question, to look, to explore, generally—where I wanted. This lack of tension that in an authoritarian family would have produced rebellion—had rather, in this semi-lax atmosphere of kind reasonableness, produced its opposite, a familial torpor zone, resulting in a lack of reasons to leave.

I have pursued my father's business, working in his hardware store in Liverpool all these years, and I am doing well, financially. I now own four stores in the Liverpool area and manage them quite well. I am a prosperous merchant, with a stable family and two healthy, good-hearted children whom I dearly love. Could anything be better than this? Yes, there is always the ghost of the incomplete. Sometimes I have the urge to leave, to move to Australia, for example, and wander through that continent, becoming a sheep rancher or prospecting for minerals in the outback. The fantasies have been endless, but the social and mental inertia has been too great.

Therefore, as you can see, I have come to your catalog and especially to your entry from Prato, Italy and the sixteen year old man who is leaving his father and his father's business and moving, secretly, to Genoa to strike out on his own. It is not a novel life. I'm sure it has been repeated thousands, hundreds of thousands, of times, but it is my life, my unlived one, that through your catalog I may gladly enter.

I have finally gotten at least some sense of the excitement of the young in their propulsion out of the parental womb. I have tasted the fear and adventure of a journey from Prato to Genoa in the late fourteen century with all its dangers and exaltations. And I have made friends, which are made when everything seems clear beyond belief, bonded by belief and the need for belief, friendships almost sealed in blood because at first we know nothing beyond our own blood, and therefore we translate everything in terms of the family, at least at first. And that bonding seems to stick, even years later because the experience of friends at that age is a powerful remembrance in later years.

To eat alone or with new friends and to pay for your meal with money you yourself have created; to wander through a foreign city, stopping at times to talk to this or that stranger, always aware of the con men and thieves who lurk there; to see a woman walking in the street and imagine a life with her; to argue endlessly about "great" questions—love, infidelity, the soul, death and birth; to sing while drunk or sober, to sing often in the midst of crowds or in the emptiness of fields; to play hard, to lose hard and to win hard; to lie in despair over some trivial matter and to rise up with the freshness of the morning and be off on another journey; to pretend with great falsity of appearance and to fall into the boundaryless pool of belief; to unravel mysteries or to seem to unravel them, and to give oneself up to those mysteries; to bend while watching the world go by and to remain rigid in the moral certainty of the self; to be amused at one moment and at the other to be brought to tears by what you think is the misfortune of another but is really your own misfortune; to explore the limits of your ignorance and then to clamp on to the ghost of your certainty—all these and more, endlessly, are there to wander through, as I wandered in those five months in Genoa, a rising young man seen from the eyes of an older, "wiser" example of our humanity.

Robert Gordon
Age 53. Proprietor of hardware stores
Liverpool, England

No. 51: Hangchow, China. March 19, 1377. [3 years; $3,575] You are a minor official and have been one for fifteen years. As a representative of the Empire, a petty judge in fact, you do not work all the time; you have many days in which you are free of your position. And during those days, stretched over the fifteen years you have been in the service, you have devoted yourself, as have others of your class, to the arts—calligraphy, poetry and painting—all, of course, related to one another.

Your mother has just died, three weeks ago, and according to the custom of officials in China, you will ask for and receive a three-year leave of absence to enter into mourning for her. It is possible that your father, also, may die during this time, and you will request and be granted a further extension of your leave, though you will not take all of it—it is frowned upon, though not uncommon.

During these three years or more you will spend your days writing and reading the classics, painting and listening to poetry and music, arts over which you and your friends enjoy spending time together. And by writing poetry, painting, listening to music, time spent by yourself somewhere in the mountains or with your friends there also, over a cup of tea or some wine, reciting the poetry of your great masters Tu fu or Li Tai Po, you will enter into the spirit of nature, into the great Tao in which we are all revolving, the spirit which is so much a part of the world. The visit to the local monastery, the fall of the peach blossom, the call of a wild tiger in the mountains—all these stir your soul and make you long even more for the greater solitude of being and the insights of the Tao. It is the first day of your leave of absence.

> *Dear Past Rentals,*
>
> *How boring it was to have been a member of the Chinese literati, well fed, "well" educated, able to move around with a high level of respect, and to observe, to follow the arts, to write, to paint, to sing and to appear (and actually believe yourself) sensitive to the stirrings of nature and the inner soul, and to look down at all those who were not like you, as sensitive, as well off, as profoundly learned in the classics. How boring, those literati!*
>
> *Then why did I go to Hangchow in 1377 for three years? To endure this "boredom," many would say, would be a hypo-*

critical act, for secretly people envy this class and sincerely feel that they, too, would have entered paradise had they been a member of this group of groups. Hypocritical for me to go, to become one? Yes, in one sense it is. But there is, as there always is, a reason or reasons for things, some social reasons to hold off the inner turmoil from the mass of social connections, from people to whom it would take too much energy to explain, and some deep reasons also, which cannot really be explained unless there is a shared experience.

I went, first of all, because there are other things than my limited life, my limited perceptions. There is always the desire to be someone else, to extend, beyond the realm of imaginative sympathy, the limits of our being. But there is another reason. There is the unfed, secret desire to be what one so loudly proclaims against, with all its overtones of taste and value and lived expectations. Here is the deeper reason, for the more I rail against this way of life—its easy elegance, its polished, almost ritualistic life of Taoist mannerisms—the more I embrace it. That desire must be relieved, for it is an unnatural opposition in the self, which cries out for resolution.

Three years, it turned out, was far too long. It might have been my initial critical momentum which, of necessity, forced me to create an almost unnatural other self. As any people beginning to find itself must appear awkward in their new role—Chicanos, Blacks, born-again Jews or Christians—I, too, felt awkward. It should be remembered, however, that I had brought with me the whole of my experience and was able to stand back a bit and compare. And as time went on, I became better, more relaxed in my new self. The residue remained, but I felt more relaxed.

After the first year, I began to fall into, to experience, those excursions into the mountains—the mist over the pine trees, the unseen music in the small hut of some lonely man

*in a lonely country. I began to see into the mist of the poetry
and the quick strokes of my brush, listening to the musical
sounds of those great poets of my people, Li Po or Su Tung Po
or Tao Yuan Ming or the others, true masters of some kind of
reverie of being in which nature is the mind of minds. I felt
myself watching the leaves shivering in the wind and falling
from the autumn trees, the blossoms in April, the stones on
the rivers, the fishermen in the mist, small specks below me
throwing their nets, like shadows onto the water. I fell into a
kind of waking dream over these moments, and my other self
spoke quickly, urgently, perhaps a little too correctively. "This
is a closed world. A needle can pierce it," it said.*

*And the needles came. In the spring, when I walked by
a row of huts and saw the peasants laughing outside, I immediately thought, "How natural, how wonderful. The beauty of
these people!" But sometimes I looked again; it was my other
self, calling. And then I saw the sores on their feet, their hands
hardened with endless work, their backs bent over, and their
bodies in rags, warming themselves with the meager firewood
they gathered with so much effort. I listened to the salt in
their conversations, the cold, harshness in their lungs, drinking when they could and beating their wives sometimes for
pleasure. And I heard them making love with great gusto and
at times, in the dead heat of summer, I saw them spread out
and asleep, totally asleep from a profound exhaustion, their
whole life open to their dreams, on their backs, with their
hands spread out as if to embrace the whole dream of the sky.*

*After the second year I could not see them without a
sense of exhaustion. I knew, from my present life, prodding
me slightly, that these people fed me, clothed me, made me
what I was; and I could feel them now, this second year,
laughing at me slyly in all their words, both to me and to
themselves, listening to the overlays of their meanings, or
what I thought were their meanings.*

I did not lash out, as others did, kicking or even ver-
bally berating them or even showing the other cheek of silence
or courtesy in their presence. I merely felt uncomfortable.
They were somehow my masters, and my whole life had been
an escape from their control, a denial of the origins of my
food and clothing and the thousand things I thought I valued.
And they had the right to laugh at me. They were the mas-
ters. I was the slave.

Therefore, the third year was boring. I had learned all I
needed, and yet I stuck on, hoping for some new level to
emerge. But that did not happen, and what I have to report
is that I learned something, a kind of humility, even beyond
the angry protest against their indulgences, their narrow
artistic snobbery. And in that I will rest, at least until the
next opposition begins to grow inside me. And then I will
search for some other balance.

Robert Castro
Age 31. Bricklayer
Los Angeles, California

No. 52: Manchester, England. October 6, 1887. [2 days; $125] You
are a ten your old boy whose parents are factory workers in the
mills of Manchester. And because they work twelve hours a day
and come home exhausted, only with time to prepare supper and
go to bed, you run loose on the streets, stealing when you can,
learning to survive in this terrible jungle, which is all you know
about the world.

Dear Past Rentals,
For years I have been travelling through your catalog.
Somehow, I think that everyone who has done this, and there

have been many (a kind of "groupies of history") has fallen into a similar pattern. I want to call this to your attention because it underlies (or overlays or permeates) all our concepts and preconceptions about travelling.

First of all, we are all travelers, even if we have never signed up for any of your entries. This basic fact of our existences—that our lives are themselves journeys—gives us the assumptions we think we need in order to return to the past, if only by proxy. But our assumptions are limited. Here, "upon this bank and shoal of time" (as Shakespeare put it) we do leap into another world. Just as the language of the English is similar to our own in many ways and we suppose that English culture and its assumptions are also similar, we will feel that because we have a history, a personal one and one conditioned by memory (and a shadowy one as well), we will somehow fit and therefore understand, on some basic level, what is going on.

Well, this is true, up to a point. But the feel and taste and smell of the past are very different. Invisible changes make us stand like a question mark under a swan-necked street lamp, lost even to the names of the traffic passing us. The strings of causality connecting us to each era of the past have been rendered invisible at times and at other times have grown thick with meaning, either imposed upon from a more "powerful" past or from a more "meaningful" future.

But these problems—and they are immense and at first overwhelming to a novice—are only a small part of the significance of historical travel. So many other elements surround our lives—elements so immediate we don't notice them and at times so vast they are invisible—we, almost automatically proceed to travel through a very narrow valley, hardly noticing, and at times deliberately not noticing, the minor tremors, the movements of the sky, the slow growth and subsidence of the earth, or the courses of the planets and stars. Countless, numberless events surround us, permeate our existences, constantly tell us, through their actions where we are going, what we are, how we perceive ourselves, how deep are the layers of phenomena through which we move or believe we move. Thomas Mann opens his famous novel The Joseph Story with the question, "How deep is the well of the past?" Yes, but also how deep is the well of the present?

I suggest that all of us try this simple exercise: We sit down in the evening and try to remember all of the things we have done that day. We start from the beginning, when we first became conscious. After an hour of "remembering," we will not be able to get past the first few minutes. Detail follows detail, thickening the heavier and heavier syrup of particulars to make room for new remembrances.

Marcel Proust was the master of this art of remembering. But the order of Proust's world, like everyone else's, expelled whole classes of particulars. It could not have been otherwise. For at a certain point we are forced, as a matter of survival, to create order out of this thickening mass. The world moves in on us, like a crowd closing in on a sinister stranger, and our sense of self disappears into the world of consciousness. The self must emerge again from some secret part which even it does not understand. That is the mystery of our sense of selfhood. Yet at times we attempt to obliterate it through this desire for exploration, this movement through consciousness. It is also true, to manipulate Voltaire a little, that if there were no self, we would have to invent one.

Now what are all these movements, forces, elements (there is no word for them all) which form a kind of negative space inside and around us and seemingly compel us to act in the ways we do? Pasteur remarked that "the organism is nothing, the environment is everything," but that environment is mostly invisible, only to be understood by a process of consciousness which, if carried to extremes, destroys the *self.*

What is that invisible environment? What are those other histories contained within it? A list—somewhat helter skelter but with some order (my order?)—may give an idea of the "other history" in which we move: the history of physical events, the history of other living things, the history of ideas, the history of crowds of physical and mental events, the history of the irrational, the history of the invented world, and other histories, meta-histories, pseudo-histories, crypto-histories, etc.

First of all, "events" going on in our bodies, the flow of juices to the pancreas, the slightly changing secretions of bile from the liver, the buildup of urine in the bladder, the production of untold numbers of red blood cells every minute, the moisturizing and drying of the skin, the nerves with their infinite or almost infinite messages, the neural network as a whole, the consciousness of all the cells in the body, the falling off of its parts, pieces of skin, hair, fingernails, the closing up of scars, the opening of orifices, the awakening of the taste buds, the tiny hairs of the inner ear vibrating, the continual bombardments of light on the rods and cones of the retina, the sense of balance through the inner ear transmitted to all the bones and muscles of the body, the tremors that run through the arms, the back, the bones of the feet, the opening and closing of all the pores of the hand, the immense power of each contraction of the heart.

Shall I stop? Yes, for this list, far too short, is really infinite. Each element can be subdivided until we are on the level of cellular events, then on the level of atomic events, then the subatomic. There are other overlays as well—created categories from which we may derive the actual ones, those that we think "really" exist. Through all of these events, we travel, sometimes more and sometimes less aware of them, but always aware of them on a miniscule level, even

when we exercise our consciousness to the fullest. How small
we are when we begin this process. This is the air we breathe.
Our conscious life contracts and expands in this atmosphere.
Even the metaphors are subject to shifting; they are almost
shadows, almost ghosts from the past, filling or emptying us.

We may travel in ways not indicated in your catalog,
not even implied. Is this travelling a limitation or an advan-
tage or a way of not filling our conscious lungs with this
atmosphere of happenings, laced with infinite particulars?
We may travel through a sea of ticks and bugs, through a his-
tory of bacteria, all of whom intersect our history at times, at
all times, or in whom we are one of many factors, a history of
atomic decay, of agglutinations of proteins, steroids, chemi-
cal vats for the storing of futures, pressure chambers of
meteorological events, moving toward some point in a pos-
sible future (as we observe it) or collapsing in front of our
eyes, which don't see it. The histories of groups of numbers,
quiet gatherings in their vast, abstract universes. The histo-
ries of pauses, pauses of all dimensions. The histories of
disasters or successes. The histories of recurrences. The histo-
ries of the echoes of events. The histories of mistakes. The
histories of confused events. The histories of elements moving
in gigantic dimensions over time we cannot conceive of. The
histories of the various hells of various living and non-living
things. The histories of the shadows of things. The histories of
jokes or of the transformations of stories. The histories of
grapes. Of melons. Of termites. Of complex sugars. Of meteo-
rological impacts.

Shall I stop? Yes, the list is truly infinite. The histories
of infinities. I shall truly stop. But when shall we stop?
Nothing ends, except as an idea of ending, an illusion of an
end. And perhaps wisely, out of our own necessity as entities
with our own possibilities and limitations, we name, like
Adam in the garden, the elements of our lives, reaching into

an invented beyond to find our arms disappearing or grow-
ing paler.

The middle life of these catalog entries can look for-
wards and backwards. They are only a suggestion of an infi-
nite sea of possibility as is our own present life, and that is
the recognition that we who have traveled so much have
come to, the point from which we emanate and to which all
things in our lives return: the living present. For Past Rentals,
though it, too, has a history, must begin with our presence
(pre-sense?), and the presents we bring to it and to ourselves
through our journeys.

Wanda Lust
Age 89. Accountant
Budapest, Hungary

**No. 53: Starting from Bario, Kalimantan, Borneo, Indonesia. May 7,
1887. [3 days; $175]** You are a twenty-four year old member of the
Penan people, who are known for their complete knowledge of
the forest. You have, with two friends, spent two years working
on the coast and are now returning to your people, your long
journey, your peselai. How you all hate the coast—the filth, the
noise, the lack of manners there—and how you endured it still
for the sake of your wives and your friends! You cannot stand the
sun and seek out the shade wherever you can.

Now you are at last entering your forest and do not plan to
emerge from it for a long time. Here you will be at home, with
your blowgun (your spear attached to it). And here you will hunt
the deer, the mousedeer, and the wild pig, and fish in the rivers.
There is always enough food in the forest. And here it is quiet.
The air of your forest is filled with understood sounds, sounds
different from those you endured on the terrible coast.

No. 54: Oviedo, Asturias, Spain. March 31, 273. [2 weeks; $450]
Though you had never fought against the Romans and had been
a small farmer all your life, you had been first conscripted into
the Roman legions and then after your first desertion, made a
slave to work in the silver mines of Asturias. Though you are still
young, your body has become thin and your eyes have fallen into
your skull. At night you have trouble sleeping. The quicksilver
has entered your blood, not a good sign, but others have the same
problem. Even the Romans say that mining is "deadly labor".
What escape is there? There are spies everywhere. And yet there
is nothing worse than this kind of work. Your family is gone, you
don't know where, and you scarcely recognize your friends. They
give you a small hut against the cold and a cheap blanket and food
that would not feed a dog. The chains are removed only once a
week so you may bathe. And bathing, something you loathe, is a
Roman custom; it is not for a true Iberian. "May they rot in their
own groins, in their own kidneys. May their words turn to dust
in their mouths. May their hands become blind eyes and their
feet wander off a thousand cliffs and disappear into the bowels
of the earth." You say these things to yourself. (The others are
full of the same curses.) No, there is no hope, only anger and
determination, and finally, death.

> *Dear Past Rentals,*
> *At first I couldn't see beyond it, a chained dog forced to*
> *lap up the food of the Romans. At first I was afraid. "This is*
> *a room in hell," I immediately thought. But a second later, as*
> *I stood in the mine tunnel, I knew two things—that I was this*
> *man, this suffering, dying man, and also that I was not going*
> *to remain in his body for long. I would be liberated.*
> *But what sympathy is there with the entity you have*
> *entered? You cannot help it. His presence is too great. He*

overwhelms you with his suffering, his past, his memories of friends, women, children, and his endless mental wanderings. Even in his dreams they appear, like the dim shadows cast upon the walls of the mine tunnels by the poor Roman lantern he uses. He trembles even in his dreams. The shadows on the mineshaft walls tremble. Only the rocks are hard. And when the miners speak in their dreams, they speak in the language of coughs and wheezings, mostly muffled from the light of the natural day. It is a language of sickness.

When I first spoke from his voice, I could hear myself the way I did as a child listening to my voice on tape for the first time. It wasn't me. But the more I spoke, the more it became me.

For a while—for a week—I couldn't stop talking. Words came out of my mouth like dead animals floating downstream after a storm, a whole living stratum skimmed off the top. Then came the shaping of the words, the contact with the eyes of others, read in the light of the tunnels: a shifting reality, a projected world of desires, most of it a kind of unlived reality, everyone speaking in a newly-fashioned past tense only, reviving the buried memories of the tangible life through a few words, sometimes words dreamt the night before under a single blanket in a cold hut.

When we came out into the daylight, or the twilight and we saw the hills of our native Asturias, our Galicia from whose soil we had risen, we blinked, as if we needed to take innumerable still pictures and recompose them through memory. And each picture was a necessary wish!

Oh, the curses we thought of! They were beautiful. Because of them some of us escaped, for they returned us to the dignity of our past lives and made us act like the living. Some of us escaped; some remained. But the curses went on, being almost eternal.

"May all the letters of their names spell the words

"disaster" or "rootless minds,"

"May their fingernails be unable to scratch the itch inside their intestines"

"May they breathe in their death and expel their life with every word they utter,"

May they lie down on a bed of poison and may their ghost be shredded,"

"Go to hell in a voiceless casket,"

"Fall forever through the blackness of your empty dreams,"

"Sleep above the smoke of the fire until you are dried out and they make tallow of your fat,"

"Rape your own body every night in your dreams,"

"Make war on your children and may they return to eat you alive."

These and so many others we uttered with an intensity of feeling which grew from the shaped air of our native land and were like swords from our mouths, burning through their stomachs, exploding in their intestines, leaving them raw in their bowels and dried out, like the old carcass of a deer in the sun. In our anger the candles we made from their hides lit the fires of our hope. We would fall on them soon one day and return to the land of our fathers, mothers, brothers, and sisters, the land salted with our tears and our curses.

Juan Gallego
Age 31. Farmer. Oviedo
Asturias, Spain

No. 55: Near the present town of Theodore, Queensland. September 14, 7,005 B.C. [One day; $74] You are a twenty-eight year old "aboriginal" living with your family and wandering around on long journeys north and south of this region. Today you are setting out to painstakingly strip the bark off a large eucalyptus tree with a stone you have fashioned for this purpose. That is all you will do today, except sit with others deep into the evening, talk, and enter into the immensely complex, intricate, and revealing story games which you all know well.

No. 56: Medellin, Columbia. September 14, 1936. [2 days; $250] All you want to do now, at seventeen, is play soccer. Every day you go out, sit around with your friends, drink something, watch the girls go by, talk, play soccer, and later drink, watching the girls pass again, and sing. (All of your friends have good voices, too.)

But soccer is your passion. You howl and scream and even get into fights, but when you are in the middle of a game, there is no one, only your body moving through the field, no mind, only the field, the goal, the ball, and the other players. "This is the life I want to live all my life," you think. You carry the thought around with you like a comfortable ghost. Your body is good and you don't have to think about it. It just does what you want it to do, better and better each day.

Dear Past Rentals,

I'm sixty-eight. It was a revelation to be seventeen. I couldn't believe what kind of a body I was in. I had forgotten. It was like having driven an old, broken-down car forever and then being put into a new Porsche for a while. I had to get used to the speed, see what it could do. And it was a magnificent one. Even when it fell down, scraping its arm or an elbow, it was up and healing right away. And the vision—I could see "everything".

That was the beginning, but it is hard to calculate how the time went. Somehow there was no time. I was in the body and then I was back in my own. Everything in between was like one moment, not a series of moments. It was indivisible. I and everything I experienced were of one piece, and I belonged to it, and "it" belonged to me. How was that possible? Had I forgotten my own youth? Yet this was a picture in all dimensions, and the picture was one, indivisible experience.

When you are seventeen, there is no time; there is only the growing. You don't reflect on anything, except if you are asked to reflect on something or brought up suddenly by some situation or directly confronted by someone. You are just too involved in what you're doing. There's no time for self-consciousness.

I remember the soccer field, not grass and not dirt, but some of both, no goal posts, only a couple sticks put at both ends of the field. Sometimes the sticks were taken away and we had to find new ones. We played until we couldn't see the ball. Then, we went to visit the girls or got together to sing. God, I had a good voice, and so did my friends. Beautiful, romantic songs flowed out of us like a thick, dark wine, a syrup, glossy and rich as the night. The girls sat and listened and from time to time offered us drinks. I was not conscious of any particular girl. My attention moved from one to another as if they were all there for me to breathe in and out as I pleased. My friends felt the same way. Then, late at night we would wander home, crawl into bed and sleep that almost deathless sleep of the young.

My mother was a big, warm woman who laughed a lot. It is hard to say that I adored her; I was incapable of conceiving the idea of adoration. But I especially remember the smell of the kitchen and the aroma of her cooking. They became a part of my body, a part of my world, inseparable from the soccer and the singing. If this was heaven, then heaven has almost no time, only immense moments, seamless and infinite in depth.

My life alternated between laziness and effort, and all the admonitions of my parents (I have not yet spoken of my father) to get me to "exert" myself were in vain. I did exert myself, but when I wanted to. There was no conscious goal directed toward effort and therefore no plan, no schedule to life and therefore no "time" for anything. To put it simply, I ate when I was hungry and slept when I was tired, leaving the food and the washing to my mother, selfish and unconscious as I was.

My father was tall and straight, quite a contrast to his wife, and the stern lines on his face reinforced this look, though there were odd moments, almost unexpected, when the lines started moving, slowly, a hint of what was to come, and he burst into uncontrollable laughter. I guess that's why he and my "mother" must have gotten along so well.

Sometimes, after work, he and some of his friends would join us for a game. We always beat the pants off them. They were really too tired to play but couldn't resist the temptation. They played for an hour and then went home. We continued playing until it got dark.

What a strange feeling this has been, like a current of innocence, a cool, refreshing wave after having walked for decades through a desert of age. The air was fresher. The trees even grew for me. And I remember the smell of the soccer ball, its strong taste of rubber. And the feeling of the ball, its give as I kicked it or hit it with my head, and the feeling of colliding with someone, falling down, getting up, and running again. Even the energy, which came into me when I fought with another boy over some trivial problem in the game— and the next moment we were, friends again. This energy was a cool, transparent fountain inside.

The air I breathed, the stars I took for granted as if they were a part of my clothing (and they were), the food I consumed in quantity (never thinking of the quantity nor the

*cost), the clothes I dirtied, the parents I worried, the strangers
I looked at with only half a sense of wonder, and the eyes of
the girls and the eyes of everyone who looked at me—all were
an endless river in which the not yet born and the yet to be
born and the already dead flowed by me and I saw them for
an instant as only a montage of possibilities rising to the edge
of the skin of the world to meet my own young skin.*

*Yes, how wonderful. Many would want to go back for-
ever. But I can not. After such a temptation I have come to
realize that another trip like this would distort my life and
everything I have lived and seen, everything I have experienced. There is another whole which is larger, another wisdom which is longer and multi-dimensional, and because it
is so much a part of me that I cannot separate it from myself
(it is myself), I must, unlike my magnificent seventeen-year-
old, see it as only a slice of something else, something which I
am still involved in creating.*

*Ayam Mohammed
Age 68. Beirut
Factory worker*

No. 57: Asuncion, Paraguay. June 15, 1819. [6 years; $4,500] You have
now reached what is to you the "venerable" age of forty and have
grown extremely restless. Sitting in a shoemaker's shop for ten
years has only filled your mind and heart with a craving for the
"northern lands," what are to become later (though you do not
and cannot know this) Bolivia, Peru and Ecuador, the lands of the
high plateau, of the Indians, whose languages are so unlike your
comfortable Spanish.

Your grandfather was a sailor who, after landing in Callao,
made his way south in easy stages and after ten years of working
at this or that, settled in La Paz, that high city whose people

you have heard so much about from your father, who, travelling further south, had settled in the town of your birth, Asuncion.

How many trades your father knew you can only guess at, perhaps thirty, and though he was not good at all of them, he managed to amass a considerable knowledge, but passed on to you a fraction of them only, because he died when you were still a young man. But the stories of his father's (and your grandfather's) wanderings still fill you with a great, and now even greater, expectation. How much you have saved and planned, only you will know. Your own son is a butcher and small rancher, who has now a fairly comfortable yet hard-working life. He visits you every few months only because he is too busy to visit you more often. The talk from your mouth is of your boredom, which leads you on to tell the stories of your grandfather's wanderings and adventures, something your son is glad to hear, though you feel by now he is fed up with this single topic of conversation. He will not miss you, nor will his wife, your wife having died eight years ago of cholera (may she be blessed in heaven).

The long awaited day is approaching. You will leave next week with a traveling merchant who is going to Sucre, and from there you will find other means of moving around that vast, high land to the north. It is time to travel, to return to the past, to wander, to learn. You have been in the dust of the lowlands too long.

> *Dear Past Rentals,*
>
> *It was a disappointment to him, not completely, of course, but when he weighed everything which had occurred during those six years of wandering through the country of his dreams, the past of his grandfather, he felt he had more than exaggerated his grandfather's story.*
>
> *It was not that he did not grow in his connection with this land. In fact, he grew a great deal. But our evaluations of what we have done are determined by the ratio of our*

expectations to our successes. In this sense my man could not fulfill many of his expectations.

He did travel, over vast distances, in fact, spending a whole year moving through the plains of Paraguay, working from time to time, and then moving gradually northward, pointing himself toward and beyond Corumba in the desolate swamplands of that area in what is now western Brazil, crossing the Taquari, the Sao Laurenco, the Miranda rivers, lying once sick with fever for weeks near Punto Suarez. There must have been something in this desolate land of low-lying jungle and swamps which drew him there, but in the back of his mind, like a completely furnished room, lay his stored vision of the altiplano of Bolivia, Peru, and later, Ecuador. Perhaps only the desire for contrast held him back, so he might make the final discovery of that land even more significant.

Then, suddenly, he made his dash for the mountains. Straight west he went, but first north to San Ignacio, a small village on the Paragua River, then to Concepcion at the foot of the Blanco, then crossing the San Miguel at Ascencion, on to Trinidad and the Mamore River, with a short detour to visit the Laguna Rogoaguado, where he stayed for three days, again poised for the leap into the high country. Finally, from Reyes on the Beni River, he climbed to La Paz (Quiquiago) where he spent ten months. At last he had arrived.

In the high country, he first deliberately, and like a fool, betrayed by his expectations, set out interrogating as many people as he could, asking them everything about the land. He wanted to learn quickly, but people there are not apt to give information on demand, especially the more they know that someone desperately wants it. And the Indians did not want anybody asking questions. They volunteered information, but information that was deliberately false. At first he did not recognize its falsity, so intent was he on learning everything.

But gradually, after many months of "inquisition," he began to "learn," settling down here and there, spending time, sitting patiently, talking, smoking, travelling casually to this village or that, hardly saying a word, but watching—waiting. Somehow, he had learned patience, perhaps out of the frustration of three months of emptiness. In that land there was hope for a groveler.

It was only after eight months of "hanging around" that he gained his first sight of the great lake Titicaca, that "minor sea" in the highlands. He spent weeks there but again learned nothing. He saw and then left, but returned months later with a friend he had made on his travels north into what is now Peru. He found ten days of peace there, only by doing nothing, only listening and watching. He let himself be noticed. He did not offer to help. He sat and watched, quiet, sullen, feigning resignation, getting drunk without joy and sad without anger. The language, the bits and pieces he absorbed, were suggestions of a world as vast as his intimations in Asuncion.

His desires grabbed these small bits and exploded them into the landscape. From this he drew often-correct conclusions but sometimes-false ones, letting his heart fall into the people and their work, their songs, their words. Then, he began to feel at ease, and then there were conversations in which he learned much, often only the ability to listen without speaking, often a sense of direction, an intention, even a mist of humor about to descend upon the world and its ultimate strangeness, as he sat, listening, both the local man and himself saying nothing.

There was a trip to the south for three months, to Sucre and the mines of Potosi, where there was another great lake, the Lago Poopo. Yet this time he did not stay by the lake but wandered south to the villages, to Huanchaco, to Pulacayo and east to Villa Talavera, wandered, listened, kept a set face until he knew where he was. There was one trip on the way north to Oruro and then to Cochabamba, where he fell in love with a younger woman but had to leave because the brothers were going to kill him.

It was now time to go north. He walked with his mule driver friend from Arequipa to Lima, a long distance but it did not matter. Time was not important. There were the coastal towns of Atico and Lomas and inland, in the mountains, Coracora and Nasca and, further north, Ica. Then, through the barren plains of the altiplano, he passed through Ayacucho and Huancayo and the rivers which flowed north through Iquitos in the far northwest and then west all the way to the Pacific Ocean, a distance he was not to travel, without the presence of an almost personal brooding he had acquired.

How quiet and peaceful was this land, dry and almost barren, cold at times, and with a wild kind of desolate emptiness. Sometimes he was gone for days, wandering, on foot through the cold, bright country, surrounded by those crude, untamed peaks always covered with snow, from whose sides ran the rivers (and sometimes the ancient irrigation ditches) into fields made fertile by waters of melted snow. He would stop at a hut for the night, pay the inhabitant, some poor Indian, money for food and lodging, sit quietly by the fire, and listen with that set face he had learned to assume so easily now. Little rags of language in Quechua or Aymara would be enough—he understood some of the language by now—to set him off, internally, never betraying a sign of interest or joy.

Sometimes, because of his stone-faced silence, there were questions: why are you here, where are you going, what do you know of Cuzco, do you like our coca?

He hardly answered with words. His silences were enough for the people he stayed with. It was a kind of pass-

word, these silences. They understood and despite themselves
began to speak—they had rarely seen a Spaniard, though
they generally were taught to despise them. (Had not the
Spaniards conquered their country and were they not the
rulers of this land? They were.) Therefore, he was a guest,
and, as such, to be treated as one. He would be given the
courtesies, and if he understood at the deeper level of connec-
tion, would be given more, words as a gift, information some-
times, but mostly the chance to observe, perhaps a fight
between husband and wife, perhaps a moment of tenderness
with the children, perhaps a method of preparing the food or
a song sung while they were working or a chance to observe a
woman at work at her weaving in the sunlight—moments
only, but expanded inside, endlessly. The quieter he became,
the more he learned, the more was revealed to him the true
nature of that land of his grandfather's memory.

There was one trip to Quito and Guayaquil and the
poetic, lush land of that high (Quito) and low (Guayauil)
country. Here he had left some of the Indians behind. There
were more Spanish. He almost forgot himself, bursting into
song, remembering his former life through the quiet country
to the south, and suddenly, in the middle of his song, remem-
bering it, becoming silent, and then remembering again
where he was and among whom he was, singing again the
songs that had been taught him and even some older ones
from his home in Paraguay. "You soy como cual oja seca que
va Rodando en el mundo".

He followed the Guayaquil River to the sea and from
there took a boat south to Lima. The trip home to Asuncion
took ten months, little of it a retracing of past visits. He lin-
gered by Titicaca again, spent only three hours at Lago
Poopo, and proceeded through northern Argentina before
travelling east to Asuncion. When he returned, his son was
hard at work on his ranch. It was as if he had never left. Six

years had passed, but his son and his son's wife looked ageless to him. And Asuncion looked the same. The mules and the horses and the wagons still moved through the rutted, dusty streets, and the men sat for hours in the cafes, drinking their mate and coffee, almost in a stupor.

When he tried to talk about his travels, his son listened attentively, for hours. He had made time for this. But somehow, there was no conveying to his offspring the history of his past, which he had wanted to bundle up and carry with him, to dispense and yet keep always in his possession, neither of which he could do. Therefore, in this sense, too, there was disappointment, no rage, however, only disappointment spreading out, like that immense high country, the altiplano, over the rest of his life, for now there was only the assimilation, the entry of the whole of this past into his life and the question, never completely answered, of what it all meant.

Cray Porter
Age 30. Chemical plant foreman
Pittsburgh, Pennsylvania

No. 58: Maoping, Zhejiang Province, China. October 25, 1978. [2 weeks; $400] Your neighbors and you are building another room onto your small house. Here, as elsewhere, house building is a communal activity. When your neighbors need to build, everyone helps them. It's all mutual. It's helping your neighbor.

You build as you have for centuries, first a frame for the walls, then the earth laid into it. Then you ram down the earth with heavy poles until it is hard. The frame is taken away and the walls stand. So well constructed are they that you can tap them with a hammer and they will ring. Then, you put on the roof, the tiles (made in the village by your neighbors and you) and the wood and glass for the windows. Finally, you whitewash the walls to protect them from the rain. You will have a big party after the room is constructed, and the people who have worked on the new room will come, and you will sing and eat and talk and, if you get drunk enough, dance. It is hard work, and there is much to be done besides building a room, much other work, but it is a good time and there is much joy in working with others.

Dear Past Rentals,

I live just outside Louisville, Kentucky. I'm a woman of thirty-five and have been married twice. I grew up in Kentucky and have never been anywhere else. That's not unusual for people around here. Although we think we're all different people—and we are in many ways—we have one big thing in common. We're all alone, and deep down inside us we all feel we're alone. Yes, we do have friends, and we do have family. And there are people we know at our work and through our work. But that's not what I mean. I mean that if we could ask ourselves, deep inside, how we felt about ourselves, we would have to answer truthfully that we were alone and, by being alone, afraid. That's not a comfortable feeling to live with, but in a very important way, it built this country.

But there are—and I've read about them—places where people don't feel alone. I don't mean that these people can enter another's body, speak directly to another person, feel directly what they are feeling. No, I mean that they feel together with the people of their village, of their neighborhood, of their culture. Americans have great difficulty doing this, in my opinion, not because we are outcasts—and in a way we are, all of us—but because of our history, because of our separate origins. I teach junior high school here in Kentucky and I have told my students about this. Deep inside they hear what I say as if it were completely true, completely self-evident. But they cannot feel what it is like not to be that way because they never have.

Therefore, my greatest wish was to be a part of such a culture. I chose catalog No. 58 because it involved work, something which I know a great deal about. I don't mean my teaching. My parents were farmers and so were their parents. I guess I was the first non-farmer in the family. And I wanted to be with farmers; I've spent a long time away from my childhood, which was a farmer's childhood.

The village of Maoping is simple—small houses, a school, a barefoot doctor who studied at a large school, a mayor who lives only 100 yards from me, and the fields nearby, where we all work hard, for life in China is not easy, even after the revolution, which has brought great benefits to all people but also great responsibilities.

I helped, also, with the house building or "room adding". We all helped. We were together. We did not think about being together; we just were. And we knew exactly what to do—we had done it many times before for others. It is really amazing to me how much people knew about building, maybe not so amazing when I think of my own childhood on the farm. But the people in cities are really ignorant of such practical things and take them for granted, believing in an abstraction (money) which they can easily pass around in order to "materialize" something. That takes all the fun and connection out of life. Maybe the barter system was in some ways better.

The lumber was there already, but we had to lay a cement foundation. It is amazing how things are arranged. We mixed the cement in a large pot and poured it into molds we had built, then smoothed out the surface and while it was drying began to build the framing for the walls. But the time the framing was ready, the cement had hardened and we were able to put up the framing.

Since wood is so scarce, we used a very old and very

effective method called "rammed earth" construction. This involves putting earth of a certain consistency into the frame-work and pounding it down until it is very hard. Then, the framing is taken away and the walls remain standing. After that, wooden supports are placed on the tops of the walls and the roof beams placed on them. The roof is thatched and the walls are whitewashed. Through this rammed earth process, the walls become so hard that when they are hit with a ham-mer, they ring. The eves hang over the walls for quite a dis-tance to keep the rain off.

Sometimes we sang. Sometimes we joked. Sometimes we told stories. And sometimes we were silent. It was almost as if we knew when to sing, when to tell stories, when to be silent. It was all in us. We had known it from childhood. This is what we do on this or that occasion. This is the togetherness of a traditional culture, and it is very comforting to all. It is hard to say how this made me feel.

In Kentucky I am generally very talkative, and I don't take any back talk from anyone. I also privately respect someone else's opinion, even if it doesn't agree with mine. I'll even tell her she's wrong, at least wrong in my opinion. But here in Maoping I couldn't do that. I wouldn't have even thought of doing that. It just wasn't done. People's opinions and feelings came out, of course. They always do, but always with a sense of an apology, as if they were sorry they had to disagree with you—no harm intended, of course.

But more than that, you are living, locally, with people you've known all your life. They are your neighbors, in four dimensions, and you know all about them and they about you. If you have secrets—and everyone does—you have to hide them deep down forever and work with the people you may not like, although there is a tendency, a strong one, to sympathize and understand people whom you don't get along with, something which is hard to do in my country because it's easy to pull away, retreat into your own private world, and in one sense, into what we call our "individuality".

We had a wonderful party afterwards when the room was completed. There was lots of drinking and thanking and laughing—a good time for everyone, with the expectation that I would give my help when another family wanted to add a room to their house. I'm reminded that America used to have this custom, too, a long time ago—quilting bees, barn raisings, etc. People sang together, worked together, gossiped together. It was a way of recognizing you were a part of something else besides your own life.

But here village life is even closer, and while you don't have to think as much on your own—the "thinking" is in some ways done for you by tradition—there's a sense of security which comes from belonging to a group which protects all its members, like one big union, and I've done something for you, like help you build your home, and you see him every day and work with him every day.

But I'll tell you something. I'm kind of selfish. I really want both worlds. I want the comfort of the village and the individualism of America. Both are good. Both are needed.

Ruth Montgomery
Age 35. School teacher.
Louisville, Kentucky

No. 59: Haddad, Sudan. April 3, 893. [2 days; $175] You are thirty-one years old, a metal smith who works making tools and weapons, which you will sell in the market when you have accumulated enough of them. Your family lives about loo feet from your workplace, but only your eldest son can enter the shop where you fashion your tools and implements.

You begin with the ore, some of which you find yourself,

going on long expeditions into the iron-bearing regions of Sudan with your seven camels, or sometimes buying it from others, who have come back with it from these places.

Then, you and your two helpers begin to melt the raw material. When the ore is melted, thanks to the continuous blasts of air from the bellows your helpers operate with you, you skim off the lighter impurities and pour the ore into earthen vessels so it may cool. Later, you will use these large pieces of almost pure iron to fashion tools and other implements by melting them down and pouring them into molds, from which will emerge the things you will sell.

Today you have just purchased a large supply of ore and will begin the smelting, a long and laborious process for which you will finally be rewarded, if Allah wills it.

No. 60: Chiente, Chekiang Province, China. March 5, 1687. [4 days; $275] There has been much to learn from the strangers who came here many years ago and who have brought new foods which you have planted, for they grow well along with your rice. Maize is certainly good, but it is better grown in the north. Sometimes you eat it and it is good. But the potatoes have come into your garden and they also are good to eat and easily grown and the snow peas or mange tout or, as you call them, "Dutch beans," because the Dutch brought them. Also, you have planted cotton, which has been good for trading. You have made your clothing from it.

This you know well, for you are the wife of a small farmer near Chiente. Besides picking the small amounts of cotton you grow in your fields, you card it, clean it, spin it, and weave it, making clothes for your husband and children and yourself.

Today you are working in the fields, planting the sweet potatoes and the snow peas ("Dutch beans"), and you will help in the fields with your son for three more days. Then there is much to be done in the house. You are, like your other female friends, very busy, but you still find time to talk and sit and enjoy a cup of tea and watch the fields blossom.

> *Dear Past Rentals,*
>
> *Why is it that no one ever teaches us to garden? I guess I'm saying this because I grew up in New York City, where the only "garden" we ever had was our view of Van Cortland Park. I heard my great-grandmother had a garden, but she lived in Pennsylvania. Everybody has gardens in Pennsylvania. All the food is packaged. The vegetables are all cleaned up and look beautiful. I love to look at them in the market.*
>
> *In school we saw a film about a farm. They told us it was a real farm, but later I found out there aren't many farms like the one we saw. On that farm the father was driving a tractor and the children milked the cows and fed the pigs and collected the eggs. That's how we all thought farms were supposed to be. We even learned a song about the farmer:*

> *O the farmer comes to town*
> *With his wagon broken down,*
> *But the farmer is the man that feeds 'em all.*

> *Well, my uncle told me the farm we saw in the film doesn't exist any more. There may be a few of these farms around, he said, but there aren't many. Most farms are big, maybe a thousand or more acres, and the farmers have big machines and they have to spend thousands of dollars taking care of everything. And they have to use fertilizers and they have to spray the fields to kill the insects. I asked him about horse manure, and he said that nobody uses it any more. They just use chemical fertilizers. They throw all the other*

stuff away.

I didn't really believe him. But one time we drove down to Los Angeles through the San Juaquin Valley, and I didn't see any farmers there, just a lot of machines, mostly picking cotton. I didn't see any farmhouses and I didn't see any kids milking cows. After then I believed him.

Now I may be a little young to sign up for one of your catalog trips, I'm only thirteen, but I read that you have junior programs for teenagers and I wanted to go to a real farm. I picked No. 60 in Chiente in Chekiang Province in China in 1678 because I noticed they grew things that came to them from Holland and they grew potatoes and cotton, too. That was right for me because I'd get to grow food that you could eat and food that you couldn't, I mean cotton.

My uncle helped me get a good book on farming in China. (It's called Forty Centuries of Farming and it's mostly about China.) I learned that they didn't have tractors or any of the equipment we have today. They had hoes and shovels and a plow that was pulled by oxen. They had rich soil because they put back all their wastes, even their stuff from the outhouses. And when there was a harvest, they all helped each other. I think that's great. No one helps anyone on the farms today. There's no one there.

I guess for a long time I've had this idea of waking up in the morning to hear the rooster crowing. And I wanted to collect the eggs and milk the cow and do all the things they used to do on the farm. This trip gave me a chance to do some of those things, but it also disappointed me in some ways I was not expecting.

First of all, I was disappointed in the smells. I expected everything to smell great, but when I woke up the first day, I smelled manure all over the place, and it was awful. Then, I woke up on a straw bed and found a hundred bugs had bitten me and my body itched a lot. Then, I had my bowl of rice and went out to the fields—no eggs or bacon, just the rice.

The first day I was there was the middle of the planting season. Well, I spent twelve hours planting rice, and when I got back that evening I was aching all over. All we had to eat was a bowl of rice with some vegetables and a little bit of fish. It was very good, but it was not enough. Towards evening I just sat and watched the fields and the sun going down and put my son to bed. He was tired, too. He had been out helping us all day. He is eleven. Even though he was tired, he still wanted to hear a story. My husband told him one. My son had heard it many times, but he didn't mind hearing it again. In fact, he preferred it. By the time the story was half-finished, he was asleep.

The night was full of mosquitoes, but the moon came up right after dark. I could see the mosquitoes dancing around right in front of the moon. We didn't stay up late. My husband and I went to bed fairly early, but I did managed to listen to the frogs and the crickets for a while. It's funny. I never saw a single frog or cricket while I was there, but I always heard them. Where do you think they came from?

I don't want to say that I spent four days working my butt off. I did, but I also had some time to talk to my women friends. We sat and drank tea in the middle of the day and gossiped and told stories and jokes. No one could read, but they sure did know a lot of stories.

There were five women with me in the fields and two of them had lost a child. One died in childbirth, and the other died of dysentery. Chen Ti's sister died in childbirth and her mother also. They talked a lot about the people who had died, just the way they talked about the people who were still living. It was all the same to them, not that they didn't think about life, but dead people were also important. Back home we never talked about my grandma, who died three years ago. My mother remembers, but she doesn't talk about her.

Here, everyone talked about the people they knew who had died.

The good part of my trip was that on the third day, and the fourth day also, I got to work in the vegetable garden. It was beautiful. I got to plant some things, like potatoes and snow peas, and I got to do a lot of weeding. The soil smelled so good I could almost taste it! And whenever I put my hand in it, I'd usually come up with a couple earthworms. Not many rocks in this soil. And no clay, either. Just good, crumbly earth. And the smell of the eggplants and cabbages and bok choy (that's a kind of Chinese cabbage) and winter melon and cilantro was just fine. I could have smelled things all day long. Even though working in the garden was hard work, it was well worth it.

Oh, I also learned how to kill a duck and pluck out all its feathers and prepare it for dinner. You know, I've never killed any animal I've eaten. It all comes in packages in the supermarket. But my woman, the one whose life I entered, did it. And she didn't waste any time either. She just grabbed that duck and cut off its neck and let the blood drip down into a bowl. And when all the blood was drained out of the duck, she started pulling out its feathers. Then, she held it over a fire and singed it so that all the places where the fathers came out of the body were smoothed off I guess. She cut open the belly and took out the intestines. She put these in a pan and started to cook them. There were even a couple duck eggs, which she put away to use later. Then she started cooking the duck.

That night we had a feast. It was a special one, a celebration of the tenth year of her mother's death or maybe it was her mother's birthday, I don't remember, but it was special. We had rice and vegetables and duck this time, and I ate well, but I didn't make a pig out of myself as I would if I'd been back home. I could see she wanted everyone to eat well, and everyone wanted everyone else to eat well. But if they ate too much, they would feel they had insulted people.

I even had some time to clean our cotton with a carding comb. I enjoyed that a lot. We saved the seeds for the next crop and put all the cotton in a basket. I started spinning it the last day of my trip. It was going to be made into a shirt for my boy and maybe into a pair of pants for my husband. I never found out. I never got that far.

Oh, I'm glad I went. I now know how hard people had to work and also see how much they thought of and needed each other and how much they remembered without knowing how to read or write. (They had to remember.) I didn't like the mosquitoes, except when they were flying around in front of the moon. I learned a lot about hard work and even about how tough life had been for them. But I also noticed how close people were to each other; they were much closer than my family is. The children ran around with the ducks, and the farmers rested in the fields, and the women sat around from time to time and talked and talked and laughed with each other. It was a good laugh, even though they were tired. They even slept a little in the middle of the day, and the kids also, when they weren't playing games like hopscotch and cat's cradle and jacks, but not jacks with a ball, only jacks with rocks. There was no fighting, but there was a lot of cooperation. Even the little kids helped out. Sometimes they even sang songs and the adults joined in, too.

I don't live in New York City any more. I live in San Luis Obispo, in California, where there isn't too much water. I'm going to start a garden tomorrow. Yesterday, I went to the nursery to get some seeds. My daddy has a good shovel and I asked him to get me a small hoe. My uncle will start showing me how to plant the seeds and when to water. I'm so excited I can't wait.

Cindy Masters
Age 13. San Luis Obispo
California. Student

No. 61: Carupano, Venezuela. December 12, 1921. [5 weeks; $650]
You are now eighty-six and you still have not made up your mind about anything—the food you like, the divisions of the week, the Catholic church, women, the nature of the physical world—anything. It all has poured itself like wind or water through the enormous sieve of your heart and brain.

"Vanity of vanities, all is vanity". You know this so well, but there remains, as you say, "a strong sense of doubt" in even this so permanent a saying. The lord provides and doesn't provide. There is morning and night—but where is noon? There is good and evil, but we invented these ideas? The value of the spider is equal to the value of the whale.

These "opinions," or the closest things you have to opinions, fall continually away, like objects and voices which loom up in a fog, are seen for a moment, and slowly disappear, leaving only a taste, a hint of their existence. You say, "There is something deep down within me which doesn't want to believe, perhaps a fear which I cannot understand, which I have spent my whole life trying to create and bring in front of you to speak with. Perhaps this is all a rationalization of something (you continue) which happened before my birth and which I must appear before, as before a court of evanescent justices in a court room filled with ghostly jurors and more ghostly lawyers."

Perhaps consumes you. It has taken over your life like a demon of infinite extension. You have never studied anything. You are not a scholar; neither are you a philosopher, or a doctor, or a man who has traveled much, only around the small village of Carupano and a few trips to Caracas. Not much, but you think it's enough.

For thirty years you were a ship builder, and you did a good enough job, even sailing out to sea with the fishermen and bringing in their catch, a poor man but not too poor, rich enough to afford two suits and a shave at the barber's twice a week, and for many here in Carupano that is to have some money.

Now, there is a small hut for you outside of town, and your nephew, who is himself a fisherman and, at times, a boat builder, brings you fish three times a week, fresh fish, which he has barbecued to perfection, and what is more, several bottles of rum which he makes from his own sugar cane, good rum, enough to get a man pleasantly drunk and not make him sick.

But even your nephew cannot understand you; no one can, not even yourself, and so it is, you think, with everyone. They are only deceiving themselves as you had done through the first forty years of your life. Vain dreams to push away the demons of uncertainty, for a man must have some certainty in his life (so you thought and so they think), or he will just fall apart, dissolve, become nothing.

You occupy your days, however, with none of these doubts. Much of the time you are at the Cafe Del Sol, overlooking the ocean, sitting with the "young ones," those men in their thirties and forties whom you listen to, winnowing their opinions as usual, silently crumbling to pieces these clods of ideas, values, visions, and pieces of sadness, and letting them dissolve again and again in a sea of events, which is, as you know (or think you know), endless.

No. 62: Mozambique. September 14, 1502. [2 months; $500] You are a cook for the great Sheik Ibrahim, and through the news which trickles down from the royal receptions given to the Portuguese, you have learned that these people are Christians, infidels whom it is important to listen to but not to trust, for they are the enemies of Allah and all your brothers. And though they have come to trade, your master, the great Sheik Ibrahim, knows that they will be back, for trade means more and more of them and they will be back, in great numbers and there will be war, eventually. All is known, and if your master did not want it to be known it would not be known. Therefore, his actions are transparent, and with great design, for the message is that Allah is merciful and that it is his will that these strangers be treated firmly and with courtesy, yet repelled. They are a great future danger.

You listen to it all during this time, for six weeks, as the negotiations go on and on. And you make it your business to find out more, through observing the Portuguese sailors, their ship, their tools, and even to talking with their cooks, trying as you can, to find out about their food, for, as the saying goes, "By their food you shall know them," and you shall. You can feel it all growing in you, the prophecy of the great Sheik Ibrahim that all shall be known of the strangers and all shall know them for what they are.

No. 63: Near Belen, Brazil. June 27, 1504. [3 years; $1050] You are one of two condemned men whom Cabral, your captain, has left here in this strange land. It has been two months since the ships departed, and though at first you were fearful of what might befall you in the midst of these savages, you now feel thankful that your fate was decided thus. Execution was the only other alternative, and you have, in the last six weeks, thanked God many times for your deliverance. The Indians have treated you well, much better than you could have expected from your countrymen. There is much to learn, and though you do not expect ever to return to your native land, you look forward each day to learning something new about fishing, hunting, and making love. The women, though shy at first, are much less so, especially since you have absorbed some of their language and customs and try to follow them as accurately as possible. Surely, there is much to be learned in this new land.

Dear Past Rentals,

How little we know when we lock ourselves into the prison of our culture, whether as Balinese, Chukchi, or residents of East Los Angeles. But when we have a chance to get out, if only for a glimpse at another way of seeing and being, we expand and, I say, add to our lives, and yet tremble with fear at that world, which lacks immediate boundaries. We come to another culture armed with our necessary assumptions and we judge it according to those assumptions. But if we are able to let them rest for a while, returning to them only later, we can, and will, grow. Growth means, in this case, taking into us another way of seeing, existing in the body, the spirit, and the mind.

I've been stuck too long in my culture, which is one among many ways of coping with the unstructured world. Every culture gives us an identity, which is paralleled and reinforced by our parents. They bring us up, first, to understand and live within their world. But, unfortunately, that upbringing also hides us from the world.

I saw your catalog entry "1504. Near Belen, Brazil" halfway through my Introduction to Anthropology class at Tokyo University, and I knew that I had to go on this journey, escape from classroom anthropology and enter a real, a tangible adventure, which would lead to my growth, even if it meant pain and dislocation. There really was nothing else to do. I had felt constricted for years and I needed to leap into the unknown if, for no other reason than to "find myself" or find my larger self and establish a connection with other possibilities.

It turned out better than I had expected. The Indians

who welcomed me, who, in effect, saved my life, were more humanly knowledgeable than my "countrymen". And after that, they gave me the tools to learn. It took me about six months to get by adequately in their language, and once I did, my life and their lives became easier for me, more fluid, more comprehensible. For example, I learned to fish with a spear, but I also learned to fish with leaves. How do you fish with leaves? I'll tell you. There's a certain kind of leaf that, when it enters the water, depletes the oxygen and stuns the fish, who come to the surface and are easily gathered. It's a simple form of fishing and practiced in lots of places.

I learned songs and stories, too. Sometimes, we sat around at night, singing together. Everyone sang and knew how to sing. There were no tone-deaf members in that community. And, what's more, they did a lot of joking, not telling formal (or formula) jokes, but general "passing" humor, I call it, things said (or mimed) spontaneously. It was "good" humor, not hostile, aggressive humor. I did not witness one hostile moment the whole time I was there. I guess the one exception proves the rule. One guy went a bit crazy. He walked round waving at things in the air, and I don't mean the mosquitoes. People tolerated him more than I would expect anyone to do in my neighborhood. They talked to him, again and again, urging him, in the gentlest way, to "come back" to them, return to his people. Up to the time I "came home," he had not returned. But even if he didn't, I liked the real gesture.

Thanks to your staff at Past Rentals, I now feel better able to move within my own culture, only because I have dipped myself in the waters of another one. I see people in a different way; even the crazies I encounter feel more a part of myself and my possibilities. I look forward to further journeys, as I both integrate myself into my "original" world and expand into other ways of being.

Nagiko Noona
Age 24. Student
Tokyo University

Dear Past Rentals,

I want to point out one problem with your catalog proj-ect. It's what could be called an absence of the big picture. Of course, you can't help it. And I don't think you could offer a "survey" either. Good for you. I'm a Past Rentals "junkie," I guess you'd call me. I've been on eighty or ninety trips, all of them valuable, though some more valuable than others. I've sampled them from all your catalogs. But only now I'm ready for the "big picture". I'm now seeing some underlying move-ments, themes, you might say. It's like seeing a lot of still pictures and then putting them together to get a movie. Or— and this is the best comparison I can come up with—it's like an insect eye, which is made up of lots of individual eyes, but the insect sees a total picture with them all. I'm beginning to see that picture now. I know my sight will require a lot more tuning, and I plan to continue my "travels," but the stretched out picture does come through now and again. It has to. I'm tied to them all. We're all tied to our ancestors.

First, every society, wherever it's been in history, has some method of control over its members. I don't mean that people don't go against what they've been brought up to accept. They do, everywhere. But, like parents bringing up their kids, people have to learn to follow one path first before they can follow any other. The problem is that almost all of them stick to that one way. And the ones that don't get more messed up. It's a hard leap to another way of seeing the world. It's like enlarging your base; you get more stable. You have more possibilities. You see, feel, understand, and sym-

pathize more. I guess a working definition of stability is the number of responses you have to any given situation. If you have only one, you're very limited. If you have five, you have more scope, more to choose from.

That's the way I feel about having gone on a lot of journeys. They've increased my base. So the big picture only comes with seeing a lot of little ones. I'd like to see your customers take a lot of trips, the more the better.

Raymondo Chu
Barber
Havana, Cuba

No. 64: Kadiri, India. December 6, 1697. [3 hours; $40] A fourteen year old woman, you have lived in the village of Kadiri all your life. You begin this day in front of the family hearth and altar, which is a cone in the center of a bowl, to represent the linga of Siva. You will sprinkle this altar with fresh water and decorate it with flowers. Today is like all days. All the rituals must be performed, bathing in the morning, cleaning your teeth, arranging your hair, reciting the words of the holy vedic texts, making oblations to the gods, to the demons and the manes, doing honor to the five domestic deities, and attending to the fire sacrifice before the midday meal in which some food for the gods is thrown on the fire and cooked rice is placed in little piles inside and outside the house for the spirits and animals. Only then do the men squat down and eat, while you and the other women wait. This you will do today, as you have done for innumerable days before this.

Dear Past Rentals,
I'm writing about your entry "1697. Kadiri, India" because of my interest in rituals. Anything that's done

repeatedly and which has a purpose to it can be called a ritual. If Lady MacBeth washed her hands to appease the gods, what she did was ritual. If I mumble a few words over a cloth doll and then stick a pin in it for the purpose of doing harm to another person, I'm engaging in ritual.

First, I want to say that I think of human beings as a species that "grows into consciousness" but still maintains the "ground base of unconscious identification," that is, an unconscious ability to act and respond instinctively to the world in which it moves. It could be called "the hum of integration" set into us by our immediate bodily responses. It also might be called "the ground base of living," "the unconscious acceptance of the world," and, of course, other things. These phrases I've created are just a suggestion of something we have with us all the time and from which rise the conscious actions we engage in, like the ritual this woman in Kadiri was engaged in each morning.

Out of the soil of the physical world, we have risen toward abstraction. I don't mean to imply that "risen" suggests any positive growth, any sense of "progress," for I don't think in that way. As a species, we've moved within what I call "the gradient of definition" and especially within the last few millennia. Our thoughts and the machines created out of our thoughts have grown increasingly more particular, more exact and exacting, a crude wagon of 16th century Italy, for example, compared with an exacting, piston driven, computer-adjusted, 240 horsepower 2002 Mercedes. The dimensions have become more and more particularized, inversely in proportion to their distance in time from the present. Imagine, to choose another example, the Renaissance clocks, big, crude affairs, accurate to within a few minutes a day, at best, and compare them with the greatest of all clocks, atomic clocks, which can measure time to within a few billions of a second a century. Exactitude. Particularity. Definition.

Consciousness. And all this developed out of the instinctive "hum of integration".

But there's a problem in all this exactitude. It's only one element of experience, the experience of the mind playing games with itself, the isolation of the mind from the body, our separation from the body of the world. Ritual, an early form of mental play, becomes an end in itself, casting off from the shore of the integrative existence, from that basic instinctive "hum of integration". The whole history of our species can be seen as the history of each member. The infant's life is the life of the physical, growing slowly and then more and more swiftly into the world of the mind, a unit of self-contained definition. I feel that the time has come when we must return to that earlier significant integration, when the defining, particularizing, exacting mind returns to the earth of its origins and begins to "think" within its larger universe of existence. Perhaps, we might value history as music, with its ground base as the hum of integration and its woven play the melody of invention, but never, never the separation. That is the ritual toward which we need to be moving.

Majid Kiani
Age 51. Tile designer
Mashed, Iran

No. 65: Near Wellington, New Zealand. November 6, 1698. [3 weeks; $400] You have been here before, with Captain Cook, who first brought you here. You have very fond memories of the time you spent with the Maoris, a people who treated you well indeed, all of the sailors on board, for they had never seen a European and you had never seen a people like this. This time things will go even better, for there are people who remember you and whom you remember. There will be dancing, plenty of food (roast dog, sweet potatoes, fern roots, sea fish, sea birds' eggs) and much to see and remember. Perhaps—and you do want it to happen— you will be tattooed, though you will not get a moka, a complete tattoo, that is. You know that some part of your body will have on it a Maori design, for they are masters at this and attribute great power to it. Most of all, you look forward to the Maori women, bare to the waist, with their grass skirts, swaying to the breeze of the music. It is a beautiful land, where relaxation and comfort and simplicity grow and expand in everything.

No. 66: Yedo (Tokyo), Japan. April 3, 1750. [2 hours; $45] You are a seven-year-old boy who has been at school for three years. Like all children in Japan who have been sent to school, you are still learning to write. It is a long and difficult process. But your teachers help you every day, and you learn, little by little. Today you must copy an example the teacher has set for you. It is a beautiful day this spring, and as you sit, looking across the garden at the blossoming cherry trees and the red and blue and green birds singing, your mind strays into a diffused world of color and warmth. You stare, almost inwardly, as children do, at the great mountain in the distance, and listen for an hour to the sounds around you.

No. 67: Slightly northwest of the Cape of Good Hope, South Africa. December 3, 1504. [One day; $75] You and your people have been living near these shores for what seems like almost forever. Last year a big ship with many strange men, people whom you had never seen before, came on shore, bringing gifts of bells, capes, jewelry, knives and other things. At that time you and the other young men brought oxen and sheep for the visitors. There was dancing and much music.

But after they had gone, you and others began to have strange feelings, not definite ones, however, about these men. Perhaps it was their stiffness on the one hand and on the other their complete licentiousness, trying to make free with the women and yet restraining themselves unnaturally, which, only later, after they had gone, aroused your suspicions. But most of all, it was their strong desires to get you, all your people, to bow down before a crossed object which they carried with them and said words over, smiling, yet in angry tones trying to convince you to kiss it, bow down to it, to say words which they repeated many times in front of it, for it is obviously sacred to them. None of your people would do it, none. They knew nothing about these people, except what they saw and heard.

When they had gone, you were left with this strange feeling of an alien force attempting to take away something in your spirits, to force you into a cave underground, to remove something, though you know nothing of what that could be. The feeling has been there for some time, and that is enough for all of you.

Now they have come again, this time erecting a large stone pillar and putting on top of it one of their wooden crossed objects. There on the beach it stands, all of them having bowed down to it and said words in front of it. Nothing happened after that. The waves and the wind and the grasses and the animals went on as before. After a few days they left, having given you more of the knives, beads, capes and bells which they had distributed before. This time the women stayed away, though there was some dancing and music.

It has been a week, seven days, after they have left and you have decided what you are going to do. You and several other young men are going to the beach to pull down their stone pillar and their crossed object. You will take the stones away and put them back where they came from. That will disperse their pretended magic and bring back the good feelings, which were there before these strangers arrived in your land.

Dear Past Rentals,

Your journey "1504. Slightly west of the Cape of Good Hope" was all about the difference between the "establishment" and the "outsiders". Of course, these guys with their arrogant beliefs were a challenge to the people they encountered. They were the outsiders. You know that long ago travelers were looked upon with suspicion. They had to pass certain "tests". They had to prove themselves. They had to go through a process of being accepted. Physically and psychologically, they represented the unknown, even though they were recognized as fellow humans.

The same thing applies within any society. Someone who goes against the grain of the society's assumptions, be he a nudist or a disbeliever, is looked upon with distrust. He's a challenge to the others. He says to them, "Expand. This is not the only world you know." But they're afraid. The society they know, the parents that taught them about the "world" have been to them a safety zone against the unknown, the uncertain, the fearful and have constructed in them what I think of as "reality walls," and if the walls came down, their destruction would cause a total re-alignment of everything they had learned. The greater the fear, the greater the ordering of belief, not necessarily on a conscious level, that's too apparent, but on a deeper level. We're mammals, and herd mammals at that. We pull together, like musk oxen, against the predators, imploding into our pooled assumptions. We explain things. We build things. We fall into each other.

Change is a hard road. It means absorbing the fearful, the unknown. Each little drop of oil floats on the ocean of the world, perfectly rounded into its own assumptions. And only the sunlight breaks it down, little by little.

Anton Roebling
Travel agent
Hamburg, Germany

Dear Past Rentals,

I have to tell you that I've been brought up as a Christian, a Methodist. I go to church regularly, have hardly missed a Sunday. I pray for people who have sinned and ask God to change their hearts and urge others to look toward, and into, Him. I read the Bible at least three times a week. In fact, in the last ten years, I've started at the beginning of the Old Testament and read clear through the New Testament—three times. I believe in the power of forgiveness granted to us by our savior Jesus Christ, who died for our sins and offered our redemption with his glory. I recognize the cross as the symbol of our salvation and believe in the power that that recognition provides.

But I had yet to experience the hostility of those people who went conquering in the name of the cross. Yes, I had read about them, how they enslaved the Indians, treated them like dirt, even after they had converted them (forcibly!) to our religion. But I had never felt the full emotional power of their actions, especially from the point of view of the people they subjugated. That's why I journeyed to South Africa on your entry "1504. Slightly northwest of the Cape of Good Hope, South Africa". I could see from these peoples' point of view how their aggressive visitors sounded. I felt how the cross was a burden to them and realized how and why they reacted it.

I am still a Christian—nothing has changed. But I see the history of my religion in another light after my journey to and with these people in South Africa. They were correct about their visitors. They felt them in their bones and they knew them from their actions, and that is why they (and I

*with them) took down their cross and returned the stones
that supported it to their original places. I say to myself, "Let
that be a lesson to your pride." And I have learned from my
humility and have not strayed from the path of our Lord and
Savior Jesus Christ.*

> *Lorraine Gould*
> *Age 47. Copywriter*
> *London, England*

No. 68: Kurashiki, Japan. May 2, 1505. [10 hours; $85] All day long you
make sushi. You have worked as a sushi chef for fifteen years. You
can make it in your sleep, if necessary. And because sushi making
is so natural to you, you are free to engage in other activities
during work, not those which take you away from the small shop
where you work, but things of the mind or conversation with the
customers or just listening to the world going on around you.

O, how full life is! The sounds and the sights of even a small
town like Kurashiki are filled with wonders. Sometimes you just
look out at all the people passing on the street, the rich and the
poor, the powerful and the weak, the sober and the drunk. They
are all the same to you; they pass and you watch, and perhaps at
times (and you know this is the case) people watch you watching.
This pleases you because you know there is a kind of fellowship
out there when you watch each other.

Sometimes you smile inwardly about it. Sometimes you
laugh out loud and people do not understand your laughter.
Sometimes, you think, they are almost afraid of it, so suddenly
does it seem to burst out of you. Several times you were looking
so hard at something which to others did not seem tragic that you
burst into tears, a sudden explosion of tears, and then you wiped
your eyes and continued looking. In fact, a half-hour later you
were laughing hysterically at something that happened in front of

you, and although you tried to communicate it to a customer, he could see nothing funny about it. You laughed at this, too, for it was funnier than what you had just witnessed.

Today, like all days, customers come and go in the shop. You continue to make sushi without thinking. You continue to look and to laugh and to cry.

> *Dear Past Rentals,*
>
> *How full life is! That's what caught my attention in your catalog entry "1461. Kurashiki, Japan". How small people have become, how narrow, how unresponsive! I've always, somehow and from the beginning of my life of eighty-eight years, felt the exuberance and wildness of the world I am more than a part of. And, by contrast, I have seen people shrink into their protective lives and look out, as if from a fortress. True, life is fearful, decisions are difficult, people not always what you expect them to be. But exactly because of these things, we get to see rather than we have to see. What a difference those two words make and what a difference the experience they carry with them has.*
>
> *Therefore, I journeyed to Kurashiki and became that sushi maker, a man who seems to many like a fool, and to others, almost on the verge of being crazy. But this man drinks in the spacious plenitude of the world around him. He watches with his whole heart and body. He flows as the living ingredient in the mix around him. The alternation between tears and laughter expands him, until he becomes the "membrane of the world". His eyes are indistinguishable from his heart, his ears merge with the sounds of the world, his touch glues itself to the skin of objects. Unfortunately, I encounter few people like this man, this sushi maker, who is far more than what his occupation suggests.*
>
> *If your readers experience this kind of person, they will*

be changed forever. They will not return to their prisons. They
will truly liberate themselves. They will leap into the ocean of
their lives.

Alim Qasimov
Age 61. Woodworker
Buhkara, Central Asia

No. 69: Burgos, Spain. September 3, 1703. [3 weeks; $300] Your wife
is seeing another man. You know that now, and by following him
around for several days, you have gotten to know his habits, what
he does for a living, where he lives, who his friends are.

Why are you driven by this passion to know him, you wife's
lover? What will you do when you find them together? You do
not possess either gun or sword, and you are not very good with
either. But an immense curiosity drives you on. You must know
everything you can about him and about your wife's interest in
him. And you will find out.

No. 70: Buenos Aires, Argentina. March 12, 1903. [4 months; $375]
You are thirty-eight and have been working for twenty years as a
sub-manager of a beef processing plant. You learned everything
there was to know about your work long ago. Your wife, who did
not have children, died six years ago and you continue working,
as before.

After she died, your spirits fell. Somehow you continued
in the same way, falling into a sterile, empty mold of life. And
it has become more and more sterile. Nothing helps—women,
knowledge, travel. You are neither poor nor wealthy. And though
you eat well, have a comfortable house, employ two servants,
have several horses, and are acquainted with many people of your
class and position, some vital element is missing.

The boredom grows. You spend days at home, going nowhere, doing nothing, engaged in trivial, mindless pursuits. Your life grows more trivial by the week, and you feel powerless to stop sinking into this quicksand of emptiness. What is life anyway? What value does it have for you, for anyone? Why do people continue in the same, faceless, boring activities? Don't they know that everything they do is useless, that they will eventually die?

How much this pulls you down, this loss, loss of more than your wife, a loss of something else deep within the nature of things. You have managed to conquer each stage of your boredom, but only with fortitude and with a rationalization that goes deep into your nature. Still, you feel the fabric tearing from within, bits and pieces falling off, parts of your life settling into the solidity of a clear and lusterless ice, and other parts falling away from you into the sea of forgetfulness.

Two months ago, out of your growing desperation, you made a major decision, a desperate one, in fact—to take off four months from work. This was not hard to do, although it did require some solid planning. You invented an excuse. And your employers, seeing no reason to disbelieve you, allowed you to go, without pay, of course. (Money has never been the reason for any of your decisions.) You are going away to a small town in the north, disguised as a carpenter, and there you plan to work and live, to build up the fallen parts of your character. It is a desperate effort. It will require everything. There is no help, except the help that will come from you, those deep, unknown resources you must call upon. You leave today.

No. 71: Michurinsk, Russia. June 13, 1749. [One hour; $45] It is four o'clock, a warm day this June, and you are lying, still, in your swaddling bands, a girl, four months old. You have not been changed for four hours and you stink, and you have given up screaming, which you have done for hours on end. It is hot in the summer field, even under the tree, where you have been placed while your mother works.

You give up and look. Above you are leaves, a whole world of leaves. You can smell them, and the earth around you. The birds sing. The sky is cloudless and there is hardly any breeze.

Dear Past Rentals,

How can we remember the brief time of our infancy? We generally recall it poorly, if at all. We may care for infants—hold them, feed them, observe the small motions of their bodies, bathe them, speak to them. But the gap is immense, incomprehensible, even for one who has entered early childhood and looks back at a three-week-old infant. I say there is only one way to leap into that gap: become that infant. Past Rentals has offered this opportunity and I have accepted.

I felt the leaves and their shadows moving. I can say that I felt the leaves and shadows, even from a distance, though there was no distance between us. The leaves fell, as if in a trance or a dance, slow motion, out of time and in a kind of eternity of falling. They fell together, separately and together, yellow shapes and their shadows half-pinned to the air—falling. I conducted their symphony with my eyes, a calligraphy of music in the air, though I could not conduct them easily, swaddled as I was.

The light—I have only spoken of the leaves and the shadows—the light was a kind of heavy, breathable burden, as if I had been suspended in it and it in me. It curved, like the bend of a tension-laden bow. The air fell on me like a kind of blanket, a second, less tangible swaddling band. It moved, as the wind moved, slowly, carefully, with its ever-changing fingers, with a skin that could not separate itself from my skin, which was, for the most part, hidden from it.

I speak of the quiet moments, the ignorance of time, and the blots of sound which came and went from my ears, blots of time, and my ears, which could not separate themselves from my body, moments when I was a single listener, an immense aural eye, inseparable from the sounding eye of the world. But I was also myself, speaking, with a cry that said, "I am here. I am testing the sound of my voice, the sound of my echoing body. Listen, whoever is there. I am coming toward you. I will come toward you. I will slowly enter you. Take heed."

These opportunities are not to be denied. They reach out and grab us. We have no choice in the matter. We must be completed. Otherwise, senses will distort themselves into all kinds of illusions. And we will not be whole.

Catherine Mboya
Age 21. Mother of two daughters
Nairobi, Kenya

No. 72: Mienyang, Hupeh Province, China. September 17, 1105. [4 hours; $95] The willows on the shore move in the slight breeze. It is late September. The moon spills over the lake and floats on the water. It is too perfect a night to stay home. You and your friend had to escape, set off on the water in a small boat, bringing with you a bottle of rice wine, "whispering to the fish," as you described your actions. Though you are a boy of eighteen, you have lived in Mienyang all your life, son of a peasant who was son of a fisherman. Tonight you will not sing the songs until you have caught at least ten fish and drunk half the bottle of wine. The full moon. And the willows by the shore. You are in the middle of a dense, dream-filled autumn.

No. 73: Suippes, France. October 19, 1765. [30 minutes; $25] It is late. The sun went down an hour ago. Your wife and you and your daughter, who is eight, have eaten your meager supper, some bread and a small bit of soup. Your daughter lies on the straw in the corner near the fire. The smallpox and the fever have been with her for three days. You have prayed, but many of you in the village have the pox and many have died. You cannot think of what is happening to you, to your daughter. It is too painful a wound to touch. When you approach it, your whole body pulls away, suddenly, as from a fire, as from a ghost.

The cold October night is calling. The moon is almost full, bright through the forest and casting long shadows over the houses and the trees. You have sat silently for more than an hour. You and your wife are capable of only a few words, which then drop like stones into the ground. They are so heavy you could use them as bricks.

The light shines weakly through the slightly open door. It calls you. It is calling you to walk out, into the village and down the road which leads to the woods, a short walk, but not too far, for there is the forest, and in the forest are the wolves and other things you dare not think about. You are safe, at least for a while, huddled by the small fire, silent, speaking the words inside you. But the moonlight calls. You walk out, down the road for a while.

Dear Past Rentals,

Smallpox is almost gone now, you know. And the bubonic plague hasn't come back in spades for a long time. We've got AIDS and other assorted diseases waiting on, or just crossing, the frontiers. And we've got other social worries—homicide, suicide, gang eruptions, divorces—you name it, we've got it. And that doesn't count just plain socially produced stupidity. I saw one example in the paper today, and you know how many there really are. (All you have to do is look.) A security guard beats up a seventy-year-old man, breaks three of his ribs and puts him in the hospital. The old man dies, not directly from the injuries inflicted on him, but certainly indirectly. The guard gets ninety days in jail. If you consider the very light sentence he received, his time in jail might even be called "cruel and unusual punishment," since when he gets out he may be prone to do the same thing again.

But anyway, that's a bit off the point of my letter to you, the only company in the real business of identification. I say this because you put people in other people's shoes, no, in other people's skins, minds, tongues, and all kinds of life situations. And that's only the beginning. Your catalog's just a jumping off platform. Each time you come out from one of the entries, you can begin to identify with others, start to leap into their skins. That's what I call humanity or civilization or whatever you want to call it. The people who can't identify with others are the ones who have the problems. They're wandering around in what I call "the fog of absence". They don't know who they are, probably because they're incapable of knowing who anyone else is. You might call them displaced people, people who have undeveloped mammalian brains. You can walk right through them. There's no grip in their handshake. There's no music in their words. There's no flavor in their instep. There's no salt in their dolor. And there's no style in their directions, that is, if they have directions.

That brings me to your catalog entry No. 73: 1665. Suippes, France. Yes, I know it's a strange one to pick—smallpox, death all around you, uncertainty, suffering, and night time, too. But this is not Club Med or the Inaugural Ball, (a ball that, by the way, inaugurates nothing). This is the flow, of that uncertain shadow around us all. As I see it, it's all part of a larger, unsifted identification. We owe it to ourselves not to look at our shadows on a dazzling screen but to walk around with them, drink down their toneless liquid, sipping the bitter with the aimless, the expansive with the needle-

*thin narrowness of temporary absence. This is my contribu-
tion to myself, to take in the others, who are also myself. If I
ever forget it, I'll end up as a shadow anyone can walk
through, without a handshake, without a musical voice,
without a style to the instep of my direction. If I forget it, my
right hand will lose its cunning, and my left hand, too.*

*Let's get real. This guy who steps out into the moonlight
has been pulled out there by some force that he does not
really understand, like all of us. Without language, without
thought, the body goes on learning the world, and only later
what it learns rises up from it as thought, and emerges
toward others as language. Yanked out into the moonlight, he
enters the dimly lit road that borders the woods, a forest
heavily populated by demons, and real creatures, too; he
enters the world of his fear and walks on with it for a while.*

*Well, that's what I did, at least for those thirty minutes
I paid for, traveling over the wrinkled rind of his mental and
emotional skin, moving in and out through all the layers of
his fears and hopes, moving with him, yes, with him, through
his dimly lit body, that understands beyond language and
therefore knows the shapes of things and their auras, their
overtones, like a rock that skips over water. And yes, there is
a bit of falsehood in this, a trance of tourism, a piece of pretend, a feeling for the fiendish, like going to the movies to be
scared, the pleasure of fear and the satisfying return to a
reinforced security, huddled in our social lairs. Keep us safe,
Mamma and Papa, though they might have died in his sight,
leaving him unclothed and alone in a world stripped of its
surfaces.*

*I do not know how many times we must dip ourselves in
that world, probably as many times as possible, as long as we
don't lean too far to one side, make of it a kind of painful
pleasure, and fall off the deep end, lose our balance and not
see anything else. But that's not a problem for most of us*

today, even with AIDS and the rising rate of tuberculosis and all the shadow people walking around us. "Dip him in a river who loves water," says William Blake. He was a man who believed that if you want to know what is enough, you've got to know what is more than enough. Well, here are the boundaries and the dark woods are just outside the humanly made road and your loved ones are dying of some disease. What will you do for them?

Mannie Bright
Age 39. Traveling salesman for Rock Bottom Discounts, International
East Lansing, Michigan

No. 74: Near Kas, Turkey. April 16, 18,861 B.C. [5 years; $10,000]
How much of your living lifetime you spend thinking. You have sought others you could think with; in fact, your life has been that continual search, like a connoisseur looking for the ultimate object, a musician, for the ultimate music, an infant, for the ultimate father.

Yes, you found those others, in fact, sought them out in your own way, a sieve of intelligence, and for the most part found them wanting, almost all of them. There were three, however, three only who could speak to you, three whom you have met over the thirty-seven years of your existence, which you think of as this indefinable substance into which you have somehow appeared. They have somehow appeared. The others have all died, and for each, you sent after them your grief, a monstrous stone deposited in the depths of the sea. And you have accepted also, with each passing, a large burden, carrying it about and then dispersing it into the world, only to find yourself enlarging, always enlarging.

But to what extent, you still do not know. And how could you, for if that last kernel of understanding, of experience, were put into place, you know you would instantly disappear, and of that you are horribly afraid. Not even to disappear, like a dot into the far-off landscape, but suddenly to vanish into everything.

You sit around the fires at night with your people—whom you have never forgotten (how could you forget those from whom you have come) and think thoughts that no one could bear to understand. Therefore, you keep silent, for no voice receives what you would say. It is difficult to live two lives, one private and one public, though you expect that it really happens to everyone.

But still you think, and think in the following manner:

"As we grow older, we accumulate more and more life inside us. Our sense of ourselves grows more defined, surrounding us with more and more of a protective self. In inverse proportion to the amount of "self" we accumulate, we exhibit less and less interest in exploration, in accumulation, in absorption beyond what we have, and therefore less and less interest in the world.

"We therefore grow complaisant. We have to. It is somehow in the nature of things merely because we have lived. Like fat, we can survive off what we have accumulated. A child has no life experience on which to rest; therefore, he goes out into the world to find his body, his self, which is a self he half-creates and half-absorbs.

"Yet even if that accumulated life of ours has been miserable, it is still ours because it is all we know, and we cling to that consolation. And a deliberately unformed life, one in which the sense of self was continually undermined? An unformed life would perpetuate "youth," incompleteness, a kind of continual neotony in which the child proceeds the man.

"Now, is this denial of 'self-hardening' possible? Can we 'de-transform' ourselves (if our 'selves' is the correct word)? Experience is a heavy sap; it sticks, even when we most want it to dissolve. We pass through the world, inhaling the sky, time, food, anger, transitions, etc. How do we ever get rid of these experiences?

Does rebellion help? No, it merely adds another dimension. Can we ever forget? Here, yes. The mind holds only so much, at least, consciously, but experience is still there, having soaked into the skin, communicated its information through subtle changes in muscle and bone, a weathering of deep influences.

"We make a general, absolute statement when we say, "Everything stays". Do we have any proof that it does? Or can we prove that nothing exists? It is easier to prove, or at least to convince ourselves, that everything we sense exists. But our growth is the cousin of ignorance. The more ignorant we are, the more there is to learn. But ignorance is itself a learned response. We deliberately create pockets of it in order to be filled, so that more of these holes of our own creation may appear. It seems to work both ways. The holes we create enlarge the world. And yet they work against fulfillment. So perhaps we must put it this way: 'We die in the midst of our harvest'.

"We cannot exist too long with ignorance, since ignorance, in its dynamic manifestations, has the same effects as chaos, and in the face of such a seemingly random distribution of effect, our identities must dissolve. 'Anything but that,' our living, ordered sense replies. 'Even fiction, a false creation (which is what we are, all living things, who are waiting to be dissolved in the flow of material or immaterial forces) is preferable to dissolution'."

Such are some of your thoughts, if they could be spoken, for much of what you think is silent, incapable of communication. Somehow you know you are special, or different, and therefore the others treat you like the man of power they think you are and leave you the place and the time in which to think. Around you, there is a kind of cave you wander into from time to time, a hole, which is only approached by others when desperate measures must be taken. But that is seldom. You are the thinker, and people will listen, but they will listen with their own understanding.

You are two miles from the sea. For three days you have camped here. You will move on to the east, follow the rising sun, and camp again and hunt. The world is in motion, incomplete, and you also move, a part of it, with the animals, the winds, the water—all of you moving. You will think, you cannot help thinking. Yours is a long life.

Dear Past Rentals,

I ask you, how does an immensely intelligent person live when he is surrounded by people of average intelligence? This, for the most part, has been, and to a certain extent continues to be, the condition of intelligence even today and has been for all times. Yes, there are opportunities for people of great intellect, that is, if they have the "proper" upbringing. Many, however, fall by the wayside, though how many we do not know. Not that schooling, by itself, will aid the intellect— it does, but only to a certain ambiguous extent.

And intelligent people five hundred, five thousand, or fifty thousand years ago found themselves in a strange situation, dislocated, in some immediate way, from their fellow humans. They stumbled around, telling people things which they could not understand, and often and as a result, created strategies to cope with their inability to link up intellectually. The emotional part of their lives played a role. And, I believe, they searched for those who would understand them, the intellectual peers, and if they found them, it was a result of a long and difficult search, helped, no doubt, by their mutual desires.

What did they think about in that long-gone past, that unrecorded time, vaster than we can imagine, when, indeed, they had much time in which to think? Because they were unencumbered by the present-day "acres" of thought with which we are surrounded and the innumerable fields of learning that that "organized" thought has created—we might call them " stiffened methods of looking": physics,

*chemistry, astronomy, literature, philosophy, history, etc.—
these people thought in ways we might find awkward, difficult, or even incomprehensible. But the advantages of that
older mental world, freed from formal categories, it seems to
me, would have been immense. And therefore, since I possess
only the most basic means of projecting myself into the
thought processes of people like that, I have opted for your
entry "18,861 BC near Kas, Turkey". I'm glad I did.*

*I don't want to give you an expanded picture of what
this very intelligent man was thinking during that five year
period I spent with/as him, but a few brief hints should convey the flavor of his thought, the flow of his thinking, the scope
of his mentally tangible world. A detailed account is on its
way to your central offices. If you have any questions about
my presentation, I hope you will not hesitate to raise them,
and I will, to the best of my ability, answer anything you are
concerned about.*

*The flux and flow of the world—this was a major preoc-
cupation of his thought. It occupied him even when he slept;
it crept into his dreams and colored them with its immense
oceans. He attempted "thought/body" experiments, such as
watching his skin move, observing a tree for a whole afternoon, smelling the flow and odor of water, sniffing his body in
the morning and again at evening to compare what he perceived as a difference in odor throughout the day. He imagined his body flowing internally into itself and then at a
certain point out again, continually, as if it were remaking
itself at every moment. There were more physical experiments. He rolled rocks downhill, observing the jagged trajec-
tory of their journeys, observed other movements across the
landscape, the shapes of things moving, or what he imagined
were their sounds and shapes, their prior journeys and the
directions they would take after he ceased to look. He imagined the attempt to observe when he was either distant from*

an event or was, given his bodily state, "incapable" of observing something with his basic senses. He imagined his intelligence as a newly emerging infant and his intelligence at his death and divided it by the time between. He measured his footsteps when he was sleeping, when he was strolling along the beach in a state of deep, suspended removal, when he was hunting, and when he was attempting to slowly walk across a shallow, shifting river. He thought about his existence before death and his existence after death, but imagined those states as "prior involutions". At one point constructed an imaginary language and would speak to himself, but he took care nobody overheard him.

I'm going to stop there, hoping this brief account will give you a flavor of his thought processes. And now I want to say something about myself. I took this journey because I wanted to compare myself with this man, who lived deep in the Paleolithic in a climate and landscape very different from our own. I wanted to know him because I, too, am, or consider myself to be, very intelligent and yet very lonely. I, too, have searched for a long time for people, both men and women, whom I could intellectually and emotionally engage with. I find that it was, and is now, a very lonely path we follow, though we may gain some comfort in the occasional traveler we meet along the way.

That Win
Age 36. Tailor
Irriwady, Burma

No. 75: Kirkuk, Iraq. November 3, 1861. [2 months; $200] At nine years old, all you want to do these days, weeks, months, almost a year now, is listen to the ud player, your neighbor, when he sits in his courtyard and plays, listen for hours while he plays for hours.

But last month, when you asked if you could come when he played, he said yes, and you have been happy to listen, knowing that even when you hear your friends playing outside or just passing on the street, you will move toward them in your mind only, just for a short time, and then return, to be lost again in the music.

What is this that has happened to you? You have sung at home from when you were four, with your parents and other friends and guests. You have always taken music for granted; it was the air you breathed, like your dreams or your sweat—never a thought about it. But now your neighbor, whose ud produces something beyond music, a weaving of some fantastic tapestry, has awakened you, and you are drunk with your awakening.

Dear Past Rentals,

As a child, I was entranced by music, just as the nine-year-old in your entry "861. Kirkuk, Iraq". Not many children fall under this spell, but those who do, possess, as I do, an uncommon musical intelligence. It is impossible to escape, for the music is calling you, like some magnetic voice drawing you toward it. Those who have been drawn by this bodily and mental gravitation will understand what I mean, for music is, as I said once in my dreams, "the body's outward, spiritual, kinetic shadow". I say it again: "Music is the body's outward, spiritual, kinetic shadow."

Life was simpler and quieter in 8th century Iraq than it is today. It flowed on in an even pace, and though the population worked hard, there were long moments, unencumbered by any detailed, overacting anxiety. For a child, especially for a child, there was time to talk, linger, dream, and absorb the slowly moving pageant of life. Concert halls? There weren't any. Audiences? The whole population was an audience, ready to descend on the unstaffed, improvised world of a great musician.

And this man was one of those great ones, though I

didn't realize it at the time, having nothing to compare him with. He played in the mornings, early, and generally for himself, as he told me years later, "for the health of body and soul". He was the pupil of a great teacher and that teacher the pupil of another great one, and thus was music handed down in an unending chain.

From the moment I sat in his courtyard and felt the vibrations fall into my ears, I knew I was to become his pupil. And though I, as Roberto Nicholini, didn't remain long enough with him, only the two months of your entry, being his pupil was, I felt, fated from the beginning.

I have a similar history; that's why I was drawn to your entry. I first heard Solomon Sanderling, the great oboist, playing next door. I wandered into his garden, and he saw me there and invited me in to listen. He was playing for himself, I suspect, for the expansion of his own soul; and for a long time, as I sat there listening, in an ever-widening trance, he took no notice of me. When he stopped playing, I stared and stared—there was no need to say anything—and he understood. A week later he came to my door, carrying a clarinet and said, "Please, start with this. Your lungs are too young now for my instrument." And I did, for three years. When I was twelve, and playing fairly well on the clarinet, he presented me with an oboe, "On loan, of course," he said. I studied with Solomon Sanderling for the next ten years, and I am, I must say, an oboist of oboists, and I now play for myself three mornings a week. I expect my own pupil to appear one day on my doorstep, and the process will start all over, the process which must be completed.

Roberto Nicholini
Age 47. Oboist
Milan, Italy

No. 76: Cuenca, Ecuador. October 27, 1889. [3 weeks; $300] How many times have you wandered through your home, Cuenca, in the altiplano, playing your flute, cross-eyed, a little drunk, a little crazy, with your one good leg and a crutch a dear friend years ago made for you, not out of balsa, that inferior tree, but from the hardest of woods—the Santa Maria tree you call it—so hard that an ax would be ruined in its cutting, or so you say, though it is not completely true.

Everyone knows you, all your twenty-eight years of living here among people who tolerate you and your crazy eyes and the clownishness you have developed which winks cross-eyed at everybody; and they all laugh, though it is hard to tell if the laughter is with you or at you, but either way it doesn't seem to matter. Living is not easy, but there is a kind of ambiguous joviality in everything you touch and see, a lightness expanding to the limits of the horizon of your small world, made light also by its size, by the size of Cuenca, your own small town, and by the eyes of everyone you know and who know you, a kind of unofficial clown, whom even the police laugh at and therefore fail to throw in jail for drinking too much or feeling up the whores, who would not have you in jail for all their money and misery. As they give you their money, you say, "Dios te bendigo" and wink. You do play that flute well, almost so automatically that the world seems to be playing it for you, so grateful is it for your music, or so you think.

> *Dear Past Rentals,*
> *All these serious entries. Don't you realize that people have laughed 'til their sides begged for mercy? Yes, I know you can tell me that you indeed have "humorous" entries. There's that furniture maker, famous by now from catalog seven (item # 129), who played practical jokes on the neighbors, the piano teacher, the English teacher, and on others*

and others and others. And there have been two or three more. But, truly, all those serious entries. You'd think nobody had ever laughed at the absurdity, the absolute, 195% absurdity of their existence. But no doubt they did, laughed with themselves and laughed with others. People had crude humor and, also, they had, let's call it "polished humor," and everything in between. And they laughed at pretension because they saw it around them (and inside them). There's the student who believes that life is lived by the logic he learned in class and applies it everywhere. There's the miser, who turns off his engine at a red light in order to save gas. Types like these can easily be made fun of, directly or indirectly, like "the complainer," "the formally formal, book-driven orator," "the beauty queen," "the 'wave-and-wink' muscle man" (strutting his stuff), "the superdreamer" (with or without words), "the transcendental mother," and lots more. We know them today, and people knew them long ago, probably in the Paleolithic, too. People are not so seriously stupid as we think.

There's always the clown. He's the usual type. This one I visited in your entry "1889. Cuenca, Ecuador" was a light-hearted human being, poor, and filled with a diffusely dreamy misery. The twinkle in his eye saved him, and the music that reflected that emotional slight of hand. There's usually one clown for every so many people, and if there isn't, then watch out: Life has collapsed and tyranny follows, like an avalanche. We know the clown because he's in every one of us. But he does his clowning in public; he says it in public. Beware the professional ones, who seem to be saying something but leave you with a suspicion you've been had and your feeling bent backwards, like an emotional mobius strip arm-twist. The real clown doesn't only make us laugh; he also makes us think, makes us look around and laugh, and in doing so recognize much of the absurdity we don't want to confront.

I guess what I'd like to get from you is a history of humor, like anthropologists talking about healing rituals or historians talking about pilgrimages. I know it's there, but like many topics—the history of defecation, the history of humming, the history of cleanliness, the history of personal deceit—it's hard to get at. All these topics are based on a profound extrapolation from our own present-day lives and the little we have available, and a lot of supposition at that. One topic that's interested me is the history of private life. It's been written about and exposed with some foundation, but it's like the usual iceberg—most of it is under water, in fact, down in the pelagic region. Another is the role of daydreaming. Someone could invent such a history. And still another historical thread might be called "The history of unconscious consciousness". There are others—many of them. But I'd like to see more of what you'd call "the profound light-hearted". There's too much of the other.

> *Ernesto Diaz*
> *Age 72. Homeopath*
> *La Paz, Bolivia*

No. 77: Besalampy, Malagasy. June 5, 1773. [3 hours; $60] You are a woman of seventy-two years on this earth. You have lived all your life along this coast, working to raise the food you have fed your children (three of them) until they grew up and went off to become fishermen and the wives of fishermen. Your husband died five years ago. Now, your best friend, a woman you have known for fifty years, has just died, and you are going to the funeral, which is in a small field overlooking the sea.

The flowers you bring with you are small, compared with the memories, and the memories are even stronger now that your friend is gone, as if through memory she had been made clearer in your presence. Still, the heaviness and the longing for her friendship and the steep decline toward death are strong within you. You walk into the small field overlooking the sea with a dwindling fistful of flowers in your hands.

Dear Past Rentals,

To rehearse your own death. I have been doing it for thirty-five years. I began "preparing" in my fifties. At that time I was told by a doctor I had consulted that I had a life-threatening illness and I would be dead within five years. The doctor said there was no cure. I went through the usual process of denial, anger, and finally acceptance, a hard road to walk; and then I began to prepare, not consciously at first but I guess I can say, imaginatively. I started to look around me, to review my life up to then. It had been a fairly good life, but with a few bumps and detours—a single bad marriage and a long, good one, a change in my interests at thirty, from mathematician to gardener, a big change I should say, and other less bumpy changes. I began to look around, first at my family, my children, dispersed then as they were, living their own lives, and then at my husband, still hardy and interested in everything, a gardener, also, by choice and an acoustician by profession. My friends were next. I had a few great, good ones and was a good friend in return. I examined them carefully, one by one and weighed them in the balance of my present feelings.

Well, that was the beginning. I didn't die, as the doctor had told me I was fated to do. But the process was begun and the severity and the momentum of this process had grown, year by year. In short, I became more and more accustomed to this preparation for my death. And, as far as I know, I was alone in this endeavor. I am now ninety years old and feel myself truly on the edge this time. Yet I still practice the rituals I have developed over the years.

I've said that I was alone in this "endeavor" or "practice". That's why your catalog entry "1773. Besalampy, Malagasy" leaped out to embrace me. Here, in this entry, I thought, was a fellow traveler, a person who had long ago begun to integrate her death with her life. For I understood that we need to wave good-bye to our friends, to bring the bouquet of our remembrance to the inward gravesite, and physically visit that place where they have gone. It clears the air of our life and lets us breathe in longer and longer waves of absorption. It allows us, also, to see the living more clearly, with greater patience and vastly greater identification. They are with us, too, though they may be behind us ten or twenty or a hundred years—what does it matter, the whole train of the living will join us in that great disappearance. So this seventy-two-year-old Malagasy woman was a traveling companion who illuminated and widened my heart and my eyes. It is good you have done this to me, for me. It is a completion, a resonant and expanding punctuation point.

Vasilica Nastu
Age 91. Gardener and mathematician
Lastuni, Romania

No. 78: Wucheng, China. April 30, 1231. [3 hours; $85] A cook's helper in Wucheng, you enjoy perfecting your own cooking, though you are by no means a great chef like your master, though he, too, is not as important as the chefs in cities like Hangchow, for example. But you are eager and young (twenty-three) and you try and are rewarded a bit for your attempts.

You also enjoy painting, something you have learned here and there and on your own, have absorbed some of the Taoist spirit and have tried to fill your paintings with it. You are a kind of hanger-on among the local literati and write poetry as well, these poems often integrated into your painting. And there are also the walks you take with others, talking and looking. And since Wucheng is a jumping off place for the literati who come from the eastern part of the empire, you make it a point of meeting them. On occasions you have accompanied them into the mountains. Your master is generous in this way and loves to cultivate your "spirit," he says.

Now you are sitting with a friend and his servant, who has just brought you some cakes and tea. You sit, overlooking a wild gorge along the river. The sound of the river is not too loud and you can still talk. It is a beautiful spring morning.

No. 79: Marsh Harbor, Great Abaco Island, Bahamas. March 21, 1841. [2 days; $240] It is March now, and you are preparing another two-day fishing trip with your friend, something you do every two weeks, except in the summer when it is too hot to go anywhere. You will probably come back, as usual, with barracuda or hogfish or parrotfish or a gropper, a boatload of fish, which you will sell, and then relax for a week, visit, talk, sit on the dock near your small shack, which is all you need here, except when the hurricane season begins (then it's to the "safe house" inland when you see the warnings), then prepare to go to sea again, sometimes with some other friend or companion. It's good to go out with others; it's less boring, and you have news to exchange in the solitude of the reef or out on the wide sea.

No. 80: Budapest, Hungary. May 4, 1916. [10 hours; $90] How stupid you think you are. You sit all day at your newspaper stand, selling the two major papers and a few magazines, a small kiosk, not even in the center of town but on a minor street almost on the outskirts of the city. You sit watching the people go by, your eyes a glass of astonishment. What are you seeing? What is this that is your life? You are almost hypnotized by everything, the colored blur of traffic, the flow of people passing, the sounds floating around you. You are at times in another world, if you could only realize this. But you cannot. How stupid you think you are!

Dear Past Rentals,

Newspaper vendors—they've been around for a couple centuries, I guess, useful people, but generally poor, especially when the kids got into the business, selling them on the streets and for some time until recently delivering them as an after-school job. For the adults, it was a meager living, usually for the crippled or those not able to do much, but it was a way to survive. And, of course, there was a lot to see around them in that life, the flow of people going chaotically somewhere and all the colors and movements of a rainbow pageant, wonderful stuff every day, if only they looked, yet this guy believed his life was a prison, and you are what you believe. (I guess I believe that.)

Our thinking is indeed limited. We adapt to the immediate. Perhaps that's the way we are—limited, near-sighted creatures. Who sees the big picture? Who sees what we are in the total pageant? Given your format, Past Rentals can't present a trip that lasts a million years. That would be asking too much. So we have this guy, "trapped" in his early twentieth century job and looking out at the flow of one small part of the species. The big picture—does anyone see it—who we are, where we have come from, how we have changed the planet, how we have seen the world through our "species eyes," how we have deceived ourselves, how we have managed to survive? Very few see it, very few.

What is the "big picture"? I'll give you my take on it,

though I know it's not the only one, and as it is, it's not by any means complete. First, we're a comparatively short-lived species. Compare us with the ants or the sharks, and we don't have to go back to the anaerobic bacteria, who've been around for billions of years—ants, about a hundred million, sharks, even longer. We've lived as a species for about a million or so years, depending on how you calculate it. That's short.

Now consider how we've operated for most of our history. We were what anthropologists call "hunter gatherers," people who found food as they traveled over the landscape and who killed what they could. We've lived that way for at least 99% of our species' history, in other words, for almost all of it. And it's only recently that we "invented" agriculture and the herding of animals and what we call "civilization". That's the 1%. And it's only more recently that we've begun to use metals in sophisticated ways. Of course, an ax was around 4,000 years ago. But even more recently, within the last fifty or so years, we've developed incredibly complex and sophisticated machines. And the measurements we can make, like measuring the distance to the moon with a difference of about a centimeter. And then you have to include the potential, what we will produce within the next fifty years, and fifty years is nothing in that big picture. It's one-two millionth of our life as a species, a blink, less than a blink, what your guy selling newspapers sees.

But what's the direction we've been going in? Where is it leading us? We didn't do much damage to the planet for at least 99% of our history. And we've made only a small impact up to the last 500 years. But during this last five hundred years, we've increasingly begun to change (perhaps I should right out say "destroy") the earth. Generally speaking, water pollution was not a big problem 150 years ago. Now, it's a major problem. Air pollution, also, was relatively minor.

Now, it isn't, and it's growing, and growing, faster and faster. Take metal extractions. We've yanked billions of tons of pure metal from the earth, and most of that only in the last hundred years. And we have to live with those metals around us. Some of them are highly poisonous, like mercury, lead, and arsenic. Some of them, like uranium, are almost impossible to get rid of.

So what am I getting at? I think you can see that we're in a bad way, and we don't even know it. We're like that newspaper vendor in Budapest, looking at the narrowest strip of that immense spectrum, trying to survive, making excuses, deceiving ourselves, rationalizing our existence, uncertain, trembling (inwardly), frightened, believing that forces beyond us will become our salvation. From the recognition of our fear, we travel inward, trying to return to a world of childish protection. And from that inward journey, we strike out with our minds (one of our only weapons) and build machines, artificial structures, fortresses (and in the mind also) which will protect us, but for a while only. We want to stop the flow of the living world, place ourselves within the cross hairs of a targeted grid of time and place, an abstracted protection. And the fortresses grow more sophisticated, from stone ax to metal plow to steam-driven boats to long-distance airfreight, from language scratched into clay to the varied inventions of paper to telegraph lines to computers to voice-activated servo-mechanisms.

All of these are expressions of our "species-being," both exacting accomplishments and successive failures at integration. We have emphasized the success of our creations; we are proud of them. We erect monuments to the telephone, the broad ax, and the bombsight. But we don't look at the other side, the total side. We don't calculate the increasing rate of destruction, which the "positives" call "progress". We are running faster and faster downhill toward the cliffhead, all of us, and we think that we are about to take off into the stress-free stratosphere, into an "outered" space in some positive journey toward the stars. From a total perspective, we are running crazy, and our life gets worse and worse, the closer we get to the present. Nuclear weapons? Enough to blow up all the planets in the solar system. Chemicals? Enough to kill us all, along with the animals. Population? Enough to destroy the earth and enough to starve us all by the billions. And everyone running around in his or her limited world, selling the limited news that we are the greatest creation since life began.

That's part of the big picture. Now, I didn't claim to tell it all or even tell it complete. I wanted to alert you to our "species problem," our narrow, and narrowing, vision, despite the recent invention of bifocals, or the telescope, microscope, spectrometer, and infrared camera. The big picture is that we're headed for destruction, and that message (written on everything) seems to say that we'll be one of the shortest-lived species on earth. I hope not, but I hope that we'll start thinking about the "big picture".

Roy Garbac
Age 30. Roofer
Zagreb, Croatia

No. 81: Near Thessaloniki, Greece. April 29, 1775 B.C. [5 minutes; $20] You are in a terrible mood today, drunk and angry. Your friend has been taunting you for the last few hours and you can endure it no longer. You turn on him and start to fight. Both of you, drunk, wrestle, slowly and methodically, as if you were fighting in thick mud and in slow motion. The fight will last for a short time and then both of you will collapse.

No. 82: Porto Velho, Brazil. September 30, 548. [2 hours; $35] You and your friend are going down to the river to fish. The rain will come in the afternoon, as it always does, but this morning for two hours, both of you will sit and whisper to each other, so as not to frighten the fish, and you will probably catch several. Morning is a good time. But mostly you like to come here to your favorite spot to watch the water go by, look for animals, and talk, of course, in whispers. You and your friend are seven years old.

Dear Past Rentals,

I'm seven years old and I went fishing. I went to your journey. It was called "548. Porto Velho, Brazil." I liked it a lot. It was quiet there. My friend and I were on a river. We talked very softly. We didn't want to frighten the fish. There were trees around us and the water was very clear. I could see the fish in the water. Some birds flew over us. I think they were herons. They had long feet and white wings. I've seen them before. My friend and I were talking about what the fish were thinking. Maybe we didn't know exactly what it was, but we had some ideas. They were talking about all the shadows they lived in and how they were each of them different. And we said to ourselves that they were the only ones who could see how the shadows were different. We also talked about how they probably had a fish-language and they were speaking in whispers because they didn't want to disturb us. We caught two of them. They were beautiful. We threw them back into the water. They swam away very fast. We didn't mind. We didn't come to the river to fish. We came to talk in whispers about the fish and their shadows and look at the trees and know that it was quiet around us. It was a good trip. I want to do it again, maybe a different trip next time, but one like this one.

Ajoy Chakravarti
Age 7. Pastry maker
Benares, India

No. 83: Near Arequipa, Peru. March 14, 829. [3 hours; $45] Yesterday was your twenty-sixth birthday. You are now a grown woman with two children, who help you prepare the fields for planting and go to market with you. Tonight you have had an ecstatic dream in which you have been clothed in brilliant, iridescent feathers in a cloak which shines out into the night and blinds all who approach you. And below your feet, many, many feet below as if deep in a hole in the earth, a dark child whose outlines you can barely distinguish squirms in a warm ball of half-light. His words are puffs of darkness, which slowly begin to extinguish your iridescent cloak, although you struggle hard against the effects of his cries. A bird comes to help, drops "eggs of light" on the child. The dawn is coming and your feathers are fading into a single color. The child is rising from its deep hole in the earth. You are awake.

You lie in bed in your hut, listening and looking around you, remembering the dream and thinking about what it might mean to you, a mother who struggles for her sacred children.

No. 84: Somewhere around Waddan, Libya. February 16, 27,853 B.C. [2 hours; $35] A twenty-two-year-old man, you have been wakened suddenly by a dream you were having, and on waking you notice that everything is very quiet, too quiet. You know enough to realize that a large animal is on the prowl. You are waking the others, who are about to start the fire, when they see the shadow of a male lion beyond the camp, walking in the moonlight.

No. 85: Wuhu, Anhwei Province, China. June 22, 1497. [15 minutes; $15] What game are you playing now, girl of nine? It is the string game. You stand with your friend, you and she on the banks of the river, watching the boatmen, dozens today, going to the great sea, beside which you stand or sometimes sit, and play this game with a string, looking through its patterns to see the boats and the river, each of you taking the patterns made by your fingers and transforming them into something else. Very skillful, you have played this game for years, as have many of your friends. Even your parents will sometimes play with you, only for a short time, since they, too, remember their childhood. Now as you play, you look out through the string between your hands at the boatmen passing.

No. 86: Maiduguri, Nigeria. August 16, 1784. [3 days; $175] Each day you wake to the terrible hunger which has lasted three weeks and made you and your family ghosts in this desert, where the wind blows without begetting and the dry soil leaves the millet as empty as paper. The whole countryside is dry. It whispers through your almost inaudible voice.

But from the coast your cousin is coming, with his caravan of food, with water and rice and millet and sorghum for all. Is this a dream? Is your cousin really coming? The day is dry. The wind blows leisurely through the tents for a thousand miles over the desert, over the dried lake, which is a day's journey from your home in Maiduguri. And your cousin and the food and the water may or may not be coming. The desert and the wind tell of yourself, the life of your family and people, blown away into shadows.

Dear Past Rentals,

To experience famine? To experience hunger? "Past Rentals, you have indeed gone o¬ the deep end," I first thought. And then I thought again and added, "The deep end of what?" On letting the thought sink deeper, I realized that hunger and its extreme form, famine, have been a recurring and major theme through history, from the Paleolithic to the present. It is only we, who, floating in abundance in our part of the world, cannot conceive of it. And yet it is, it has been there, tangible as air, water, and the recent full loaf of bread. "Give us this day our daily bread," I thought surely meant something for the time of our history after the baking of bread. "Give us this day our daily rice. Or give us this day our daily millet. Or potatoes. Or roots. Or freshly killed antelope."

Yes, I said, I am going to immerse myself in the past. If I am going to identify with the lives of others, I am going to feel as they felt, hunger as they hungered, hope as they hoped. And therefore I came to your entry "1784. Maiduguri, Nigeria (Chad?)" to experience what those people felt. I tasted their pain, their sorrow, and even their sacrifice. I don't know if the cousin arrived from the coast. I know only their suffering.

Mary Adams Waysit
Age 49. Cannery worker
Guyaquil, Equator

No. 87: Malatya, Turkey. November 14, 1374. [4 days; $250] How much regret you have suffered over your parent's death these last ten years. Yes, they died in a terrible fire. And you, their only daughter, were saved, with great courage, it should be said, by the neighbors, who have taken you into their lives and made you their daughter, and even more than that, their deep friend. Allah is merciful, they say, and yes, Allah is merciful, but how much regret you have suffered over their deaths, how much memory comes to you—their voices, their movements, their singing, their tears even—everything comes back. Grief, unending grief, when will it end, when will you throw this terrible burden over the endless chiffhead and into the sea of past events? It is your fondest wish, the wish at the center of your suffering heart.

No. 88: Chingpien to Chihtan, Kansu Province, China. April 17, 548. [2 weeks; $450] You are returning to Chihtan from Chingpien on the Great Wall with your lover, a trip he has made to inspect the provisioning of the garrison stationed there against the northern barbarians.

It has been beautiful this late April, and you often stop to look at this scene or that, at the flowers on the almost barren hillsides, the hint of a new moon in the west, or the color of the few trees that suck their juices from the evening sky. You pause for long conversations about almost everything. You are full of each other, and the time of your life is rich and expanding.

No. 89: Taegu, Korea. February 5, 1501. [2 years; $1050] Contentious, bitchy, complaining, moody, loving at times, only to irrupt with a volcano of false accusations—you are certainly a difficult wife. But because your husband has taken the only course open to him, that is, to spend his time with other women, and increasingly so in the last few years, you have decided to do away with him.

For three months you have been slipping small amounts of poison into his tea, not enough for him, or anyone else, to notice, but enough that, taken over a long time, will kill him.

And, in fact, this "treatment" has done just that. Last week your husband died, in his sleep, fortunately. And the doctors you have called have attributed his death to his carousing, drinking, running around until late in the night, and to other superficial evidence, glad that they can find something to which they can attribute his death.

But what will you do now? How will you spend the next twenty years of your life? Now forty and too old to marry and certainly not wealthy enough to attract a rich or even a well-to-do husband, you will languish in Taegu, the only town you have known. And people who know you (and many do, through intense gossip) will secretly suggest that, though there is no proof you killed your husband, you have purposely done him in. Yes, what will you do now?

Dear Past Rentals,

How many murderers have you had in your catalogs? I have counted four, in catalogs 3, 7, 8, and 11. One was a woman who murdered her newly born baby, not an unusual occurrence, considering that millions have done so, almost all out of desperation. Another was a member of a gang who sent him out to kill a man who wouldn't give them his house to use, a terribly mindless crime. Another happened because of a quarrel with a neighbor over land. It all took place on the property line, you know. And the last one was terrible, a son murdering his father. Of course, you could understand why. The father was a son of a bitch, worked his son only to get money to drink with, and beat him every day, whether or not he did the work.

Why am I interested in these murderer entries? The reason is that I am myself a murderer. I am serving a life sentence at the Fellow Springs Prison in Heffenwise, Texas and have now been here for about sixteen years and eight months. I'll die here—there's no doubt of that. But in those sixteen years and eight months I've learned something. I've taught myself to read and write—I couldn't do that very well

*before I was incarcerated. And I've done a lot of drawings. I
knew I was good at artwork before they caught me, but I've
had a lot of time to improve. And I have improved. In fact, I
think I'm pretty good at what I do. I'm sending along some
sketches I made of those trips I just described. You may see
how deeply I've involved myself in the subjects, because I've
gone on all of them. They weren't cheap, but I had sponsors,
Murderers Anonymous, an organization we have right here
at the Fellow Springs Prison. We have twenty-five members
and we meet twice a week. We've been meeting for the last
eleven years. It's an important organization, and I feel good
about being a member. Our organization decided that I
should go on all those trips, for my own good, and after I went
on two of them I totally agreed. I've learned a lot, and it's all
in the sketches I'm sending. You may use them for whatever
you want. It would also be nice to have them exhibited somewhere out there, if you can arrange it.*

*It's not hard to describe what I've learned on those trips
to the four murders. But it is hard, I think, for people to see
what might be missing in these people that would cause them
to commit the same crimes or crimes like them. I'm going to
say it as simply as I can: People kill others, deliberately kill
them, because there's something missing, something that
didn't get filled in somewhere along the way or sifted out. I'm
a good example. I never learned to feel that other people were
there. My parents set it up so that I saw them as people who
were always in the way. I had to get around them. And when
I couldn't get around them, that's when I let loose. And that's
why I'm here now.*

*Now this last trip, my fifth, to Taegu, Korea in 1501
was—I have to say—the same thing. It told me what I'd
already known, that there was something missing in that
woman, and that something built on something that built on
something else until there was a mountain of layers ready to*

explode. And, of course, it did. Killing your husband? A lot of women have done that. That's why I didn't feel I learned much from this one. But I want to tell you what I did get out of my fifth murder trip, and it's important, very important.

I have to say I got one thing. I learned that I didn't need to go on any more of these murder trips. I realized that I was making my whole "murder history" even stronger. I realized that I needed to get into something more positive. I can't believe it's taken me so long to realize this. But is has. Since I've returned, I've started thinking about the positive trips I want to take, and I've got about thirty lined up. I won't be able to go on all of them, even if they're spread out over the next ten years. But with the help of Murderers Anonymous here at the prison and a grant we're getting to help many of us travel through your catalog, I'll probably be able to visit a lot of people, situations, and places. And, most important, I think these new trips will help me a lot. I've grown in the last sixteen years and eight months, but I'm looking forward to growing even more, now that I feel I'm on the right road, a positive one.

Remember to let me know what you think of the sketches. I hope you can use them.

Robert Findley James
Age 45. Prisoner, Fellow Springs Prison
Heffenweise, Texas

From: Past Rentals
To: Robert Findley James
Fellow Springs Prison
Heffenweise, Texas

Dear Mr. James,

We were extremely encouraged to receive your forty-five sketches at our clearing office in Fort Wayne, Indiana and have passed them on to our Integration Bureau in Philadelphia. We have been in touch with them for the last week about your drawings. They like them very much. At first, they didn't know how to make use of them. But someone we know in the art world in California suggested that we create The Past Rentals Room of Retrieved Artifacts within the Palace of the Legion of Honor in San Francisco, and we are on our way to doing that. As soon as we open that exhibition room, your drawings will be the first items to be exhibited. We also hope that we can display copies of your letter to us while the exhibition is in progress. Please let us know.

More important, we have come to another epiphany— that's a kind of important realization. We would like to know if it would be all right with you if we featured a part of your life in prison (not anything before you were arrested) in our next catalog. If this would be okay with you, please sign the enclosed papers, have them notarized, and send them back to us, care of our Philadelphia office.

Sincerely,

Andrew Askit
Program Director for Special Extensions

No. 90: Bucharest, Romania. June 30, 1916. [7 hours; $50] You are a thirteen-year-old boy who, along with two of your friends, has constructed a small, crystal radio. However, once you have built it, you interrupt your listening for long periods to do what you cannot help doing—telling long and involved stories, in fact, cooperatively telling them, for as soon as one boy goes on for a time, according to the rules of your games, another interrupts him, continuing the story in his own way.

The radio, however, interrupts you with its startling news of the First World War. Then, you listen. But no sooner have the vital facts been presented, than you are off with a new turn, a dramatic climax or anticlimax, yet all of it somehow coming from the news, which increasingly provides the information for new turns in your endless story.

Dear Past Rentals,

I was that thirteen-year-old boy. I was, I was. I swear to you I was. I built myself a crystal set, those old, home-made radios with wire wound round a toilet paper roll and a crystal you bought and a set of head phones, and you had to move the wire across the wire-bound roll and tune in on a station. Sometimes you got them and sometimes you didn't, and sometimes you just had to wait. And I was that kind of storyteller. We told stories all the time, made them up, fantastic as they were, with strange names and stranger places and perhaps stranger motivations for the characters. Stories like "Whippoorwill Hollow Jack and the Tremblers". (Sounds like a '50s band, doesn't it?) It had a character named Whippoorwill, who had the habit of disappearing all of a sudden, not when he wanted to, but just for no reason, gone. And reappearing again, hours or weeks or years later in different places. Once, we had him disappear in the middle of Australia (Alice Springs) and appear two days later in Bangor, Maine. (And, believe it or not, we practiced our geography that way.) Once Whippoorwill was going to be inaugurated as President of Halftax (not Halifax—we knew that place already), a country whose name we invented, along with a partial language and a geography, and a kind of weather pattern. Of course, he disappeared right in the middle of his swearing in as President. And re-appeared four years later just when the "new" President was swearing in. Of course, it was all crazy. But it was great fun at the time, and now that I look back at it from a period of forty years, I still think it's fun, and I still think it would have been great to have continued that game at twenty, at thirty, at forty, and at fifty. What do we think we are, adults? Well, yes and no.

But when we heard the news of the outbreak of the war on my crystal set (it was the outbreak of the Second World War, the Japanese attack on Pearl Harbor), we listened for a long time for as much as we could and then tuned into my parents' radio, which had much better reception, and listened for more than an hour or a day, listened for at least two weeks. Maybe that's why the stories stopped, at least for a time. Reality, and a terrible reality at that, intruded on our imagination and carried us with it.

It was this intersection of the imaginary world of young boys and the reality of the "grown-up" world that interested me in your entry, "1916. Bucharest, Romania". And, of course, it was also the remembrance of those wonderful days of imagination and, I should say, technology that drew me to your entry. I believe that these two worlds, the world of imagination and the world of, let's call it, the "real" are more alike than we want to admit. They really cannot be separated, though we try. I think we would not understand the "real" world without the power of the "shaping" imagination. Childhood provides that, but, unfortunately, that shaping sense in us seems to die out with age. You brought it back to me with your entry. I urge all your readers and participants to enter their world fully armed with that shaping imagination.

Diego de Ortiz
Age 53. Garbage collector

Bilbao, Spain

No. 91: Naples, Italy. March 26, 1921. [2 hours; $30] You are a twenty-three-year-old woman, a clerk in a large governmental building. You work in an office in charge of regional engineering projects. Since becoming a typist, you have been in charge of preparing interdepartmental memos and letters.

But despite your workload, you find yourself engaged in personal memoranda. Sometimes, when you begin to type a letter, you find yourself transforming it into a love letter addressed to someone whom you can imagine but have never seen. The letter is, of course, never sent, but you keep it in a personal file and from time to time read over the growing collection, as if it were a novel. (There are many dozens of them already.)

Two new male employees have become a part of the office, and you have been strongly attracted to them. They have been included in your letters, along with the imaginary ones. You are now writing one of your letters, this one about the second man in the office.

No. 92: Wrightsville Beach, North Carolina. August 16, 1881. [9 hours; $105] You are a young woman of nineteen who has come to the beach for the day with her girlfriends, all of you on your one day off a week, and a beautiful day it is, just perfect for sitting on the warm sand, watching everything around you and being watched (and, hopefully, admired.) You have all brought food from home and rented a small tent under which you can sit to watch the beach traffic, especially the men.

Dozens of bathing machines into which you will "send yourselves" as you say, when you want to go into the water, are ranged below you. They are really "modesty machines," as you call them. A man enters this device, changes into his bathing suit, and then walks into the water. When he is ready to come out and needs to change, he changes in the bathing machine. Sometimes, however, the tide goes out and the man must run, nude, to get to it. This delights and thrills you, and, of course, you watch for it when you are standing on the cliffs overlooking the beach.

And there, as you watch the people who have come, are the other girls, all wearing what you and your friends are wearing—laced sandals, sailor collars, short skirts and matching pantaloons. A variety of yells, calls, songs, and whistles fills the hot August day. There will be much to see and later to talk about when you return in the evening on the horse-drawn tram.

No. 93: Warsaw, Poland. April 6, 1902. [3 weeks; $450] You are twenty-two years old, a young woman who has worked as a telephone switchboard worker at the main telephone unit in Warsaw now for about six years. You work a ten-hour day, six days a week. There is nothing to sustain you except your work. Although you live with your family, they cannot feed you without your work, for they, too, work long hours and live under the same conditions.

Six months ago, a union organizer, disguised as an operator (a young woman), began to speak to the girls. Everyone was afraid, and they had good reason to be. They could be fired and never again get another job in Warsaw. This was a real possibility, for the employers had much power and were organized, as the workers were not.

However, the idea of a union made you hopeful, and little by little, secretly, you began to collect dues, sign up members, and hold meetings. Finally, two weeks ago, feeling ready, you went to your employer and asked for an eight-hour day and a raise in your salaries. You pretty much knew what the employer would say, but you also knew that he would be surprised. No one had told him you had organized a union. You felt proud of what you had done, even though you knew that difficult days were ahead. You would have to fight for everything you wanted, fight even harder than you worked, and that was hard enough. When he heard your demands, the employer was quiet, asked a few questions, and then left. The next day, twenty telephone operators were fired. Immediately, you held a meeting and decided to strike. In ten minutes everyone was out on the streets, picketing the main telephone unit so that no one in Warsaw could call. Within a day, other units in Poland had gone on strike. Almost everyone was out. Only two or three women, afraid of losing their jobs and not being able to support their families, stayed at work.

Now it is the third day of the strike. You know the employer is going to bring in strikebreakers. But your husbands are behind you. They are organized and will frighten the women away. You also know that you will be out of work for a long time, but you know there is support for you in many areas and there is much to be done in the next few weeks.

Dear Past Rentals,

You're damned right, and I wish you had more about labor and labor unions and organizing. We've been the people who've built this country. We're the people, as the bumper sticker says, who gave you the weekend, and would like to give you more. And it's more than a shame that workers aren't really organized, that they've sold themselves down the river, that they don't know anything about their history and the struggles that people went through to give them what should be their rights.

How many people can feel, really feel what people 100 years ago experienced when they worked? It was more than the lack of food, the poor wages, or dangerous working conditions. It was that, too. But it was the insecurity—have a job today and lose it tomorrow, get sick and get fired, say the wrong thing and get the ax. That's what it was like and that's what it's going to be like if working people don't get together. I don't mean only get together into unions, but go beyond unions to the political world and organize a party by and for labor. Little by little we built the forty-hour week, and we finally got it in 1932. But little by little we're losing it, losing the power and momentum we had, while the rich are getting still richer and the poor even poorer. America's top 1% now controls about 65% of the wealth; America's top 5% controls about 98% of the wealth. That's not democracy. That's oligarchy. In fact, it's robbery. And the workers don't even realize what's happening to them. They believe that they, too, can "inherit a factory," "strike it rich," get better off through their own efforts. All that, of course, is bullshit. It's a lie that's fed to people to keep them from disrupting the way things are going, from equalizing the wealth and therefore the power. And, of course, you can see by what I'm saying that that's got to change.

Your entry "1925. Warsaw, Poland" roused me to return "to those thrilling days of yesterday," thrilling in the expansion of hope through struggle. And it renewed my own hope in the working people of my time to equalize society, if only to give us a guaranteed decent minimum wage, a thirty-five hour week, job security, an end to the military (which robs you of half your federal taxes), and a big role in decision making. And these things can happen, and more, if working people wake up, like the woman in your Poland entry.

Happy St. Claire
Age 43. Paper mill worker
Eureka, California

Dear Past Rentals,

It's amazing how decisions are made. From reading what passes as history, what's called "the history of America," "the history of the French Enlightenment" (I'm looking at two books with these titles), you'd think that action and change rose out of various kingly acts of, I guess, powerful people, an insult, the death of a ruler, a mistake, a disagreement, or an act of aggression. These were important, of course, but the groundswell of history is seldom recorded, the immediate reactions of people in a particular situation or a particular class or the climatic conditions which effected them go virtually unnoticed. What about a particular person at a particular time under a particular set of conditions? Are that person's choices (or absence of choices) ever described in detail? History does not deal with the particular conditions of particular people, or so we are told. But look closely and at that middle distance of observation at your own behavior. You will get a better understanding of what makes people passive or active with regard to the conditions under which they exist.

These women at the telephone station are no different than women working in groups anywhere. People, to give them credit, exist in several worlds of decision making. They are continually weighing each decision, as if they were walking with a multiple balance beam all over their situational bodies. They suspend each item, judging their importance on each occasion. They move some to the back burner, while others may "flare up" into importance, and still others they don't think of at all. Within these choices are all sorts of implied threats and rewards. For example, the Warsaw telephone operators talking in public about their working conditions was certainly dangerous to their economic well-being and, perhaps, to their bodily health. These workers had all kinds of worries, such as heating their homes (or rather their shoddy apartments), shopping for food, relating to their neigh-

bors, helping their children grow up in a significant and healthy way, contending with the police, the garbage, battling rats and various insects, having time to themselves, worrying about the possibility of being robbed, dealing with their feelings of greed and envy, and so forth. Each person everywhere today, and perhaps throughout history, has carried around his concerns in "baskets" of varying weights and sizes.

I find it interesting that people will rationalize their actions (or inactions) and do them naturally and instantaneously, without thinking. For example, they will leap to the defense of their country in a foreign war, which has nothing to do with them, rather than think about what percentage of taxes they are paying or how much say they have in selecting candidates to represent them. People are dragged along in the winds of their times by forces that control them and which they do not know control them. Today, the world they know of in my country, the United States, is the only one they know. But, more important, this world that more people are living in is a manufactured one, removed from their daily lives, and people make choices on the basis of that manufactured world and not some real, tangible one! The media gives them a world and they proceed to act within it. And, oddly, it is the only world they know, and it carries with it a freight load of assumptions, and on those assumptions they act. It is the most absurd thing we have ever encountered at any time in history. One hundred years ago people knew what was real, dealt with it tangibly, felt their tired bodies at the end of the day, and more or less knew their neighbors. But people today are as ghostly as the images fed to them. Propaganda? Yes, the most subtle and pervasive one ever developed. No dictatorship has ever had a more sophisticated program of thought control as we have today. The Russians? The Russians were crude by comparison.

What's interesting to me is how people make changes,

how they react to their situations. I wonder how long people in my country can go on suspended in this thought control. The women in your trip to Warsaw were not of this type and could at least feel the conditions of their lives. Their choices were active. Ours are not.

> *Maria Straight*
> *Age 26. Public defender*
> *Billings, Montana*

No. 94: Brno, Czechoslovakia. July 5, 1843. [3 weeks; $150]   After having been in jail for six years, you have just been released. What will you do now? The world you knew is not the same. Many things have changed. Many friends and contacts are gone. And you still do not have a job. What choices do you have? Is this prison, with its filthy food, its fleas in the mattresses, its smell of urine and feces, and its grumbling inmates, a better place? Sometimes you think so, but your body says, "No, of course not. Anything is better than a prison cell." You have a sister in Brno, and you will stay with her for a short time. She cannot keep you— she is poor herself. You enter Brno, free but uncertain.

No. 95: Borobudur, Java. September 16, 901. [One hour; $35]   Now eighteen, you work with your father in a field about 1,000 yards from the great temple of Borobudur. In fact, you have grown up in sight of the temple and have heard stories of its construction from your grandfather, who heard it from his grandfather, a miraculous achievement in honor of the Buddha. Of course, you have been to the temple many times and have seen, in effect read, the life of that man whom you wish with all your heart to emulate, in fact, to become.

Even now, you meditate in the fields outside your house,

where your large family lives. You sit, at dawn, facing away from the temple toward the east for an hour each morning, as does your twelve-year-old brother and your cousins and your father. And then you go to work, in the land you know and believe in. You are now sitting down to meditate, as you have for the last ten years.

No. 96: Bogota, Columbia. February 3, 1903. [6 hours; $75] You never liked stealing. Though you never think about why you don't like it, you just do it. There's hunger, of course, but there is also the quiet fraternity of the other thieves, whom you meet at least three times a week, and the fences and the arguments over price—all these things are events which form a whole, moving into themselves, solidifying, to the point of hardening, into a fortress whose walls may become more dangerous than the one which this life protects you from.

But there is hunger, and therefore you don't think too much about what this all means. Hunger means something, as does the use of your whole being in the execution of a theft, and also, and perhaps most important, the presence of your partner who, after the death of your parents, taught you how to survive and made, as he says, "an honest thief" out of you. May God protect him and bless him. (You read because of him. The others cannot.) You know something of a few trades—ropemaking, carpentry, small farming—through his patience, and you forgive him his curious depressions and his occasional wanderings into the lowland jungles where the Jivaros still hunt and take human heads.

Today you will wander around the large market in Bogota with your partner, and he will point out (although you already know how to do this yourself) the "marks" for the day, a bit of hustling and con man activity, you being the poor boy who cannot find his way back to his parent's home and they being the "good" people who will lead you there, through the alley, where both of you will set upon them and run away with their watches and their money.

Dear Past Rentals,

I've never met a thief. I've never wanted to. I don't think many people really do, though they may dream about it sometimes. I've also never thought about a thief as a person. Somehow he was rendered dead by being placed in some abstract social category. When I read your catalog entry No. 96, I got started on another train of thought. Who is a thief anyway, and what kind of thief and how old and from where and why? Then I thought of my own life, how I had stolen money from my father when I was ten, how we'd steal candy from the market when we were kids, how we winked, knowingly, at other kids who had stolen something, as if we were both in on a secret, both a part of an in-group which made us special people.

Beyond these small, personal instances, I thought about corporations who steal "within the law," who can afford powerful accountants and attorneys, who, for instance, don't pay for the damage the pesticides they spray produce. Then, I really began to think about thieves, different kinds, big and small, and their own mindsets, their own "necessary" worlds. There was a lot to think about. And then I went to Bogota on your catalog entry.

I learned that things are more mixed up than I thought. Put a thief like this one in another context and he might turn out to be a saint. Put a saint in another place and he might turn out to be a thief. But there's another layer, too. Some people like the excitement. Without necessity, life's boring. Necessity keeps intelligence alive. Our animal instincts and our intelligence demand it. Now, the illusive sense of moral clarity is hard to pin down. It's all mixed up because every-

one has a lot of different impulses in him, even the most "righteous" person. That's why seeing this young man from the "inside" (and inside the pages of your catalog) opened me up.

Bogota, where this boy and his mentor carried on their "trade," was a quiet, grimy, hardly developed city, the capital of a big and empty country with its usual graft and its usual poverty. Some classes of people fall a bit, some rise, and some see people rise while they are falling, and some are just born into poverty and others are just born into wealth. And there's not much middle ground.

My young boy was intelligent, but fallen into necessary poverty. His parents died when he was fairly young, and there was no one there for him, except a thief, his mentor, a man who had his own intelligent quirks, but who nonetheless "saved" him from starvation. The needs of a young boy for a father can be transferred to another out of necessity, yet woe be unto him who does not succeed in "adopting" one. He will seek him everywhere, to the point of inventing a father. That is how it is. And our young man was no different. Once the meld had been made, he grew in the soil of his needs.

But there is a special relationship between the mentor and the student, one not connected entirely with their "profession," but rather with the personality of the teacher. "Our" teacher was a man of secretive moods, sometimes caustic and satirical, sometimes expansively melancholy, sometimes clearly practical. I remember that day he told me that he had gone down river with some Jivaros and had eaten part of a human body. For a split second I believed him, but then I caught something. His head turned down and one of his eyes looked up at me with that sheepish glance, that "Who do you think I'm kidding" look. And then he pushed me over the small stone I was sitting on and laughed. But he had indeed gone somewhere into the lowlands for a few weeks and had come back with a whole suitcase of stories about marginal people in the tropics who ate almost anything that walked and who sat for hours looking at the river and who slept in hammocks and who were not bothered by the mosquitoes.

It was not so much the material itself, but the way in which he related these things, half as a matter of fact and half as news from a reporter sent to the scene of a comic disaster. Sometimes he presented his material clinically, like a doctor reporting the precise procedure he used to remove an appendix from a struggling crocodile. I got the feeling that he went away in order to return with these stories, rather, these ways of telling them. The return, I felt, represented more than the journey.

As for the young man, he had been hardened to their absurdity but not to their appeal. Every time he heard one, he laughed, since they were told with such a ridiculous air about them. But his laughter was a "cut off" laughter. It was intellectual, a laughter of appraisal, a judgment of the show being put on for him. This was his style, though he was capable of some feeling for others, of course.

Yet despite this compassion, the young man was always nervous. When he ate, he had a habit of furtively looking around him, and when he defecated, it was the same, a quick glance to the side, like a bird on the ground, hunting for worms, nervous ears and a slightly tensed body. All three—the eating, the looking, and the laughter—are vulnerable moments; they have existed from our beginnings as a species and perhaps from before. He gave with a kind of generous, compulsive giving and yet at times felt suddenly offended by some small and inconsequential action: an apple unpromised, an appointment not kept, a restaurant which didn't serve good food (although he knew it didn't). Being a thief made him nervous, careful, as if those feelings that needed to emerge from him had to be kept at bay lest they reveal him for the small boy, who was still a necessary part of his being and had not entirely left.

Not so his mentor. He had somehow come to terms with the boy and the young man inside him. Perhaps the trips were ways of organizing his life through artifice, for his stories revealed a studied manipulation. It was hard to say. In Bogota there were many types, some like his mentor—but all kinds. In fact, it was the abundant variety of people who impressed me. And out of that variety came a whole spectrum of reactions to that backwater capital; and indeed when his mentor fled for long periods to the emptiness of the tropical lowlands, I understood deeply within me the reasons for that flight.

So being a thief is not as straightforward as it might seem. The burden of being outside the law all your life is a great one. But yet we forget how much a burden being only within the law can be. Your catalog entry showed me the entrance into a people I had never believed in or thought about much or sympathized with in any way. It showed me that thieves, like all of us, belong to the same source, and the return to that source bring backs a primal sanity which furthers our sense of being human.

Primo Danielovic
Age 38. Printer
Trieste, Italy

No. 97: Harrisburg, Pennsylvania. December 10, 1911. [10 hours; $75]
You are a seventeen-year-old woman who works in her parent's grocery story in Harrisburg. You have worked there since you were six and you will probably work there for as long as you can imagine. There is nothing else to do here where you live. Business is not wonderful, but with all of you working it is enough to keep you going. Your family and you live in a small apartment above

the store.

In the winter you go ice-skating with your girlfriends, ogle the boys, and talk—endlessly. When you have time at night, you read mostly long, soupy, romantic novels, which your friends pass around. You wander through your teenage years, moaning over this or that man, longing, romantically and effortlessly, to be taken away from your daily life.

It is winter, and for a few minutes at lunchtime you are sitting near the coal stove in the apartment above the store and, while you eat your lunch, reading another novel. Your mother will call you and you will come downstairs and begin to work in the store until about eight o'clock. Then, you will spend time with your friends and go to bed, for work starts at seven o'clock tomorrow morning.

Dear Past Rentals,

Oh, I wanted to work in my parents' grocery store in Harrisburg, Pennsylvania. I wanted to go ice skating with my girlfriends and ogle the boys and talk and talk and talk, romantically, longingly, anything to escape from the drudgery of daily life. Oh, adolescent girlhood, how I miss you. Returning to that time was a true pleasure, a true remembrance, and a true indulgence, and I loved it. I just loved it.

I want more entries like this one. You don't know how many burdens they relieve. Magazines aren't enough. Movies aren't enough. Rock stars aren't enough. None of them are enough. It's the real thing I want. I want to be there. I want to feel those soupy, romantic novels soak into me while I'm lying in bed on a cold, blustery winter night. I want to feel warm and protected, loved and protected, cared for and protected. Oh, bring them back. They are my breath and my ocean, my lifeblood and my nectar. They are what I need more than anything else.

Rosie Connerly
Age 43
Fort Wayne, Indiana

No. 98: Chicago, Illinois. December 4, 1893. [10 hours; $100] Now, at forty-five, you have been a road sweeper for fifteen years. At first you started out sweeping the gutters with a large broom. After seven years, the city brought in mechanical sweepers, large cylindrical brooms turned by horsepower. Now, you drive the horse around the streets, sweeping the refuse into piles, where it is later picked up by others. Chicago is cold and overcast today as you are operating the street sweeper, as usual, a pint of whiskey inside your coat for extra warmth.

No. 99: Rajahmundry, India. November 29, 1559. [6 hours; $85] You are an Indian girl of fourteen, brought up as a Hindu, like your parents. Since the time when you first began to listen, and later to overhear your parents and their friends discussing philosophy, religion and mathematics, you have become obsessed with "the meaning of things".

From these discussions you have begun to write down your thoughts, original thoughts but ones elaborated from family discussions. You have not written notes from what others have said. These are your own thoughts, preceding from the base ground of the discussions and extending farther out, much father than anyone participating in these talks would have dreamed of going. If your parents had read what you have written, they would have either misunderstood them, found them incomprehensible, or else thought them heretical. Therefore, you keep your writing to yourself.

Now, at fourteen years old, closeted in a small hut on the

edge of the forest, and overlooking the sea, you write, lost in the abstract arguments passing through your head like a pageant of magnificent latticework. Your writing is an elaboration on the paradoxes of being one, being many, being born alive in others, being a part of others, a part of things, or of animals. It is strongly influenced by the Hindu religion, to which your family belongs, though you might yourself deny it. And yet it is something abstractly so, if that is one way of saying it. The form of the abstract argument weaves itself in, out, and through all things. When you write, you hear everything around you; you are alive and inside of everything, not merely removing the outlines of things and setting them apart, but somehow intellectually attempting to find the essence of all things through the philosophy, mathematics, and religion from which you began.

Dear Past Rentals,

A fourteen-year-old girl studying philosophy? I couldn't believe it, until I met a fourteen-year-old girl who was doing just that. My grandmother wanted to study engineering, but her husband prevented her from doing so. My older cousin in Bainbridge, Massachusetts twenty-five years ago wanted to study surgery, but her father got her into nursing school, after which she went through the usual progression, working at St. George's Hospital out there, marrying a doctor (a surgeon, no less), and settling down with two children, not a bad life, but one with some big gaps in it.

All around me now I see intelligent women asking intel-ligent questions, but something is missing in them, curiosity. How could they find the questions to ask and the answers to those questions if they did not go somewhere, inside them-selves, to find them? It's the journey, the exploration, that matters. How is it that men want to do this but women feel timid, afraid? More important to me, how is it that some women have managed to follow that path of curiosity and thereby answer the questions they have, themselves, asked?

I noticed, also, that this young woman in your catalog entry ("1559. Rajahmundry, India") did all her thinking in secret. What would have happened if she had had a group of like-minded, equally as intelligent, young women with her, even an elder woman or two, stimulating them, stimulating each other? Would they have been destroyed, or would they have just been laughed at, or would they have been ignored? So many brilliant women in the past have been consigned to lives of subservience, peeking out of their purdha at the world they might have, perhaps absorbing secretly what they could not absorb in public and directing their new knowledge inward. Their attention was absorbed into the immediate, the practical, and perhaps for the better, for what use is all this abstraction, even The Theory of Relativity, to most people? When we feel the earth under us, don't we know something just as important as the Law of Falling Bodies or Leibnitz's monads?

I have thought that perhaps this young woman's interest was an aberration, a distortion of her normal growth, a way of escaping from problems like sex, friendship, and feelings. Of course, men also may move away from these things by becoming "philosophical," but their activities have been considered more acceptable.

There may be a biological reason for this. The man participates biologically for only a moment in the process of reproduction. A woman first bears a child for nine months and then raises it, emotionally and biologically, for the next fifteen years. The man is under no biological obligation. In some ways he is freed into what might be called "a biologically useless existence," which leaves him empty. To fill this emptiness he must create his own rationale for being; he must show that he is someone.

Some of this energy will be siphoned off by the woman in the home and by child raising. But there is still plenty left, and men have found ways of allowing this energy to play itself out—sports, travel, philandering, science, self-exploration, etc. Most of the time these activities aid the development of new generations, when men are able to express this energy. When they are not, chaos results. Wars break out. Whole populations become depressed or occupy themselves with labyrinths of trivia.

But where childbirth and child raising are made easier, that is, where technology has eased the burden of living, then the possibility of mutual participation in both child rearing and in the larger world, exploration for both men and women, becomes possible. Today the conditions exist for this mutual identification and merging of roles. These conditions did not exist in the mid-fifteenth century when this young woman lived. What men have created, then, may prepare for a dispersal of roles beneficial to both sexes, and women may not enter more and more the older world of men but enter an exploration that merges the concrete with the abstract, and that, it seems to me, is basic philosophy.

I hope I have explained myself clearly enough. I do not mean to detract from the importance of this young woman's endeavors, from the significance of her own exploration. But I did want to fill out a larger picture that remains barely understood among both men and women.

Lisa Alejandro
Age 49. Astronomer
Santiago, Chile

No. 100: St. Petersburg, Russia. January 3, 1841. [4 hours; $95] A six-year-old girl with light, golden hair, thin, and with eyes that wander everywhere, you have come to the market in the suburbs of St. Petersburg to buy meat. Your family is not rich, yet they come here to save money, since the animals people buy are those that have died of the cold.

The animals lie here frozen at 20 below zero. Scattered around you are dozens of sheep, cows and pigs. It will be necessary to work quickly when they are partially thawed, for the meat will not keep long. Therefore, your family and a few others will share it, using as much as possible. Your father is going to buy a pig today. He is looking over the possible ones, and you are wandering around the market, looking at everything, since you have few opportunities to come even this far into St. Petersburg. Everything, including the frozen animals, fascinates you.

Dear Past Rentals,

Oh, what a cold place. Oh, it was so cold! And I was so wrapped up I could hardly move. I was a six-year-old girl on my trip. I'm ten now. Four years ago I was six. I don't remember how I felt being six, except starting school and learning to ride my bicycle and eating fresh bread from the oven. St. Petersburg was a cold place, but I live in a cold place, Minneapolis, Minnesota, where the temperature can go down to a minus 30 or more. But St. Petersburg was even colder!

I remember my father. I don't mean my real father. I mean this man who was my father. I could smell all that liquor coming out of him. I think it was vodka. And my mother, too. They were too interested in buying one of those frozen animals—I think they bought a frozen pig. I mean they were too interested in the animals to pay much attention to little me. This little girl liked eating meat. Me, I like it, too, but I like things like pizza better.

The market place was exciting. There were so many

booths there. People were selling all kinds of things. Of course, someone was selling hot tea. I know the Russians drink a lot of tea. We read about that in school. There were booths for getting your shoes fixed. There were booths where the gypsies would tell your fortune. There were booths that sold old clothes. I don't think the clothes had been washed. There was a booth that sold live chickens and fresh meat. There was a booth that sold hot soup and it smelled very good. I wish I could have had some. There was a booth that sold books. But I couldn't read. My parents couldn't read either and they couldn't send me to school—we were too poor for that—so I could only look at the books. I was sad about that. There was a booth that sold old jewelry. I spent a lot of time at that booth. There was a booth that sold paper. People bought the paper by the sheet and not by the package. There weren't any packages of paper. There was a booth that sold wood. There was a booth that sold cabbages and beets. There was a booth that sold tools. Oh, I spent all my time just looking. It was fun. I learned a lot.

P.S. Thanks to your Young People's Program, I was able to go on this trip. I have a suggestion to make: You should publish a special catalog just for us young people.

Cynthia Albert
Age 10. 5th grader, Thomas Edison Elementary School
Minneapolis, Minnesota

No. 101: Bjorko, Sweden. November 1, 847. [One hour; $25] Your wife has died, at fifty-eight, and you, at sixty-one, are soon to follow. You stand by her grave with your hoard of silver, which you have accumulated from the scores of raids you participated in for the last twenty-five years and prepare to lay them down with her body.

It is a cold day and you feel half-ready to throw yourself into the grave and lie beside her. You look over the cold, low hills this November and know that you will not be prepared for the winter, whose first wave is here upon you. You will not be ready and are not ready. You stand with these thoughts beside your wife's grave and with the hoard of silver in your hands.

No. 102: Srem, Poland. November 2, 1779. [2 weeks; $450] You are twenty-seven, a peddler who travels around western Poland, selling what you have, staying a few days in each house and making clothes for the whole family. The cloth is woven from wool from the farmer's own sheep and is therefore cheaper. In this way, you are able to sit and talk and gossip (the farmers like nothing better than this) and sometimes seduce a woman or two, for they do not meet many men like you in these small villages, a man who has been to a great many cities in Poland. Maybe you will never get married, but at least there is the occasional adventure, which is a kind of clearing in the chaos of your loneliness.

On Sunday you go to church to eye the women and generally see what kind of a village you have come to. Most are miserable, but the farmers are happy to see you because you do good work and do not charge exorbitantly.

> *Dear Past Rentals,*
> *I had a great time. I wasn't looking for it, but it hap-*
> *pened. That's the way it usually goes. When things are*
> *cookin', they're cookin'. And when they're not, well, you just*
> *have to wait for the food to come. I don't mean to say that it's*
> *easy being a traveling salesman. It's not. It was a rough life*
> *for this guy, but it was the only life he knew, so what the hell—*
> *it was his life, and I was sharing a part of it, and there's noth-*

ing like gettin' to know someone from the inside, where it counts.

It was gettin' on toward winter, about November, but nobody really paid much attention to the date. They didn't even have calendars. And no clocks or watches. And the homes. They may have had a couple chairs and a table, and they probably made them the hard way. Not much money around either. Proud people, though. They'd treat you like a prince, just because you were from a big city and were passing through their territory, small as it was. They'd kill the chicken and bake a loaf of bread just for you. Now that's what I call being treated like a special guest. You don't get that everywhere. And that may be because the people don't have much, and what they gave they gave as part of their own lives. I like that. I try to do it myself, as much as I can. I've done it a lot more since I've come back from your trip. It's made me a better person, so hurrah for Past Rentals, and I mean that.

But your guy, this peddler I partly became, was not a happy camper. He carried around his sadness the way some people carry around their body odor because they haven't washed in weeks. (These peasants didn't wash much, but all of them smelled, so you didn't smell any one of them much.) He was a sad guy and he needed these people to show him some warmth. And they needed him, too, wanted to catch a glimpse of big city ways. Many of them thought of going to Warsaw or Poznan or Bialystok or Lublin or Krakow.

The men wanted information about the restaurants and the wines and the theaters. The woman wanted to know about the clothes. That's where this peddler came in. He had been to these cities, in fact, even lived in them for some time. And he'd rattle off the names of restaurants and the foods that were served there and tell them the way the waiters were dressed and describe the people who came there to eat, big shots, rich people, and they'd eat it up, hang on his every word.

He'd mostly tell the truth. But when he couldn't remember a place or a person, he'd make up something that would fit the situation. It wouldn't quite be a lie, but it wouldn't exactly be the truth either. It seems he had to get good at telling them about these places, and he wasn't good at the beginning. Sometimes he'd get himself into spots because he got carried away with his descriptions and told them something that seemed even too fabulous for them to believe, like the time he said there was dancing in the streets in Poznan in April. "How could that be?" asked one man, It rains most of April and the dancers would ruin their beautiful clothing." My man was forced to be quick. He said, "No, I mean the end of April, the beginning of May, and only on absolutely clear days." Then he went on to describe in great detail the dances, the costumes, the food sold in the stalls, and the colors and sizes of the horses and carriages people came in or on.

But underneath all this quickness, all this inventive behavior, was a great sadness. Only at the end of my two weeks did I get an inkling of what it was that had made him so sad. It was the death of his son and wife ten years ago. The colera got them. And whenever he heard that old Polish curse "May the cholera get you," he shivered. It was too painful.

I felt sorry for him, but he tried to get as much as he could to make him feel better. One day he would go back to Bialystok, where he was from, but not for a while, not for many years. He liked the peasants, and they liked him, too. He went out of his way to help, when he saw they needed help. When I was with him, he stayed a whole day at one farm to help the farmer repair his barn. The man had hurt himself the week before and couldn't use his right arm. My peddler did all the work.

I just hoped he'd find something better, I mean some-

thing that would get him out of his sadness. But he had no place to live, except what the peasants gave him, a bed for the night, and no close friends in Bialystok—they had most of them died, some even from the cholera. What was he going to do, move back to a vacant city? He tried to think of it as little as possible.

Every time I pass down Highway 5 through the Central Valley in California, the richest farmland in America, I wonder where all that life went, people who saw others and lived with them. They're all living in cities, cramped up in the suburbs or in trailer camps or living in new apartment houses. Would they invite an almost stranger into their houses? And what could he tell them that they didn't already know or want to hear? It's another world and not especially a better one. Just a bit different.

Let it rest there. There's more to say, but it's unnecessary. People have lived all kinds of lives, lived with all kinds of disasters and, not to get too heavy, with all kinds of joys, too. It's not a good idea to concentrate too much on the negatives but also not to get too Pollyanna constructing some pie in the sky world. As I said earlier, "When things are cookin', they're cookin'. And when they're not, you just have to wait."

Gerald Brownie Brownelle
Age 53. Hardware store clerk
Lancaster, Pennsylvania

No. 103: Chinan, Shantung Province, China. August 19, 1791. [5 days; $250] A poor scholar you have been for these last fifteen years, writing the government pamphlets, and when you have had a chance, painting, speaking with your friends of the classics, reading the old poetry, and writing some yourself.

But evil times have fallen upon you. You have been thrown

into jail for something you know nothing about, and your worst fears have been revealed to you. Here there are no windows. The prisoners are chained side by side to benches, yourself included. Urine and excrement are left inside the cell, and prisoners who died in their sleep are still chained to the living. Though you have not seen this yet (you expect to see it, however), starving prisoners will eat the bodies of the dead.

You have been here for a week, and you do not know when you will be released, if ever. You are filled with despair, and yet, somehow, you cling to the illusion of freedom, or to the freedom you had before you were brought here, to that of a poor scholar living a simple life. Maybe your friends will rescue you, but for now there is only this cell and the other miserable prisoners chained to its walls, hopeless and faint with hunger among smells that are almost beyond you.

Dear Past Rentals,

I've been working in a plastics factory for the last ten years. Before that I worked as a plasterer in Bari. I like being near the sea or wandering out to the mountains with my family. I've worked hard most of my life. I can't say that I've been a man of leisure, but I've had my leisure, too. "A good Sunday is worth two Mondays," I say. Though I've wanted to do something very different, I didn't know how different your catalog entry No. 102 would be. This trip has been the greatest shock of my life.

I couldn't believe the misery I experienced. I wouldn't wish it on a dog, on a mosquito, or on my worst enemy. I was chained for five days next to a dead man. I was "deliberately" half-starved, in fact, left to die. The cell I was in stank so much I almost fainted when they first put me there. The nights were hot, and the stench of the others chained together with me was almost more than I could bear. And the guards—they were so "sympathetic," they never came around. They just left us to rot among the mosquitoes, the flies, and the rats. At the end of five days I was sure the man I had become had lost at least eight pounds. What did these poor people do to deserve such misery?

Beyond the physical there was the personal. I was a minor government official, a man with at least pretensions to culture, one who could read and write, an intelligent man, who wanted, like other men of his background, to live the "simple life"; that meant a life of leisure—poetry, painting, conversation—that kind of life.

This "scholar" had never dreamed there was such a place as that prison and never thought he would encounter those conditions. And he never really woke up to it either! The shock was too great. Something in him, the will to live, kept him alive, but that was not living. I know. It was really a kind of suspended death. Chained to a dead man? Living in your own excrement? No. That was a torture without torturers.

After a short time the shock of going to this place made him remove himself to another world. And I don't mean to heaven. He retreated into that world he had always wanted to enter, the world of the wandering scholar, and he stayed there pretty much for the five days I was with him.

Now why did I do this? I know it's not the kind of vacation a man of my circumstances would take. The truth is I made a mistake. I wrote down the wrong number and you put me in China in 1791. And in this jail. I could have left, according to the rules, but something made me stay, probably curiosity, and knowing that it would end in five days, and knowing that I wouldn't die from it kept me there.

And, believe it or not, I was fascinated by everything, frightened and fascinated. First, I paid a lot of attention to everything, including the five other men manacled to me and to the dead man. (He died on the third day. When I woke up and realized he was dead, I shook the chains and cried out to the guards, but it was no use. They never came around. I saw them only four times, and they never removed the dead man.) But because I was there as a "tourist" so to speak, I could step back a little, even though my body was caving in from hunger. What saved me was a visit from my cousin, who brought me a little food, some of which I shared with the others. Thank God for relatives!

Also, after I got "used to" the physical conditions, I began to "move around" in this man's body. He was small but fairly fat, and that fat must have helped him, at least for the five days I was with him. He must have lived off it, because he didn't eat much. His mind made that curious transition. First, he protested aloud, then to himself—long strings of thoughts about his innocence, his devotion to the Empire, etc. Then, he poured out oceans of tears about his wife and children and his parents and others. After that, thoughts about his salvation rose up inside him, fantasies about help, long petitions composed in his head, filled with patronizing allusions to the classics.

These got strung out for three days. On the day when he discovered the dead man next to him, his mind went inward; he built a fortress, which began, slowly, to deny everything around him. First, the 'utopia' he "invented" was a kingdom created to right the wrongs of the present world. Then, he meticulously painted a mental picture of an earlier age, with just rulers and prosperity, etc. There was a place for the peasant, for the artisan, for the government official, for the literati, for the merchant, for the traveler, for everyone. Everyone had his place there, and if he didn't move from it, he was all right.

Then, there gradually appeared a particular image of a more sheltered part of this society, a kind of utopia within a utopia. And, of course, he was there. But even in his fantasy he had to be admitted there through a strict examination, quizzed on the classics. How good was his calligraphy? What kind of a poem could he really write? The poem he wrote was, in his opinion, magnificent, though there were criticisms. I guess you have to want more than you can get, even in your dreams, and the comments must also help.

But even though he came by degrees and with a certain strategy to this world of his own making (it was easy to understand the logic behind it), he was, at times, suddenly jerked into the present, the "real" world, and I could sense the terror, the full confrontations with the horror into which he had been thrust. He tried, to his credit I'll have to say, to look at it openly, and for a while he did, a while meaning a few hours at best. But back he went. Most of the time he was in his fantasyland, but he woke up from time to time and even forced himself to wake up, to look around him at the cell. (The other prisoners may, for all I knew, have been going through the same processes.) At the beginning he spoke to the others, and there was some attempt at conversation, especially when he came out of his dreamland. But conversation, under those circumstances, was, to say the least, difficult.

I don't know what became of him. He probably died there. It would have taken a miracle for him to have been released, but sometimes miracles happen.

Even though I made a mistake, I'm glad I went. I see more now. I look at the police in a different way. I look at all of us in a different way. I'm not so safe any more. There's always the possibility that I, too, will be put in one of those places. I, too, could fantasize about some utopia of my own. (I know I've got it there.)

Something has changed. My wife looks different to me. And my children, too. They'll never understand what I've been through. And I've tried, many times, to explain it to

them. Maybe when they "grow up". But today I feel more—
both ways. I feel closer to others, to the possible misery of
others, and I feel more afraid of what could happen to me in
my present life. That's why my needs are greater now. I was a
simple man before I left. Now I'm not. There's too much
around me to be frightened about, and also too much around
me to love.

> *Luigi Formica*
> *Age 30. Worker in a plastics factory*
> *Bari, Italy*

No. 104: Pontivy, Brittany, France. February 27, 1722. [5 hours; $75]
You wake, one morning ten months after your birth, here at
Pontivy, a young girl with dark eyes and light hair, in the single
room farm house where your older sister (age six), your parents,
and your mother's parents live. You have plenty of time to look
around as you lie in your cradle, four feet from the large, glowing
hearth, where the evening meal is cooking.

Here in this granite building, protected from the wind
by large clumps of elms and oaks, you exist with the cows and
chickens and pigs. Your parents sleep in a small partition built
into the wall near the hearth, and on the earthen floor, worn hard
by years of being walked on, separated by a hurdle, lie the animals.
You can smell them. Their odor is strong, almost overpowering,
compared to even that of your mother. You will spend much time
exploring these strange creatures.

Hams and baskets of cheese and chestnuts hang from the
rafters, and although everyone is gone from the house and you
are alone, you can hear the voices of people outside calling to
each other. You will be here all morning, alone near the fire.

Dear Past Rentals,

Have you ever thought about what it was like to have been an infant, maybe four months old or so, and we've all been one—that's what we all have in common. Yet how many people have chosen this kind of entry? In the sixth catalog I counted only three, and in the ninth catalog there were only two. I checked your indexes for the other catalogs, too. I could only find eleven catalog entries as infants.

That's a shame. Infants, anywhere from three weeks to ten months old, are raised in a variety of climates and places and cultures. The Russians, for example, wrap up all their small babies in swaddling bands, probably to protect them from the winter. But, you know, they also do this in the summer. I know that's hard to believe, but they must have some reason—maybe only tradition.

This little guy, at least while I was there, had a comfortable place. It was a cold, February day during my five hours "residence," but I was well protected, set in a small cradle near the fire so I was warm. Sunlight coming through the slightly open door warmed me and felt good. Since my "parents" lived on a farm, they also, like everyone else, lived with the animals. The pigs and cow and chickens got the other half of that room. That's how it was. The outhouse was outside and only one chamber pot for the whole family. It must have been a pisser (I'm not playing with words, mind you!) getting up in the middle of the night to use the chamber pot.

From where I was situated, I could, of course, smell the animals. If you start at an early age, you get used to their smells and you like them. Those animals were also keeping the place warm. There was a big pot of something, probably beans or stew, cooking on the fire. They probably let it cook all morning while they had a few slices of bread and went about their way. And later on they'd eat the stew or the beans or whatever they had. I'd get my mother's milk, of course. (No formulas then.)

Going back as an infant is the most pleasant journey you could imagine. You get a chance to feel and smell and hear things, lots of things, the animals near you, for starters. I loved hearing the pigs grunt and the squeal of the piglets. A cow just shifting his place a few feet is a pleasant sound. The crowing rooster and the scratching hens—these are all great sounds. Also, my blankets were a bit scratchy and probably had fleas in them, but after a while they felt extremely comfortable next to my skin. Remember, all those blankets were made right there on the home loom and had all their sheep's old, lanolin-soaked wool in them, and the smell was strong and pleasant.

I'd suggest to anyone that before they went off to some exotic place as some exotic person, they should check out the infant program and find out what it's like to be there at the beginning. Then, they might be able to move on to other things.

Max Seifert
Age 24. Gardener
Beverly Hills, California

No. 105: Medellin, Columbia. April 16, 1802. [2 weeks; $200] You do not feel intimidated by the bandits, who may station themselves along the way from Medellin to Bogota. Every two months your friend and you drive four mules laden with supplies, which you will sell in Bogota. You carry a dagger each and a long rifle for protection, and you know the road, have traveled it many times these last eight years. And by now the people along the way know you well, even the bandits.

Today you are about to leave on another trip to Bogota. You have carefully packed the four mules and are ready to start. It will take about two weeks, walking, but the weather is good and people in Bogota will want you to visit them, and that is good, too.

No. 106: Heidelberg, Germany. June 15, 1802. [3 weeks; $400] You are an eighteen-year-old student at the University of Heidelberg. Now, after much hard studying, alternating with great bouts of drinking and carousing, your examinations over, you are prepared to depart on a three-week walking trip through the Bavarian Alps. You will sleep in the open, since there are few inns, and those you might find are on the poor side. Besides, the weather will be good and your companions and you will feel the fresh air and be able to sketch many glorious scenes along the way.

No. 107: Near Wellington, New Zealand. July 15, 1701. [4 hours; $85] A sensitive, beautiful, and uncommonly slender, nine-year-old Maori girl, you sit in the long hut with your mother and two other women, all of you weaving a mat. On the ceiling hang hundreds of dried fish. Along the walls are the tattooed statues of the ancestors. Several men are at the other end of the hut, talking. You can't hear what they are saying and it is not important.

The smell of the burnt wood from the fire fills the long house and leaves you in a dreamy atmosphere. You work at the weaving and at times look up at almost nothing, yet search with eyes long gone inward. Thoughts in a haze of vision pass and change—just as smoke changes or clouds pass—and pass on to other visions, vague and indefinable. All of it hangs suspended in the winter atmosphere like a vaguely changing shape, some force inside and outside your life, a power you may communicate with through a small effort of release. It is very pleasing and broadening to be with this power.

Dear Past Rentals,

Days of quietness: The mind expands through its hazy dreaming. The work goes on, amid the smells of smoke and fish. The cold day and the warmth inside. I needed your journey. I know I can always daydream at home, pick any cold day and let the carpet of my mind unravel. Dreaminess can be found anywhere. Yes, I know. But there it was life with others, all of us expanding in that dreamy state, half-suspended thoughts and feelings that drifted within the collective space of the long hut. The smell of the dried, smoked fish gave everything a tangible odor, and for a nine-year-old, it made dreaming more meaningful. Anyway, I loved it, the movements of the dream, images flowing from some world I shared with others, shared thoughts and shared feelings.

It started with the image of wetness over the forest, liquid seeping into the trees, and the patches of foggy vapor lying on the low, vague, bushy shapes of the plants below them. Half-formed mouths emerged from that part air and part watery world, floating among the huge trees, resting on the slender branches, settling into intermittent, open patches of land. Frogs floated above the surface, as if they had entered the boundaries of the eyes from an unknown place (eyes both below and above the water), images of these slow-moving animals, invisible before and now made visible by an expansion of time and distance. Words appeared as slow, shifting shapes, words that stretched out in an elastic landscape and spoke, slowly, carefully, into my ear, or into something I thought was my ear. The words merged with the trees, the whole forest, which later rose carefully into the sky, and the sky itself had its large, expansive word. These floating words, locked in their vague outlines, spoke of a moon that fitted perfectly into the palm of my hand and crumbled the bound shapes of innumerable tattoos that soon were dancing on the walls of the air, and brought to me suddenly the grip on the oars of the longboat and the strain of its motion.

They spoke of many things, as I fell back and back and back into endless waves of dreaming. The images came and went, not only in my eyes, but in my ears, tongue, and skin, through my extended, almost-indefinable body that went with them, traveling. It was more than relaxing. I existed in something larger that floated slowly within that self of everything I knew. As soon as I felt it, the whole body relaxed. Your entry "1701. Near Wellington, New Zealand" made it grow in me.

Martha McCullough
Age 78. Retired travel agent
Glasgow, Scotland

No. 108:   Amersfoort, Netherlands. February 14, 1605. [5 hours; $50] What you like best, even as a woman of thirty-one, is the carousing, the drinking and the singing, and even the men, lustful with wine and conversation and song. Tonight you will be in that world after this day of general depression, hardly able to rouse yourself after the strange letter you received, delivered to you this morning by your maid. It is a cold, blank, windless, winter day—hardly one on which to receive the news that your cousin will be arriving next week from Amsterdam, a cousin who talks too much and does not listen, a bore (and a boor, too) whom you must put up with for a week, not something to look forward to at all. But tonight you will spend the evening at the inn, where there will be much singing, excited talk, wine, beer, and men. And you know you will feel better, much better.

Dear Past Rentals,

Somehow, we are too serious about our drinking. We want to arrive at our destination without feeling the landscape. Too serious, I say. But your Netherlands trip ("1605. Amersfoort, Netherlands") was more than a trip to the tavern. It was a way of life, a journey into the life of a thirty-one-year-old woman who is alive and who feels that her cousin will get in the way of her exuberant life.

The cousin, it turned out, was ten years younger and had grown up extremely protected, with hardly a chance to speak to anyone outside her family. Guarded against strangers, she was primed to be married off at the first opportunity, and the opportunity was, indeed, on the way. There was something in her visit that this older, more mature woman wondered about. Did this cousin want to discuss her upcoming marriage? Was she attempting to break free of her family? My woman well knew her father's sister's family, rich and controlling, pretentious in their wealth, filled with outward status and inward confusion. And she suspected that that was the aim of her cousin's visit.

She thought of what she might do for her, perhaps introduce her to her friends, bring her down to the inn, engage her in the intense conversations into which my woman loved to enter. There were good people there, a bit free, but understanding. They would act as a tonic for her cousin's heavy, empty soul. This, she knew, would be good for that younger woman, but there were other problems, the family, her family and her father's sister's family being the main ones. This rolled around in her head. It would take this woman of some intelligence and heart more time to decide on a course of action than I had with her. But I feel that she will make the right decision, though all decisions do not work out in the way we want them to. You have again introduced another life-problem to me and to others. May you present more in future catalogs.

Svetlana Chernachevsky
Age 34. Cook
Vladovostok, Russia

No. 109: Yedo, Japan. March 3, 1747. [6 hours; $95] You are a geisha, a pleasure woman, and have been one for about twelve years. When your parents died and you became an orphan, Mrs. Yashimoto, a woman who is known for her training of geishas, brought you into her world and taught you everything you needed to know, an education of many years.

When you look back on your childhood, despite the tragic loss of your parents, you remember your training as good, in fact, very good. You learned to sing well (you have a charming voice, people tell you), to write poems spontaneously, to dress with great taste the way a geisha should dress, as Mrs. Yashimoto has shown you many times, to make tea and to pour it properly, and most important, to speak well. All these talents a woman may learn, she says, but if there is no spark, if the true nature of your actions is not rooted in insight, then it will lie flat and empty like a shadow. Toward this aim, Mrs. Yashimoto's work has born great fruit, and you are destined, many say, for a great marriage.

You live in the Yoshiwara, on the outskirts of Yedo. It is the center of the Ukiyo-i (the floating world) with its theaters, restaurants, baths, and teahouses, usually patronized by the chonin, wealthy merchants, the real power in the country, by the sons of great families, sowing their wild oats for a while, and by a few sporadic samurai. Tonight you will dine with a screen merchant. You take the kuruma, a rickshaw drawn by a porter, to where you will meet him. You are, at twenty-two, almost at the height of your powers, and yet you are full of profound restraint and true imaginative declaration. You will surely make a good marriage.

No. 110: Tomot, Russia (on the Aldan River). July 23, 1834. [3 weeks; $850] What could have possessed you, a woman of twenty-five, except the excitement of youth, to move 3,000 miles from your home in Rostov, to this settlement, hardly a village, on the Aldan River in lower Siberia, a place of hunters and trappers, where there is only a small community enlivened occasionally by a wandering trapper or surveyor.

Nothing could have persuaded you to move, except the vision of a life you had already made, something you found you enjoyed and which came from a deep, unknown part of you, an adventure, a world that presented you every day with a challenge. This challenge raised you, in your own mind, to heroic proportions, as it did to all with whom you lived.

Now, after five years of being in Tomot with your husband, a district official for the Tzar, you have begun to trap and hunt on your own. It is July, and like everyone else, you have been luxuriating in the warmth of the land and the cooling breezes which blow down from the pines into the small clearing where your cabin rests. It is quiet, except for the birds, the river and the wind. The sounds of this land agree with you, for they come from those animals from which your clothes, hats, and shoes are made, and what you eat comes from them, from what you have killed, whether fish from the river, or deer or bear from the forest.

Today, with several women and their husbands, you will travel down river to Ust-Maya where there is to be a big wedding celebration. The niece of one of the women in your group is getting married, and none of you would miss it for the world. There is very little of this kind of excitement in your life, and any chance is seized, even if it means a long journey.

You plan to boat downstream, stopping to hunt along the way, set traps for lynx and silver fox, and then check your traps on the way back. There will be vodka and dancing. But since this is your first trip to Ust-Maya, you want to remember the land so that you may again hunt and trap in this vast region of forest and river.

Dear Past Rentals,

First, I want to tell you something about myself because what I am has effected my journey to Tomot, Russia (catalog No. 110). I am a thirty-four-year- old woman from Egypt. I have lived in Egypt all my life and plan to remain in Egypt 'till I die. I love my country and have traveled extensively within it. And I have seen much that I admire and even much that has revolted me. I was born into a wealthy family and I have married a man of my class. My place is secure. Servants, whom I treat well but who are still servants to me, take care of my needs. They have their life; I have mine. I love sitting in the courtyard of our home, listening to the sounds of the fountain and reading book after book, in this way travelling where I want and yet remaining home, where I feel protected, comfortable, and in control of my life. I have grown used to this life. I have grown very used to it.

But there is always the other side, the face behind the shadow. And I am curious. I am afraid but curious. I want to know but I do not want to be frightened, even by the thought of what lies out there. The more comfortable I become—and I can become extremely comfortable—the more terrified I get, the more I feel my life is an immense emptiness, but a comfortable emptiness nevertheless. But as I have said, there is always the other side. In my dreams I leave my body behind and travel to the Zagros Mountains in Iran, to the Canadian Arctic, to the Bahamas—everywhere, but only in my dreams, from which I may, in time, awake, safe and comfortable. But, as I have said, there is always the other side.

I have, of course, read your catalog many times. In fact,

it has become for me the starting point of many of my dreams. But I have also been afraid of actually going. How could I live as a servant girl in Spain, as you describe this woman, or as a wife in Korea who poisons her husband and gets away with her crime and then, afterwards, suffers? How could I? I am a very respectable, upper-class woman, almost automatically a slave to my upper-class assumptions.

But then again there is always the other side, which has become an obsession with me these past four years. Mental shadows surround me. Strange, yet fascinating, creatures come out from under them. I am being sucked into their dancing, swirling world. My body has begun to desert me, seduced by forces beyond my control. "What will I do?" I asked myself last November, as the waves of these feelings fell upon me again. I wanted to pray to Allah the merciful to relieve me of this burden, but my own self held me back while page after page of shadow rose from the floor of the world, like a vast, unloosened skirt of sand in the desert.

So it was something uncompleted within me that put my request through to you. I thought about journeys, and I finally chose one which was as far away from present-day Egypt as I could find and yet one which was, it seemed to me then at least, not beyond my comprehension. The journey to Tomot called me. I heard its voice inside me, moving my slender, comfortable body toward the north, toward the vast forests of Siberia, which I had only known through reading and now was to experience directly, though with the promise of return. "What would happen to me if I could not return?" I have thought, as I am sure others have. But you have guaranteed my return and have never lost a traveler. I believed you. That assured me, and I went.

But now I am here to report my complete disgust. I know you have received letters from people who have praised their journeys or even from those who have been ambivalent, having received some insight but who had had troubles adapting or had chosen a catalog entry by chance and arrived, not knowing where they were or not being able to identify with the world they had, in some way, entered.

That is not my case. I entered this world, knowing where I was going, or at least I thought I knew where I was going. But it was not in any way a world I wanted to enter. I had come, laden with previous illusions, half-held hopes, and, of course, fears. I blame my limited, upper class Egyptian world for that. I am too well-protected, in body and mind and spirit, to have entered a place in which I had to work, to struggle and always be aware of the reactions of a people who lived in a totally different landscape—rough taiga, forests of bears and wolves, dangerous rivers, sudden rainstorms—all this even in summer, the most idyllic time of the year.

There I was, the wife of a minor Tsarist official, torn by choice from a comfortable life in Rostov and placed in a vast backwoods of small, crudely made cabins and a self-sufficient population. She had made the adaptation, in fact, gloried in it. She it was who wanted to go hunting herself, without her husband and their friends, right into the heart of the forest. The forest has shadows. The eye must grow accustomed to the light or its absence. There are swamps and dead branches and animals everywhere. One must be careful at all times. It is only possible to walk for miles across a flat, clear plain, having no obstacles in your path. She must be continually aware of where she steps. A hunter must know where he placed his traps. He must know how to return, or he may become lost in that vastness.

And here was this woman—crude, full, and open— wanting to go out with other women and hunt, kill even a dangerous animal like a bear, probably place traps and hunt deer and yet remember where she was at all times. She wanted to open the dead deer, take out its entrails, skin it,

*and preserve it, and right there make camp in the middle of
that forest, where at night she could listen to the wolves calling to one another and the shadows of the campfire rising
into the trees.*

*What bravery, or what foolishness this woman had
within her—I could not distinguish between them. The
Egyptian within me rose up and trembled at every step she
took. I was looking over her shoulder at all times, even when
she slept. What else could I do, having dragged my own background with me?*

*Moreover, her manners and those of the others around
her disgusted me. They wore the skins of animals—bears,
lynx, otter, deer—and they loved them next to their skins.
Indeed, they were beautiful, but all of them smelled of bear
grease and deer fat and the smoke of the fires they had sat
next to all their lives. When they traveled, they carried a rag
to wipe their behinds, and when they had the opportunity
they washed it in the river. But mostly their "portable toilet
paper" smelled. And bathing was almost an impossibility.*

*There were also the mosquitoes. They were worse than
wolves and bears. Though she did not seem to mind them,
they made my life miserable. And I suppose after a while it is
possible to become accustomed to their continual need for
blood. They came in large, dark swarms and descended, at
once, on any unprotected part of her body. And she made
almost no attempts to drive them away. Only near the smoke
of the fire were they nearly absent.*

*But most important, everything about her and the oth-
ers was crude. All of them cooked their food over the open fire
and ate it half-raw, and then threw the bones to the dogs,
who fought over them immediately. They practically slept in
the remains of their meals. And they ate far too much meat.
There were no vegetables. How could anyone live on such a
diet? At times, they would leave an animal hung up from a*

branch for weeks until it developed a fine mold, and then they would cut off a haunch and cook it. They preferred it that way, and with the mold on it! How disgusting!

I longed to return to my comfortable homeland. I was fighting my transference, almost fighting for my life, though I knew I had only to wait and I would be brought back. Yet the time spent tramping through the mud, fighting off the mosquitoes, eating the meat with its layers of mold, and feeling the forest and its dank shadows moving around me, day and night, was too much. I am indeed weak. I cannot stand the hard connections, the relentless, physical life of struggle with a powerful world, which demands strong muscles and a strong, relentless vision. I have returned, defeated.

Have I learned something from this experience? Have I grown larger, wiser, from my Siberian adventure? Have I at least brought back something, which might help me understand my own situation, my own life? Though I have thought about these questions a great deal these last seven months— I have little else to do—I have no answers powerful enough to reach me. I remember everything that happened, but I see no connection between the forest and my life here in Egypt. Instead, I feel an overwhelming sense of revolt, of disgust. I wish the whole thing had never happened. I sit in the courtyard and read or listen to the fountain and its cool serenity. I feel the beautiful blue tiles under my feet, and I know I am secure, protected. I am not in danger. There is nothing to attack me in my own home, which is my own world. And I will remain here until I die, though there is always the other side, I know now, the other side.

Kawsar Elshenawy
Housewife
Cairo, Egypt

No. 111: Heves, Hungary. June 12, 1899. [One day; $75] You have met him again, your lover from thirty years ago, by accident, at the railway station, in fact, bumped into him in the crowd, dropped both your bags and began apologizing to each other. Then, you truly recognized each other. Your faces lit up with that strange, full, abstracted gaze of memory, trying to recall, or at least trying to allow the flow of your lives to enter. Then silence for a moment. Then more talk. Then the chance to meet again.

You did not expect this to happen and now it has. Something strange has descended on both of you. He is as struck by this encounter as you are. You will meet tomorrow, but for the rest of this day this remarkable meeting has been on your mind so much you cannot think of anything else.

No. 112: Turbat, Pakistan. November 30, 775. [10 minutes; $15] At two years old, standing in a field, you look down at the earth, your eyes fastened on a large, moist worm. You notice it does not return to the earth, but remains for some time on the surface. You stare at it blankly for several minutes, then turn your gaze toward the bare winter meadow and the few blackbirds in the field.

> *Dear Past Rentals,*
> *Standing alone in a field and looking at a worm for ten minutes is certainly not anyone's idea of a trip, even if it is to Turbat in Pakistan and the year is 775. But it is my trip and it is deeply significant, even though it may be short and the experience, to some at least, trivial. I want to tell you why I chose this trip and also what I experienced, because I believe that all experience is important and therefore all journeys do not necessarily require "traveling".*
> *Much of my life I have stood alone, looking and listen-*

ing. My mind suspended, I became a part of what was around me, a kind of unmoved mover and eventually a part of the place, which surrounded me. If I did it for long enough, I became invisible—indistinguishable from the landscape. I don't mean that no one saw me, but that no one took notice of me, like the mailman in one Father Brown mystery that no one noticed because he was just too familiar to be noticed.

I remember such a time when I was three years old, and I can go back even a bit earlier. I was in the back yard of a house in Detroit, Michigan, where I lived for the first few years of my life and I was looking down at the earth, discovering it for the first time (or the second or the third). It was almost spring, probably the end of March, and also a damp day. I was wearing a wool coat and rubber boots with wool socks under them. I was certainly warm enough. I was looking down, in that timeless way a very young child looks, suspended and completely out of time. I saw a perfectly clean, red ball near my feet, a little bigger than a golf ball but perfectly red. I looked at it the way a hypnotized person looks through a wall, at something else beyond, or else at its essence, as if the ball were really in him, as if he were the ball. And yet I was looking at the ball. When an infant looks at something, he does not only look the way an adult looks at something. Adults have learned to look and therefore look with, you might say, rather than at something. And in this sense, you might also say, the adults are looking with their minds and not with their eyes. A young person is the thing he looks at. It is only on repeated lookings that he separates himself to become "the observer".

We may try to reach back with our own minds (now completely conditioned) to those moments, but our histories get in the way, blurring the true outlines of experience. Perhaps those things we looked at, experienced as children, are lost forever, but yet, if we reach back to something else *rather than to the thought, we may recapture some of that moment, although never the whole of it. If we look back from our adult lives, history becomes an illusion (or, at least, the looking of an adult). I can tell you that the experience of that ball rests inside me, in my cells, and can be unlocked only through a combination of smell and touch and sight, and even sound, not really through language.*

When we are young, our sense of smell is sharper, perhaps because our noses are closer to the ground. Our world is activated by our nose, not by our mind or our language. We are lost in the world of smell, and we find dog shit, for example, as important as clover. The damp earth pushes up its small tongues of grass and begins to breathe. The leaf mold, mixed with the earth, rises into the air. Last year I remembered the smell of a damp towel thrown out on a mound of compost. I held it up to my nose and I began to remember. I remembered digging holes and tunnels in the earth. Maybe I remembered it just so I could return to that smell. And I remembered thinking how it might feel to be buried and dead in the earth with no coffin except the soil around me. Thoughts of a child, once absorbed, then buried.

These are not morbid images sprouting from the head of a demented insomniac. They are thoughts that expand my lungs or my touch—every sense of my body—and return me to some other time and place before the invention of language or the allotment of territory on an earth previously empty of boundaries. And this is parhaps far stranger than it seems to our minds when we "think-follow" the partially abstracted road of language. Therefore, when I saw your catalog entry No. 112, I realized, and I think wrongly, that I could identify with it, completely, since that was the place I had been wanting to go back to since my early childhood.

To say that I liked the experience is to place it in words, and I don't mean I liked it. I mean what happened there was a way of returning to an original place, to experiencing my body at that age. The smells returned, and the worm and the earth tasted of worm and earth, and there was nothing around them, no accretion of memory, no fissionable half-lives in which memory turns to lead over time. There was something eternal about it, as there must have been in that first clean and clear space when the ball I saw at my feet did not appear red or smell red but tasted red. I can still experience that color today, and your trip to Turbat helped the taste come back.

It was quiet in Turbat, and I wore clothes that I had had, it seemed, forever, rags mainly. I hadn't eaten for two days, a child of three, and I was hungry, very hungry. I was a child who fell into hunger as a stone falls into the earth, and for the rest of my life I would continue falling into it, becoming its familiar. I could feel the newly plowed, wet soil under my bare feet. The plow had made the soil shiny, and in my small world its churned up mass stretched for a long way. The air was dry and clear, and when I looked in one direction there was nothing to see but the flat land.

No one called me for those precious ten minutes, and I expected no one to call. I had neither father nor mother. There was no one, except what I saw coming out of the earth, that single worm, neither beautiful nor ugly, neither danger-ous nor benign. It was just what it was, a worm turned up by the plow, come up to the dangerous surface world of its life to feel the air, before returning to its home. I could see the ribbed patterns on its body, made so it could tunnel only in one direction, like the valves in the veins and arteries to help the blood move only forward in time and the past, grasped at, to become a created fiction.

I saw it also as separate from the earth it inhabited and which yet was a part of its being. And I also saw it apart from everything else, glowing with a dull, opaque shining, like the soil that absorbs but does not reflect its light or heat. The soil tasted in me like earth in the mouth of a dead man, plain, good earth filling him forever. And the worm moved on that earth, swallowing it as it continued its life—always forward. But here it had paused, as I had paused to look at it. It still moved in a kind of suspension between two worlds, neither upwards toward death nor downwards to its original world, which was pure food for it, and which it would continue eating all its life, earth made to be eaten, which gave itself wholly to be eaten. It was not conscious of me or anyone above it, or perhaps it was conscious in a way in which I was conscious, relieved of thought or the burdens of its life, now that it located itself on the border of its own existence.

I saw the motions of a tube stretching in all its parts, like a man half awake in the morning, stretching, and then falling back into himself to rest, and then stretching again. How open this stretching was. The stretching was a way to touch beyond itself, a reach for more through a kind of uncertainty about existence or perhaps an inability to know itself. (The night air might have done that.) And I remained suspended, expecting nothing to come out of that world or return to it. It was all there, washed and clean in the looking.

I said earlier that this was a mistake. It is also clear to me that any experience, when it is defined, becomes an illusion. Our conscious life is made of such illusions. And necessarily so, if we are to maintain a sense of our living and, I should say, a sense of our trembling uncertainties. For the edge is everywhere. Objects shear off. Experiences crack, divide from their original. And then they come together and we don't know why, a kind of continuous miracle.

But, strangely, we stop the world with our infinite fear. We create cages in our zoo of zoos because we continue to admire those cages so we might possess the terror inside them, shake hands with it, but on the wrong side of the mir-

ror, a denial necessary for survival. And so I say that in one sense my "journey" into myself and into another was also a mistake, the mistake we all construct by expecting that something will save us from our ultimate destruction in the ambiguous borderland between life and death. And in some way I can't explain, I saw the worm thinking the same. The fact that this experience appeared to me or that any experience appeared to me, was enough.

When I returned, I thought I had had an experience of great insight and purity. But there I was, back in the world I had left, soon to be looking at memory as I had always looked and recognizing the impossibility of seeing myself in the same place at the same time, though I had invented space and time. This is the great folly I have committed in my innocence, of forcing myself into the middle of things—or into the muddle of things—wanting to escape to an invented purity, leaping from the purity I had always been wandering inside and did not know it. I know that each of your catalog entries is a compartment on another, worm-like train and that we may go from one to another. But the exploration is infinite and illusion proceeds it like an intangible John the Baptist, always in rags. Fortunately for me, there is nowhere to go, and if here did not exist, I would continually have to invent it.

Richard Bakker Handcock
Age 43. Grocery clerk and typist
Los Angeles, California

No. 113: Hanchung, China. April 3, 831. [6 months; $525] Your son has gotten married. His wife is the daughter of a middle farmer, sixteen years old, tall and thin, unusual for Hanchung. You have been living in your son's house for three months and, as you expected, your daughter-in-law is very ignorant. She comes to you for everything. But there is hope. She will learn to manage the house, cook, take care of her husband, and respect the neighbors. She will learn because you are there for her and for your son, who is not in the house all day and who needs a wife to give him the honor he deserves. You will teach your daughter-in-law everything because you, yourself, had a mother-in-law who taught you everything. That is the way life is. That is the way it will be.

Dear Past Rentals,

Where do we start when our children leave us to raise their own families? No, they don't leave us entirely, but the reminder of their leaving is perhaps more painful than it would be if they actually, completely left. They are not clear. They are divided in their localities and loyalties. We are no longer what we used to be and must content ourselves with being guests in our children's houses and overhearing their conversations, impotent to help where we know help would succeed. Our children confront the new with a mixture of arrogance and ignorance while we sit watching the mistakes only we can see coming. Each of their experiences rests on our bed of memory. There are more things to come, we know, even more intolerable things.

My own son was treated well, perhaps because we had much to give him. We were not bathing in money, but my husband, who owned a liquor store in Washington D.C. not far from the Senate Office Building, made a very comfortable living. I can say that he sold liquor to a great many influential men. David went to good schools; we could afford it. We ate out often and went to the Adirondacks or to Florida or even once to California for our vacations. David dressed well, had his own room, and had good friends, nice boys and girls who didn't get into trouble like some of them today—drugs, alcohol, drunk driving, sex at fifteen—thank God he didn't get infected.

And then he met Shiela, who is certainly a nice girl. And, of course, they got married. And there's nothing wrong with that, mind you, nothing at all. We even helped them find an apartment in Virginia. And he has a nice job working as a chemist, checking pollution samples for the Department of Interior. But there's something wrong here. He seems to be too well settled. He has the perfect baby girl. Sheila's had no trouble with her, and their daughter is over a year old now. They're all in good health. And they have friends and they seem happy. But I know there's something wrong. I can smell it. Maybe not now, but in five years or in eight—I don't know, but it's coming. What can I say? I can't interfere. Sheila has a mother, too, just like me; and she's probably suffering in the same way as I am.

I have looked at your catalog many times. I have even pondered over some of your entries—I wanted to go so badly. But I've always ended up being pulled toward home. There were too many things to do, to see, to respond to. I've gotten involved in politics, and as a result I am aware only of the immediate problems. But most of all, I haven't gone because I didn't need anything. It takes a lot of need to put yourself in another time and place. I just didn't have the need.

But your new catalog has an entry, which drew it to me immediately. It screamed out for me, grabbed me by my soul and pulled me in. I couldn't wait to hear from you. Here was a chance to be a grandmother, to have a strong voice in raising my son's child. I would be the teacher, and there would be no problems. I felt so good thinking of it that I was almost happy before I took your trip. And although I had never been to China and knew very little about the Tang Dynasty and Hanchung, I felt that I was indeed qualified and ready for the challenge.

First, I liked the house. Though it was not large, it was clean. I even had small "kang" for myself. The baby slept in a cradle near the main bed. It had "fortunate" eyes, so I thought. My son's wife was young, sixteen, nervous and worried. Sometimes she would drop a bowl of rice, then hurriedly clean it up, throwing it all to the chickens and then deny she had ever dropped it.

First, she had to learn to cook well, so I became her teacher. In one month she was making significant meals, considering what they had to eat, mostly rice and vegetables and occasionally a little fish and chicken and maybe pork once in a while. I was patient and firm and made her practice several times and remember everything step by step. And she was eager, almost too eager; in fact, I had to slow her down, teach her to take her time, give her a lot of self-confidence. I remember how I was at her age, though I wasn't yet married. I probably knew less than she did. I taught her to dress well, to shop properly, and to husband her resources, to make baskets, to plant an herb garden, to eat quietly—God, she was a noisy eater! That all took place during the first two months

Then, I began the more important lessons. (Remember that I had six months. After that she was on her own.) Well, I taught her how to look at her husband. That's an art in itself. Then, I gave her hints about sex. I couldn't very well get into bed and show her, could I? She eventually confided in me and described her lovemaking, in great detail, mind you. I gave her suggestions. In a few months she didn't need them. She knew very well what to do.

After that, I "improved" her sense of humor. When I first met her, she had one, but it was crude, just plain crude. It might have been okay if there was some bodily gusto behind it. I like that kind of humor. I guess I taught her how to wait for the right moment, and I provided the opportunities, with my son, her husband, and with the neighbors, and at times in the market when we went together. It took her at least three months to start raising an eyelash in the proper way so people stood up and noticed her. By the time I left, she was at least on her way and managed to get off some penetrating remarks, which set people back on their chairs. Even the neighbor children started to laugh with her, and even sought her out, waiting.

Once, toward the end, I came upon her with two teenage girls both doubled up with laughter, rolling in the dirt, laughing so hard it was painful—you know what I mean. Their mother was calling them and they couldn't get up. Finally, they stumbled off to the next cottage, still laughing. I was proud.

There were also the problems of people and their "manipulations"—I can't think of any other way to put it. All people have different aims, and in order to understand them we have to get on their wavelength get under their skin and see the world from their side for a while. That means you have to leave yourself behind or be in two places at once. For a young girl, that's difficult. The humor helped. It allowed my daughter-in-law to distance herself a little in order to make connections. But establishing the proper distance, and the proper closeness as well I might add, required a sense of style, a developing of personality, finding out what you could or could not do, and maybe most of all, patience. I can't say she succeeded much here, but she was still very young and her personality had not really begun to take shape.

But something was happening by the time I was ready to leave. Once (this was five months into my trip) an angry, drunken neighbor suddenly bumped into her as they both came around the corner of the house. Both were knocked down. Both were unhurt. The drunken woman began to berate my daughter-in-law, towering over her with her huge body, (My daughter-in-law was short and thin.) What a strange sight, a mountain of a woman practically wrapping herself around a little trickle of a child. But my daughter-in-law carefully stepped back, and in full possession of herself announced, "I want to do that again. Let's fall down again." The woman, still half-drunk, looked at her, puzzled, and softly, as if only a breath of words came out of her huge body, said, "Fall down. Fall down," then louder, almost shouting the words and shaking the volcano of her body, repeated, "Fall down. Fall down. Okay. Okay. Yes," then walked away, still crying out for the whole village to hear, "Fall down. Fall down. Okay. Okay. Yes." But this was an exception, a pine tree in the middle of a barren tundra. But I could see by this that the forest was marching forward.

Strangely enough, their child was easy. She slept regularly and played quietly and had no illness while I was there. I showed her mother how to talk to her and taught her many simple songs, which she could sing at all times of the day and night. I believe you should always sing to your child. Music is good. And talk too. Talk is also good, if only for the music in it. Also, your child should know you're there, and when you are not there, it should feel comfortable. That's important. Sometimes I remembered being absent for David, and I regretted it. Also, hold your child. At this, my daughter-in-law was good. At first, she had some problems when the infant and the cooking demanded attention at the same time. But as her clumsiness gave way to confidence, she could do both, talk to her child while she cooked and keep an eye on it if she were washing, for example, or cleaning the house.

There was more. I was able to tell many stories at night. In fact, we all told stories, but since I was the oldest I was given preference since I knew more, and my son deferred to me even when he had heard the story a few dozen times. And I improved as well. I could see my mistakes coming and I tried to avoid them. Most of the time I did, and when I "fell on my face," they all forgave me because I was the grand-mother.

Now I am back in Washington. I was certainly sorry to leave. I felt I was being filled with insight and ability every day I was around my grandchild and my daughter-in-law. I felt wanted, and I felt useful. My life had meaning, deep meaning. For a while I have "had my fix," so they say. When I visited my son and his wife and child, I was carried on the wings of that experience and therefore could watch, held up by the warm waters of my giving. How little we are able to give. How much we want to give. Without giving, we would crumble, like poor soil that has lost its humus.

May Feldenkreis
Age 56. Housewife
Washington, D. C.

No. 114: Cangombe, Angola. 1631. [3 weeks; $225] Though you are fourteen years old, a young, tall, and thin girl, you have been washing the clothes by the Cuando River for many years now. Today is no exception. Proud and erect along the path, you will go with the other women to the river, carrying on top of your head your wonderfully colored clothes. There, at the washing stones the women will assemble, laughing, talking, gossiping, and telling stories. The children will play around you, shouting and throwing up the water into the morning air. And occasionally you will all see the young boys following the path along the other side of the river, off somewhere, but managing to pass by where you work, the young boys, one of whom you will marry.

Dear Past Rentals,
My name is Merri-Lou Terricy. I'm sixteen and I go to

Tennyson High School in Fulton, Kansas. My parents, like me, grew up in Fulton, and they own a hardware store in the center of town. (The whole town's really quite small.) Every day after school I spend a few hours at my parents' store, helping them out. It's nice there. All the people in town come through at least once a month. Most come just to talk, especially in winter, 'cause we have a fine cast iron stove and the stove heats up real well.

I'm also working on a quilt with my friends Betsy and Reina and Jill. We get together twice a week and sew. And talk a lot, of course. We've been making that quilt for about two years, started it 'cause our moms gave us a lot of material and we got together anyway just to talk. So now we're making this beautiful quilt and talking anyway. Reina's seventeen and has a steady boyfriend, Jack Daniels, who's going to work for his father as a hide tanner next year when he graduates. She doesn't know about getting married, but she sure wants to. Betsy's seventeen also, but she doesn't have a steady boyfriend. She says she doesn't want a steady yet. She just likes being asked. I don't have a boyfriend and I haven't been asked much. Maybe I'm not really that pretty. I'm not shy, but I'm a little afraid.

Betsy and Reina both talk a lot about boys. In fact, that seems to be all they talk about. Betsy tells us about all the boys she's been out with, and she gives us all the details, too. Sometimes I get so excited I start crying. And later I imagine what it would be like to have a boyfriend. But I get sad again and start moping and my mother asks me what I'm doing or how I'm feeling and I just say a few words kind of low and walk away. In the spring and the summer and the fall I take walks. I like being out in the country and just looking at the wheat fields and the blackbirds and the dust swirling up on the road. I like the wind on my face and I like to think about all the insects and the mice and the snakes living in the wheat field, and sometimes I try to find them, but I can't. I feel better when I'm out doors. I guess I don't have to worry about boys thinking about me and saying no. But I'm happy, too. I like living in Fulton and I like the people here. And I even get pretty good grades in school and I sing in the school chorus.

One of my history reports was about women in Africa. I wrote a lot about what they do every day, I mean the women in tropical Africa, in the forest, near the river. I even heard a little of their music and I like it. I talked about how they ground up their millet and how they sang when they were working. And I explained how the children learned to sing at an early age. And I even had some photographs of the cloth the women made. It's very beautiful. About a month after I handed in my report (I got an A), I was looking through your catalog and noticed No. 114. "Congombe, Angola, the life of a 14 year old girl". I began to dream of the girl's life and I couldn't stop. I wanted to be there near the Cuando River with the other women and my friends, so I went, thanks to your junior program. I learned a lot on my trip and I want to thank you. When I say I learned a lot, I mean a lot about myself. Of course, I learned something about these people in Angola, but I really went because of my fear of boys and what they think of me. When I came back, I felt I had something that would help me a lot, and I felt stronger about myself.

This girl had a lot of friends. They didn't all do the same things together all the time, but they often did things a young girl would do, like playing games and talking, just like Reina and Betsy and me. I guess in some ways people are the same all over the world. When my mother and I were pounding the millet in the millet mortar, my friends would stand around and sing with us or just talk about this man or that or what happened in the next village or who lost his chickens or about some wedding in the area. A lot of what we said was just jok-

ing, but it was fun because we made a whole story out of it. The next time we got together we threw in lots of things that didn't belong in the real story. After a while the story got so big that we had to start smaller stories from the main one. And everyone knew something about all the characters in the stories. If the man lost his chicken, we made him go out and look for it, sometimes all the way to the ocean. (We live a long way from the ocean.) And on the way he would meet people like Mr. Rain Tans Your Face or Leaves Like You or Snake Whip Trap. And some of them would help him and some would make him fall into the mud or urinate on his feet to cool them off.

Sometimes the story was funny and we all laughed because it made us feel we knew what we could do. It gave us power and made us see more about the world and people in general. Sometimes the story was sad. Oh, we made it as sad as possible. We made it so sad that we started crying ourselves, even though we knew what we were saying wasn't really true. That's how strongly we felt.

But I noticed after a while how much the stories came around to the young boys that we saw all the time, but especially in the late afternoon and evening. They wandered in and out of our stories, and we always played games with them. They either fell into the river and were chased by a crocodile, or they had to climb a tree because they saw the shadow of a leopard.

We also made them into heroes, funny heroes. They could stop a crocodile's mouth from opening by just talking. Sometimes the birds would tell them to shut up, but they wouldn't until the thunder slapped them in the face. There was also "the boy with the third leg" who was blind but had an enormous penis. He used it as a cane to find his way around the village. Once a girl fell down right in front of him and he just walked over her with his "cane," only his "cane" went down right between her legs. After he had walked on a few feet, she came running after him and fell down in front of him again. We laughed a lot about this boy. In fact, we made up dozens of stories about the boys in our village and the ones in the next, who we also knew.

No matter how much we put down the boys or built them up as heroes, we knew we were just trying to control things because we were excited. We went to the river more often than usual to wash the clothes because the boys passed by on their way into the forest to hunt. We liked to see them walk by. And of course we called out to them and they answered. We liked to tease them, and they liked to say funny things about us. We pretended we didn't like what they said, but we really did.

After a month or so we started a kind of, I guess you would call it, a "dialog story". We would make up stories about what would happen to them in the forest, and they would continue the story where we left off. At night we would sometimes continue the story with the boys. The boys were pretty good storytellers, but they were different. Sometimes we would invent stories that would make us laugh, and sometimes we created stories so sad they made us cry. We tried hard to do both because it made us feel better after we laughed and cried. Sometimes we sang songs together and sometimes we even invented songs together.

You're probably wondering when I was going to meet a boy who would marry me. Well, that really didn't happen, but it didn't matter. The boys were all around us and they paid attention to us all. I didn't feel left out. And because we were together in a group, we could say all kinds of nice things to each other. But there were two boys who said more than I expected to me. One gave me a hat he had made. The other sang to me behind a tree one evening. I was feeling good and we all had a wonderful time, even if no boy wanted to marry me or be my boyfriend.

Everything kept getting better, and I felt more and more that I belonged. Then I had to leave. I didn't feel sad leaving because I knew I carried all those days and nights with me and I would be able to have them whenever a boy looked at me and I could tell him something funny or invent something he could laugh at, that is, if he had any fun in him. I don't think many of them do.

It's funny that when I came back everything was the same. I still went to my parents' store after school, and I still sing in the school chorus, and Betsy and Reina and I still continued working on our quilt and talking. But I know that the world I went to and the girl I became made me feel what it was like to live the way I want rather than the way I do, even though the way I live is still alright with me.

Merri-Lou Terricy
Age 16. High school student
Fulton, Kansas

No. 115: Columbia, Pennsylvania. May 3, 1846. [2 months; $365] Now that the boys and your brother's son have gone off to the fields and you have finished your morning's tasks, the big pot of stew on the wood stove and the children fed, gone off at last, you and your daughters will await your three neighbors—Rachel, Rebecca and Judith—and you will all set to work again on the large quilt you have been making this year, work, quilt, and talk—some stories to hear, some to tell, a bit to eat, of course, and gradually complete the quilt for the barn raising this September.

Dear Past Rentals,
How good life feels in Columbia, Pennsylvania in 1846.

The farms are beautiful and it is May and spring is here. Oh, I feel so filled with everything, the fields of wheat coming up, the colors of the dogwood trees and the lilac, and the birds singing around me. Oh, I'm full of the sap of life. I love watching my husband take the boys off to the fields for the day, watch them disappear in the distance, and at times hear them shouting to each other. And all the quietness around me—how wonderful this peace. It makes me sing hymns at times and sometimes just sing funny songs while I'm cooking or sewing or feeding the chickens and pigs or just sitting in the sunlight, feeling my body pulling it into me. O, how wonderful!

All this is wonderful because I live in the middle of Tokyo, Japan, where I am a typist for Toshiba Electronics and work fifty hours a week in a forty story office building and live in an apartment, and there is no garden. The trees and flowers are locked up in the park and I have to travel by subway to be with them. My life is drudgery, I know. I help support my family and my husband and I live a pretty comfortable life. We have good food and a nice apartment. We even go to the theater from time to time and wander in the park with the children. But it is all very clean and carefully controlled—everything, my work, the subway the park, the traffic. There is no room to breathe. There is a careful attention to detail, to people and to what they feel and think. I guess that's true everywhere, but it's perhaps more true here in Japan or, at least, we have to pay more attention to it here. Therefore, this trip. Therefore, I really don't want to go back. I know I have to. But I really don't want to return.

Here in Columbia, Pennsylvania I love cooking on the big wood stove, which heats our small house. I don't "have to" start the fire. I "get to" start the fire. It is indeed a privilege. I am such a good cook. Why? Because I can bake bread in the wood-heated oven. I have to know the exact temperature and keep it just right, but the bread comes out perfect every time. The children sleep in the loft all together. We don't have much space, so they crowd together. I often look in on them when they're sleeping. They huddle up to keep warm in the winter, even though we keep the fire burning. I make wonderful stews, and sometimes, when my husband and the boys are working hard in the fields, I bring their lunch to them. The house smells of food!

We all of us like to sing. Sometimes we spend a couple hours singing all kinds of songs. Mr. Ralphson, a music teacher, was here two years ago and taught us how to read music, recognizing the shapes of the notes, and we've all learned dozens of songs, and what's more, all of us know all the parts. The children often sing to themselves when they're working or playing and I love to listen. I sing to myself when I'm working, and I'm usually working. When I'm not working, I sit in the sunlight and listen, usually to the silence or to the birds.

Yes, there have been the usual problems, loneliness at times, fights with my husband, the usual childhood diseases—thank God all the children have survived—and the general burden of work, which goes on all day, except on the Sabbath. But my husband and I love walking to town (it's only five miles away) and just talking about anything. Sometimes there's a dance and everyone goes. Sometimes there's a visiting preacher, and we all huddle into the church (it's so tiny). We're so tightly packed that we almost don't need a fire in winter. And sometimes we just sit and tell stories and jokes and play games with the children.

I love the hard work. I like feeling what my body can do. I love sitting in the sunlight on our porch. I love listening to the birds and the sound of the wind. I love cooking. I love sewing. I love working in the garden. There is nothing here I don't love, even if it's painful.

Today Rebecca, Rachel, and Judith came over. These quilting get-togethers are even more wonderful. When company comes, we feel so happy with one another. And our talk and work suits us very well. We don't talk about much, but just the chance to talk is a great pleasure. We are more than friends. We are almost a family. When they come, Rachel and Rebecca bring their children, and my children go off into the woods with them and don't come back until evening, and my friends and I are alone with one another. How wonderful. And the children have a good time, too!

The quilt we are making is going to be beautiful. It's a log cabin design. We've collected scraps of all kinds, and since we've been sewing since childhood, we are experts. We all do something different, and yet we work together. I can't do a really good job describing the quilt, but I can say that there are squares within squares and squares within those squares. And the larger squares make diagonal patterns as well. The border is not geometric. It's a flowery pattern, which contrasts with the central log cabin design. Our quilt will be the glory of the county.

I can't leave Columbia, Pennsylvania in 1846. I don't want to leave. This world is paradise to me. I don't want to go back to Tokyo, to my job and my husband and my children. I want to be here where the air is clean and there is silence and the trees are blossoming and the friends are warm and comfortable. Oh, I really don't want to return.

Seiko Ishikawa
Age 26. Typist
Tokyo, Japan

No. 116: 200 miles west of Omdurman, Sudan. February 25, 1903. [4

hours; $75] You are a very young (eight year old) Kababish girl wandering with your few camels and sheep in the great desert of the Sudan. There are forty people in your travelling group. You subsist on the roots and edible plants you find along the way, as well as on trade, journeying from water hole to water hole, living in the tents for the hot days and venturing out in the late afternoons and mornings (you get up before dawn) to milk the camels and to travel.

You are on the move a lot, often walking twenty miles in a day, wearing your sandals and carrying your few belongings, hardly disguising your contempt for all settled people, whom you term "slaves". You are free to wander, to walk, which is the desire of your dried out but hardy bodies, and to sing and dance at night by the fires (if there is wood for a fire) and to tell stories without end, which will go on until the last Kababish has vanished from the earth. And dream and look up at the bright, very bright sky in which all the constellations are etched and in which the history of all the worlds is recorded.

Though you know very little, you listen. You have learned many songs and can dance with the other children at night. You are young, you are learning, you are wedded to the ways of the Kababish and to the Kababish women.

Now it is night and it is almost cold. There is a fire and your uncle is telling you about the great wanderings of the stars before you were born. You listen, almost in a trance, to the voice of your uncle and to the voice of the fire, sometimes looking out at the blackness of the desert in which you live and then at the perfectly etched stars above you. Your feet are warm by the fire.

No. 117: Lerwick, Shetland Islands, England. March 17, 1780. [4 hours; $75] The children are gone. The last one went to live in Dundee three weeks ago. You and your husband are alone in that thick-walled, rammed earth cottage with its inset windows, which offer protection against the raging winds, alone again with your husband with whom you have spent all these long years. You are forty-seven, past childbearing, and are sitting near the hearth this March evening, knitting again as you have done for decades, remembering everything, the growth of the children, the storms, the food you prepared, the warmth of the evenings when the wind blew around you. Remembering everything.

Dear Past Rentals,

I don't know how most people survived the loneliness. Everything they did with their hands, their bodies, looking, estimating, weighing their actions, waiting. Not holding back, not anxious, but patient, patience over a lifetime, waiting, and when the waves came in, as they did every so often, they rode them. And if they found themselves stranded on some bleak shore—a famine, a war, a disease—they would wait, for eventually the wave would come and wash them out to sea again. And all their actions every day were repeated, almost an eternity of repetition!

And the stupidity, acres of it, all the way to the horizon. Everything the same—the same sheep, the same enormously cold winters, the same births and deaths around them. And the stretching back of generations, remembered in stories— harvests lost, marriages and weddings and early deaths— everything alive from the past through which they moved like a familiar stranger through the unseen rooms. So the genera- tions were linked and the knowledge of who you were was to be sustained. If there was wisdom here, it was in survival, allowing the storm to blow over you, to remain patient, while the wind tried to pull up the earth itself, almost its own lever, and the earth its fulcrum.

They remembered the smallest things, objects and

events of little consequence to us today, like the way her sister started a fire one day with coal dust, or the discovery of the accidental face of a dragon on a rock dug up from the field, or how the cat lay on the chair in front of the fire, silhouetted against the light. And after the remembering, they defined and refined and ultimately, confined the memory until it fit-ted neatly on the shelf they had created for it in their minds, like the carved, little dolls and the knitted clothing which occasionally fell into the fire and were consumed—all neatly placed in a row on the mantle.

Her husband and she never quarreled, though they beat the children from time to time as they would beat a lamb that was in their way or would move a rock from a field. The children, it seemed, were quiet afterwards, believing they needed a quota of physical punishment, and would return it when they were adults, the privilege, or necessity, of survival. And afterwards they would continue playing by the hearth as if nothing had happened. Eternal childhood? No, they would soon become adults. There was not much time for playing. O yes, there was time, but not much.

She remembered the midsummer sun hovering close to the horizon for so long, and would stay up for its setting and then sleep for a few hours and wake up in daylight again, hardly aware of the darkness. And she remembered the win-ter sun setting quick over the horizon. And the long winter nights, like a kind of hibernation. And the sound of the winds blowing for weeks, when the ocean became the color of slate and the few trees screamed from their roots from agony. Then, there was warmth, and the Bible was read for plea-sure—all those stories of the Old Testament. And all the while the knitting went on, eternally. The house was inherited from her husband's great-great grandfather, who built it, its six foot thick walls and its inset windows, thick, to keep out the wind and yet to provide light, for the darkness was almost unbearable, a weight that oppressed them far more than the cold days and the hard labor of sheep herding.

And there was the memory of the death of one child— something she ate, they said—and the refusal to have more children for a long time and then the joyous birth of another six years later, the last one, born almost bald and screaming to fill its lungs with the new air. And now she was gone, to another's home, and all the children were gone, no, not entirely, for they came to visit and they remembered and were required to remember their parents, the now almost-old ones who would eventually die in that solid, thick-walled house and, most undoubtedly, in the winter when the wind was blowing.

How difficult a life, and for how many ages was this life repeated? Forever, it seemed. Whole generations passing like the flowing of fox-gray waves onto the shore, deformed in the process, almost identical, and reformed, to attempt another passage, and always a failure. I saw all the generations till now, my time, like waves formed far out in the ocean, travelling toward land. How we have lived. How we have died. The same. Always the same.

Sigrid Hamburger
Age 56. Film developer
Mainz, Germany

Dear Past Rentals,

I found her a good woman, calm and careful in everything she did. True, the limits of her world were circumscribed, painfully so. She did not know anything beyond them, only the hearth and the steep, cold, rocky grasslands and her husband and the sheep and the children. The world ended almost at the ocean's edge, slate-gray in what seemed an endless winter.

She knitted beautiful things. I loved her knitting. Mostly sweaters, thick with the heavy oil of the sheep still in them, and worn for a long time by them all. She could knit in her sleep—she had done it for so long, and her mother before her.

Those small, squinty eyes that mostly looked out at a dim interior, even in summer, were like the deep-set windows of the house. From somewhere inside, there was a preservation, a holding on, a tenacity as formidable as the almost constant wind that furled its hundred mile sheets against the land and the puny people who managed to endure, generation after generation. That is admirable, more than what we may find important in the city dweller, alone and protected by streetcars and bicycles, umbrellas and fountain pens, steam heat and telegraph messages. So many things between them and their mortality, and yet there is more fear, more need to create even larger fortresses.

The limited nature of their wants and the limited number of their possessions—these are admirable. Here there is no golden age of simplicity and comfort, nor even heroics, battling the north wind and the sea, no, nothing like this, but only some deep warmth kept burning somewhere in the cells, a candle protected by a body and the body protected by a house and the house—unprotected, battered and low and almost eternal.

Yes, there is something in this life, persistence, the need for honesty as a wall against chaos, the fortress of memory to extend the daylight of the seasons, and the word made flesh through action, every day the struggle that makes us know what we are up against, and the recognition of that other wind, invisible, which would eventually blow them away into another world which they could not possibly conceive of and the imagination of which was merely a projection of need. And all this to remind me of the world I live in, fleshed away of all the layers of fear, almost to want to stand naked against that material wind so that even later I might stand naked against the other wind, which will blow me, also, into another world, like them, to become something I can never know and may never create from my own longing.

Svetlana Ismailova Petrovna
Age 61.   Billing clerk
Sverdlovsk, Russia

Dear Past Rentals,
I can't believe a prostitute like me would want to spend four hours with a sheepherder's wife, and forty-seven years old at that. Well, I did, and I didn't know why, at least when I chose your catalog entry. I guess I've been getting tired of being a whore. It does get boring. The same old men wanting the same old thing. I try to please them and I often do. But it's empty. I guess that's why I needed something to remind me of living on the ground, not in the air of somebody else's breath, and bad breath at that.
I loved the house, small as it was. It was dark and cozy and the wind was blowing as if it never would stop, but I felt warm and protected. The wind, after all, was out there, and I was quietly knitting, and there was no rush. I could go on all day watching the sweater I was making get longer and longer and feel the fire behind me warming my back and the pot of slow-cooking mutton on the stove simmering and me not even hungry, just relaxed, as if I was knitting eternity. I know that sounds strange, but I felt I was in the middle of an enormous space, almost like a big room, a very, very big room that seemed to go on forever in space and time, and I could go on knitting and knitting forever and never want to stop.
The rough planks on the floor had been worn down to a

smoothness and shined. I guess all the oil from those wool rugs had gotten absorbed and the floor had been polished by the rugs. There was no phone, of course. There was also no television. There were no visitors. There was nothing. Nothing. And I loved it. I didn't have to do anything, just knit forever and listen to the wind and smell the food cooking in the one large pot she owned in which everything was made. I could hear the trees, what there were of them, creaking in the wind, not a desperate sound like someone who's being tortured and begs for mercy, but an easy sound like someone who's used to stretching and bends with everything. So, I imagined I bent with everything, just staying inside until it all blew over.

Besides the wind and the sound of my rocker, there was nothing. Quiet. Just like I like it. Quiet forever.

Marta Pontevecchio
Age 26. Prostitute
Spoleto, Italy

No. 118: Bristol, England. February 10, 1919. [4 months; $875] You were married once before, and your husband, unfortunately, died after eight years of married life. You have been married to your second husband, a carpenter in Bristol, for three years. You recently went to a doctor because of some vaginal irritation, and the doctor told you that you had syphilis. Of course, you confronted your husband with your condition and he replied, matter-of-factly, that all the women he slept with were clean. Shocked and appalled by his verbal and physical effrontery, you found yourself on the point of assaulting him when, to your complete surprise, he began to attack you. You managed to get out of your apartment and call the police, who came quickly and removed your rampant husband from the premises, temporarily locking him up in jail. You are planning, of course, to ask for a divorce, which you will certainly receive. Your sister lives in Worcester and it is to that city that you are going as soon as you can pack your bags and be off. Your life will have to begin again, though you don't know how.

No. 119: Ploiesti, Romania. January 5, 1659. [7 hours; $100] Your father is a butcher, and you have, in the usual manner of the times, followed his profession. Now sixteen, you have worked with him for seven years—since you were nine. Always it is the same thing, the cows that you cut up, the chickens whose necks you cut off, and the pigs, which you kill with a sharp knife across their throat.

You don't think much now about killing the animals or cutting them up, although when you were five and watched your father killing a cow that first time (that is, the first time you realized what was happening), you went behind the shop and threw up. You were sick for a week. The picture of that "first" killing comes back to you even though you have yourself killed hundreds of animals.

Today you are planning to kill a pig, which was brought to you the night before, a monster of an animal. It knew its death would come soon, it had been crying all night. Then, the work really begins. You will hang it up by its hind legs, slice through its belly and remove its guts, then remove its skin, dipping it into a hot kettle outside the shop this cold January. There are a few hours of work waiting for you tomorrow.

No. 120: Gent, Belgium. January 11, 1699. [One day; $75] You are an apothecary, as were your father before you and his father. It is not unusual for the trade to be carried on from father to son. Since you were six years old, you have known about this strange business, its secrets, mysteries, delights, and even terrors.

The stuffed alligator that hangs from the ceiling is a reminder of the origins of your craft, whose beginnings go back, so you believe, to the land of Egypt, where medicines and concoctions were made for thousands of years. Your aim, at times, is to re-discover these simples, elaborations from the essences of things.

Several times a month you leave Gent, going out to the countryside to gather the herbs which you will need to make medicines for your clients. You receive other substances from various sources, too various to mention, many which indeed cannot be mentioned. You pass on secrets only to others of your brotherhood, your guild of apothecaries. From your shelves come ginger from Alexandria, cinnamon from China, cloves from the East Indies, pepper, nutmeg and perfumes and hundreds of other herbs and minerals and spices, arriving through secret routes, through a chain of trade which extends an enormous distance from your native Gent.

Today is really not different than any other day. With the help of your apprentice, you will proceed to make up the potions which have been ordered by several ladies in Gent, hoping that what you make will not incapacitate or kill them or render them speechless or give them hallucinations or menstrual cramps or any other disorder, but by some miracle unknown even to you, will make them well.

No. 121: Cremona, Italy. July 23, 1448. [3 hours; $65] For three years, though you are only nineteen, you have been the wife of a prosperous grain merchant in Cremona. Your parents, from Ferrara, are also grain merchants.

Yours was an arranged marriage. When you were first introduced to your husband-to-be, you inwardly shook, hiding your trepidations with a clear and calm exterior. But now that you have been his wife for three years, you have grown accustomed to your status and also to your duties in the household.

You must supervise the servants, who are slaves from Africa

and Tartary. This means informing them each day of what you wish them to do, although your instructions must be planned in great detail, or, at least, had to be at the beginning. (Now, a few words suffice.) You must also allot the money for shopping, yet only you must decant the malvoisie wine from Cyprus, which you consider a great joy and luxury.

You wear a purple velvet gown lined with green cloth, and your hair is plaited around your head in a severe, though beautifully severe, style. There is something about you, you believe, that shows respect, even in its severity. This is good for all to see. When you go out, you put on a mantella and cover your head with a hood. In winter you wear a beaver hat and in summer a straw one.

You must prepare the salting tubs full of meat, a task which only you supervise. And you will go out with your maid regularly to shop; it would be impossible for you to carry by yourself all the things you buy. You are so slight of build and so careful with your hands and face that nothing must be allowed to blemish them, especially the dreaded smallpox.

Your greatest joy is in your faience dishes, a great prize which, you are sure, others are jealous of you for having.

Though you do much work, there is time for leisure, visits with friends of your own sex and walks with your maid, and even, from time to time, visits to Ferrara, where your parents live.

You have grown to taking your mother-in-law for granted, not a good thing to do, for she is jealous of your attentions to your husband. But you are growing in her esteem. Every day you learn something new with which to entertain her, and though she cannot walk well and must spend most of her time sitting by the fire in winter and in the garden in summer, she delights in the stories you tell, in fact, cannot wait to hear the next one.

Today you are both sitting in the garden. It is July and the weather is wonderful—no other word can describe it. Your husband is not home, and the servants are relaxing—somewhere else. Now you settle down to tell your mother-in-law a story even more fabulous than the others you tell her, a story you have heard from a merchant's wife, her husband having just returned from a business trip to Greece, a story brought to Greece by the people of Cairo, who love to tell such stories of wild men and heroes.

Dear Past Rentals,

Even in a fairly wealthy home, one with several servants, the lady of the house had much to do. Housewives, today, do not even understand the drudgery of everyday life, which people in the fifteenth century had to contend with, and as a matter of necessity, too. As a housewife, I work at least two hours a day taking care of our home. I mop the bathroom and kitchen floors, vacuum the carpet in the living room, wash the windows at least once a month, and do the dishes daily, and, of course, shop and cook. Those "labor saving" tools—the vacuum cleaner, the automatic dishwasher, the refrigerator, and the gas stove, not to mention the recently installed sink with its indoor plumbing and the bathtub and indoor toilets—have made life far easier for the housewife. And I should also mention the conveniences of shopping and preparing food.

This woman from Cremona, despite her servants, had much to do. She probably also had a garden to tend and perhaps a dozen or so chickens and a pig or two or three, even within the city. Shopping was both an activity which required some skill at bargaining and a game which gave pleasure and maintained contact with familiar faces, an entrance into the larger urban community. And this was a woman of some substance, part of whose work was done by servants.

The storytelling was less enjoyable than I expected—I must say that. But I loved moving about in the coolness of that house in July, cool in the shadows, with the light stream-

ing in through the windows, and everything as open as it could be. I would sit alone, watching the birds come to the small garden we had or the maid scrubbing the wooden floor 'til it shined, and smell the meat cooking as the rich smell floated slowly down the hallway and entered my nostrils. The sounds of carters, draymen, and peddlers shouting their wares flowed in from the street, and all this took place behind high walls and a locked gate that led out into the street. Work surrounded me—always. There was an intense industry going on, keeping everything clear and pleasing, and even in my exhaustion, there was a great pleasure in all of it.

Mary Carson
Age 31. Housewife
Kansas City, Kansas

No. 122: Cairo, Egypt (Part I). February 1, 1372. [One day; $100] You are the only wife of Abu-l-Hasan Al Hahshab, who has lived in the city of Old Cairo for forty-seven years, was born there, and expects to die in his beloved "carnival of wonders," as he calls it. Today is your day to go to the hammar, the bath and beauty parlor, where you will first take a steam bath, then receive a massage, and then a shampoo and a pedicure. Afterwards, you will relax with your friends over a cold lunch you have all brought from home—meat pasties, salads of eggplants, honey cakes, peaches, and coffee, a good meal and a satisfying one, especially when it is eaten with friends. Then, you will receive a facial treatment and a henna rinse, and you will have your eyelashes darkened with indigo, kohl put around your eyes, and your nails varnished red. When you are ready to go home from this day-long visit to the hammar, in the evening when the day has cooled off somewhat and the bright desert stars have come out in all their glory, you will look like a princess, a jewel in the starlight to rival the evening or the morning star, and your husband tonight will be pleased with you, immensely pleased, for he is always pleased when he sees you after you have returned from the hammar.

No. 123: Cairo, Egypt (Part II). February 1, 1372. [6 days; $495] You are a merchant from Padua making a trip to Cairo. You will be staying with your old business friend Abu-l-Hasan Al Hahshab, in a city governed under the sultan Saladin. Every time you come to this splendid city, so different from your native Padua, you are amazed at the tall buildings, four or five stories high, with their mousharabielas, balconies protected by wooden lattices and protruding from the walls onto the narrow streets, and behind these lattices, the gorgeous houses, with their wonderful tiles, their fountains, and their unseen women. All this turns your head, as your friend Abu-l-Hasan Al Hahshab expects it to do.

Now, your first day in Cairo begins. It will be a busy one, for your friend's wife will go to the hammar, the beauty parlor and bath, and her children will spend some time today studying the holy Koran at the mosque, reciting aloud by heart from the holy book. And you and your friend will spend the morning quietly drinking coffee and eating the fresh dishes brought to you, talking of this and that but not yet of business, which, you have learned, requires patience, many weeks of patience, before everything is concluded, and for this you thank the world in which you have found yourself these last eight years, a world slower, and yet more beautiful for being slower, where arabesques of politeness flow into the deeper meanings of things and the cry of the muezzin is echoed in the baths and the fountains, and flows across the vast desert in an unending, silent wind of comfort and intent.

No. 124: Kobe, Japan. August 22, 1491. [9 hours; $95] A street sweeper does his job well. He is a public servant of the municipality. There is much to be proud of, to make the places where people walk look clean and be clean. You take much pride in your work. When you look at what you have done, and often at what others who do your work have done, you feel satisfied that you have given something to others.

But, as you know, filth can be discovered everywhere, exists everywhere. It is strange that only the public places are to be kept clean. It is not difficult to discover, everywhere you go, the private filth that accumulates wherever people do not care. They push it away, but it remains. They use perfume, but do not bathe. They speak the right language but do not do the right things. Everywhere you see this and you are not deceived, though you may be only a street sweeper for the municipality. You see it in your son's words and actions and try with patience to help him overcome his burdens, which you understand is everyone's burdens. Only with your son, who is closer to you, it is more difficult to see clearly.

Today you are working with him on the edge of Kobe, this large, beautiful city. And you want to impress upon him, somehow, what clear, clean acting and thinking mean.

Dear Past Rentals,

Why is it there is always a problem? Everything we do is a problem. Getting our food, raising our children, talking to the neighbors, shopping, eating, sleeping, growing, looking, studying, playing—everything we do encounters something else, something beyond it or which it is attached to. And this thing that we encounter has an equal claim, in fact, cannot, in an absolute sense, be detached from the thing we call "the experience".

We detach. We say, "These are the boundaries. What I have made is separate, and the world cannot cross my line. I say it and it is true." This drawing of boundaries is an abso-

lute assertion, and, like any assertion, it pushes away the rest of the world, creates an island, admits, in the doer, the limits of doing. It establishes, through an act of "cosmic nerve," a sense of self, a separation.

But only for a moment, the merest instant. This act of health creates a vacuum, an imbalance between what is defined as such and what is beyond definition. And the outer world, the unknown, pours in, almost immediately. Even through constant definition, constant assertion, the world will invade the asserter, either consciously or unconsciously.

Cleanliness is an act of assertion. It says to whatever forces may be listening, "Here is my order. It extends to this point and no further. I will not cross over. I will not dissolve myself in something I have so defined as chaos, but something which I cannot, will not, do not desire to, comprehend; for comprehension has its limits, and to preserve myself I will set those limits. Thus it is with every creature, every living thing.

Your catalog entry from Kobe made me wonder about this street cleaner, especially his "social criticism," his way of looking at others, his strength and his helplessness, equally balanced in him. It made me think about the others, the ones he despised, and about his son, who would grow up with the same internal sense of definition, of clean and dirty, of order and disorder, of them" and "us".

There is nothing "evil" or "unnatural" in all this. Even the people he looked upon as "dirty" (and, by extension, disorderly) had their limits of order and cleanliness. There is a continuum in all this. Some would pick up specks of dust from what most would consider an immaculately clean floor. Others would let the dust accumulate. And all draw the lines in different ways.

But this man's sense of pride in his work, his desire to pass on that pride to his son, and his desire to do for others gave him a warmth that few people today, at least where I live (in Lynwood, California, a "suburb" of Los Angeles) would possess. And, from what I have been able to learn, few people possess this public sense of pride, let alone develop standards, values, a worldview, which includes the public and the personal.

Last night I saw the street sweepers riding their machines pass my house. It was, I realized, just a job for them. And how could it be otherwise? Consider the amount of things people accumulate and the rate at which everyone accumulates the things of the world. Born to shop, born to buy, born to accumulate. At this rate of accumulation we will gobble up the world in less than a hundred years. I think we are like cancer cells, reaching out to absorb the surrounding cells for our food, and growing, and devouring more and more cells, until all is eaten up and we are left alone. Our boundaries have grown; we have stopped having boundaries. We create and create in order to devour the world. And this is, to say the least, unhealthy.

Now, your man in Kobe lived in a smaller, less rapacious world, rapacious though it was. And his reaction to the "disorder" he saw around him, to people's lack of public cohesiveness, was like Voltaire's reaction to the world of superstition he saw around him and the consequent need for order, for a sense of boundaries, and also, eventually, for cleanliness.

Our world is disorderly enough. And the disorder is caused, paradoxically, by an inordinate desire for order, for control of the things we continue to produce, thinking these things, like a dike we built against the inevitable encroachment of the sea, will save us. They are not our life preserver, our ship in the storm. They are our planned confusion, the "orderly" city in complete disorder. Manhattan is the best example. Everything is structured and the people are themselves constricted, and the garbage accumulates.

I always feel that having less would return us to the true connections, the kind of "order" this street sweeper in Kobe thought of as order on a human scale. I would want to eliminate an enormous amount of what we now have—the military, the automobile, the airplane, all totally and almost totally unnecessary goods, all bureaucratic inefficiency and waste, all redundancy, and more, too. I would reduce the population of the world to at least one-tenth its present number and bring people together in tight, small communities. I would like people to do things on their own and not have things imposed upon them. I would like people to relate to the natural world and to each other. The human scale would suit me just fine, and, I think, your street sweeper in Kobe as well.

Your entry has set me thinking again, something I can't help doing. Without a sense of real order, the order that comes from biological need, not an imposed order, not an order created to maintain an outmoded way of doing things and an emptied relation to the universe in which we find ourselves, we will all be devoured by the larger process of that same universe.

> *Mary Eng Simpson*
> *Age 36. City planner*
> *Lynwood, California*

No. 125: Livorno, Italy. April 27, 1778. [6 hours; $105] The sign of a knife-grinder, they say, is a missing thumb. So, they ask you, why is your thumb not missing, why are your hands and body in such good condition? And why is there usually that smile just forming on your face when you hand back the perfectly sharpened knife and you say, "That will be twenty-five lire please, signora"? Nor do you know why your thumbs are still with you, or why you begin, only begin to smile when you ask for your money, the lawful fruits of your labor. You can only say, "Here I am, the son of a poor man, a butcher by trade, who has had to go out into this world and earn his bread," and, you add silently, "his wine and his women".

God is watching you. Maybe that is why you still have your thumbs and why you begin to smile. The smile begins because you think God isn't watching, that you, only, are watching yourself. And it ends, shortly after it began, because you somehow realize that if God is there, and if he is omnipotent, he is surely watching you and knows everything about you. It is only when you realize this fully—and you do not do it very often—that you break into a real smile that fills your whole face and extends through your hands and into the rest of your body. It is then that you burst into uncontrollable laughter, as if you and God understood the joke you were both playing on one another, a joke so big and so overwhelming, that both of you cannot help bursting into laughter.

The church must hear nothing of you, you say to yourself. The church must hear nothing. It cannot understand. It is too poor, sitting there with its big buildings and powerful robes and incense. God and you both understand. Today, you call out in a shrill whistle that you are here to sharpen all the knives and axes and for very little, too. You sing a little "smart" song, as you call out, to sweeten the offers you make. You would sing the song anyway, even if it did not result in more business. And now here are three young ladies in front of you with their knives, three beautiful, young ladies. And, at least to begin with, you suppress the smile, which you feel forming on your face.

No. 126: Yagodharapura (Angkor), Cambodia. 1241. [One day; $105]
Your husband works as a fisherman near the city, and you sell in the marketplace what he cannot dispose of to the villages. When you are selling fish, you wear your pleated cotton skirt, your silver

necklaces, and your hair tied back in a bun, tight. Like other women at Angkor, the lobes of your ears have been stretched and they are beautiful, for everyone admires them. You call out to the passersby in a singsong voice, which you have developed first to entice them into buying. But also you like to "create small conflicts," to engage in arguments. You have not even thought about why you do this, even though you find it pleasurable, almost like a need to scratch when your skin itches.

> *Dear Past Rentals,*
>
> *Please know that I love being in the middle of a crowd. If there's something happening, I want to know about it. My motto is "Born to Gossip". I'd rather gossip than work, and I'd rather argue than gossip. I can't understand people. Why don't they like to talk, to feel themselves in the middle of things, know that they're part of a larger body? Being in the thick of it makes me feel comfortable, not nervous.*
>
> *That's why, even though I don't know much about Ankor Wat (and from what I've been able to find out, very few people do, either), I wanted to be in a time and place where people strongly needed to be with people, if only to bump up against them, or smell them, or listen to their words or their noises or their shuffling around. Not to mention a real hungering for news—news or gossip, what's the difference?*
>
> *And argument-that's the right line for me. Some people will bet on anything—the time the sun rises, the exact arrival of the next train, the length of the next passerby's fingernails—you name it, they'll bet on it. I'm like those people. I'll argue about anything, especially if it's as clear as the earth from outer space. I've argued over the average weight of sparrows in spring. I've argued over the average size of a man's penis or the size of a particular man's penis. I've argued over the value of the English language. I've argued over everything.*

But like all addicts, I have to push things one step fur-
ther. That's why your market woman in Ankor stimulated me
so much. She was a champion. She picked her subjects,
brought them around to what she wanted to argue about and
then jumped in, all of her. When she argued, she used her
whole body. She waved her hands around as if she were
brushing off a herd of flies. She perspired when she talked—
she was a large woman, too. When things really got going—
and she had her own group of master arguers around her,
and an audience, too-she'd stand up right next to the person
she was arguing with so she (or he) could smell her (in fact, so
they both could smell each other—now that's closeness) and
talking, sometimes shout at each other, but often, to be really
effective, whisper. I never realized until then how powerful a
whisper could be until I hear her say, "The waste? There's no
such thing in you. No such thing." I know this doesn't sound
like much, but when it was whispered, it sounded like thun-
der. And her body reeked of sweat and food. O God, I loved
it!

And who wouldn't? That's what we are, and the sooner
we admit it, I say, the sooner we'll see ourselves for what we
are, big, loving, powerful, expanding, gregarious bodies, like
elephant seals on the rocks, all pushed together, feeling each
other's presence, communicating in the most basic way pos-
sible, listening to the buzz of intelligence in the species, not
the suburbs, no, not that madness, the other extreme, isola-
tion, anger, helplessness—lost, lost, lost.

That day a man came up wanting to buy some vegeta-
bles. She said, "Vegetables. What do you want with vegeta-
bles? What you need is a good, long walk in the sun to make
your head get all soft. Then you can come back and soften the
vegetables.

The man looked at her (he had known her for years) and
replied, "I'm going underground so I can avoid you. I'm cover-

ing myself up so I grow lots of vegetables from my own corpse. What do you think of that? Forget about the sun."

My woman replied, "It's not just the sunlight you're going to need but a way of finding your wife's vagina." (At this point she made the sign of the fig.) "And, if I were you, I'd go hunt down a hut where you can sleep off this heat. Your head's swelled enough as it is."

The man replied, "Better a swelled head than a shrunken one. Better a cool underground than a hothouse above ground. Wait till the next rain and take a shower. You've just reduced the price of sunlight." And so it went, day after day, and this man was no exception. He had known her for years, and to argue with her was the easiest thing in the world for him to do. It was his way of having fun. And he seemed to be having a lot of it then. And so was she.

Ankor was the place. This market woman, this master human being, was the heart of us all. And, for a short time, I was that heart.

Mary Ann Fishing
Age 36. Saleswoman: Reality Productions
Des Moines, Iowa

No. 127: Norwitch, England. July 13, 1889. [2 days; $200] Though for ten years you were a naavy on the streets of Norwitch, for the last two years you have become a part-time boxer. Before you turned "professional," you had gotten into a number of fights and developed a reputation as a real scrapper, who almost always came out ahead. But now the "good" ones have come after you, for there is money to be made.

At first you fought your opponents with bare hands. But since Broughton invented boxing gloves and, after 1867, the Queensbury rules gained in popularity, the gloves have become standard equipment in your part of England, and you all wear them, as well as follow the rules set down by the marquis of Queensbury. Eighteen out of twenty wins this last year have made you a regional boxing champion, and people come from far and wide to see you in action. You are almost famous. Even when you went to Hull, just for a visit mind you, a few people knew you.

Tomorrow night is another match, this time against a man you knew ten years ago, Brian White, whom you know you can beat and will beat. Not many fighters can come up to you in punch, movement, and stamina. You feel good about yourself and you like people noticing you, even if it's only over a small part of England, your Norwitch.

After tomorrow's fight there is a young lady who has been watching you a great deal lately. Who knows what will come of this?

No. 128: Hull, England. 1700. [10 hours; $50]   Although you are thirty-one years old, your life is about to end. You have been convicted of impersonating a royal pensioner, and the penalty, as it is in so many other offenses, is death by hanging. You are in your cell. All around you, you hear the moans of other desperate men who, in a short time, will also be hanged.

How will you spend these next few hours, for you have only ten hours left before they come to take you to the gallows, where you will hang as surely as the sun rises in the east and sets in the west.

Dear Past Rentals,
What does it mean to be condemned to be hanged? What goes on in the mind and heart of a man about to face the ending of his life? These were the first thoughts I had on reading your entry. And because I wanted to know, I went to

experience this man's final hours. (I must say that I didn't stay around for the actual hanging. That was an experience I didn't intend to go through with.)

But even though the man himself interested me, he was not as important as the crowd, which came to see his execution. What started our in my mind to be a solemn event, the ending of one life, and for a trivial crime, one which today is merely a misdemeanor, carrying a jail sentence of not more than six months, turned into a spectacle, a theatrical event, an outward expression of public frustration, of deeply seated animal instincts let loose, a kind of cock fight or bear baiting.

And the condemned man was expected to act his part. He was again being judged by his "peers". Was he going to face his death with dignity? And since he was the main event, would he "play" to his audience, like an actor on stage? The crowd, who had within them the history of those who had done just that, expected the condemned to play a role that they, the crowd, had in their heads. The condemned man was, in this sense, unimportant. He was merely a creation of the mob, a representative figure, a sacrificial representative of some level of humanity. And this was, to me, far more interesting, even though I did keep my "eye" on this poor man, about to end his life dangling from a rope.

Afterwards I wondered how we do things today. Certainly, the 500 or more crimes punishable by death have been reduced to only a few, and long prison sentences have become more and more uncommon. Parole, time out for good behavior, and overcrowded prisons have kept the sentences light, that is, in comparison with those of the past. Therefore, a new outlet must have been created for that mob, which, deprived of its instinctive expressions, had to flow into new containers.

Besides the television and movies, where violence is tamed, removed from the physical world and placed in the mind, which further removes it from satisfactions enjoyed in the past (now making that mob a "mental" mob), sports is still going strong. But even here it has been made a creature of television, removed from the actual, physical experience. And there is business, which is a kind of instinctive outlet for the animal within us.

Still, I wonder where all that energy has gone. People in the 18th century and before (and even up into the 20th century) worked hard, physically hard, and their bodies came home at night tired. They worked long hours and they struggled, physically, with physical things. They lifted things, they moved the shuttles of the looms back and forth, they held onto the plow, they dug, they rowed boats—in short, they worked their asses off, and that was life.

I cannot imagine how a football game, watched on television, could generate that much instinctive energy. Jogging and working out, for some, provide at least, a kind of release. But for most people, there is no outlet. I imagine they could use something like an execution. At that execution, where I was the main performer, I felt the urge to respond, to go out with true expression, not like a wimp but like a man. I wanted to bow to the crowd, to parade up to the gallows, to embrace the hangman, to dance for a moment so all could see me, an insignificant clerk in his few moments of glory. The crowd provided that for me. And I, to oblige them, provided their entertainment.

Where will our species go from here? Will our basic, animal instincts wither away? Is the next stage in our history the "Era of the Wimp"? Or will we find a way of expressing what has been with us from the beginning (and even before our beginning) and which we cannot, at least in the near future, dispense with or even would want to eliminate.

George Fars Malanthon

Age 29. Clerk
Hull, England

No. 129: Pontefract, England. 1687. [4 hours; $85] You are a wine merchant, receiving, overland from Liverpool, wagonloads of wine from Portugal and Spain and mixing what you get with cheaper wines. You manage to make a living selling this wine to the local merchants in this small village in the West Riding.

Today you are delivering a hogshead of Spanish Sherry to a house of a local knife manufacturer, who will also invite you in to share some of what you have sold him, and you will sit for an hour or two talking of this and that, but especially of the impending political events which both of you expect to occur within the next five years—the King, Holland, and the possible revolution.

1687. Pontefract, England. 4 hours. $85.

Dear Past Rentals,

To sit and talk and not to worry about time—that I miss and miss dearly. I am a low-level corporate executive for a large midwestern insurance company, and I account for every second of my time, even when I'm on the toilet, even when I'm eating. And at home with my family, I often think about loose ends, or I fear that loose ends will appear, and they often do appear, even in my dreams, or especially in my dreams.

I imagined that, in the past, because people worked longer, they took the time to be with one another, to sit down and talk about other things, assured of their lives, that they were not going to change, in fact, that they were fixed, and therefore though they were poor, they would maintain their relationships with others, and the quiet continuity of exis-tence would proceed unchanged, protected, as they were for much of their lives, from enormous upheavals of technology, which we "suffer" from today.

Time was "slower" in those days. Things had to get done, but the anxiety of planning every minute did not exist. People were buoyed up by tradition, by a relatively unchanging sense of self, formed by a relatively unchanging society. And there was, at least for me, a profound sense of comfort in all this.

First, I felt like a participant in the world in which I lived. The man whom I talked to and I shared roughly the same political opinions and therefore could speculate in the same directions. And we knew there were many others who shared our desires and points of view. Our conversation focused primarily on the replacement of the Catholic king James II with someone else. The talk was that William and Mary of Holland, good Protestant rulers, would assume the throne and truly re-establish the Protestant reign and suppress the Catholics, who, we felt, were a threat to the country and who reminded us of the Catholic threat of 1588 from Spain, when our good queen Elizabeth ruled.

We knew it would happen, but we wanted to know when and how it would occur. And we speculated on the Catholic reaction. Would the forces of James III, uncrowned as the lawful successor, fight to regain the throne? And how would the Protestant forces resist this "rebellion," since that is what it would be called? Would the new rulers place severe restrictions on the Catholics and other dissenters who did not belong to the Church of England, or would there be a new era of peace among us all?

We could not say, but the wine was good—after all, it was my wine—and the cakes we ate were fresh from the oven, baked by the merchant's wife, and wonderful. Such relaxation everyone should enjoy. It is a part of being human. The rest of our lives, without this human comfort, will turn into a

disease and destroy what we are, or should be. That is why I
say that accounting for one's time is a terrible way to live, in
fact, is really not living.

> Michael James
> Age 38. Accounts Executive
> Minneapolis, Minnesota

No. 130: Halmstad, Sweden. July 16, 1629. [3 days; $275] Somewhere, through the village priest and through your own effort and the efforts of your parents (both illiterate) and your distant uncles, you learned to read and write. You have always read books when you could get them, good and bad ones, on every subject you could find. And today it is no different than it was twenty-five years ago when you were a young man of fifteen, running around absorbing everything.

But times are not very good, and since you were wounded in a battle which you certainly did not want to have any part of but were forcibly conscripted into, you have been unable to do farm work or any other work which requires a strong body capable of decisive movements. Now you are a public scribe for the city of Halmstad. People come to you, almost everyone comes to you, to have you write letters, copy contracts, write agreements, love letters, poetry, notices, and perform many other areas of writing which you half compose for them and half take down from dictation.

Now that you cannot move about as you used to, you take an interest in your customers. You cannot help probing a bit, striking up a conversation about things wholly different from the subject at hand. People are more than willing to talk. Underneath the surface of their lives lies a force of loneliness ready to explode. It is only necessary to know how to let it out without the explosion.

And through the years, you have become a master at this.

People tell you everything, their fears, their loves, or the objects of their hatred. They do not hold back. But one sure sign of a person who listens is that he must never divulge anything. But the patterns of life, hidden and revealed, enlarge themselves and you cannot help revealing what you know—this desire to tell all has tormented you now for three years.

But despite your dilemma (or because of it), you have found a way of both revealing your information and keeping it private. You have resorted every night to keeping a written commentary of everything you have heard that day, a diary of the thoughts and fears and hopes of the people who turn to you for confidences, to unburden themselves. And, in addition, through your diary you have also begun, lonely creature that you are, to unburden yourself, and in doing this you are even more able to listen to all that people tell you. How wonderful and amazing the fabric behind the fabric may become!

Dear Past Rentals,

How can anyone listen to the private thoughts and feelings of another and not unburden himself to himself or to another? Here are some of the things this Swedish scribe wrote down about the people with whom he came into contact. I will give only a small sampling, since there is no fear now of anyone discovering the secrets of these people who revealed themselves to him.

One woman, twenty-eight, a housewife and seamstress: "I'm afraid of the somewhat older gentleman who lives across the street from us. He looks at me from his window. When we pass each other on the street, he does not merely greet me, but engages me in intense conversation. It seems he wants to talk, has much to say, and overflows with thoughts. I do not know how to reply to him. He needs someone to listen to him, but I am, unfortunately, not the one who can hear him properly. I don't know what to do."

A young man, thirteen: "Every day I am tired. I work and work. There is no time to do anything else; I can't even daydream. If I do, I will make mistakes, and my master will beat me. I don't want him to beat me. But I can't help it. I need to dream. Last week I imagined I was in the air, high above the church, floating and invisible, except the birds were talking about me. And I understood what they were say- ing. I told them I needed to be a part of the air, and they told me, 'Go down, return to your home, your street. You don't want to be here.' I woke up just in time to get back to work, for my master came in a few seconds after that. I feel that I will lose me mind."

Myself: "I cannot help them. I can only listen. Maybe they will help themselves. Maybe they will really know how to solve their own problems. Maybe they only need to hear the words coming out of their mouths. And I want to help them. Why do I want to help them? There is a reason, but I don't know it."

Myself: "The squirrels are chasing each other. They need to play, but they then gather less food for the winter. One activity interferes with the other. People are the same way. They need to play, to absorb their world, like a hug they give it or a hug they allow the world to give them. But their work pushes away that enormous hug. How will they, I mean, how will we balance the two?"

Ibrahim Muhawi
33. Jeweler
Beirut, Lebanon

No. 131: Guadalajara, Mexico. March 4, 1701. [9 hours; $80] For fourteen years you have been, what we would now call, a travelling salesman. Now you are twenty-eight and you have wandered, especially through the north of England, selling all kinds of things. For the last few years you have sold scissors, needles, thread, spectacles, combs, almanacs, religious images, and other small items from a kind of display case you carry from your shoulders and which stretches down in front of you.

As you walk through the streets, you shout out your wares and at times make up jingles about them, and, literally, whistle up trade. You do not make a very good living, but you have never suffered from lack of interest. There are always people to meet, women to watch, and from time to time a few encounters with some of them in a stable or in a room, somewhere, wherever it is convenient.

Although you do not even think it, all the people you meet are amazing, and you would, if you knew how, almost bow down to any of them, even to the crazy or the pompous. The pageant of life overflows through you; it is always beyond your expectations. And though you would not say or think this, somewhere inside, you believe, through your actions and your responses to people, that good and bad are meaningless. They are categories—a strange idea. If this thought ever came into your head, and it never has, you would reject it as you would reject fish offal if it were served to you.

Today is just another day, but without the just or the unjust. Rather, and plainly, too, it is another day, and you never know what will happen, only that it is all happening in such profusion that you cannot take it in, except in your poor and always limited manner. But it is wonderful, beyond belief or explanation.

No. 132:   Rennes, France. November 29, 1705. [3 weeks; $200]
You are now thirty-seven, poor and unmarried, but you have managed to eat well enough, even when times have been hard and the harvests have failed. You are a porter and carry things on

your back all day. Though you have become strong at your work, you lie down at night exhausted. You would be more tired if you did not take frequent naps when you have no work, or if you did not spend your time talking with other porters, or with bakers or goldsmiths, with almost everyone, as everyone else you know does.

The main talk today has been about the bad harvest. It has been the principle topic of conversation for weeks. Things are growing tense. People know that conditions will grow worse if something is not done, but nobody believes the rich will open their storehouses, that the church will provide food for the hungry, that food will be found.

There is a growing nervousness everywhere. You have sensed this for weeks, and yet you and those around you talk, only to continue talking, continue putting out feelers, only to establish an atmosphere of certainty around you. The rich have hoarded their food; you know they do not go hungry. You have seen the insides of their houses. You have also seen the faces of the hungry poor, the farm laborers and the poor of Rennes, and you and the others around you know it will get worse because the rich will never give their food to the poor. They are too frightened, too removed, or too absorbed in their snobbish tastes to help anyone, and the church is the servant of the rich. What will you do? What will all of you do? You know the results of breaking into the houses of the rich. But what is to be done? You are all growing desperate. There must be action soon.

> *Dear Past Rentals,*
> *When I read your entry about the hoarding of food by the rich and the poor who were not able to get food because of a bad harvest and who were growing desperate, and I read at the end of your entry the question "What is to be done?" I, too, asked, "What is to be done?," for I and many in my vil-*

lage and in my country, Indonesia, have asked the same question. We also, when the harvests do not come and there is no rice or vegetables or fruits, are also desperate. We know who has and who does not have. We know the rich have and will not give. What is to be done?

The government, of course, sees our discontent, but it is not our government. It is the government of the rich. Still, to head off discontent or eventually outright rebellion, it must make some concessions. Its dilemma is that it cannot antagonize the rich and it cannot afford to outwardly suppress the people. Therefore, like a crab, it moves sideways. It is presently re-settling some of the population of Java (the main island just next to mine) by forcibly moving people to West Irian Java, where they face extremely harsh conditions.

We have too many people in our country, but the government does not undertake a birth control program because most of the rich and a large percentage of the population are Muslim, and this religion does not believe in birth control. My country has great deposits of oil, but the money does not go into the public good. How can it when the rich control the country and the wealthy countries control the less wealthy?

I understand the desperation of those people in France. I imagine that if things got much worse, the people would rise up and take what they needed, but with terrible consequences. Many more than participated in the rebellion would be killed or tortured or thrown in jail to rot. The same would happen here. But we do not have any other choice. It is either rebel or die.

Everywhere over our country the powerful business interests trample the people. And even if there were no domination, we would still have serious problems. What is to be done? Indeed, what is to be done?

Ajan Warjan

Age 27. Farmer
Kelapang, Indonesia

No. 133: Utrecht, Holland. September 30, 1618. [4 hours; $75] Though you are now fifty-three, you have not stopped being a maker of cheeses, which is your lifetime profession. But like all the people you know and have known for many years—cheese makers, clothiers, carpenters, and the other workmen who cluster around your life—you enjoy playing bowls, smoking tobacco in your clay pipe, and drinking beer, but only when the weather is nice, and it is not often nice in Utrecht.

Today, however, happens to be an unusually beautiful day— clear, autumn weather, and even a little warm. Everyone is feeling good. Your juices are flowing, the trees are beautiful, yellow and red this autumn day, and you can't wait to begin.

No. 134: Augsburg, Germany. November 1, 1502. [2 hours; $80] You are one of the greatest brewers of German beer, a rich, smooth beer, which you serve at your inn in Augsburg, where travelers and merchants stay on their way through the region. Today you are describing to a traveling merchant just how the beer is made. You have just sat down, both of you, to dinner and, of course, to several pints of your new beer.

No. 135: Venice, Italy. May 27, 1499. [6 hours; $75] You have been a gondolier for fifteen years. Still single because you do not have enough money to get married, you spend what you have on your favorite pastime, gambling. You gamble on the cockfights. You gamble on the ships coming in. You gamble on almost anything. With three gold coins in your pocket you are going to the cockfight where, you think, Marcello Giuliani's cock is bound to win. But it doesn't matter. It is the sweat, the noise, and the excitement of the crowd you enjoy, win or lose.

Dear Past Rentals,

Where do you see a good cockfight these days? You can't, unless you hear it through the grapevine. I now live in Saskatchewan in central Canada, but I used to live in Aquila in Italy. There, every week you could go to a cockfight. And they were truly wonderful. I don't make any apologies for the treatment of the birds. They are really tortured. But something wonderful takes place during a cockfight. And because I miss them so much, now that I am in Canada, I wanted to go back to Italy, at least through your catalog.

This is a man's activity, mind you. The women stay at home and glower at us when we return. And even if we don't tell them where we've been, they know. First, there are the cocks to be looked over, discussed, argued about. There are gross and fine points to kick around. There is money to be bet and agreements to keep. There is the noise and confusion of everyone talking at once, arguing, shouting, laughing, and looking each other in the eyes. And this is just the beginning, but it is as necessary as what follows.

Next, the fighting begins, and there is much shouting. People shout at their cocks, urge them on, sweat from anxiety. Some have even had heart attacks in the middle of a cockfight. They smoke. They drink. They stand up and practically throw things at the arena. They are excited. Everyone is excited, so much they don't really know what they're doing, and often pickpockets can work the crowd greatly to their advantage.

I'm no different than anyone else. I shout and stamp my feet on the rough boards of the stands. I argue and shout and sing the praises of one cock or another. I eat and drink and sweat and am at times ready to throw things into the arena.

But once or twice I have stood back and just watched. The whole thing is more like a spectacle than a betting arrangement. People need to lose themselves in the noise and excitement. They have had difficulties during the week. They are worried about their work or just bored with it. Or they have nothing else to do. Or they would just rather come here than go out and play soccer. Or they would rather do both. It's impossible to explain it completely. But just as in the past, people need an outlet for their bodily feelings, and they can't get it at home around the wife and the kids. I guess they need to feel alive in the world.

Your man interested in betting, especially on the cocks, turned out to be a fairly contentious fellow. During the six hours I entered the life of this guy, he practically got into two fights, but the gambling got the better of him and he held back. He was caught up in the fever as much as the next guy was. That night he lost, not big, just a few florins. But he went home happy, or, at least, satisfied. He had had his fix and that was enough. In two weeks he would be back. But during those two weeks he would have bet small amounts on almost everything, especially the ships coming in, but also bet on the color of his neighbor's wife's dress, the number of gondolas passing the Grand Canal in one hour, the kind of beggars in the piazza in front of Saint Mark's church, on almost anything it was possible to lose or win money doing.

> *Mike Francesco*
> *Age 33. Carpenter*
> *Saskatoon, Saskatchewan*

No. 136: Madrid, Spain. March 7, 1788. [2 hours; $45] It is cold in Madrid and the weather is atrocious. As they say, "Nueve anos de invierno, y tres de infierno" (Nine years of winter and three of hell). But March is better than the cold, blustery days of January and December. You are a shoemaker, twenty-nine years old, and your shop, a very small "hole in the wall" somewhere off the Plaza Mayor, is somehow even colder than the day. The pile of blowing coals helps warm the small room of your shop, a room that is almost the size of a large closet. Your sheepskin coat helps, too, but when you sit all day, as you do, the cold gets to your bones and your fingers begin to get numb. Therefore, during the afternoon, you walk, show yourself on the street, stop to talk to everyone, conduct business even, and find out what has been going on, as well as give out the information you have absorbed in your afternoon walk. The sun is out, after a few weeks of dark, gray skies, and you cannot wait to be walking near the Plaza Mayor on the Avenida de la Incarnacion.

No. 137: Granada, Spain. September 24, 1572. [5 days; $250] You and your ancestors have lived in southern Spain, particularly in Granada, for many centuries, as long as anyone in your family can remember. You speak Spanish and Arabic, as do your children. Eighty years ago the Spaniards took over your city, but your great grandfather stayed on. He did not go into exile in North Africa, as did many at the time. The Spaniards needed you, the people they conquered, for you knew how to make things, to work. You have heard this many times: "The infidels are lazy. They do not know how to make things; they do not know how to work. They know only how to conquer." You believe this without question. You are twenty-three, but you know how to work brass, silver, gold, and other metals, as well as to produce tiles and to construct fountains. All your life you have watched your people doing these things and, even among them, your ability is greatly prized.

All of you, in order to stay in your native Spain, your native Granada, have had to convert to the infidel religion, but, of course, you do not believe in their ways. It is easy to deceive them. You have known the words and rituals of the Catholic faith for many years; it has been all around you. But still, in secret, you prostrate your body toward Mecca and utter the prayers to Allah, who commands all things. Much is revealed through the will of Allah.

Yet today, despite all you have tried to conceal, you have, without warning, been seized by the Inquisition. They do not feel that you are really a Christian, and how could they believe otherwise, with their suspicious minds? You know they are not going to believe you, no matter what you say or do. You give yourself up to your god, in whose hands lie all mercy, understanding, and compassion. You rest now, in jail, with others, waiting for the severe questions and the terrible tortures you know you will face from these devils.

Dear Past Rentals,

Do you know what fanaticism is? It's killing everyone who doesn't believe what you believe. And eventually it's killing yourself after everyone who doesn't agree with you has been eliminated (or, at best, converted). Fanaticism is ultimately self-destructive. It kills off even the fanatics. It "purifies" everything in order to "purify" itself because of the fear of living, the fear of an enemy the fanatic himself has created. And ultimately a fanatic is afraid of himself and the unconquerable ambiguity in existence.

And the people who chose, for one reason or another, to live under the rule of the fanatics—how did they cope? How did they hide? Everywhere this has happened, minorities cowered under the power of the rulers, and the rulers used the people to carry out what they could not directly accomplish. People rationalized what they were doing, what they were told to do, perhaps not directly, but still told, still forced to do. And the cowering ones, the ones who hid, they, too, produced their reasons, like a shield, to protect themselves from the forces surrounding them.

In the case of the Jews in Russia, cowering under the terrible peasants around them, and in Spain, the Moslems and the Jews cowering for decades because of the Christian fanaticism which had overthrown them, the practical ones, who had made Spain the glory that it was—these people hid themselves. They led two lives, continually, all their lives, and at the same time, secretly, they strengthened their religion, or so it seemed.

However, when you are forced to live this dual life, you are also forced to get good at imitating your enemy. In order to do that, you must become him, not just outwardly, but, more importantly, in an inward sense, you must actually be him. In short, you must become a Christian in order to hide yourselves from the Christians. And if you are "liberated," if you escape to a land where you are not persecuted, where you do not have to hide, do you still remain a Christian? Or when you return to your original religion, do you maintain some of the feelings of the other, "outward" religion?

This man was not troubled by his fate. He was troubled by his ambiguity. He had lived among Christians all his life and had yet been a Muslim, and a proud one as well. Yet something had crept into him from the Christian world, something he could not help feeling as a part of himself. In prison he still bowed toward Mecca five times a day—secretly, of course. But when he looked out at the church near the prison, he involuntarily crossed himself and said a few quick words in Latin. This troubled him more than the tortures, for he knew he would not survive them—no one survived them.

Yet even in the midst of these double worlds, he maintained the pride of his work, his skill at being a master carpenter and a still more magnificent maker of fountains. He could look back on the things he had made and remember them with pride. Then, his life and his work merged and he felt whole again. He remembered his traditions and glowed over them, caressed them in memory and through them remembered the beauty and grace and depth of what he and his ancestors had done on this beautiful, barren peninsula which they had conquered over 600 years before.

> Junichiro Tanazaki
> Age 63. Saki brewer
> Kobe, Japan

No. 138: Catania, Sicily, Italy. April 23, 1648. [3 weeks; $225] For some reason you did not know what you were doing during those two weeks of mourning. There was nothing between you, nothing that anyone could see or even that Sofia, his widow, could notice, though you cared for her greatly. But for the funeral service you wore a blue suit, not a black one and you cried too much, showing something which could not be proven but was suspected, even though nothing had passed between you.

You tried to apologize later, but you were met with silence, and you knew what that meant—they were coming to get you. Because you could not answer the questions they asked about you and Sofia, you could not convince them in the least, though you knew you were telling the truth. You did not want to admit anything—it was too risky—and their suspicion fell on you even more because you were a young man and had lived next door to her. They were out to get you now. What were your chances of surviving? You had lived in Catania all your life. You did not know any other city in Sicily or in Italy itself. But you knew you had to leave, and immediately, too.

A cousin in Bari, you believed, was your only hope. Tonight, carrying only a small bag, you have secretly left your room, making the bed as if you were still asleep in it. Fortunately, your brother's sailboat is in port and there is a wind tonight. You untie the rope, enter, and sail out into the sea, north toward Gioiosa Ionica, which you hope to make before morning, then onwards, slowly, to Otranto and then to Bari, where your cousin will give you sanctuary.

Dear Past Rentals,

Well, how close can you get to your neighbor? This guy was not that close, but he got dunned anyway. Maybe he wasn't too bright. Or maybe he just got carried away. One thing led to another, and before he knew it, they were after him. In some places, at least, you can't be too careful what you show others.

Once I was like this guy, but things didn't turn out as seriously. A friend of mine had a girlfriend whose sister I liked to talk to. I wasn't interested in "going after her" as they say in my part of Spain (near Murcia, which is in the south-west). And I was only twenty-two and didn't know my finger from a fence post. I just wanted to talk, and she did, too, a lot, in fact. We spent hours together, alone, and I didn't realize what others were thinking. I got a rude shock when my friend told me that her brothers were looking for me, and not to take me out to dinner either. Fortunately, I left town quickly, spent a few weeks visiting my cousin in Elche, and with his help wrote her a letter to be delivered to her brothers, then called them, explaining what had been going on. Fortunately, they accepted my explanation, but I didn't see this woman much after that.

Well, living in Sicily is much worse. You don't just smile at a woman or stop to talk to her in a private place or meet her for lunch or, God forbid, spend time with her in her bedroom. People there do more than talk. They act. They feel bound, by older ties than they can conceive, to have to kill you. That's right, kill you. Now isn't that weird?

The worst part is that this guy will never be able to come back to Catania or even to Sicily again. And more, he'll have to hide completely because there's always the chance that some relative will come looking for him to settle what he thinks is a "dishonor". And, what's not said, those relatives are scared to do it; they don't want to do it. But if they don't, they will also be punished, and they fear the forces of their society more than they fear killing someone. How strange all this seems, how strange it feels, especially to an American, a German, a Swede, who were never raised with these traditions and would not think twice about what happened to this young man who overstepped the boundaries of his unwritten culture.

    Federico Martinez
    Age 28. Boat builder
    Murcia, Spain

No. 139: Karnak, Egypt. February 20, 2134 B.C. [One hour; $45] You are a sandal maker, as were your father before you and his father. It is something you did not think about, but even at four years old you knew you were going to follow your father's work. By the time you were nine, you were turning out sandals and wearing them yourself or selling them to your friends or anyone who would buy them.

Now, your sandals are made for all classes of people, from small farmers to laborers, and though you have some contact with other sandal makers in Karnak and nearby, you do not collude with them to fix prices, as they do. Therefore, your prices are slightly below theirs, which makes you popular with many people but not with the other sandal makers. Today you are in your shop, which is really a small hut. It is late afternoon and you are beginning to work, after a long lunch, which you have eaten behind your shop, where your family and you live. One person is waiting for the sandals you are now working on.

No. 140: Torino, Italy. March 5, 1983. [One day; $75] Perhaps you have thought too much about the problems of the world, of mankind. But they depress you and it is not just for a few minutes or an hour. This brooding has been going on for years and you cannot stop. You feel as if you are sleeping under layers and layers of blankets, which should have suffocated you long ago, and yet you will not pull off the covers. You feel you would betray yourself if you did this.

The problems, indeed, are real. There is the problem of the world's population, 6 billion and still increasing. There is the problem of radiation and nuclear weapons and nuclear waste. If people inhabited all the planets of the solar system, there would be enough radiation from the present nuclear stockpiles to kill everyone and kill them perhaps many times over. There is the decay of the ozone layer, the rise in carbon dioxide or general industrial pollution on the land and in the oceans. And finally there is the problem of each of us, that we will die, sooner or later, and we will leave this life, which is incomparably strange, neither good nor bad, but strange. And there are all the little problems, tiny fears, tiny projections of self, tiny strategies, little griefs, little angers, and the little excuses, all for the intricate purposes of living. They are small, very, very small, but equally as important.

And today you wake up in the same way and with all of these blankets upon you. You can hardly breathe. You will go through the day, sitting down to your breakfast, walking to work, eating lunch by the river with your friends where you will laugh and joke about everything in order to pass the time, and the problems will be rehearsed again in you or in conversation, and they will accumulate and you will return home with them, as usual.

Dear Past Rentals,

I feel the same way. What's so odd about this guy? We should be worried, real worried. And yet so many people are not, or if they are they hide their worries by not knowing. They worry about smaller problems—what the children should wear, their relation to the neighbors, the massacres in Bosnia. Either they know nothing or they want to know nothing. And you can put most people in these two categories.

I think this guy is a hero and the most important kind of hero. He sees through his body. He worries through his body. He looks through his body. And he puts it all together, not just mentally, but emotionally and physically and intellectually. He doesn't see an isolated famine in Ethiopia or a conflict in the Near East or an attempted return to democracy in Russia—he doesn't see these things alone. He looks under them, through them, beyond them. And he sees the species, the growth of the species, our species, and the destructive effects of that growth. And he wants something else, something far more integrated, more human, something, which combines the past and the future into the present. And yet no one hears him, no one hears him completely. And in this lies his tragedy.

Well, there are some of us like him. And it's good to know that we exist, for as much good as it will do us, and probably not much. The forces are enormous, so enormous they are beyond comprehension. That's why when we begin to communicate what we "see," projecting what we see into the near future, we can never say enough. Everything is tied to everything else. And those who would want not to be disturbed—and that is all of us—will question anyone who sets off on this direction, because it is a threat. It reminds us of the coming tsunami building at the center of the ocean and moving inexorably toward the fortress we have created to protect ourselves all these years. But the knowledge that it is coming is as certain as the knowledge that we will die, though we prefer to ignore that fact and think of the immediate world.

There is almost a law governing this faulted communication, one paralleling Isaac Newton's inverse square law of gravitation. It says that the importance of anything varies inversely with its distance from us. How can we worry about the world's population when we are confronted by layoffs and homeless people on the streets? How can we think about the history of our species when we are worried about the boss or the people we work with? It seems we were not meant to go beyond our immediate boundaries of space and time.

What solutions could we propose (we who "see" as this man "sees")? Solutions exist, but they would require a re-looking, a re-alignment of what we are, a re-turn to a far greater simplicity, in fact, the elimination of much of what we have today. But more important, we would have to re-align our whole way of looking at the world while maintaining a standard of living which does not cause us to sink into a barbarous past, not to mention the threat of starvation. In short, we need an adequate standard of living with only about one-tenth to one-twelfth the world's population.

How is it possible to tell people that this is only one of many things, which must be done to avoid a total collapse of life on our planet? And if we mentioned other things—the elimination of the military, the virtual elimination of advertising, the automobile, the airplane, a vast reduction of manufactured goods—we would be given the same old "practical" answer that it is not practical, that no one would do it, that it cannot be done. The inverse square law is in operation again.

Therefore, I understand completely what this man feels and how difficult and how lonely his existence is, for I am also that man who cannot cry or laugh at what is happening to everything around him. If there were many of us, we might speak, but, alas, there are so few, and that is the tragedy.

Mohammed Ben-Yusef
Age 44. Health inspector for the city of Oran
Oran, Algeria

No. 141: Luxor, Egypt. June 14, 1483 B.C. [12 hours; $75] You are a servant for a small prince, a medium sized landowner near Luxor. You work in his kitchen every day, preparing the meals for your employer and his guests. You also prepare meals for the servants, so your day is filled with much work.

However, you also have many things to do within your workday. You need to go to the river to find a duck for today's meal, though that will not be the only animal they will be eating. Behind you are the kitchen implements, oil jars, spoons, pots, containers of barley, and the large pots in which you will cook tonight's meal and the meals for the servants.

You are young, only fourteen, but you have managed, through your cleverness (some of your friends say your stupidity) to be appointed to the kitchen of the prince. Here you will eat well and watch what comes and goes, for nothing passes the attention of the servants of the prince. You enjoy this life, for what comes to you in the way of information and gossip comes from close and far, from as far away as Goshen or Upper Egypt or from the land of the Nubians. You hope to accumulate knowledge; in fact, you are starved for it and seek it out even before it arrives at your door. The kitchen is hot, but outside in the shade the servants come by to talk, and while you are preparing the duck for the prince and his guests, you will listen, sometimes inside and sometimes outside the kitchen, to the talk around you.

No. 142: Ur, Chaldea, Iraq. October 5, 1875 B.C. [10 hours; $90] You are eleven, a young schoolboy, conscientious in your studies because your father supervises your lessons. You recite from a tablet during the day, come home for dinner, and after dinner get a fresh tablet and fill it with writing. At night you will receive your next day's lesson, your recitation, and your writing assignment. You will recite this lesson to your teacher and also to your father.

On your way home, you linger, watching without thinking about them, the low, one story unbaked clay houses with their blank, dark, rectangular windows (there is no glass) and wander through the bazaar where carpenters, basket makers, goldsmiths, potters, cloth makers and other trades make their way. Some of these people you know. You stop to talk to them and to the boys your age, with whom you run off through the city in search of new adventures.

Tonight you will sit at your father's feet and recite your lesson, which you have prepared well, and your father will indeed be pleased with your work. For dinner you will eat a broiled fish, cucumbers, marrow cooked in oil (a favorite of yours), grasshoppers on skewers with cheese, and to drink, barley wine. This is a good day for you, but it has only begun. You are now on your way home from your teacher.

No. 143: Kandi, Benin. March 17, 669. [3 weeks; $325] It has been a good season for millet, and you, who are now fifteen, and the other women also, have managed to raise a good crop. The harvest is tomorrow. For the next few weeks you will let the plants dry, shake out the seeds and place them in large earthen containers, which you will carry on your backs to the granaries, where the millet will be kept free from rats, other animals, and insects. And then there will be beer for everyone.

No. 144: Somewhere near Moura on the Branco River, Brazil. February 3 (late afternoon), 752. [3 hours; $55] You are fifty-two, but are still useful, even though you do not accompany the men on their hunting trips into the jungle. Your eyes and hands have worked the wood of the forest for almost all of your life, and today is no exception. You are fashioning a top for your granddaughter and it is almost finished. You like to see her watching you work. Every few seconds you look up and smile, and your granddaughter in turn begins to smile but is too caught up in the fascination of your work to continue smiling.

> *Dear Past Rentals,*
> *Where is the Branco River? Where's Moura? Of course, I know where Brazil is. But as I found out, it doesn't really matter. Old people and their grandchildren are the same everywhere and anytime. This man was the same as I am with my grandchildren. He just happens to live in the Amazon rain forest on the Branco River near Maura in Brazil.*
> *The day was very quiet—that's the first thing I noticed. After all the noise of the traffic in Hyderabad, in the center of India, where I live with my son and his wife and their children, I felt strange, at least for a while. But then I began to hear—the sounds of the macaws and the monkeys calling out to each other and the creak of the hammock in which someone was resting. And then this old man's whole world collapsed into me and I felt at home, as if my ancestors and I had been there for a thousand years. I felt protected. I felt noticed, though there was no one around. And I felt that I was known as someone with a history and there were stories*

to tell about me. Therefore, when someone knew me, he knew my history, my sorrows and my happiness. He didn't know me as an abstraction.

And I knew how to do things, knew how to carve, and not only the top I was making for my granddaughter, but there was a history of carving in me, from childhood when I first began to make things, like everyone else in my tribe, whom I knew as intimately as they knew me. What a relief from the noise and confusion and human complexity of Hyderabad.

As I carved, I looked at my granddaughter playing with her dolls and later with her jacks (not the kind of jacks we have today) and reciting as she played and sang and recited the poems and songs of children her age. I remembered some of them, too, for I had heard them when I was young, and remembered the ones I had known and recited when I was six or eight or twelve. There was nothing to do there but remember and carve and listen to the birds and the monkeys, and when it rained for a short time during my "stay," listen to the rain. There is nothing more peaceful than listening to the rain falling on all the trees of the forest. So it must have been like this over the centuries for people who lived here.

Martin Singh
Age 71. Retired waiter
Hyderabad, India

No. 145: Near the present town of Burgos, Spain. July 12, 15,602 B.C. [**3 weeks; $350**] You are a twelve-year-old girl who has watched the carvings come into your life, carvings that your people claim are endowed with magic. Secretly, one day, and for three weeks thereafter, you fashion a small piece of wood into the image of your mother, and indeed it is an almost perfect image. You hide it from the others, looking only when they are away. For months you rub your fingers over the wood until it becomes perfectly smooth. Because of the animal oils you use, it has taken on a smooth, glossy appearance. Finally, you can stand it no longer and show it to your mother, innocently, of course, for you want to present it to her. It is, in fact, her image.

Her face is full of horror when she sees it. She does not want to touch it. She spits on it. She is afraid of it. She does not know what to do with it. And yet she is certain there is something powerful in your wooden figure and that her daughter is endowed with great magic, with power, especially over her mother, which she considers, in the depths of her soul, beyond her comprehension.

You gradually begin to realize what effect you have produced on your mother by carving this image of her. Images have power. What will the others think of this? What will they do to your carving? What will they do to you? You await their answers as you begin, for your own protection, to fashion your own image inside you.

Dear Past Rentals,

What is the difference between the power of a real person and the power of an idol? Teenage girls swoon over their favorite rock stars. Writers are held up as idols. Some are respected merely because they have a "position" of power. Others have a reputation. But behind them or beside their beholder, there is a fixed image, which is the creation of desire, a projection out of need. These, then, are the living idols, which the Book of Exodus warned us about, as did the second commandment.

But we are a symbolic species, and outward representations of inward states function in us as the objects of realia. Hence, the differences between 15,602 BC, the date of your catalog entry, and 1993 is, in its most basic sense, superficial.

We are still those symbol creating people, and therefore their dreams, reactions, creations, phantasms, projections, animism, etc. ring inside us, among us, around us, today as well as in the past. The only difference is the technology. We have folded ourselves into the many worlds of our creation and shut out the world we didn't create, the natural world, while they had integrated the natural world into themselves. Perhaps, it now occurs to me, they had a greater need for the creation of artifacts as symbolic projections of inner states than we have. We are surrounded by the artificial; they were not.

Where does the artificial lead us? It has become the crutch we have increasingly leaned upon and, at the same time, the protection we have created against nature. They lived without these artifacts, but their life spans were short. Ours are much longer, but we have accumulated immense burdens, which threaten to drown us, both physically and psychically.

Shall we return to those "thrilling days of yesteryear" when our people wandered over a vast landscape, increasingly equal to, but also in certain ways inferior to the animals which surrounded them (and, at times, entered them with disastrous results)? A deep romanticism adheres to this wish to return to the Paleolithic. We desire to become, as Shakespeare's King Lear says, "naked, unaccommodated man," to return to that world of direct, immediately felt experience, felt through the body directly and vibrating within us and turning outward until the whole landscape has become indistinguishable from our beings.

How wonderful and liberating this feeling is. But it is wonderful perhaps because we think of it in our warm houses and because we are clothed against the winters of the world. Despite, or because of, the hypocrisy of these desires, we are possessed by an ambiguous universe, caught between safety and adventure; and in a world, today, in which we are more and more cut off from nature, we have become more and more "artificialized".

We are surrounded by the things we have made, our progeny, and have even changed what has come through our hands and our technology, to the point of our transformation of the natural world—corn, for example, transformed from its smaller, earlier, perhaps more succulent beginnings; grass for our lawns remade in our image; new species of vegetables, hundred pound cabbages and squashes, giant heads of lettuce, grapes that no one 1,000 years ago would have believed could exist.

And the products of our minds have been effected also by these changes. Wilderness is a word, not an experience, perhaps made impossible once the word is fixed in our linguistic landscape. Animals, as well, have gone down under the arrows of our conceptualization. An immense buzz of concepts floats around the world as an artificial atmosphere we breath every day, even in our sleep.

Therefore, we can understand that idol, that statue of her mother—which this young girl, proud of her production, had carved in secret, her outward embodiment of an inward love. That statue would have had serious repercussions, for her and for everyone around her. Today as well, too, the massive weight of our symbolic world must be thought of with the same care, lest we flounder in illusion, worshipping ourselves and therefore reducing our essential beings to the sum of the tiny cells of the body, and making our world an artificial wilderness rather than the immense breath of our spirits, which are coterminous with the world in which we are born.

I hope this clarifies something in a journey, which extends up to the present and into our future and therefore can be thought of as no journey at all.

> *Mary Harper Rowe*
> *Age 68. Traveler*
> *Adelaide, Australia*

No. 146: Neander Valley, near Dusseldorf, Germany. January 23, 27,847 B.C. [One day; $100] You are a six year old girl who cannot do much, except watch (and this you do very well) while your father, his brother, and two other men newly arrived in the camp chip flint for axes and spear heads. While they chip away at the rock, they also sing, and at times during these days, you have begun to sing these work songs with them.

> *Dear Past Rentals,*
> *Just a note to tell you that chipping flint is hard work, and to register a protest against the view some anthropologists have expressed that civilization is the measure of its progression in tool making. Art, I believe, proceeded tool making. Singing and social gathering were coexistent with the construction of artifacts. They were not merely the lubricants that aided the work, like the radio turned on to increase production in the factory. They were equally as important and incapable of being separated from the labor. This absurd idea, that tool making came before culture, is an illusion created in the present and projected onto the past.*

> *Chen Liu Chung*
> *Age 36. Metal worker*
> *Manchuria, China*

No. 147: Southeast of Bundaberg near the Burnell River, Australia. July 16, 1307. [3 days; $215] No longer a young man, now at seventeen, you hunt, fish and gather food with the rest of your small band, your own large family. Tonight is the corroboree, where you will gather with many others, from other clans, who have come from great distances to sing and dance in order to allow the spirit of a young girl who has died to come to rest.

You will communicate with that other world, which comes in and out of your life and is still indivisible from it. You will eat and talk and sing, and you will meet the young women whom you have not encountered before, and they will meet you. You have been to several corroborees before, but each is a surprising and exciting time, both in and out of time. All night you will dance and sing and talk and laugh and see what is to be seen, and the next day also.

This is a good time, not because it will make you happy or that it will fulfill some small, immediate goal of your life, but you will "see," your knowledge will increase, and you will become richer, fuller, more understanding, as you enter more and more into the spirit of the ancestors, that other world of the corroboree.

No. 148: Bakhtaran. In the Zagros Mountains. December 24, 1225. **[3 hours; $90]** It is December. The nights are cold, but the sky has been clear. At night the stars look like a plateful of salt in the black sky. You and your father have been herding the sheep to a slightly lower pasture.

Around noon clouds begin to roll up into the brightening sky, until by three o'clock, two or three hours later, a sharp north wind sets in. You hurry on, knowing what is coming. It is a storm, and a heavy one, too. There is no shelter here. You must walk back for about twelve miles with or without the sheep. You are fourteen and your father's youngest son.

Dear Past Rentals,

Would they make it back home, walking those twelve miles? If they didn't go all the way, would they build a shelter and wait out the storm? Would anyone come looking for them? Would they be found? Why didn't they recognize the coming storm? What sound and feeling would the storm have for them?

I asked these questions when I read your entry No. 148, a trip to "Bakhtaran in the Zagros Mountains, 1225" I'm sure many people at one time or another had been trapped in a coming storm. What did they do? Living in Manitoba, I've also had to deal with blizzards, where they are far worse than those in the Zagros Mountains are.

Well, even though I was scared, they were not. They knew exactly what to do. They didn't make it back in time and had to weather the storm. Tradition told them what to do. They built a shelter from branches and placed them tee-pee style against one another. They then crawled inside and waited, actually slept until the storm was over. When they realized they wouldn't be able to make it back in time, they had to work fast. My father knew what to do and so did I. I hadn't had any direct experience with making such a lean to, but I had heard it described many times before, and I just followed my father's directions.

The sheep were left to fend for themselves and they did, of course. Our sheep dog, however, just curled in with us in the shelter. The storm was a heavy one, and we spend part of our time before we slept just listening to the wind. When we woke up the next morning, we had to dig ourselves out, so much snow had fallen in the storm. Our dog was the first to emerge, barking and yapping with delight at the clear weather and the brightness of the snow. Snowy "mounds" of sheep, very much alive, "littered" the meadow. I felt as if I was born again, the way my son, my real son, felt, being born in our home on the afternoon of a very bright day, the dazzling sun-

shine pouring into the bedroom where he first "saw the light".
*   And the people at home in the village didn't look sur-*
prised as we came walking in, a bit tired from the storm but
bright and fresh as the day. We sat down and had some mut-
ton stew and tea. Then, we felt better and began to talk of
gathering up the sheep before the wolves got to them.

> *Frank Clarke*
> *Age 37*
> *Minnedosa, Manitoba*

No. 149: Near Cambridge Bay, Victoria Island, Canada. June 25, 1889.
[9 hours; $70] You have just turned thirteen, already a companion
on many hunting trips, and a small hunter yourself. The goddess
of the sea, Iliaktuk, and the spirits of the land have been good
to you and your family. You remember your mother and her
warmth, the feeling of her closeness, her face in your face. And
you remember your father and his brother, your uncle, intent for
hours over a seal's blow hole, patient, waiting, such expert, alert
hunters, and you want to be so much like them. And you know
you will.

But last night you had a dream that came from a map a man
from the south showed you three months ago. Pointing to the
map, he showed you what he said was the whole of the Arctic. He
pointed out the others who lived in your land, peoples you did
not know but in your dream yearned to speak with, to learn from.

In your dream, you were travelling over this land, around the
globe, east through King William Island, then further east to the
last land of eastern Baffin Island and then on to Greenland, that
huge land of ice. The journey took years, not days, but this did not
matter. You were tireless as you walked on, visiting everyone you
met, talking, listening to the land and the people. As your dream
ended, you were in the Russian Arctic. You had arrived among

the Chukchi in Siberia.

Your dream ended, but it has stayed with you all day. And tonight you have an overwhelming feeling that you will have the same dream. Throughout the afternoon you have felt that it will be necessary to complete your "journey," to "return" home and also deepen the connections you had established. You lie down on the bearskin of the small tent your family shares. Soon you will be asleep.

> *Dear Past Rentals,*
>
> *Wouldn't it be wonderful if we could put together an anthology of the dreams of all peoples from the beginning of our species? We know that certain animals dream, but they can't tell us much about their dreams. We also know that our dreams are often touched off by events of the day—a purse spilling open, the sound of a truck behind us, the colors reflected in a wet window after the rain. But we also know that dreams hold the immediate world together, attempt to "knit up the raveled sleeve of care," as Shakespeare put it.*
>
> *But they are deeper than that, even though they include the more immediate world. They seem to say something about a sense of knowledge that antedated our existence. That's why dreams have been examined for their prophetic power. This young boy's dream seems to fit into this latter category and also into the previous ones. He was shown a map, which he must have absorbed entirely and at once. This was the immediate cause.*
>
> *But where did the travelling across the Polar Regions come from, the recognition of people and their ways, which he had perhaps, at best, only dimly known about? How did he find the Laps or the other Polar peoples of the Russian Arctic, and later encounter the Chuckchi, who are almost as far to the east as he could possibly go without returning to his*

place of origin?

I think there is a possible explanation on practical, historical grounds. The peoples of the Arctic have been in that region for a long time, perhaps tens of thousands of years. And they must have traveled long distances, not everyone, but a few. In this way knowledge of the lore and traditions of other peoples remained after the actual visitors had left.

But I don't think this is the whole explanation. This boy had not been exposed to much information about other Arctic peoples. Something else might be involved, some kind of racial unconscious, though I hate to use that expression. It smacks too much of Karl Jung and is perhaps tinged with fascist thought. But perhaps more remains than we think. And, to give the practical its due, the similarities of most Arctic peoples are greater than their differences.

And, to support the practical interpretation, in the second night of dreaming there were many elements the boy would have known about—an image of the sea full of fish, fruitful and ready to harvest, an encounter with two huge polar bears rising out of the water and shaking themselves, drops of iridescent water forming a rainbow around their bodies, empty kayaks ascending the summer rivers. These indicate the practical world.

This was a journey that I would not have undertaken in the "real world"; for, even if possible, it would have required many years of travel and under dangerous conditions. But this dream journey took only half of the night and perhaps not even that. I remember the vastness of the land, empty of anyone, even of animals, and the continual walking, as if forever, an eternity of walking. I remember the glow of the summer sun, which refused to set over the horizon and I remembered the sound of the silence around me, a silence so deep and vast that I felt that I was a larger part of it.

I would like to visit this region again, only this time in

person, for a few months, and go with those who live there,
have lived there all their lives and with their ancestors as
well, with everybody who has lived in that vast, empty, dan-
gerous, but serene land.

Helmut Schmidt
Age 22. Student
Freiburg University, Germany

No. 150: Hyrynsalmi, Finland. March 31, 1259. [2 hours; $45] You live alone with your family near Hyrynsalmi, which is hardly a town, a few houses at most. The people who live near you, the few dozen scattered through this area, visit each other for a long time, staying a week or two and then returning to their solitary lives in the forest, the forest, which is everything. You all say this when you speak of your life, "The forest is everything. There is nothing but the forest."

In the winter, the wolves are hungry and you must be careful. Twice you have had a close encounter with bears. Since hunting for deer is not difficult—there are so many—you will eat deer meat most of the year.

Life is not easy, but there are many things to see around you, "to sense," as you say. The forest is alive, and you are alive in the forest. Occasionally a stranger will come, and as many of you as possible will gather together to listen, ask questions, and generally have a good time, get drunk on whatever you may have around or can beg or steal.

But no one has come for months. The forest is still; you can almost hear it breathing in the wind, near the water, near the lake. You walk out to cut trees for a small storage shed near your home. It is almost spring.

No. 151: Nanyang, Honan, China. March 25, 103 B.C. [4 hours; $50]
You are now eighty years old, the oldest woman in your village, perhaps the oldest person in Honan itself. Because of your long memory, you are called the "historian of Nanyang". And because you have somehow unofficially been "assigned" this position for the last thirty years, your memory has indeed improved.

You sit in front of your great grandson's small house and close your eyes, remembering something from forty years ago, trying to recall the smallest details of the experience, the colors of the clothes, the shape of the landscape, the smells, the colors at every season, the voices of the people and their small and large gestures—everything.

This, in fact, has become an obsession. Hardly a moment passes when you are not trying to bring to life the events you remember. It has even made you a great teller of what you believe to be true stories, things that have happened to you and to others, pulled up through your memory. All kinds of people come to you, even the judges, to ask you questions about times which they can only dimly remember from their parents, and they will listen for hours as you talk on and on.

Tonight is one such time. They have brought a bit of rice wine to warm you as you sit under the protection of a small lamp in your grandson's house and begin to tell your visitors of something that happened sixty years ago, something you can recall to the smallest detail. You will talk for three or four hours.

Dear Past Rentals,
Have you ever tried this experiment? You lie in bed at night, trying to remember everything you have done that day from the moment you woke up (or perhaps even before). Every time I have tried it—and I've done it many times, it's an obsession with me—I can't get past the first hour. Sometimes I can't even get past the first twenty minutes. I'm

reminded of something my mathematics teacher told me forty years ago when I was in college. He said, "Imagine an infinitely twisted or bent line. Now straighten that line. How long would it be? The answer is that it would be infinitely long since the line is infinitely bent." That's how memory is. It can extend forever. We just keep filling in the details.

This very old woman was a history book for her time. When Su Ma Tien, the famous Chinese historian, came to write his history of China after the First Emperor, the founder of the Qin Dynasty, who ordered all the books to be burnt, he had to rely on people's memory and on folk tales to re-establish the history of China. He would have relied on people like this very elderly woman in Nanyang.

She was frail, very frail, but had a thin boned elegance to her, which gave her bearing—her voice and her gestures and her movements—a dignity, which few had achieved. All this, perhaps, was reinforced by the respect in which she was held. But there was a deep sense of pride in her. She never raised her voice to scold nor lost track of the general within the specific—everything was related to the direction in which she was going when she began to speak from her memory.

She told a strange story that evening. When she was seven, she used to play with a boy whose back was deformed. His head and neck turned faster than his body. And when he wanted to turn around quickly, he used his arms as a kind of windmill, flinging them out as he turned, as a diver might use his arms to twist his body around. He had bright, penetrating eyes, but a strange, high-pitched laugh which made her, she said, shiver for an instant as if the world had been suddenly, and only for a tiny amount of time, transformed, shifted a slight distance, which way it was impossible to determine. (Of course it would be impossible. Consider those questions in which you are asked to determine if the universe had changed when everything has been doubled in size.)

This boy disappeared suddenly one day and was not heard of for five years. When the villagers saw him again, he was taller and his back was almost clear of any deformity. There was, however, a slight hint of his prior physical condition—he had the same way of turning his body around, "the windmill movement," I'd call it. And the laugh, that shivering laugh, was still with him and the dark eyes, too.

He said that bandits had kidnapped him. They had treated him well but forced him to accompany them on their raids on the villages. He was not required to participate, only to watch. He saw them line up the villagers and force them to undress, all of them, even the children, while the bandits went through the clothing and then through the houses, looking for money first but also for food, rice mainly.

But ferocious as they appeared (they seemed to want to make that impression on him and on others), they were really trying to show him how "good" they were. They ordered the peasants around, but they treated them kindly. They seized the baskets of rice, but they took only enough for their needs. When they found money, and that was seldom, they counted it, laid it in a heap in the middle of the village and made the villagers look at it carefully. They asked them to guess how much money there was. Then, in a mock contest, they gave half of the money to the villager who was most accurate in his estimate. And then, as they were riding away, they threw the remainder back in the hands of the children. They seemed to be toying with people with the aim of receiving something for their "good" behavior.

As the young boy grew up, they often placed large planks of wood on his body and stood on them, as if they were trying to compress him, to straighten out his crooked back. At the same time, they recited poems and played music "of an unearthly kind" (as he remembered) and danced and shouted at something beyond his hearing as if to communicate with someone on the far edge of a territory in which they felt they were safe. It was to tell that entity that he was not to cross some imaginary line, not to enter their practical world, that their world was theirs and his was his own, not theirs. Property rights, you might say.

The purpose to his kidnapping began slowly to dawn on him. He was their sacred object. They were telling this entity from the "beyond" that he was not needed. They had their own sacred resonator, whom they would cause to see for them and defend them and account for their actions, and they would help him correct the deformity which had made him sacred and thus, eventually, ask this other entity to return, but much later. First the curing and then the return.

The "board press," the warm baths, the "stretchings," the dancing, the songs, and the poetry did help. During the last two years of his "captivity," the boy had almost grown out of his deformity. He had become a man, and a very strong one at that. And he did feel very grateful for what the bandits had done for him as anyone would have felt grateful who had had a deformity lifted from his him. To show his appreciation, he not only accompanied the bandits on their raids but took an active part, more than imitating their actions, in fact, going beyond them in acts of terrible boasting and fantastic, unexpected generosity. The actor had learned well, very well, from his teachers. During the warm baths he received, he sang aloud the same songs that had been sung to him and recited the same poetry he had heard for years and laughed and danced and shook even with terror at the appearance of the soldiers who hunted them. But, he knew, he was not, at heart, a bandit though all this adventure and magic thrilled him.

Then, when he was fifteen, the bandits raided a village they had entered dozens of times, but the soldiers were waiting for them. The villagers had not betrayed them; they had been forced to conceal the soldiers. It was also clear that the soldiers, after they had captured the bandits, would strip the village of its food and leave the villagers hungry. The bandits knew this and fought hard, for they were not fighting only for their own lives but for those of the villagers, whose mock enemies they had been for so long.

The bandits were outnumbered. Half of them died in battle, and a dozen of them were captured and sent off to the capital for execution. But the boy was saved from either fate. The villagers, who had seen him over the years, first as an observer and then as a gigantic participant, hid him among the compost heaps, where he practically suffocated. But he survived. And after the soldiers had gone, stripping the village of almost everything, they pulled him out of the dung heap, washed him off, and sent him on his way, back to his village, which he still remembered the name of though not the direction in which it lay.

The old woman told this story with great language and a bewildering variety of gesture, but also with her voice, now loud with terror to imitate the bragging of the bandits, now soft with compassion for the kidnappers and the boy. And at the end, waving her hands into the imaginary landscape, she recited, simply, the words I will always remember, "That boy, who became a man, and a good one, too, was my dearest friend and my husband. But his voice will still shake the world slightly when he laughs, and I will still tremble a little when I remember him."

There is no moral to this story. Perhaps there is, but I don't want to attempt to create one. It is a story pulled out of the endlessly curved string of memory, no more fantastic than any of the other possibilities which daily confront us but still resonant in me as I remember my journey.

Ivana Curcic

Age 35. Mathematics teacher
Belgrade, Yugoslavia

No. 152: Arhus, Denmark. February 3, 1700. [3 months; $325] How you know how to cheat and lie, how you have learned to withhold information and parcel it out to your advantage. You use others, and then, when you are finished with them, excuse yourself from their company.

But your abilities have their limits. It is impossible, in a small town like Arhus, to continue for long without getting at least a bit of a reputation. People are beginning to close in on you, avoid you, even talk about you behind your back. And you are beginning to feel nervous. Your wife has moved away from you, if not physically, then emotionally. Your brother, his wife, your uncle, and your grandfather have hardly spoken with you for the last six months.

It is apparent that you must do something, but you do not know what to do. How can you undo the habits and actions of so many years? You have contemplated running away, but where would you go, and how would you leave? And worst of all, you do not really want to change. You actually enjoy doing what you do, and you cannot contemplate another way of acting toward others. Yet something, something must be done, and very soon, too.

Dear Past Rentals,
It was a temporary solution, I tell you. His problem will never be solved, except by suicide, if that is any kind of solution. He had been at it too long and it had become so much a part of him that giving it up would have been like giving up his breath. An addict saying no to heroin? A lifetime smoker suddenly giving up tobacco? Impossible.

So he compromised, at least on the surface. He began, however difficult it was for him, to tell the truth, offer help, quietly, so his actions would not be noticed much but still noticed, and noticed, talked about. He gave, not much, but something and did not make a point of giving. Yet he knew people would notice, and of course they did, just enough to lift the edge of his reputation. For over two months he continued in this way, giving, helping, but only a little, and quietly.

This was certainly a calculated action, but it was also a desperate one, for inside him his behavior cost him great pain. He actually forced himself to be honest, generous, and helpful. When he acted, to hold back the forces inside him which were ready to burst out in all directions, he had to recite to himself exactly what he was going to think, say, and do, acting out in advance his little drama. Alone in the fields or inside the barn, he would be forced to say what he was thinking, say to himself his exactingly private thoughts.

Of course, he released some tension in this way. And people did begin to notice and talk. Still, his grandfather, his brother, and his wife remained aloof, biding their time, preparing their judgment. Even here, when they witnessed his actions or heard about them from others, they did not accept even this small amount of change. But they did store within them all the basic positive acts he "committed". And these acts of his did begin to weigh in his favor.

Of course he knew what he was doing. He was too calculating a person not to know. But he also knew that what he was doing was indeed impossible. He could not believe in the goodness of others and in his own goodness, at least enough to carry off deceiving himself, for once deceived, he would be able to deceive the others. And in the last few weeks, when he meticulously rehearsed his little plays before acting them out, he also began to rehearse his "older" self, the one dying to break out and soothe him with familiarity. Those actions of the "past" were acted out as a counterweight to his future actions of pretended good, and they came to be more artful, more beguiling, more fully real than these little charades. He was a man who had fallen down a steep slope and in trying to climb back could not gain a firm foothold—the earth kept slipping beneath him.

I did not stay to see his eventual, now almost absolutely predictable, fall. But it was coming as sure as the tides would rise with the moon. He was indeed helpless. The emptiness was again entering him. He was falling, even in his dreams. But his denial, the dyke he had carefully placed before the overwhelming sea of appearance, was finally breaking, a crack here and a crack there. No, nothing could save him, except a complete collapse.

Now that I have returned, I see people like this all the time or, at least, more and more, or at least I think I see them. I am haunted by their collapse, their fragility, their desperation. And I am frightened at my inability, in any way, to help them strengthen themselves, to help them move in a correspondingly humane direction. I am not this person, I say, but how many of them are there out there, how many?

Ingrid Petterson
Age 66. Gardener
Norrkoping, Sweden

No. 153: Greifswald, Germany. March 27, 1557. [3 hours; $50] You are a seven-year old girl who was blinded two years ago from an accident; your eyes were seriously burned in a fire. You accept your blindness. What else can you do? Every day, you are careful to perform your duties, as much as you can. You will carry your own weight.

You do everything with great deliberation. The way you wash

yourself, sit at the table, or eat—all is performed with a grace that comes only with a long and deep awareness of the body and its movements, an awareness, indeed, that dates from your birth.

Though you cannot see your father and mother and brother eating with you, you imagine them eating with the same deliberate motions you use. And the others—you imagine them through your own actions. They become you, or you enter them through the projections of your bodily awareness.

You feel your body sitting on the stool and sense the weight and texture of the spoon you lift to your lips. You feel the coarse wood of the table and in summer the warmth from the tongue of sunlight in the open doorway and the sounds of the other children passing outside in the little village which you know by your smell and touch and hearing.

But most of all, you listen to and speak with all kinds of people, old and young, sick or well. You love talking with them, and you talk and talk until your mother takes you by the arm and brings you home.

But it is especially with your grandmother that you like to exchange the sound of words. Today she is in the kitchen, where you help her with the midday meal. As you work, you speak, quietly and yet deliberately. The light comes in through the open window, the shudders are drawn back, and the kitchen, though it is still late March, is warm.

Dear Past Rentals,

She was such a good girl, such a wonderful light to everybody. Oh, that I had such a daughter—warm and delightful and understanding and with a desire to bind us all together in a warm ball of sunlight, to hold us close through the net of her voice. Such a daughter is a jewel. Though she is blind, what does it matter? My daughter is blind, though she "sees" or thinks she sees, wandering around the house, all

thirteen years of her, blind as midnight, but with the arro-
gance of those who think they can see.

Not a word to me my daughter speaks which shows me
she sees anything. From dresses to swimsuits, from gossip to
dance tunes, she dresses down the world, dresses it down, not
up, pulls a curtain over it and never shows her feelings. She
eats as daintily as a bird and then goes off to gorge herself
with junk food. She talks exaggeration behind everyone's
back, even behind her supposed best friend's back and behind
mine I am told. She does nothing, but pretends to be doing
everything. She "presents" herself when she wants attention
but cannot present herself when others need help. She is
indeed blind, totally blind, and yet she has eyes.

Oh, this girl, if she were my own, I would give my life, my
heart for her. I would be filled with her voice, with her warm
voice, even in the depths of winter, and I would be made
whole again, instead of this dishrag which my daughter has
made of me.

Andrea Catano
Age 39. Debutante
Rome, Italy

No. 154: Satun, Malasia. November 25, 335. [3 hours; $65] Although
you do not live in Satun, it is a place you return to for days on end,
drawn to the conversations with the old men, there near the sea.
Although you are not old yourself, scarcely thirty, you feel a need
to be with them, for there is something about their style which
opens you, and even though they taunt you, call you a person
who has no desire to change—a "ne'er-do-well," a "beachcomber,"
"a lazy man"—you do not care; for when they begin to ignore you,
to talk among themselves about this and that, they forget your

existence, and you can sit back and listen to their fishing stories, their ruminations about youth, their travels (some of them), and the extended stories of their extended, eternally extended, families.

All the time away from them, further up the coast where you live alone, begging a few fish to eat and working now and then at one job or another, work that is not in your soul, you yearn for these circles of old men. Today you are returning to them, to the village of Satun, to listen, and be reviled for a short time, and then to become anonymous, and, of course, again, to listen.

No. 155: Genoa, Italy. March 3, 1116. [7 hours; $75] Today you are going to the feast of Saint Elias, patron saint of goldsmiths. You will spend most of the day with others of your guild and profession. Yesterday, your son and you swept up your shop, and undoubtedly, although you have not sifted any of the sweepings, you will find much gold (and silver), which you will, of course, use again. Although your wife and son will eat at home, by themselves, you know what you will be served at the banquet. It will be goose, chitterlings and jugged hare flavored with herbs, carp, boar's head and suckling pig, and glasses of claret to wash down your feast. You are looking forward to this great day.

No. 156: Los Teques, Columbia. February 3, 1886. [3 days; $175] You grew up in Los Teques, but when you were thirteen, your parents moved to Trujillo, a larger town, where your father found work as a butcher. By the time your parents died six years later in a flu epidemic, you had learned your father's business (you worked for him for three years almost every day) and also something about mathematics and engineering, as well as a little chemistry, a dabbler you thought of yourself at that time, but nevertheless a very intense and interested one. From Trujillo, you went to

Caracas, where at night you studied mathematics and engineering and chemistry.

But it was not until six years from your semi-academic beginnings—with one man who has remained your close friend to this day, Miguel Ortigas, and who "gave" you your education, almost free—that you were able to leave the world of study and enter the world of work. And though there were setbacks— the death of your first wife shortly after your marriage and the destruction of your house on the outskirts of Caracas—you rose steadily, but never too high in the economic ranks—there was too much jealousy around you.

For the past fifteen years you have lived a comfortable but not ostentatious life. However, in the last two or three years you have been drawn to the town where you were born, Los Teques, a small town, nothing special about it, dusty streets, clay houses, a school, a few churches. Of course, there doesn't have to be anything special about the town where you grew up; what is special is that you grew up there and the memory of childhood stays with you, like a bright, primary dye on the clothing of your life. Now, finally, after many delays, other turnings in your life, you are at last in Los Teques. You have just entered the town.

Dear Past Rentals,

What is home, anyway? Some insects have no home, at least the way we speak of it. Home exists only as something we would desire to return to. It is a kind of retreat, like a funk hole or, though perhaps not biologically necessary, like sleep, a comfort station of mind and body.

What makes it so ungraspable is that since adolescence we have been moving away from it, and only through the deliberate force of memory can we at least simulate a return. And we do, in ways that we are only faintly aware of. We marry and introduce the home on another level, using the assumptions of our childhood and our newfound knowledge and power to re-create what we think is our home. And it is.

But home goes deeper, much deeper. It is buried in our memory of the womb and even earlier, through an almost limitless regression, a stepping back through "deep time" to the origins of all living things and perhaps to the origin of the universe itself. (That's the big picture.) So the home we think of as home is only a way station, one of many homes, rest spots for the weary on their almost infinite regression to the beginning of beginnings in the search for all their origins.

But it is difficult to produce the intense memory of the home in which we were children, a home filled with parents and warmth and relatives and fears and surprises and sudden spurts of tenderness and retreat. There is too much of our vulnerability in that time capsule. One whiff of memory and we are back in a world we are now little prepared for, wandering through a time and place which only a child may manage and then only with help from others.

But the desire to return to that first home, because it marks a sense of completeness to our lives, is irresistible. That is why we return so late in life, never after we have left, never after marriage. Pushed, expelled, or projected from the warmth of our ten or fifteen or twenty years of comfort (as we were physically pushed from our mother's womb), we believe in our velocity toward a goal we cannot even imagine. We are blind to our backsides, see only what is ahead of us, and only later gain a 360 degree vision and only sometimes and only for some of us.

Our biological propulsion away from our homes is genetically necessary. We are pushed out, like the seedpod's germines, scattered or blown by some invisible wind inside us, to find ourselves on another shore, another soil, which we must cultivate by our presence. Only after we have opened our seed and produced our garden, sent out shoots ourselves, can we begin to open our backsides, our memories.

Los Teques was like all places seen from that vantage-point. Though it might appear to others as the dirtiest, dustiest, most distasteful place in the world, it was not to this man, whose body I entered for a short time. He carried within him its fructification. Here, he planted another seed, though one which will not grow, except inwardly. The parents may have been terrible, the friends an illusion, the beauty of the landscape untrustworthy. But all was swept away by the inward, implosive rush of memory, the bondings which held him in his own growth and the sights and sounds and smells which exploded inside and were absorbed into his cells, his vibratory molecules, his peculiar way of looking at and responding to the world, all things which have made him what he was, unable to pull himself away from these events because he and they were the same. It is indeed true that "the apple never falls far from the tree."

I, Francisco Jimenez, am an orphan. I had no parents. My mother died as I was screaming with birth, and my father was unknown to me and perhaps to my mother. I was raised by an institution, where my "parents" were other children and the adults were reduced to the status of caregivers. How will I return? What home do I have to return to? Where will I find my origins?

Francisco Jimenez
Age 56. Social worker
Guadalajara, Mexico

No. 157: Adelaide, Australia. May 3, 1784. [3 weeks; $300] You have come from England with your mother to this strange land by a two-month boat trip. Your mother, a convicted felon, has taken you with her. Her husband, your father, died slightly after he had gotten her pregnant with you.

You stand here with two bags in your hands, all the things you have in the world besides the clothes on your back, and look out at the new land you know you will die in some day. There on the dock, with a hundred other convicts, you wonder what you will do, as everyone else wonders the same. You are ten years old, a young, and relatively healthy boy.

No. 158: Sinop, Turkey. August 20, 1708. [One day; $115] From Antalya, where you were born, you wandered to Konya, then to Cihanbeyli, and on to Ankara, which was far too large a city, but in which you stayed for three years, somehow being able to study mathematics and history with a good teacher, who kept you for this time, though in poverty.

When you could no longer stand the noise and confusion of this monster of a city, you moved to Safranbolu, where, teaching this and that to children, you managed, with money you had saved, to move slowly northward, first to Artin, then to Daday, and finally, now, to Sinop, where you have been for twenty years, somehow having escaped both the terrors and the joys of marriage and having come as far north as you can go, a long journey to this small coastal town on the Black Sea, quiet yet filled with a continual hum of gossip.

You have moved through the shadows of this vast land in which you were born, through its skin, so its seemed, and its center, managing to appear almost inconspicuous, moving as you know, through the shadows of the social world as well, among men and women of all classes and conditions. And now to have come to this land's end, and in these last few years, now that you are almost fifty, to have continued dully teaching the young boys of this town, having made only a few friends, because, in your heart, you know that you are an outcast, someone who sees but does not change things, watching life go on around you like a shadow of an echo, a hint of things, almost a useless being.

But still there is this life, not without its strong virtues, this borderline existence among half-strangers and almost-friends. It is the virtue of looking that you enjoy, the delight in being in a kind of middle distance, storing the memories of innumerable passages within the warp and weft of events, of time and its magical distances. Allah, the merciful one, will understand you, for you are a part of his wandering, he, too, the wanderer, the partly absent one. Today you sit for a while and then move slowly through the town, stopping, beyond the tight confines of the passageway in which you find yourself, to stare out at the bright slit of the sea and then, turning your back, look with profound disinterest at the few people going by on their half-serious errands. You even watch a small funeral procession pass you, as you stand in the shade of a woodworking shop for a moment in the intense light and warmth and clarity of August.

No. 159: Atlantic Ocean. May 27, 1679. [3 days; $175] Born in Portugal and a sailor most of your life, you are now working on the Santa Inez, a Portuguese slaving ship which has taken aboard it African men, women, and children and placed them in shackles in the slave quarters below, sunless, hot and salt-dry, where many of them, you know, will die of disease, if not from the meager food you dole out every day or from the rotten water you give them to drink. But slavery is profitable and you are promised a good share of the profits from this voyage, and, besides, your family is not doing well in your country. You have steeled yourself twice already—this is your third voyage—and after this one you want no other.

It has been hot the last few days, and the stench below has gotten worse, even though the slaves are brought up once a day on deck so that they may relieve themselves. Some of them were almost dead this morning when they came topside, barely able to be dragged up by their chains, and cursing them does not help. What will you do with the dead, for you are sure there will be many, perhaps half the slaves who came aboard from the coast. You sit on deck, watching and waiting, and imagine, again, as on the other voyages, the price you must pay to feed your family.

Dear Past Rentals,

What pain inside a sailor's heart? And there was pain inside this man, great pain, pain even worse than the pain of other, more "normal" sailors, which was great enough in those days. But, nevertheless, pain greatly suppressed, stuffed full of thoughts of the future, of the life of his family in Lisbon—or was it Coimbra he hailed from? Everything but the present, the herding of people, an occupation far from common even among the Portuguese poor, sucked dry and required, for their own salvation, to sail across an insane ocean and, as desperate people themselves, to deal with others locked up and practically starving, certainly diseased and dying. It was a wonder the sailors themselves survived under their own conditions, let alone those of the slaves.

But there was a conflict within him, and that suppressed battle, that argument that went on in the lower levels of his psyche, made him, if not an angry man, at least a one-dimensional sailor whose thoughts flowed toward Portugal, not toward the holds of the ship and its terrible cargo.

But those sailors did irrupt, in anger, at the human cargo they were carrying. His dreams, which I can attest to, were terrible. They were like those of Macbeth who, after killing the king, is haunted, along with his wife, by those "terrible dreams that shake us nightly," allowing only a fitful sleep and, during the day, a preoccupation with the unraveled elements of his conscience, a continual battle to push those feelings out of sight and mind.

*Even the brawls, which were blamed on the slaves—
though locked in the hold they could not have provoked anything—turned them against their cargo, blaming the Africans
for the "whole stinking mess," especially during the hot,
almost windless days when the hold stank and the odor of old
or rotting flesh rose to the deck. They beat them, but it didn't
help and they knew it. Nothing would help him, my sailor,
except to return to his city and work as a fisherman or a
carpenter or a tile maker, at anything but this filthy nightmare.*

*While I was inside him, one dream itched at the scalp of
his psyche, itched where he could not get at it. To escape from
this terrible ghost that had entered his life, he worked harder,
worked so hard he almost collapsed. It was a repeated image
of millions of slaves, who had become the waters of the ocean,
rising up in the form of a giant mouth, to devour the ship, a
mouth hundreds of meters high which repeatedly swallowed,
not only the slave ship, O Incarnacion, but also the armadas
of ships traveling westward with their human cargoes. And
when the mouths, in the form of a wave, retreated, they left a
dense saliva whose odor turned his skin to parchment, not
like the sun, but rather as if the water were an acid slowing
dissolving his tissues, not to the bone but to the heart, the
feelings, even to the memory of the half-rotting past within
him. Again and again the waves rose until he could no longer
bear to look at the ocean. Then, in this dreaming, he vomited
up his past, image by image, until there was left only a darkness from which the stars had been puffed out and the darkness itself a cold gelatin which fell on him, making his body
shiver until the whole slave ship began to shake and the
timbers loosened and he fell into the mouth of the giant maw
which haunted him.*

*Yes, the slaves suffered more than he did, much more.
They died, physically died, though half of them survived,*

barely. But the nightmare was loosed and there was no stopping it once it began. Though the others seemed to show nothing, how could they help but be infected by the same disease, the same visions? That boat was more than their prison, though it was that, too. But, I am sure, long after he returned to his native city, the dream persisted and made him a kind of living corpse, all the warmth of his natural feelings having been taken out of him and replaced by an emptiness, as it was, I suppose, in the others, poisoning the land also, since they found no relief from their suffering.

I traveled with this man because I have also, in a very small way, mind you, been a prisoner of my work. I have toiled as a clerk in Ankara for twenty years, confined to an office where the records of the dead are kept. I had to file them away and account for each one, every working day, for twenty years, and the atmosphere is so like a tomb I could no longer hear the traffic passing in the street above me, and even the sounds of others passing in the hallways were muffled, absorbed into the stone of the building, until the world outside was no longer a world and going home had become like going to work, not home to freedom at the end of a day or on a weekend, but a journey to another part of the prison.

I have "escaped," fortunately, and am now retired on a small, a very small, pension. I am out of that soundless world with its own kind of nightmare. Yet still, in dreams, I wander through those long, silent corridors, muffled and dumb like the dismal forms I placed in the files, one by one, like the dead whose names were buried, as were their bodies, in this tomb, for a second time.

Niyazi Misri
Age 71. Former clerk in the Office of the Dead
Ankara, Turkey

No. 160: Yermolayevo, Ukraine. Somewhere near the Belaya River. February 27, 1779. [3 hours; $45] You have been a peasant since you were born, as was your father and your father's father. There is nothing different about you to distinguish you from other peasants, except a certain desire to carve wooden figures of the saints on winter evenings in the small hut you and your family, your wife and two children, a son and daughter, inhabit, all of you sleeping on straw with ticks in it and eating from the single pot over the immense stove on which, in the winter, you all sleep.

When you drink, and it is often, you beat your wife—it is expected of you, you are a peasant and peasants beat their wives and their children also—but it is strange, somehow, the remorse you feel afterwards. And, as always, afterwards, you beg your wife's forgiveness, down on your knees, holding her legs, telling her, swearing by all the saints that you will never, never do what you did that night. Of course, you know that all the other peasants near Yermolayevo do the same thing the day after they have gotten drunk, but that does not stop you from doing it, too. God is merciful, and you are blessed for your actions, though you may beat your wife until she almost cannot get up and you are so tired and confused you lie down from exhaustion.

But this last year—you are now forty-one—something has taken hold of you, some spirit. You do not beat your wife and children any more. Instead, you get drunk and look at them, longingly, indeed, look through them, at something beyond their bodies, some spirit you feel you are communicating with. At times, in your drunkenness, you speak to this spirit because there is in your mind one spirit and protective of each person, and that spirit you need to communicate with through your own spirit, and that spirit you see is behind you, in a place you cannot see. God is merciful. He gives you your spirit; he speaks through your spirit. And when you have spoken with God and the spirits have vanished, as they will after a while, you grow confused and fall on the floor and sleep.

It is an evening in late February, and you have come home, after visiting the local vodka dispensary, still with a bit of that "spirit" left in your bottle, winding your way along the road under the moon three-quarters full between the snowdrifts in the white farmland of winter to the warm home where your wife and children and their spirits, with whom you will speak tonight, are waiting.

Dear Past Rentals,

Was this guy fooling himself, believing he could give up boozing just like that, once he'd "seen the light" or whatever I thought he saw when I went on your trip. It's not that easy; it's never easy. I know because I'm a recovering alcoholic who's been on the wagon for fifteen years (still recovering), and it's not even easy now. Part of my desire to enter this guy's life was to experience what it's like to stop, stop doing all those terrible things this guy, you said, did, like beat his wife and children. I wanted to remember what I went through when I stopped. I wanted to experience the pain again. I'm not a guy who likes pain—I'm not that way—but I felt it was necessary to remember.

And I was also curious about the visions you said he had, visions of some spirit behind each person, a kind of guardian angel. Funny, but I believe in that stuff, I really do. I can't explain it, but I can almost see it at times, even when I'm walking down the street and I look at the people coming toward me, all kinds, happy or sad or old or young. And sometimes I see something around them, a kind of light. At first I thought I was having the DT's again, but I knew that was impossible because I hadn't had a drink in fifteen years. But when it kept happening again and again, I began to get into it and look—I guess that's the word I want to use—but it was also a kind of feeling looking hearing smelling tasting experience, everything at once coming at me and glowing.

This guy had the same experience. I couldn't believe it at first, but it was there. I watched him feeling the bodies of people glowing in that incredible cold that only a Russian winter could make. Everyone was glowing, and it wasn't from all the vodka they drank—everyone drank it. It was something else, like the Northern Lights I guess.

He thought of this glow as "spirits," and at first I made the connection with the vodka. That seemed logical. But he had stopped drinking weeks ago, in fact, as soon as he realized it wasn't the DT's coming back at him or some vision the devil had placed in his way to tempt him. He began to be filled with joy—that's the only word that fits what he felt, joy.

But he had another stage to overcome, just as I did when I noticed the glow in people. He had to get beyond the "conversion" stage, for right then, when I came into his life, he was hot to tell everyone and get them to see it, too. But they wouldn't—I know—and he would try harder, in fact, want to beat it into them, and then he would be back at the place he started, the beating, not the beatitude, not the holiness. I don't know if he got beyond the recognition stage, but I sure hope he did. It's hard to tell about people, whether they'll make it or not. You have to sit back and watch them and not interfere. And who knows why some make it and some don't.

Cesar Braeckman
Age 49. Janitor
Oostende, Belgium

No. 161: Alula, Somalia. March 3, 1877. [5 hours; $85] What is it to be a poor merchant, to look out on the Gulf of Aden day after day in search of the land beyond, which you cannot see? And the heat!

It is almost unbearable. No wind, or even a breeze, only the warm ocean and, west of where you are, the powerfully hot land. You are near the cape of the Horn of Africa, near Cape Guyardaful. The boats that round it on their way up the Red Sea are usually Dhows from Lower Juba and also from as far down as Mombasa, a long journey, and longer still through the Red Sea.

Some of the Dhows unload at Alula, some continue further west to the towns of Andala, Bosaso, Malf, and Karinon on their way to Djibouti. You were in Djibouti once, and it seemed to you a big city, poised as it is on the Bab el Mendeb, the passageway into the vast Red Sea.

What else can you do here but gossip with everybody? It is one of the only real pastimes, as it is in other small towns along the coast. People come and go. A trickle of news comes through. When it comes, you will hear it, a trickle at a time, sitting at a small cafe overlooking the Gulf with a few friends and a cup of strong coffee and sometimes, when you have a little money, smoking a hookah, either tobacco or hashish (you prefer hashish).

Today you are sitting with two friends at the cafe, drinking your small cup of strong coffee and, fortunately, for you have made a little money this month, smoking a little of the hashish which has come by boat from Kenya. There is the ocean in front of you and there are the boats passing, and a few more boats offshore.

No. 162: Bialowieza, Poland. March 3, 1821. [6 days; $575] You have come here at last, all twenty-five years of you, to live in the Bialowieza forest, in Eastern Poland, the last virgin forest in Europe, the remains of what once was an immense kingdom of trees covering most of Europe from northern Italy to Scandinavia.

Then, in that vast kingdom, people lived the life of the forest, worshipped the gods of the forest, and breathed the air of the forest. Now, cities and farms have obliterated its memory; and the people, too, who live in these places where once the forest peoples lived now think and feel differently.

What attracted you to this place (you are not even Polish or Russian) was something negative—a disgust with the cities and with your own childhood, growing up on a farm in northern France. There, the trees are new, perhaps at most a hundred years old, and when you enter these "pieces of wood" as your father contemptuously called them, you emerge a short time later, again into rolling hills and farmland. Looking south, you can imagine this landscape of forest going on for hundreds of miles, indeed all the way to the Mediterranean.

And though you have spots of fond memory of the farm and village in which you grew up, there is another side to you which craves the older world, which you sensed, even as a boy, when you walked through these thinned out woods and open fields planted with everything except trees and acorns.

For hours you have been approaching this remnant of the vast, ancient forest. There it is, ahead of you—you know it well. A feeling of welcome comes over you, the forest welcoming you and you welcoming the forest inside you. You know this is your home, the place where a large part of your heart belongs, not all of it, but a large part of it. You feel relieved, even as you approach it from miles away, relieved even more with each step you take toward it, your home, your mother, your ancestors, your long history.

> Dear Past Rentals,
>
> Yes, what was that forest like, the one that covered almost all of Europe a thousand years ago? It's almost all gone, that original growth. And I hope you offer a trip to America back when the forest was still there. They said that when Columbus landed in the New World, the forests were so thick that a squirrel could have gone from the Atlantic to the Mississippi without touching land. And now look at it, or

them, all the forests, cut down, hardly any original growth left, and in such a short time, too.

I'm glad somebody wanted to see what it was really like, though I think he was eventually going to realize that it really was gone and he would, only in his imagination, be able to recreate what that world was really like, though I don't know, having been with him for only six days. Maybe his imagination merged with the forest and made it larger. I hope so.

I've been tramping through forests for twenty-five years and have come to know them, lots of them. I've made it my life's work and my life. I've seen Alaskan forests, mid-latitude hardwood forests, scrub forests, tropical forests, timberline growth, washed out land where forests used to be, fossilized trees, trees a hundred million years old—I've seen almost all of them. And they're all beautiful and all a great and wonderful mystery.

But I've missed the old growth. Of course, you can still go to British Columbia and Alaska and the fast disappearing forests of the Amazon and Ecuador and to Siberia and what they call there the taiga and see it as it was or as it is. But you have to travel a long way, and you shouldn't have to do that. The forest should be next door, the way it was in 1840 in western Oregon or even in northern California at that time. Trees that stood for centuries, bears and mountain lions and wildcats and skunks and beaver and birds you couldn't believe existed in such numbers. They were there.

I'm not a loner. I like people, like their sweat and their swearing and their mistakes and their faults and successes. I've tried living the life of a hermit, first in Alaska out on the Kenai twenty-five years ago and later inwards from Knight Inlet where the Bella Coola live and have lived for thousands of years. But I needed people, as much as I love the forest and the quiet and the wind and the rain and the storms and the wood fires in the cabin. No, a clearing is a good thing, but too big a clearing is not, and that's what we've got today, too big a clearing, too much of a manufactured wilderness where all the important things are done at a distance—from people, from animals, from storms and warm weather, from trees, from forests, for the body.

This guy was returning to some earlier time. He was putting himself into the spirit of those trees and the shade and the sunlight and the wind that had visited them for a long time. He was going to be content. I hope he found what he was looking for, even if it might have taken a large chunk of imagination to do it in such a small forest, to imagine one that was so much bigger then.

I guess it won't come as a surprise to you what I'm going to tell you next. On Wednesday I'm leaving for that forest. I know I won't find much—I'm not expecting much either. But since I've been there through your catalog entry, I think I'll go there myself this time. I've got a lot of imagination stored in me now.

Kent Feldspar Anderson
Age 57. Freelance environmental planner
Eugene, Oregon

No. 163: Coventry, England. April 6, 1731. [6 hours; $80] You are in rags and almost penniless. Your children are starving and your husband has been sent to the poorhouse, for he, like you, has squandered his wages on drink, specifically gin, its cost placed on the tally and taken out of his wages at the end of the week. And you, too, must have it—there is no end to this misery—two, three, four glasses a day, a bottle when you can get it. What does it matter? You will lie in the gutter and drink or drink at the Geneva house nearby when you have the money, or buy it from almost anyone. Your children are going to the poorhouse. And you are going to hell, to hell, with your gin bottle, weaving your way on the street, which moves, rather than you.

And, of course, you are not the only one. All of them are drunk, and even your children want it—you've seen to that. Maybe the dysentery won't come, but the food is not on the table, and your children tell you they are hungry and you don't care. No, you don't care.

You are at the Geneva shop today because you have got some money from a man whom you persuaded to come home with you last night, five shillings, and it will all go for the gin. Then, you will beg again, and it will never end, until you get to hell, the street to hell paved with all the gin bottles in the world.

No. 164: Talsi, Lithuania. May 31, 1833. [3 hours; $75] You are ten, the daughter of a carpenter who has been known for several years as a fine cook and an expert in dying cloth. For three years you have raised a pet kestrel, a wild bird which you have had from almost the time he was born. He is often tied by one of his legs to a tall stake in front of your house. He and you have been great friends. When you loosen him from your hand and watch him disappear in the distance, you know, always, that he will return.

Now, ten days ago, you came out to find him lying on the ground—a good thing the dogs hadn't discovered him; they would have torn him apart—dead, from what, you do not know. All day and the next your heart sank, heavier than a stone. You saw and felt nothing except your loss. Your great friend was dead—that was all you knew. At night you fell asleep crying. Your friends could not console you, nor could the adults—parents, aunt, grandmother and grandfather—even as they promised you another bird, a kestrel even. No, they could not stop your tears.

After a week of grief and grieving, you decided to bury your friend. This was fine with everyone, but when you proposed a funeral, a long procession and everyone wearing pieces of black, in mourning, the adults smiled, almost outwardly laughing at you, a child who wanted a funeral for her friend, just like those for people in the village.

But through their smiles they, too, felt something; for they had had their own pets who had died and they had buried them also, thinking of some ceremony but never proposing it or putting it in action. Somehow they had felt that yes, this is what they, too, had all wanted. There were words they had wanted to say to the animal that had been their friend—dog or wolf or bird or pig—whatever it might have been. But they were at first too embarrassed to ask for that ceremony or prepare a funeral or a funeral speech.

However, when the day of the funeral ceremony arrived and the children, your friends, had begun to assemble in the procession, which was to come to rest somewhere near a low hill on the edge of the village, the adults, all of them wearing black, fell in behind the long line of mourners, as had been prescribed.

All of you, children, adults, and the old grandmothers and grandfathers even, had something to say inside them, that was not said many years ago or, more recently, about the death of the beloved animal they had lived with. You were at the front of the procession, and you would speak first.

Dear Past Rentals,

I'm so happy you made this catalog entry. I think it was done for me and maybe some of my friends. I'm only sixteen, but your journey taught me a lot about pets. I felt so happy for the people, especially for the kids, because they got to say good-bye to their pet birds or their pet cat or dog or whatever. I just cried and cried inside that girl. And yet I felt so happy that she and all her friends and the adults were also there.

When I returned, six weeks later, my yellow finch,

Mamasu, died. I think she just got to be too old. I found her on the floor of her cage (a cage I made for her three years ago when I got her from my uncle), and I held her in my hands and cried, harder than I cried when I went to Lithuania. Of course, I had told my friends about my trip on your junior program. They were the ones who suggested a funeral for Mamasu. And, of course, the adults were smiling, just like they did in your entry. But we all got together with them and told them about my trip, and when we finished they weren't smiling in the same way. When we had the funeral—it was on a hillside near our village—they all came. They all brought something to lay on Mamasu's grave, and all my friends did, too. And we all said something about our pets. It was just like it was in the journey to Lithuania. I felt better afterwards.

    Konde Kouyate
    Age 16
    Gagnoa, Ivory Coast

No. 165: Galap, Palau. April 22, 1025. [3 hours; $75] Thirty-seven years old now, you have lain in bed awake for the last few months, off and on, half thinking, half seeing, half feeling forces, moods, shapes, configurations which you have either repressed or never seen, vague riders let loose by the night, the seams of your life opening, and something entering into you, expanding.

At first they were small, these intimations of a kind of beyond, but they have grown and grown until in the middle of the night they fill you completely. There was a moment, rather a few hours, three weeks ago, when you were terrified, and you lay till dawn, looking, immobilized by the experience.

But gradually you have grown to welcome them, these perceptions, which are always different but remain strangely the same, for you have felt yourself growing, as large as the world they represent, far larger than your tiny island in the Pacific, far larger indeed than the whole world itself, with, it seems to you now, its petty rumbles, its tiny voices, its endless successions of day and night, and the common rounds of activity, work, and the social courtesies.

Though these are not gone and you know they will continue until you die or your son works for you and you may sit and dream over the fuming ocean which surrounds you, these messengers of necessity have taken on a new significance in comparison to the nightly visions which come upon you until you cannot wait for them to arrive.

Tonight, however, your wife is sick, and moans, turning over again and again in her semi-sleep, adding now this other dimension to your nightly visitations. Perhaps she, too, is dreaming the same dreams.

> *Dear Past Rentals,*
>
> *I know it's a big subject, dreams, but I want to suggest that dreams have a history parallel to history. Yes, dreams come and go. They arise through something in our daytime life and emerge, veiled and transformed, in that other world of expanded sleep. They are a kind of conversation we enter into with the waking world. Two worlds go on, parallel to each other, and at times, merge, and when they do, something else expands in us.*
>
> *I think we could establish a history of dreams. Dreams are a byproduct of history. They occur because history happens. They are a construct, just as history is a construct, for history is, after all, an abstraction, like a line or a point in geometry. We construct it because it is somehow necessary. And dreams, also, we construct, or our inner processes construct them for their own purposes. If so, then a history of those sleep-driven experiences is possible, except, I must add,*

for one important element shakes up and blurs this comparison: Dreams cannot be easily accessed and recorded. I put aside for the moment the problems of interpretation. But they are a world parallel to the waking one and in that sense can be seen as a further commentary on daily life, on stretches of time, on history.

Your entry No. 165 (Galap, Palau) provided me with a chance to see the historical dynamics of dreaming. The man in this entry nightly reached out beyond his tiny island in the Pacific toward other places, other situations. His isolation troubled him. Others moving about the globe passed through him like shadows, all with a history. He saw and heard them—I might say, like your catalog entries—speaking on all levels and in various orders of suggestive keys and commentaries. A particular woman, far off in Guadalajara, a widow of three months, revealed an account of three generations of her family—a farmer in the first, a merchant in the second, and a minor official in the third. Another, in Colombo, in what is now Sri Lanka, wordlessly reminded him of the ritual of washing and then led him onto the "journey into the soiled body," people everywhere through history, unwashed, incapable of washing, or else ignorant of it. A third voice led him toward a catalog of journeys, short and long, purposeful and purposeless, journeys through vast deserts, travelers who perished in the snow of high mountains and lay there, perfectly preserved beneath twenty feet of ice, travelers with people and travelers apart from people.

These parts of the dream world, echoes of the waking world, commentaries on history, repetitions and overtones of events, broaden and shape all levels of perception. If they could be brought together, if the data could be assembled, we would have another history, a further commentary on a combined, much larger historical panorama, which would reveal further levels of community.

Tao Yan Ming
Age 39. Anthropologist's helper
Xian, China

Dear Past Rentals,
History is a tricky subject, and you people at Past Rentals know it better than most. It's a slippery one because it's mostly a re-creation, based on what looks like definite information, of course, but one which includes the creator, the historian. Historians would not admit that they make up history as they go, that it's a complete fabrication (although some have done so, presented history as myth). But many would say that they play a part in its presentation. Two historians may operate from similar materials, have similar assumptions, and live in the same "historical period". And they may present different pictures. Of course, that's true of everyone. Two witnesses to the same accident (who says it's the same?) may have two differing opinions about it. People see each other differently. Or someone who happens to be transported to a different culture sees through the eyes of his own social assumptions. Agreement can be thought of as a "leap into faith," to borrow a famous phrase. That world of the common is a very slippery one, and some philosophers have argued that that world does not exist.
But I want to go one step further. Someone could, and perhaps has, put one over on us and written an historical account that is pure fabrication and makes us believe it through its inner consistency and nothing else. Everything in his account is invented, and there is nothing different in his account from a work of historical fiction. Suppose I write a short history of the 630's in France. I create the names of people at that time. In some detail, I show them thinking and

acting, indicate their journeys, refer to things they wrote, to the food they ate, to people with whom that came into contact, etc. And if you had little access to knowledge of the period, you might believe everything you read, so much is taken on faith. That will to believe, to accept much that has the feel of consistency about it, adds to our identity, something which we cannot do without. And, I imagine (no pun intended) that much of that which we encounter in print is based on the gravitational attraction of the consistent, which rests on a whole set of known and unknown assumptions we have absorbed from birth.

Past Rentals, I challenge you to present such an item, to hide it within your next catalog, and wait for the reactions; and you will get them, letters from people who will claim to have "discovered" much in their travels. The entry would reveal the tenacious grip with which we cling to that consistency, and, simultaneously, it would lift the lid on the "real" world.

Andre Kertesz
Age 40. Farmer
The Puzsta, Hungary

No. 166: Lini, China. November 4, 986. [2 hours; $30] Now, after the harvest is in, the tax collector will come. He will take much and you will live on what you have hidden, the way you hid your sons when the recruiting officer came two years ago.

The recruiting officer took away many from your village, as he had done for years before that, young men, and older men, too, taken away to fight at the northern wall against the barbarians. Gone, cut down, never to see their families again. How long will it go on, the endless deaths, the endless separations? The emperor is strong, yet the northern barbarians will take from you more than the emperor and his officials will steal.

What can a poor peasant do? The ancestors do not hear. No one hears. Only the endless sorrow, like the rain, the eternal rain on the fields of the barren winter hills. The sorrow of the Middle Kingdom. The sorrow of the peasants, the sorrow of the vast ocean of the people who inhabit this land.

You are in your hut when the tax collector comes. One of your sons, the youngest, is at home. The other is away in another village.

No. 167: Pompeii, Italy. October 4, 195 B.C. [8 hours; $105] Being a servant for a wealthy merchant in Pompeii, you are now engaged in preparing the evening meal for about ten people, family and guests alike. You have eaten little since the cena. Like others in your town, you do not eat much during the day. The evening meal is important. The guests and the family will eat in the trichenium. After the guests seat themselves, you will bring round the ewers with water, with which they will wash themselves. Then, they will be served hors d'oeuvres of pickled sow's udders and oysters from Jarentium. For the main course, they will have roast dormice sprinkled with honey and pollyseed fritters and later some dried fruit. They will eat heavily, and afterwards the guests will show their appreciation by belching as loudly as they can. After dinner, you will see them dicing by the light of an oil lamp, and then they will go to bed. Meanwhile, you will have a chance to eat what leftovers the cook has saved you. You will put everything away, and then you will go to bed.

No. 168: Somewhere near Choyren, Mongolia. September 10, 1501. [12 hours; $70] You are fifteen, a young Mongolian who set out this morning very early so that he might arrive toward evening at his uncle's yurt sixty miles from his home. It is not a long ride—you have ridden much further in a day—and you have taken food to eat, good food, which will sustain you. But you have lingered on the trail.

You are seized with the spirit of autumn. In the afternoon, after eating lunch, you lay down and slept. When you awoke, you remained for a while looking at the low hills in the distance and the small white clouds above them. Now you have stopped again, to look. The hills are closer but still distant, for the plains of your land are immense. During the winter you do not wish to stop and look. It is a different landscape.

But beyond these facts, which determine your life because they control the rhythms of your body, you are feeling your eighteen years, which inflate you beyond your body, a feeling you sense as a loss of boyhood, a time when you lingered, not knowing why, but as children do, just lingered.

Today, even your horse wants what you want, not to rest, but to feel everything around you, not in the mind, but in the body, to be connected with everything in your life, but primarily with the unmeasurable, immense joy of the plains of this giant, slowly rolling land in which you, in this lifetime, have found yourself.

No. 169: Malanje, Angola. March 3, 1927. [3 weeks; $575] You are an eighteen year old Mormon missionary who has now spent about six years in Malanje, Angola about 400 miles inland from Luanda on the coast and about five days journey from the largest town. Missionary work was expected of you; you knew you were going to go somewhere to work with and to convert people to Christ and Mormonism. Though you had some idea of the difficulties this would involve, these notions were mainly abstract. In effect, it was what was expected of you; the great unknown of your adolescence lay out there, with all sorts of feelings and ideas floating through it. God called you less than your body did. And so it was with all the young men of Ogden, Utah, your home. Some of your friends from high school were off to New South Wales, some to India, others to China.

You had always had a fascination with the tropics, or what you thought was the jungle, and so, more unconsciously than not, you picked Angola, which you thought was right in the middle of the hottest, steamiest jungle in the world. You traveled by train to New York, where the Mormon mission put you on a boat bound for Tangiers, where from there, you boarded boat after boat going south down the African coast, eating almost nothing because of the recurrent diarrhea you contracted.

You finally landed in Luanda after a series of boat trips lasting about two months. You passed the mouth of the Congo River in a fever, and when you finally debarked at Luanda and were met by your Mormon brethren, you had to spend three weeks recovering from your travels and the bodily disasters you had picked up on the way. Here you were, surrounded by black people everywhere, something you had never experienced in Ogden, even in New York City or in Morocco, and you spent days and days gazing at the people who passed you on the street, themselves staring at you in bewilderment and surprise, roused only now by the push of your desire to spread the gospel of Jesus Christ and his forgiveness to those who had not known his mercy. God was merciful, but you knew he was testing you. Why else would he have made you suffer so much on this journey?

Almost a week after you had recovered, off you went to Malanje, a five-day's trek which left you, again, wracked with stomach cramps and other disorders. But you arrived, finally, at the small village where there was a hut for you. The last missionary had suddenly departed for Utah, called, as they said, "by urgent business at home," and you have inherited his hut.

After four months, you learned some of the rudiments of the language, trying to "see" what is "going on with these people," whom you had no idea, not the slightest, of what they thought, felt, believed, feared, or desired—only what they did, or seemed to do. You fell to your knees each night, praying for their deliverance, but what they were, what they wanted, you were ignorant of. The greater your ignorance, the more you prayed, calling upon God to enlighten you, as if in a flash you would come to understand these people who had somehow "allowed" you to live among them, as if asking for deliverance.

Several months after you had arrived, you came upon a girl, naked, of course. (At first you could not have endured it, their nakedness, but now you have grown so accustomed to it, that it does not matter, though you proceeded in your chaotic activities fully clothed, oblivious of it.) Somehow, little by little, through gestures and small words and songs, she was chosen to help you because, as you could gather, they felt pity for you, isolated from your people, always on your knees and in a pitiful state of health, both in body and mind.

Over the next seven months she managed to teach you a great deal of the language, helping you learn about her people, finally sending you on hunting trips with the men. You played games in the village with the young boys, learned songs and stories about people and trees and animals, learned how best to sleep at night, how to protect yourself from insects and snakes, how to drink, to eat, to defecate even, and finally how to make love, quietly alone in the forest or in your hut with her. And beyond these you learned how to feel for others, how to communicate your desires, how to relax (which you had never learned before), how to be polite, and finally how to see everything living, even the earth and the sky and the rain, as well as the animals you had known, hunted, and eaten, learned to take pity on them who were killed so you and the others might eat and live.

At first you thought this young woman, graceful and quiet and assured yet firm in her purpose, was being sent by God to teach you; indeed, you firmly believed this at the beginning, at least for the first six months with her. But gradually you became accustomed to the world around you, to the continuous ceremonies, which, at first you would have considered monstrous, the long speeches and stories and songs, the women laughing and laughing until they fell over with uncontrollable mirth, every day the absorption of life through your pores, your intestines, and your dreams and the disgorging of those dreams to the young woman, who was now your significant, deep confidant, your controlling presence.

There were moments when you woke up shivering, thinking, "What am I doing? Why am I here? How have I turned away from God? What is God? Where do I belong?" Yet at times, dreaming of your home in Utah, remembering the dry, flat, and high, clear spaces of your boyhood among such a different people, you started yelling at the villagers, cursing them in English, which they, of course, did not understand, and they always, even the children, looked at you quietly, and then, after you had finished with your tirade, offered you a glass of weak beer to calm you down or perhaps some jungle tea to relax you, in your tears, your trembling, your hysteria.

And so, you noticed, it is with others in the village when they go berserk; they, too, were treated in the same way. You are no different. Your skin is different, but you are no different. God, you now believed, was clearly on their side, their compassion, their patience, their tolerance, and their knowledge, which, they feel, comes from knowing and being the world around them, something that had never entered you, except, abstractly, as doctrine, but now as something you know in your body, in your blood, in the larger vision of your selfhood.

After a year, your body became relaxed, almost fluid. Former vestiges of your earlier self all but faded and you laughed with the children at their games and even wept when someone was hurt or sick, learning a little how to comfort others or even how to tend them in their illness. You cried at funerals, at the passing of the old ones with whom you had eaten and with whom you had wept, and to whom you had told your stories and wandered with into the forest in search of game and plants and even danced with.

Clothing was no longer a problem. You now went around almost unclothed most of the time, though you had occasional "relapses" when you would appear totally clothed, as if asserting your other, earlier self. You no longer asked, "What has become of me? Where is God? What is my purpose?"; for you knew, somehow, what your purpose was, though you could not explain it.

Though there have been occasional white visitors, other missionaries who have come to see you in Malanje—you have "dressed up" for them, putting on an enormous show, all the more preposterous by being observed by your friends in the village (almost winking to them at times, or suppressing a wink)—you now knew that you did not, could not, return to your former life. God is understood, though he is ineffable. You have learned something which you do not care to lose, would not lose, even at the cost of your life, though letters, brought from the coast, arrived from home every month. These you answered, carefully, with great style, giving long accounts of "your village," the people here, the landscape, etc., but somehow leaving out the essence of life, which made it the central place of your spiritual existence. You lived a double life, then, giving long lip service to pious exclamations of virtue and religion (though you do not for once believe them) and at the same time allowed the non-verbal feelings, the inexpressible, to enter you.

But last week your father himself arrived on the coast, wanting you to return. The letters he sent, asking you to come back, at least for a while, had all but gone unanswered, at least were verbally turned away or avoided because you did not want to return, in fact, you could not return. The thought of entering that older world of your youth would now seem to you like entering this village for the first time, only more disastrous now, knowing what you now know. What will you do? How will you communicate with your father, whom you have not seen in these last six years. How will he understand your life here, which you must explain, putting aside all pretense, opening the veil in a few weeks which you have only opened these last few years? You call now upon the strength of your people, the people of the village, not upon the older God, but upon something larger, though you do not know how something can be larger than God. Now, your father has arrived. You are there to greet him.

No. 170: Southern Algeria, Tassili-n-Ajjer Plateau. March 1, 12,901 B.C. [3 hours; $75] You are an eleven year old boy who is now wandering with his family around the Tassili-n-Ajjer plateau, wandering slowly through these vast grasslands, as you have done for years, hunting and foraging. Animals of all kinds abound here. Your father and uncle hunt them, and now you accompany the men, walking the long distances, stalking the animals you will kill and eat, observing their habits, learning how to move among them, how to recognize the spoor of predators and the spoor of prey.

Danger, of course, is around you everywhere, and you must, as your father says, "be everywhere at once and still be in yourself". You do not think, you act. Everything seems to enter you through the skin. Even at night, camped on the plains, you must be "everything and still yourself," even when you sleep, even in your dreams, which will tell you where the animals are hiding.

You want so much to be like your father, your uncle, and other men you have seen hunting, who feel and see the sacred vision of the world. You, too, want to have these visitations. Twice you thought you had them. In your dreams you saw animals, immense plains filled with them. You saw one of them choose you, die for you, since that is its fate. You are completely attached to it now. It is yours, and you belong to each other. It is your fate, too.

You have come to the great cave at Tassili-n-Ajjer, high on

the plateau where your father is about to show you something he thinks you are now ready to see; you are now old enough to see it. He knows of your visions, and also of the knowledge that has been pouring into you for years, and he feels that you are ready to see them, the animals painted on the cave walls, the magic animals which will renew you. They will show you the immemorial hunt, whose rhythm is the rhythm of the world in which you have your existence, which breathes into itself as you breathe it into you. Now, the cave.

No. 171: Rome, Italy (the Vatican). December 1, 1281. [5 hours; $100]
For thirteen years you have been a scribe attached to Pope Nicolas III, starting, as you did, when you were twelve. During your years of employment with his Holiness, you have, on occasions, come into contact with the Jews of Rome as well as Jews from other areas around the Mediterranean. Although at first you did not speak or read Hebrew, the language of the Jews, you still wanted to translate into Latin some of their works.

Finally, after years of study, first by yourself and then with learned Jews of your city, you mastered the language and read, first, the Old Testament in Hebrew (knowing it quite well in the vulgate of Jerome's translation) and then several areas of the Mishna, and later the Zohar, all in Hebrew, since there were no translations of these works into Latin (though you still dream of translating them, a lifetime project, you know).

Recently, however, you have come into contact with Abraham Abulafia, a Jewish scholar born in Zaragoza, Spain. You have heard his lectures and have admired, indeed secretly practiced, his Gematria, the giving of the letters of the scripture a numerical value and thus deducing events through a numerological translation and evaluation. Abulafia's messianic zeal, even as you still remain a Christian, has inspired you to visions of the Book of Revelation. You yearn to talk with him about it. You now have your chance, for Abulafia, foolishly driven by his desire to transmit his ideas to the Pope himself, has been thrown into prison. You have obtained permission to visit him in his cell.

Dear Past Rentals,

Abulafia? Who was he? I guess that only a handful of people, mainly scholars of the Cabala, would know of him, if not know his ideas. I had heard of this man, casually, and only by accident, through some book I had read on the Apocalypse, which seemed to interest the Christians more than the Jews around that time.

First of all, I didn't take this journey to find out about the man in jail, Abulafia. I went because I was curious about why some Christian would want to learn Hebrew. Well, I found out and I didn't find out. Along the way I learned a lot more, mainly about the way those 13th century Christians thought about things.

They didn't believe in the history we think today is history. Everything in their world was fixed. You had only to read the right books or listen to the right appointed authorities to "find out" what was the true structure of the world. They, the authors and the authorities, would tell you. It would be like going to the politicians, the senator or the mayor to find out if the sun would rise the next morning. Believe me, it's hard to get adjusted to this kind of thinking.

Out there among the stars everything was the same; it never changed. Down where they were, everything did. The stars were immortal; the people on earth died and went to heaven or to hell (and only a few to purgatory). Your job in this existence was to get around the devil in you, that is, your original sin, your disobedience, something that happened long ago but is still with you. That immense organization, the "universal" Catholic Church, headed by the Pope, was the judge and the guide in all religious matters.

Now Rome was a second rate city by our standards, filthy and smelling of garbage and human wastes, all kinds but mainly shit, which they often just flung out the window into the street. You could be walking along and if you weren't paying any attention have a pile of it land on you. People were cooped up in what would appear to us as tiny boxes, where they managed to live, in rooms no bigger than a large closet and with nothing in them, one room per family, that's it, and no furniture, just some straw for a bed, a table maybe, and a spoon and a knife for eating, and not meat either, mostly grains. (Remember, pasta didn't come in until around the thirteenth century, when Marco Polo brought it back from his trip to China.)

Most of them, if they hadn't died already, looked like shit when they got to forty. They worked hard and they beat their children, and the children died young, too. They wore their clothes till they fell off them; then they used them as rags, used every bit of them. And those who had looms and could get wool made themselves whatever they could. You could hear the shuttles going back and forth as you walked down those narrow streets and sometimes you could hear the moaning of the sick and the prayers for the dead and the bells tolling in the churches. People were being born and were dying all around you, as far as I could see. Funerals and going to church and gossiping (and maybe screwing and drinking) were the main sources of social activity, though they must have done other things, too.

Well, in that world, what do you expect? A new guy in town, someone this man I became had heard of, perhaps had read people who had spoken of him—this was a kind of special attraction, someone from a distant land, made more attractive by his pure foreignness. But I have to hand it to that guy. He took a chance visiting this man, put in jail because he was a Jew (those Christians were more than suspicious of Jews) and one who had dared to propose an audience with the Pope himself and about the Apocalypse, something the Vatican didn't want to hear any more about in those days.

One hundred and fifty years before, they had heard enough. All kinds of apocalyptic fervor was breaking out. And 400 years later there would be more, and they didn't want a bunch of "radicals" disturbing the status quo. Therefore, they threw Abulafia in jail, where he would rot, of course, jails being worse places than the squalid rooms people lived in.

This "brave" man was filled with all kinds of vague stories of the Jews and especially with that Christian legend of "The Wandering Jew". This Jew denied Christ on his way to Golgotha and Christ put a curse on him, that he would wander until Christ returned. And whenever a Christian saw a Jew passing through town or just some stranger who might have been Jewish, he thought of the wandering Jew. On the one hand, they couldn't touch that man since Christ had already "claimed" him— his future was fixed, at least till the end of time. On the other hand, he was something bad, someone who had denied their "savior". So they were ambivalent. They did not know what to do. This man might even be holy and filled with importance. Let the church decide, and the church did. It tortured them or kicked them out of town or let them rot in jail. Heaven would decide. The buck didn't stop there.

This guy asked Abulafia a lot of questions, in Hebrew no less. And the guy answered them, but in a peculiar way. He didn't give any yes/no answers. He really said, "find out for yourself." Or "I'll tell you a story and you figure out what it means." This guy wanted to know when his savior was coming, the exact date, give or take a morning or an afternoon.

"What are the signs of the coming of our blessed savior?" he would ask, fervently, expectantly, wanting the guy to pull out a calendar and point to a day. Abulafia told the story of Jonah as if Jonah knew, but didn't tell this guy how to find out what Jonah found out, if Jonah had found out anything. He told the story of Moses and the curses brought down on Pharaoh by God, the plagues, the serpents, the killing of the first born, etc. This guy had heard that story a thousand times, but he wanted to know how it related to the coming of Christ. Were these actions of God signs, like the pestilence in the Book of Revelation? Was Moses a kind of second John the Baptist? Was Moses, born in a cradle on the Nile and under obscure beginnings and dangers, like Christ, a kind of harbinger of the Coming?

This guy kept asking questions, to the point of interrupting the answers Abulafia was trying to give. At a certain point, about six hours into the "interview," he practically hauled back and hit Abulafia but was constrained by, well, I guess, the Legend. Maybe he thought Abulafia was the wandering Jew himself. You can't hit a guy who had been "touched" by Christ and who had undoubtedly seen the crucifixion.

But after that—and Abulafia saw the anger behind it—the "wandering Jew" just shut up, wouldn't say a word, just kept smiling and humming to himself, looking up from time to time with a twinkle in his eye. Then he'd look down, shake his head, and continue humming and bobbing his head and reciting prayers in Hebrew. My man left an hour later, in disgust, probably to tell the Pope to torture the Jew.

I find it amazing how people lock themselves into a perceptual room as small as those dwellings I saw in Rome and as filthy as well. Fear drove them into their cloaca publica and they ended up throwing their shit on others whom they basically invented and then did away with. It happened then and it is happening now, too. We call it fanaticism.

Rodney Dangerfield
Age 37. Bricklayer
Des Moines, Iowa

No. 172: Gulkana, Alaska. January 13, 1899. [6 hours; $75] Rough, chunky, a bear of a man, you lived in Seattle, working as a drayman for several years before you heard of the gold strike. Loaded with as much equipment as you could carry, you took the first ship north. Along with hundreds of others, your aim was to get rich quick, although you knew almost nothing about mining gold or mining anything else.

Along with 95% of those whom you accompanied, your gold expedition was an almost complete failure, except for a minor strike, which netted you about $3,000, easily reduced to about $900 through your recklessness, spending it on women and beer and the frightfully expensive practice of boasting.

The fights you got into were legendary. People made bets on you even before you began to pick on someone. The more you drank, the more combative you became, and then the more you tended to lose, because, big as you were, you practically lost your balance, and if you won, you probably succeeded by falling on your opponent and smothering him with both your body and your breath, which could be smelled clear across the room, or that was what they said, much of it legend, collapsing on a tiny bit of fact.

One day you left town (Moose Pass) and headed northwest, somewhere around Mt. Blackburn, propelled by some wild talk of silver and (so they said secretly but enough for you to hear them) platinum. They could read the dollar signs in your eyes, and it was not hard to egg you on until you spent almost all you had left on supplies and headed out to an area almost no one had dared to enter. There you found nothing—no gold, silver or platinum. It was almost absent of people, except for an occasional prospector who wandered into the region and, seeing nothing of value, left.

But somehow you stayed, building a cabin, laying in a supply of firewood and meat for the winter, and in so doing isolated yourself for a whole year. At first, you didn't know why you did it, but later you understood. You were tired of wearing yourself out with drink and fighting. Something in you wanted to bury itself from people, from loud cities and the boisterousness that was eating its way through you. Here, around Gulkana, not even Gulkana yet, you put down your traps, wandered through the mountains when you could, and brooded by the fire for months and months, waiting for the anger and chaos inside you to subside. Here, you were calmed by the wind, the blizzards, the calls of the animals, and the wonderful, terrible silences larger than anything you had experienced before.

Today is like any other day in the winter. You are sitting by the fire, carving the stock of a gun (your old one had split two days ago), and letting your mind wander, as it will, everywhere.

Dear Past Rentals,

It's all a matter of getting rid of your anger, and I know all about it. I grew up with it. My father was one, mean, angry son of a bitch. Sometimes he'd come home so mad we fled and left him alone in the kitchen, not bothering to eat our suppers. Sometimes he ranted for hours, yelling and cursing and screaming obscenities at everyone, from the gardeners in the park to the President himself. Sometimes he'd realize what he was going to do and run outside into the woods (even in December) and throw rocks at the cows and lift up the calves and throw them around. And he'd scream and yell at the cows, even try to strike up an argument with them. He wasn't too successful. And, of course, sometimes I got it, with his belt, anywhere he could find to hit me. And I'd scream and yell as loud as I could to magnify my pain so he wouldn't hit me any harder. (He hit me hard enough.)

I'm not bragging about my father or what he did to me. I knew other kids whose fathers hit them. Some had their arms broken, even their ribs. I knew one guy whose father actually put him in the hospital. But who else are you going to model yourself after? I tried to escape him when I was around fourteen or fifteen, but after that I just ran away, stayed with friends or slept out in a tent in the woods (in summer, of course). However, when I became a teenager, about sixteen or seventeen, I started to turn angry. I didn't hit anybody, but I felt like I wanted to. I yelled. I called people names. I didn't even know what the names meant. I just had to exercise my voice.

I think you can see how I identified with your drayman from Washington who goes off to live in no man's land. I'm not anything like him now—I've changed a lot—but he had a lot of energy that just burned off him in waves, and when he had no way of getting rid of it, like my father, he'd get drunk and start a fight and wake up the next morning with a sore rib or a black eye or bruises on his face and chest.

It's funny how people select the right thing for them after a while, choose it without knowing why, and things get better. Their body tells them something their mind can't communicate. They become swimmers or weight lifters or long distance runners or football players, anything that will burn off that energy. Their rhythms go up and down. They work hard and they play hard. And after many years they don't have the energy they had before and they get calmer. It's strange to say, but the most content and well put together people, the calmest people I've ever met, were guys who had gone through a lot in a war, mainly the Second World War and mainly in the Pacific. That experience either crippled them or healed some-

thing in them. I've felt all along that all the talking in the world wouldn't have done them any good.

My man was that way. He didn't belong among people. They just provoked him. Now, the place he found was just perfect. He could survive there, cut his own firewood, hunt his deer or bear or fish, build what he needed, and, most important, just sit and let his body calm down by the fire or look out at the silence of the long, deep winter, watch the trees weighed down by the snow, listen, from time to time, to a branch breaking off from that weight, and feel content.

That's what a man who's angry needs. And there've been plenty who haven't had the opportunity to get that solitude. They were the unlucky ones. They took out their excess energy on others. If they managed to hold back the anger just enough and were smart enough to do it, then they could carefully, in a very controlled way, let others have it. They didn't believe in the Golden Rule beneath the Golden Rule: Don't give unto others what you would not want given unto you. These were the trapped ones who didn't know they were trapped, the torturers, the savage policemen, the sadistic husbands or wives, the sly judges twisting the sentences to fit their inward turmoil, and the demagogues, all of them, who couldn't find a clearing for their pain.

> *Tumaru Fukuoka*
> *Age 32, Sumo wrestler*
> *Kyoto, Japan*

No. 173: Algiers (in Punic Ikosim: Owl or Thorn Island), Algeria. January 4, 278 B.C. [6 minutes; $20] Your father is a fisherman, and you are four years old, spending time mostly with your mother, who cooks and helps repair the nets and sings to you in the mornings with a soft, high voice, accompanied only by the waves and the sounds of the sea birds which hover around the fishing boats and stab the water with their beaks. You sit playing in the sand for hours, watching the sun come up and the light fill the shore and later look toward the soft, dry land on which your small hut is built.

The flies increase. Your mother covers you with a salve to protect you, singing you songs, and, later when the sun is high in the sky and you are ready for your mid-day sleep, she tells you stories and recites poems about strange birds, fish, and rocks which were once people who had, somehow, taken a false step somewhere. Then you fall asleep and vaguely dream of them, sometimes all of them together, speaking, arguing, with the waves in the background washing their voices in a cape of sound, soothing and relaxing, until finally in your sleep you blend with everything and are carried to another land and another time, in another logic, perhaps the logic and time of the noonday sun with its enormous power and presence and the waves trying to creep up the shore again and again.

You are playing by the water with a small stick. It is early morning. The sun has just risen. It is not yet warm. There are shadows everywhere. You walk for a while and then sit down, tired and musing. Then, you walk back and sit again, less tired, more alert. There is a boat by the shore. Your father is getting out of it. You are running toward him, laughing with joy.

No. 174: Bousso (on the Chari River), Chad. February 21, 766. [5 hours; $60] You are an old woman, how old, you are not completely sure, but you have had three children, one of whom has died. Now you have three grandsons. You have worked hard and enjoyed much in your life and you are not sorry to leave it, sorry, perhaps just a little, for who would not, in the expectation of future generations, be a little sorry.

One of your sons is almost an old man himself, perhaps fifty, and he has been away for over two years, somewhere in the west, near Maiduguri, working for those who have cattle, "the rich men of the west". He sends presents home to his family, which somehow arrive, through a traveler whom he has befriended, through a merchant who will happen to pass your way, always home to his mother, wishing his friends there a happy life. May they prosper, may they see and speak well of others, etc.

The other son, however, is both physically and spiritually closer to you. He, also, was born in Bousso on the Chari River, the source of all the millet and wonder of this world. He has traveled and worked hard. He has known many people in this vast, hot land through the southern reaches of the enormous desert and the northern reaches of the great forest. And he has always come back, especially during these last five years, returning with stories and gifts, for you and for others.

He never forgets anything. He is blessed with a full memory. And more than a memory, for he pictures things to you and your friends, as you sit around the fire at night, drinking millet beer and laughing, things that open the cracks in the shadows where the light is kept at night, open your hearts and even the pores of your skin, even to the wisdom of the kidneys and the liver, which, they say, is found in the phases of the moon on its monthly journeys.

Tonight you listen to your son as he talks and sings. You look out at the vast moonlit landscape, flat, with its tiny ghost bushes beyond the Chari, listening to the few cattle, with bells on their necks, wandering near the water, and fill yourself with everything you have known and loved in this life.

No. 175: Tabati village, Cameroon. April 6, 1544. [7 hours; $100] You are an eighteen-year-old girl who lives in Tabati, a small village near the Sanaga River in the highlands of Cameroon. An idiot child, you sit all day in the shade of a large tree near your home in the village, and listen. And look. Sometimes you defecate right under the tree and then watch the flies gather. You smell the tree. You smell your own feces. And later you come to smell the cooking, though you have no part in the preparation of food.

Despite your sedentary position under the tree near your home, you are visited frequently by other children, adults and old men and women. They take a kindly interest in you, offer you food, a toy to play with, and sometimes the children or the elderly will sit down and enter into a game with you as they would play with a child (one of the games they remembered playing as children). You like to see them smile because the shadows which cross their faces enchant you. You like the shine of their clear teeth in the shade. You show them things you have found—some stones, a piece of a cooking pot, beetles, ants. And you offer these to them as presents. They often say no, but they will hold them, especially the beetles, examining everything carefully, and then, politely and kindly but firmly, put them back into your large hands.

It is cool under the tree, which is your home during the day, and you can look out over the mountains and the lands beyond, though you have never been there. There is something in you that moves others to approach, something in the way your body shapes itself, light and soft, empty and almost weightless, with no hint of the heavier, darker, more congealed and confusing perplexity of the others, people who move about on their necessary errands, filled with fears and complications, which, in you, are virtually absent.

> *Dear Past Rentals,*
>
> *We live in Khemisset, a small village in Morocco, near Meknes, which is near the town of Fes. We can travel to Rabat, about an hour by bus from our village, and visit the ocean and the big city with all its noise and energy. But we*

usually stay in Khemisset, except if my husband, who makes and sells shoes, has business in the cities on the coast.

Mostly, we live in the village, quietly, because it is quiet here compared to Rabat or Casablanca, which is even noisier, live with our two idiot sons, twenty-four and twenty-six years old who have a good life here. I have been to the city and seen how people treat the idiots there. They look at them like dirt. They treat them like strange animals in the zoo, animals who, they feel, should be teased. I think they are afraid. They imagine it is terrible to be an idiot. Some of them, the young ones, have even thrown things at my sons. They have no respect for life, for people, for plants, for anything. And you can't explain anything to them.

But in my village my sons are kings, not because everyone is less intelligent than they are. No, people just know my sons and treat them with dignity and respect. When people know you, they are not going to hurt you, unless they are crazy themselves, and people here are less likely to be crazy than people are in a city like Rabat.

My sons don't work much. They help us a little, do what they can, but mostly they wander around the village, sitting in the shade, eating fruit, watching the goats, listening to the humming of the flies around them, looking at the flowers, and just being around, not much by most people's standards but an exciting life by theirs.

The villagers take care of them. Sometimes my boys start crying as if the rain were falling from their hair. They can't help it. They are moved by something. It might be the men singing on their way to the fields. It might be the sound of the rain falling on the roofs. It might be almost nothing we can figure out. But they cry and cry and cry. There doesn't seem to be an end to their crying. The villagers sometimes sit with them when they cry, and sometimes they just bring them home to us and I hold them and they stop crying, these twenty-two and twenty-four year old boys.

At other times they just smile at everyone, and often everyone smiles back at them. People cannot resist smiling if someone smiles at them, that is, when they have the time and the comfort in their lives to smile and to feel a smile. My husband and I know my boys are safe and well taken care of, and my boys are happy to live in such a place.

Even though my intelligence is normal, I feel the joy my young men give and receive. And therefore I decided to go to the Cameroons to become this idiot girl. I was not surprised. I think I had known how she would feel. After all, I have had twenty-six years of experience. I found that there is some-thing very pleasant and down to earth about being an idiot girl, one who, like my boys, is very well taken care of by others and who lives in a safe, comforting place.

She did not think as we do. Her thoughts, if she really had them, came and went, half formed. But her responses to the soil, the slight breezes moving the leaves on the trees, the journeys of beetles, the colors of the sky and the earth, the passing of people, the sound of their steps and their voices, the smells of dung and of cooking, of the earth held to her nose, the colors of the walls of the houses, and the colors of the clothing next to the colors of the earth—all these were rich with a closeness I envy. And she, too, when she smiled, was smiled at (or with). And she, too, when she cried, was held or taken to her parents' house. Such is the life of an idiot child in a comforting village. I know that for many, many years, people who were born with less intelligence than most had a place and could feel a part of life around them.

(Woman's name withheld)

No. 176: Changsha, China. April 19, 1388. [5 weeks; $95] You wander around Changsha, unkempt, seemingly empty, appearing (yet only appearing) confused, with a kind of deflective effervescence about you as you stop to talk to all kinds of people—merchants, carters, herdsmen, jewelers, potters, wherever you may go in a city you have known for seventeen years, living everywhere, finding your lodgings for the night wherever you can. And under your broad hat, your eyes are always noting the people who live here, their voices, gestures, habits of mind, and temper.

Anything but fastidious in your outward appearance, you are meticulous in your observations, writing nothing down but remembering everything. For you are a professional spy for the sub-prefect of the emperor Chu Yuan-chang. Your reports are made irregularly through a little house on the edge of the city, usually at night when you can send word ahead. And if not, you will sit, for hours sometimes, sheltered from the rain, waiting and listening and watching the rice fields extending into the mountains and feel the rain, outside, for hours and days, renewing the land.

Dear Past Rentals,

You might think that the life of a spy is dangerous, and therefore, exciting. Well, it depends on when you lived and where. Today, a spy's life is neither dangerous nor exciting. He's really a kind of drudge, writing down information and sending in reports, most of the time simple, ordinary things, not imminent invasions or atomic secrets.

The spy business, like any other today, has become specialized. The most lucrative ones, the private spies, are the corporate ones. They manage to get a job in a technically sensitive area, a large lab of a large corporation, for example where they can steal information and get paid for it. Or else a scientist or a lab technician is recruited to deliver information to another corporation. It's done all the time, internationally and nationally. Thus, information is disseminated.

In some ways spying was the same in the past, but long ago it remained on a more immediate level. In the fourteenth century in China, for example, people wouldn't have called a man a spy if he passed on information about an industrial process, if he smuggled a few silkworms out of the country, for example. Spies were primarily political spies, checking out the temper of the people, looking for discontents, agitators, and sometimes criminals, if they could find them. And they were the equivalent of our survey teams, out to check out the political and the social market.

Some spies, I imagine, must have had it easy. They did their job, sent in their reports, and spent their time "checking out the landscape," so to speak. They could go anywhere if they blended into the landscape. What an ideal job for a novelist because, in a way, they are spies. And, by extension, everyone is a kind of spy. We are all trying to get "the low-down" on people, find out how they operate, as if they were really any different from ourselves. (They are, and they are not.)

As you can tell, I have had some experience in the world of spying. I'm not going to tell you where and how and why, but I will say this much— I've been around. Now this Chinese spy in Changsha in what would have been the Middle Ages for us westerners was a sharp cookie. He did his job well because he didn't leave any traces. Others wrote down what he reported, and he made sure he wasn't seen entering that house on the edge of the village. He didn't get paid much, but he made enough to survive and he didn't need much in the first place. Food, wine, tea, clothes, a place to live and a little spending money— that's all a spy got in those days, not like today where some are sent to school to learn their "trade," become expert scholars in the "art" of spying.

Because his job was fairly easy and because he knew that if he wanted to keep it he'd have to water down his reports and not say anything terrible about anyone—he didn't want to finger even the critical ones—he'd often make things up and then follow leads which would get him nowhere and end up making excuses for not finding the people he reported on. His work was all so tedious he had to do something to liven it up. But it took an agile mind to do this.

But through that facade of his, old clothes, a foolish, don't care at all disguise, he soaked up a lot of information, noticing everything and blending everywhere. He had the freedom to keep his ears and eyes open and at the same time to let himself go with others. He had one fundamental problem, however. He had no friends. He couldn't have, since anyone who got too close to him would begin questioning his life, asking questions like where he got his money, how he managed to live, why he had so much time to spend talking to others. Therefore, he had to make the best of things, take his friendships on the wing, so to speak. But his was a basically good life and fairly secure. It was just that loneliness that shaped him as it probably has shaped spies through every age and society.

Jean Martinon (Real name withheld)
Age 39. Business executive
Marseilles, France

No. 177: Calcutta, India. May 6, 1757. [14 hours; $105] You are a soldier in the pay of Siraj-ud-Daula, a weak, vain ruler surrounded by many who would rather depose than support him. An army of 1,000 Europeans and 2,000 Sepoys are gathered against him, and you believe, from what you have been able to gather listening to others in the army, that they will be successful. You have made your plans and are on your way to join the Sepoys, who are only twenty miles away.

First, you changed your clothes, placing your sword in a box so you would not be known as a soldier, and walked away from Calcutta. Unfortunately, you have gotten sick from something you ate the night before and have taken refuge in a small shop, where you have asked for tea and some herbal medicine.

After sitting in the front of the shop for hours, relaxing and gently chatting with the shopkeeper and his customers about many things, none of which really interest you at the moment, you eventually see them coming, the Sepoys and the European soldiers under Robert Clive, the Englishman, whom you had hoped to serve. They are strung out along the road for a long distance, marching surely toward their destination, but in no hurry. First, the Europeans and then the Indians. Guns, cannon, lances, swords. They are an inelegant group, but you know that they will carry the day, and you would like, if only for your own advancement, though also for the hatred you bear Siraj-ud-Daula and his whole miserable gang of petty flatterers, to achieve some personal glory. But you are not fated to succeed. You can only watch as they pass you by, while you sit there, sick and immobilized, this bright June day, thousands of them, as they go to their death, in the usual relentless march of conflict which you have come to expect these last ten years, from the way that life around you has been falling apart.

Dear Past Rentals,

How many boring, stupid, erratic rulers have people worked for, putting up with their madness and their whims, even with their insecure generosities and overblown imaginations. Our man in Calcutta had had enough of this. But he would have put up with his ruler forever if it had not been for the British. Tyrannical as they were, the British were different, exotic, a bit less so on the surface, a big attraction for a hanger on at court, especially one who was breeding his resentment the way a bacterial infection multiplies in a wound. He was ripe for recruitment.

He wasn't terribly smart. He just went with the flow. He was comfortably well off and didn't realize it. He looked around him and saw only himself as he would see the world, not as others, the poor or the merchants or the farmers would see it. His lens did not allow for other lenses.

But there's always disease to hold up an army. It has been said that Chang Kai Chek's army, recuperating in Canton in 1949, would have been demolished by the Communist Red Army on their way to do just that if it hadn't been for a particular bug which immobilized those soldiers and gave Chang's men enough time to make the leap to Taiwan. Thus, whatever we think of the Communists or of Chang's immensely corrupt forces, a little microbe, something beyond the reach of the eye, changed history, as it has done so many times.

This guy, although he didn't know it, had his cake and got to eat it, too. He could sit on the sidelines with no danger to himself and see the British forces on their way to take over, and the British would, for they were far superior to the forces they opposed. This guy just had a little tummy ache. A little intestinal bacteria had gotten into him, something that happened to everyone in those days (and even today). After the smoke had cleared, he could step out and denounce the ruler he had served and work for the British, for he knew the works. He would survive, thanks to the bacteria, which laid him up.

One more thing I thought of when I was there. It's a wonder the British survived in that climate, unprepared as they were, wearing those heavy clothes and wanting those cottages and gardens in a country and climate that can't support them. And expecting people to act British. And yet they changed the nature of India in some important ways, introducing a bureaucracy and an educational system which uni-

fied a land, which only in the broadest sense could have been called a country. English, up to very recently, has been the unofficial official language of a "new" nation. The British did this, along with, it should be mention, their many atrocities.

Aulis Saalinen
Age 50. Clerk, municipal court
Turku, Finland

No. 178: Konya, Turkey. February 16, 1368. [3 hours; $50] You are a sixteen-year-old lady who has been educated at home by her mother, her grandmother, her aunt, and her older cousin, all of whom have, for the past three years, been concerned with your matrimonial future. And it is the same with all your friends. They, too, have been primed for marriage. To this aim you have met several young men on certain, almost socially arranged occasions, though you have been kept relatively secluded from any "chance" connections, and, of course, like any young girl of your age, you are "curious".

How could you not be? You have learned how to weave, make carpets, cook and do other things, which a woman of your class and age should know. Subtle matters have been placed in your way, among other things, how to look at a man and how to avoid his glances, how to dress for various purposes and occasions, how to sing (you have a beautiful voice), and how to dance. With your friends, when you visit each other, you will practice these ways of being a woman, though what you do is really what you would call play, frivolous activity, yet still a way of learning the behavior of a young, eligible woman of your age.

All of you will talk endlessly about this or that man you have seen, though you hardly know anything about him. "What kind of man do you want? How should he dress? What kind of house should he have? Where should he live? Etc. You give yourself over to these questions for hours, days that extend to weeks, And you must fight against their "utterly consuming passion". You can see it in the voices and sighs of the other girls, and you know that they, too, can see their desires in yours. When will he come to me? When will my father tell me of a suitor? What will I wear at the marriage ceremony? What will my dowry be? How will he speak of me to my father? What will my mother say of him? All these questions are part of the language of your sixteen-year-old life.

But now, one day, when you passed through the market with your cousin and aunt, you saw, again, the young boy sitting in his father's shop. You noticed him again, and what is more important, you noticed that he had been noticing you. In the shop, you hardly dared look at him, but you could feel his eyes on you, as if your skin were glowing where his eyes alighted. And when you were leaving the shop, you heard from almost behind you a few words of parting from the young man, as if he had wanted to say more but could not release the words. You looked back at him and smiled. You could see that he, too, was smiling and looking. And then you left. Now you are at home, thinking. You cannot help losing yourself in his glorious interest.

No. 179: Hankow, China. March 23, 978. [4 hours; $90] You make your living as a porter, carrying things all over the city. You have been doing this for five years, having lost your job as a cemetery caretaker. This was the only thing you could do to keep your body alive. Life is difficult, but you live, and even though you work hard and there are many who almost spit in your face or abuse you with the unkindest of words, there is always time, with a friend or two, for a cup of tea and a few cakes at the teahouse, and there is the shouting, the talk, and the pleasure at eyeing the women who pass by the window on the narrow street of the tea house you frequent.

Today is no different, except that the rain is falling, heavy, as if the whole sky were visiting the earth. Therefore, it is warm in the teahouse, almost too warm, with the sweat and noise of bodies coming in out of the rain. You will not go to work until the rain clears. Instead, you will sit here with a few friends, who are almost always here at the teahouse, and talk and talk and talk and when you think you are finished, argue and talk and argue again as you have always talked and argued every day of your life.

Dear Past Rentals,

Gossip makes the world go round. We love it. We couldn't get along without it. And for most of our history it was almost the only source of entertainment, that is, listening to and being with other people. Today, gossip has taken different forms, mainly through the media and mainly through radio and television and, of course, the "gossip" magazines. Some programs can be thought of as almost pure gossip. Some, like the news, are just disguised gossip.

But despite the media, the word gets around. It penetrates, everywhere people congregate. Everyone is nervously trying to tell everyone else what's on his mind or even what just pops into his mind. We need to be gratified by somebody else's ears, listened to as the infants we once were. We are so narcissistic that only the crazies go off to live and die alone, and even they want to tell us about their lives.

But in the past, that is, before the arrival of TV and radio and mass-produced magazines and newspapers, when word spread by voice, not by electronic circuit or printing press, conversation was an art and an enjoyable one at that. Some were more sophisticated, others far cruder. But all were aware of the form of discourse and even the topics.

Your porter was a powerful, uneducated man who struggled hard to survive and therefore pushed aside the tangle of necessity to sit in this clearing of a teahouse for an hour or two, greeting this and that friend as they passed through on their way to or from their own work. The departures were also important, as were the greetings. Both are the boundaries of a new state, artificially set aside and protected by the actions of saying hello and good-bye. In this way we disarm ourselves and settle down.

Have you ever noticed an American conversation, a typical one, that is? Or have you ever compared it with an English or a Russian or an Israeli one? It's important to notice that they all reflect the basic assumptions of the culture. The Americans, for example, agree to listen to the I of the other, waiting their turn at the "feeding trough". There seems to be very little objective matter—most is subjective. Americans agree to allow others the right of free speech; and their conversations, if they can be called that, are, so to speak, "inter-subjective". The English, on the other hand, depending on class, tend to be more concerned, at least outwardly, about their interlocutors. They are also more objective, talking not about themselves but about other things, and, at worst, walking around each other's toes. The French also, may spend their conversations arguing, ranting and raving, at times, about politics, or economic conditions but, again depending on class, leaning often more toward form than content. Perhaps these are stereotypes, but, taken as such, they generally hold true.

What is the best, the healthiest conversation, the most satisfying for all? One in which people talk about something objectively most important to them. Whether it's the condition of the streets, new styles in women's clothing, the price of food, or garbage collection, it does not matter. It does, of course, but the form, I feel, provides the possibility for fulfillment. It is amazing how sometimes the most trivial subjects may become the most satisfying, only because of the structure each conversation tends toward, an arrangement in which everyone has the chance to speak, to contribute to the general "dance". That's what we want the most, to make a contribution and be recognized.

Therefore, the topics this porter and his friends talked about in the teahouse, though important, were not the substance. The satisfaction of being with friends, of sitting down and watching the world go by, and especially of feeling you are a contributor and the enjoyment of having people respond to your contributions—these make a conversation significant, link you to others, and make you whole.

There are other matters, too, subtle ones hard to talk about—a film would be better. But Past Rentals has not as yet developed a method of providing visual evidence. I'm talking about the musical qualities of conversation, its tensions and releases, its monophonic and homophonic aspects, its tempos, antiphonies, beginnings and returns, its crescendos and decrescendos, its action as dance. And what about the silences? They are equally important. And the ambiance. Equally important. And the comfort or discomfort of the chairs? All, equally important.

One must be prepared for conversation. Otherwise, it will not go well. If you are feeling sick, or are worried or angry or in love, you will distract yourself and others and tinge the color of the interaction. If you are an impulsive person or are always busy and cannot sit still, or if you present a personality uncongenial to the company you are with, then you, and perhaps the others, will go away with some sense of incompleteness in you, and that sense will build in you all day and emerge unknown to you in the most remote places of your life.

Therefore, the connoisseur of conversation must practice self-awareness and awareness of others, must indulge in exercises of integration, without which nothing can be accomplished. If he can proceed in this way, he will increase his health and increase his perception of himself and of others, find himself both more contented and more responsive, and at the same time more fulfilled.

> *Marya Antinoini*
> *Age 36. Owner, Cafe Barri*
> *Avellino, Italy*

No. 180: Kiev, Russia. May 31, 1241. [2 weeks; $395] The Mongols, led by Ogudai Khan, have been besieging Kiev for days. You are thirteen years old, a young man who has told his father he is prepared to fight in defense of the city. But your father has another plan. He has heard of the cruelty and barbarity of the Mongols and knows that if Kiev falls, and he thinks it surely will fall, all the inhabitants will be slaughtered. He has, therefore, cleverly concealed you in a section of wall, which he has built just for such an occasion. It is invisible, although it contains barely enough room for you to lie down.

But it has saved your life. Your father, you are certain, has perished with the other inhabitants of the city. He had brought you as much food as he could, a few week's supply, some warm clothing and as much money as he could gather, enough to keep you well for about a month, long enough, he hoped, for the Mongols to do what they came to do and depart.

When the soldiers finally broke through the city gates, you quickly sealed yourself into your living tomb, remaining there day and night while you listened to the screams of the dying and remained silent while the soldiers searched and looted your father's house. Fortunately, they were used to living in tents, not houses, and therefore, they did not notice how your hiding place had been constructed.

Finally, the screams subsided, the city grew quiet, deathly

quiet, and though you remained for a few more days in the midst of this ominous silence, you slowly ventured out. There was no one in the house. There was no one in the streets, though for the first two days you only looked out the windows. Then you moved slowly, secretly, from building to building, looking for more food (you needed more). When you found some, you then moved back to your father's house. You heard only silence for days, for weeks. Then a few faces appeared, those who had also been hiding, fearful people like you. None of you spoke to each other for a long time. Instead, you spent your energies looking for food.

Finally, you moved out of the city and went looking for the peasants, those who had not been touched by the Khan's army. They fed you, and you worked for them for three months. They gave you food, some sheep, a cow, and thus you and the remaining inhabitants survived. The winter was terrible and you had to work doubly hard to keep yourself warm. You burned some of the buildings for firewood because there was no energy or time to gather wood from the forest.

Now, the spring has come and you are repairing the damage to your father's home. This is the easy task. At last you can begin to relax a bit, though the city is almost empty, a ghost town, and all the bodies the Mongols left as a warning have been buried and prayers have been said over them. Now, you are sitting upstairs in front of the bedroom window, looking out at the great city of Kiev, its wooden houses, its great gates, at the countryside beyond, and thinking, obliquely and vaguely, about the life which existed here before the barbarians and murderers had come, remembering the city as it was, each particular of your life and your father's life in it and your father, and his sacrifice.

No. 181: Crotone, Italy. September 31, 1098. [3 weeks; $450] You are twenty-eight and have settled in Crotone, Italy, after having left Strasbourg eight years ago on your way to the Holy Land to recapture it from the Muslims. You and the others started in early spring and passing through Besancon and then through Lyons and Beaucaire, finally arrived at Marseilles in mid-summer.

The journey to Marseilles was difficult enough, but things got worse. The boats were not yet seaworthy and had to be repaired—a delay of at least two months. Then, they had to stop along the French and Italian coasts, gradually making their way eastward. Storms in the early fall made sailing difficult, if not impossible. And though you had heard stories about thieves in the Italian towns, you only realized how dangerous things were when you discovered your shipmate's body dead, as you came out of a tavern one day after a two week layover in a small town in western Italy, his throat cut and his purse taken. You ran quickly to the boat and stayed there until it left.

The inhabitants of the towns were unfriendly, even hostile, afraid of you, while others took their revenge in unprotected places. You used your time, however, as well as you could, learning as much of the native language as possible, and by the time you reached the southern tip of the Italic peninsula and were ready to pass through the Straits of Messina, your knowledge of the language was passable, though you noticed how the language changed as you moved southward.

It was there that you were set upon by pirates. To protect everyone, the captain drove the ship toward shore, beaching it there, whether by accident or design you do not know. Ashore, you ran for your lives—no one knew where they were running, though they certainly knew why.

You managed to make your way northeast, helping the farmers and shepherds with their crops or their flocks or both, working as hard as you could for your food and a little extra, which was not much, and finding yourself, finally, in Crotona, a small town made up mostly of fishermen. There, you found work helping to mend boats (you had learned something from your stay in Marseilles) and load ships. You lived in a small hut, which was mostly a ten-foot hole above the earth, and you were hard pressed to keep it dry when the rains came.

Slowly, you began to settle here. The desire to wrest the Holy Land from the Muslims was forgotten and crumbled in the daily work of the town, whose inhabitants you came to know intimately and one of whom you eventually married. Now, you spend your time sitting with the other fishermen in the days between fishing trips, drinking the local liquor, and talking, about almost anything, getting drunk, singing, and walking everywhere, through the wild, dry, hot land you had come to through many accidents.

No. 182: Pula, Dalmatia, Yugoslavia. September 1, 162. [6 weeks; $500] You turned pirate six years ago, raiding the Roman shipping routes, and then retreated into the mountain strongholds of the Adriatic, slipping in among the islands for protection if anyone came to pursue you. You take what you need—grain, cattle, sometimes spices—and then return to one of several islands, and in this way have managed to accumulate enough to "retire," for you do not enjoy what you do and prefer the life of leisure you live from time to time on the islands of your choice.

Last week, however, your crew and you visited a small coastal village in Istria, a trading village, where you noticed, first, an almost total absence of people. "What had happened?" you wondered. Then you saw the villagers, or what was left of them, and the bodies lying in the huts and some down near the sea, distended, awful, bloated, putrid. The stench began to effect you. The villagers seemed used to it, and most of them were too weak to retreat to the mountains for what seemed to you some sort of safety. The place stank of disease.

You ordered your men not to touch anything or anyone, and in this way you made your "retreat" to the boats and then home again, still bothered by what you had seen. Two weeks later you noticed one of your men vomiting. In two days he was dead. Then, three others developed the fatal symptoms. Then another. And another. Was there any ending of this visitation? Maybe the gods would be merciful, but you deeply doubted it.

Five weeks ago you became so frightened you left, taking with you only a few provisions, and made your way up into the mountains to a small hut you had built two years ago, determined to live in isolation for as long as this dreaded sickness would last. You have been in your hut for eight days, with ten sheep and a cow and several baskets of grain. You communicate with others, when you see them, from a distance, asking them about the sickness, if it has gone away. But the air is good and the weather has not yet turned cold. You will wait here as long as necessary, and then, you hope, you will pick up the pieces below. Life holds many mysteries.

No. 183: Chara, Persia. May 6, 327. [8 days; $325] You are a hostler, supplying food and other provisions for traders, whole caravans of them coming from western India. You have supplied them for twenty years, have seen all kinds of people pass through your own world in Chara. They stay a few days, a week, sometimes two, and then move on. You will see them, some of them at least, on their eastward journey. Thus, you get the news both ways, and news is your main business, not yielding a financial but a personal profit. You glean as much as possible out of every scrap of information, weighing it all against everything you have heard before and even projecting into the future what you will hear and even what you expect to hear. For in this small town there is little else to do, except listen and exchange information.

Yes, of course, there are the local women and there are dances and food and music, which you love, but somehow the world for you ends twenty-five miles outside of town, the physical world you inhabit, that is. Yet the world comes in on the wind, on the breath of others, from afar, from the kingdoms of India where the Mauria emperors rule, that fabulous land of wealth and learning and story, and on the other end of the earth, in the west, from the vast empire of Rome, whose goods are transported, literally, across your doorstep, and whose great emperor Constantine has sent to you the breath of news about his people.

Each month a new breath arrives, to be unwrapped on your doorstep, and you and a few other friends who assemble to sit, listen and give information are the true recipients of this wind blowing from afar, news to be carried even further, along with the information you yourself have added to the travelers' other burdens and from which you receive your own life, a life midway between the empires of India and Rome on the mighty trade routes which fertilize the world and bring their nutrients to others and to you.

A new caravan has come today, though you have heard of its coming for two days already and are prepared for its arrival. Still, there is much to be done, but you look forward to the tea and the ritual toasts under the tents, the blazing fire in a sky of intense stars, and the conversation, stories and information you need to keep you truly alive, the breath of information blown into you.

No. 184: Yorkshire, England. July 22, 1605. [12 hours; $125] You are the housewife of a large farming family, which includes your husband, three children, age six, eight, and eleven, your mother (your father died two years ago), your husband's father and mother, a cousin who has come to live with you, three servants, two milkmaids, three plowmen, two cowherds, and several day laborers, a considerable family, even in your own parish.

Yours is a prosperous family, but there is no leisure for you. You must see to the nurture, training, and disciplining of the children—you are their schoolmistress as well as their mother. You must prepare the meals, bake, clean, wash, and instruct the servants at their daily tasks. In addition, you supervise the brewing, the gardening, the nursing, and at times perform these tasks yourself. And, in your spare time, you will spin flax or wool. You rise at four or five in the morning and you go to bed at eight or nine o'clock.

> In winter at nine, and in summer at ten,
> To bed after supper, both maidens and men.

At dinner, in addition to supervising the servants, you are continually on watch for bad table manners, especially by the servants and laborers. They must not be allowed to talk saucily at the table, must not reach out for food, and must take their share of what has been provided.

> No lurching, no snatching, no striving at all;
> Lest one go without, and another have all.

Though you are a very capable housewife, things do not always run well. Last year one servant got pregnant and you had to resolve the paternity of the child. And there are always beggars who come to your door, asking for work or food or both. How you deal with them is important. You cannot turn them away rudely— that would not be godly of you. Nor can you become the target of their long-reaching network. As in all things, you must draw a middle course, between charity and rudeness. Also, there are the problems of the health of the children and the servants. They are not always well and you are not always successful, though you have learned through your mother and other women, some simple remedies, which you are often successful with. Some calamities, however, are only for God, who, in his infinite mercy, takes and gives. In religious matters you are hardly knowledgeable, though from your upbringing you have absorbed a great deal of biblical lore, mainly through having been read to by your father when you were a child. Now, your husband reads passages from the scriptures to everyone, including the ploughmen and threshers and milkmaids.

Today, you are supervising the servants in the preparation of the evening meal, though a dozen matters lie around in the back of your mind, still other things you must do. It is always a matter of choosing, of judgment, of organization in the complicated world in which you live.

No. 185: Millerovo, Russia. march 14, 1851. [3 days; $200] Now you are seventeen years old, a young, broad and laughing girl who is going to get married. Ever since your parents have told you the svakha, the professional matchmaker has come several times to talk about your future husband. You know who he is, and though you are happy about your coming betrothal, you are nervous with anticipation.

You have seen several of your friends marry and have shared their excitement. Now it is your turn, and all of them are as excited as you are. You know you will spend much time sewing your wedding clothes and singing as you sew. On the dievitchnik (the evening of the wedding) you will pretend to be sad, as all girls pretend; and after the wedding, on the way home from the church, you will endure the jokes about your wedding night and enjoy the banquet prepared in your honor. You will be worn out by it, for it will go on for several days. There will be dances in the meadow, many dances, if you have anything to say about it.

No. 186: Wiltshire, England. August 26, 1589. [4 hours; $65] You are the wife of a poor tenant farmer a few miles from Marlborough. You must tend to the cow and the chickens and your one treasure, the pig, which you feed with whatever scraps are left from your food and send the children into the woods to gather acorns for it.

You must also tend the garden, for your work is an extra source of income, and important, too. You will also increase your family income through spinning yarn. You have to mend the children's clothes, cook the meals, and clean the small, one room cottage. The herbs you grow are for your own consumption and most of the food you raise, although some of it will be sold at the local market, along with what you have spun. Your children have something to eat—for this you are thankful enough— and you have a roof over your head, something the poor day laborer does not have, having to build himself a makeshift shelter somewhere. You work hard, and your children, too.

Church service is almost nonexistent—you do not have the time, and none of you can read or write. This is true of most of the people you know or meet. Everything happens every day, immediately—feed the chickens, milk the cow, tend the garden, spin, clean, and mend. There is no time for anything else, a few moments, perhaps, to spend with your husband and children on Sunday and occasionally the market place and the meetings with others. You feel the land and the houses and the woods with the time of your body. They are a certainty like no other, more certain, even, than God. Now you are out in your garden in the morning, tending it with your eldest daughter. It is late August.

Dear Past Rentals,

This is the life I love, the busier the better. I can't stand sitting around doing nothing, like my husband, that slug of a man, who wants to "relax," as he says, but spends most of his time at home talking to his friends, watching the football games on TV, and sitting outside in the backyard. How could anyone be happy doing that? (Or not doing anything—that's what I think it is.)

I'm not like that. It's a wonder we get along as well as we do. For me, if somehow there's nothing to do, I think, "Oh, oh, something's wrong," and I remember—there's always something I want to do, not mentally, sitting around thinking about this or that, but physically, putting in a garden, keeping the chickens, shopping for the right clothes, helping the children with their homework, cooking, and these are just the basics.

My husband's the problem when I start working, which is most of the time. He doesn't want to pitch in or do practically anything that requires a bit of extra work. I needed your "vacation." I felt at home there, and I had the working companionship with my "husband". That's how I want it to be now, but I'll have to settle for four hours in Elizabethan England.

It seems strange to me how seriously people take their vacations, considering how little they work. The people in England at that time (and for a long time before and after that) could have used a good few weeks of relaxation; they needed it. But today, for most, it seems psychological. People want to do serious, necessary work. They want to feel they're contributing to other people's welfare. But, let's face it, they're not. Most people work for somebody else, and that person makes the money. They're bought off with things, which they are persuaded by advertising that they need. They really need what money can't buy—friendship, love, connection, a sense of being a part of something as everyday as growing some of their own food, washing their own clothes, and even making some of the things they need.

My husband's just one example; he belongs to the empty majority. If he had to survive on his own, he wouldn't last a week. There is much to be done, but the serious things of life are just not done. People are in full flight from seriousness (and even from serious humor). This little journey returned me to the long world of the necessary, one that's been around for far longer than the 1980's or 90's.

Rachel Falk
Age 28. Housewife and part time bartendress
Portland, Oregon

No. 187: Hsi, Shansi Province, China. October 2, 294 B.C. [2 days; $110] Your grandparents used to farm around Taiku, but there were too many people for the land and your parents had to move. They struck out to the west and a little to the south. You were born near the village of Hsi, still in Shansi Province, though your grandparents are no longer alive and your uncles are still farming the Taiku land. Here, the empire of the state of Qin has prepared agricultural handbooks and distributed them to the farmers. They have given you low farm taxes and high grain prices, and in doing this they have stabilized the empire, you believe. Though your father cannot read the government pamphlets, the government information has been passed around through others, orally. He has profited some by them, but more by his own hard work, something all of your family, all of your "people," have known how to do. "Life is hard and hard work is life," you all say, and it is true. The land is not as good as the Taiku land, but with good methods of farming, your father, with your help and the help of his wife, can live. Barley and wheat are good crops, and nearby is the mighty river, the terrible, mighty river. Fishermen come to trade their fish for your wheat, and sometimes you eat well.

Meanwhile, you wander in the hills with the other boys, hunting or just lying in the sun or playing games and drawing pictures in the earth, watching the grasses and the few trees and the farmers on the other hills planting and singing, and singing, yourself, in the autumn and spring, and telling stories, old, old stories of strange people who lived long ago and who did mysterious things with or without the help of others. Today you are twelve years old.

No. 188: Boston, Massachusetts. August 4, 1647. [4 weeks; $325]
You had sailed aboard The Defense four months ago, having impulsively (you are eighteen) signed a paper requiring you to work for five years in Virginia to pay your passage and the cost of your "food and lodgings". You had never been to sea and did not know what to expect, though when you met your new shipmates and heard the stories they told about the crossings, you were tempted to escape, but a fever you contracted before you had boarded kept you there until the boat sailed. Fortunately, you managed to take all your worldly goods and a small amount of food—ten pounds of bacon, several loaves of bread and a gallon of ale, not much for so long an ocean voyage.

And so it proved, though it was not a bad one by the standards of those you talked to when you arrived, just an average one. This did not mean that you did not suffer, severely—seasickness was endemic and several died because of dysentery. You spent eight days riding a storm in mid-ocean, but though there was barely enough food for all of you, you still managed to arrive in fairly good condition, not to Virginia, as you thought, but to Boston, as a result of the storm, which drew you northward.

Now, on your second day in this "city," not much more than a few wooden houses, you walk around, still gawking, almost terrified, at the wilderness you have arrived in. The forests are thick with trees—it would take hundreds of years to clear them—and the strange savages, whom you see walking among the Englishmen, are almost naked.

You have been waiting for a boat to take you to Virginia. It will arrive in three or four weeks. Meanwhile, you have made yourself useful, receiving your food and a place to sleep from a carpenter building a large house. It is early August, and it is almost hot where you are working. There are deer in the clearing near the house, and a fairly large garden is almost ready to be harvested, that is, as someone had said to you, "if the deer don't arrive first and God gives us corn."

No. 189: Saragossa, Spain. March 30, 1094. [3 weeks; $495] You are a slave in the household of Mohammad Al-Kadir, a man of some importance as a merchant in Saragossa and with connections in the countryside. When you were sixteen, you were captured by pirates, who had raided the coast near Anzio where you lived and taken you to Spain, where you were sold to the household of Mohammad Al-Kadir, who treated you well. You lived near the Aljaferia, a building you much admired for its workmanship and beauty. Whenever you could, which was quite often, you visited the building.

A friend of your master Al Kadir had noticed you there several times and, on speaking to you, found out that you greatly admired the beauty of the Aljaferia. He proceeded to talk to your master, and in a few weeks you were apprenticed to a carpenter, with whom you worked for twelve years, until you were thirty. Though you are not a literate man, you have admired the carved and inscribed writing on the walls of many of the buildings of Saragossa and have heard fabulous stories about the other buildings of El-Andaluz, especially of Cordoba. Now, for weeks, your master has been planning a trip to Cordoba. He intends to take you along, if only so that you can see it. You have left Saragossa and are a day's journey out of the city. It will be eight days before you reach Cordoba.

No. 190: Messina, Sicily. June 5, 10 B.C. [3 weeks; $300] You are a cook on a Roman trading ship going to Sicily. You make the trip every few months, spend a week or two on the island, and then return to Ostia, where the crewmen will unload the grain and the other things you have brought back from that place you call "the fabulous land". You are in a small minority on board your ship—most of the crew can't stand the place and always grumble with you about why you find it something to speak well about. But you tell them to go to hell.

You know why, even though you really can't explain it to them clearly. All you know is that the four or five women you visit there are glad to see you. They cook, dance, sing, and take long walks into the hills with you, where you make love and then return at sunset to stay up all night drinking the local wine and beer and getting intoxicated from the incense of the hemp plants brought from North Africa. You love them, all of them, and the others you meet, for after the soft, lapping journey through the Tyrrhenian Sea you need to let out all the body, spread it out in the sun and the hills and fill the land with yourself.

Maybe, in some other lifetime you were born here, and you secretly think you will die here, too, when your time will have come. Now you have spent five days in Messina drinking and making love and singing and talking to everybody. You are sitting on the top of the house of one of the women and looking out in the distance at the few small islands north of the mainland and almost doing nothing, just sitting. It is four o'clock. A bit later the sun will set over the land. You sit there, your mind nowhere. Nowhere. But everything is here for you.

Dear Past Rentals,

Work, what a drag! All these guys out there working their asses off and for what, to buy another TV, get a micro-wave, buy a newer car, go to Palm Springs, or gamble away their money in Las Vegas. Who knows? It's all crazy. These guys don't know what to do with themselves. They're running as fast as they can away from everything that's real, valu-able. Everything disturbs them. Touch them and they shake.

When they have a day off, they don't know what to do. Someone has to tell them what to do. Hell, no one's ever been as crazy as people today.

This cook worked hard when he had to, and when he didn't, he just sat around and collapsed into himself. The way I see it, when you're working, you push everything out of the picture. When you're not working, everything collapses into you again. Most people can't let that happen. They build a wall against it, and therefore the pressure to let everything collapse gets greater and greater.

This cook was what I want to be, a man who knows how to enjoy himself and feels good about others enjoying themselves, too. First, he stopped in town and bought up as much good eatings as possible—bread, cheese, you name it. Then, he walked to the house he'd be staying in, put away the food, sat down, and just looked out at the sea for an hour or so. No one disturbed him. He had done it lots of times before. Then, when he had begun to relax, things started happening, but slowly, quietly, carefully.

His first woman was five years older than he was, and her main interest was the news. For three hours, she pumped him for it. And he sat back and let her, loving to watch how she did it—sudden, staccato-like questions and then long, soft, descriptions of what she and the others had been doing while he was at sea. Then, again, one after the other, she asked her other sharp questions, trying to take him by surprise. But when he was relaxed, he never lost his balance. That's what the real relaxation does for you.

Slowly, over the next few days, people started showing up, friends, a few of his other women, a musician, until the house was humming, softly, with their voices, everyone speaking quietly trying to listen to the whole tone of the "gathering" This "tone" got deeper and deeper. It was as impressive as the sound of the sea at night under a full moon. It gave peace to an already peaceful gathering.

Gradually, people dispersed and then came together, not through any arrangement they had made, but someone knowing a good time when they saw one. And then, after ten hours or so, they went off again on one errand or another, finding their way back when they were finished.

My cook, also, left the house, the gathering, and wandered with one woman or another, or sometimes with a friend, into the hills to sit with them and listen to the wind or see it gently blowing the wheat fields in one direction. There was no rush. There was nothing to do but to be there with someone and with the place, wine to be drunk, yes, and food to be eaten and love to be made, but mostly, over everything the feeling of deep serenity to be fallen into without effort, just an existence.

These people exist, even today, among the many who live, as an American writer once said, "lives of quiet desperation". The few—who don't need much, except each other. They know where they are going, but they are going nowhere. They know what they are eating, but the eating is all involved with everything else. That's what I like to call "style". This man taught me, though he formally taught me nothing. I felt like a young kid who understands in his body the presence of someone secure, who responds to the person who lets the world flow through him like an endless wave.

Mike MacArthur
Age 49. Construction worker
Belmont, California

No. 191: Shiraz, Iran. March 30, 1793. [8 hours; $85] You are eight years old, a slave to a house of weavers or carpet makers. You started working there, almost sold to them, a year ago by your mother. You work ten hours a day in front of the loom, knotting the rugs, tying the hundreds of knots, Senna or Geordis, into the warp and weft laid out on the large loom in front of which you now sit. You know, when you finish, you will get an extra meal, though your fingers are sore from the tying, and it takes months for the three of you, all young girls, to complete a carpet. The masters are strict. They threaten you every day, and the older ones are seduced. But by then their usefulness is gone—their fingers have become too large and they cannot tie as many small knots into the carpet. Allah is mighty, you hear, but the ones who say it are rich or afraid, and they join in the beating of all the children of Shiraz.

Oh, to play a little in the sunshine and to drink a glass of soured goat's milk, to sleep in the sunlight and dream of your mother, not these nightmares of twisted lines and children eating weeds and foul air and leftovers from the rich man's table.

The carpets are beautiful, however, and as the pattern grows, you wait, expectantly, as do the other children working with you, for the finished work, then to be trimmed and washed in the river and laid out on the rocks to be dried; you have seen it done many times. Now, you are knotting the last small piece of a medium sized carpet, and you will soon, this day, in fact, be allowed to go out to the river with the other children to see the carpets washed and to play and walk and swim in the water. Your fingers ache and your stomach feeds on itself. You will soon be free, for a while, at least.

No. 192: Nottingham, England. February 1, 1737. [10 hours; $95] Up to the age of thirty-eight you had first been an ironworker for fifteen years and then in the last five years owned a small business, which is quietly growing. Now, for these last four months, you have developed molds for casting screws, something you think will be in great demand, and you hope to make your fortune this way.

But there are still problems to be worked out. The cast screws are crude. Therefore, you have been working on a refinement in the molds, which, you hope, will require that less processing be done after they are removed. You have constructed the molds so that when the screws have cooled considerably, you may release them, by the hundreds, where they will fall into a long trough and be polished through being turned inside a centrifugal barrel containing a fine sand, the sand then drained from the barrel (to be used again) and the screws inspected and improved upon if they are imperfect.

There is great excitement in this work, but there is much worry. The consistency of the iron needs to be improved, although the melting process is almost perfected because of the high-grade coal you use. And the molds need to be replaced every few months because they wear out. But all this is overcome by the excitement of the process and the conversations you have about it in Birmingham with the "club," the friends in your inventing-manufacturing world you see every three weeks.

Now you are in your workshop, preparing a new mold, which will produce an even more refined screw, and waiting for your friend, and helper, Samuel Franklin, to arrive.

No. 193: Leipzig, Germany. January 14, 1368. [6 hours; $75] Your parents, merchants in Bruges, have sent you away to the University of Leipzig, where you are studying law. You have been here for two years and, of course, are bored. The entertainment consists of singing hymns, and even that activity is restricted. You may also play with a soft ball in the courtrooms of the inner buildings, but that is all. These account for the legitimate entertainment; the other activities are all done at a risk, meaning reprimand, dismissal, fine, or corporal punishment.

But all the students have given themselves to the illegal, if only out of boredom. The law is tedious. The professors are a single monotone of befuddlement. The lecture rooms are cold. And the lecturers must be bribed. Money speaks, as it does in your native Bruges. Locked in your small rooms all day, you feel like prisoners, as indeed, in a way, you are.

It is no wonder that you go out on long drinking sprees, and half or three-quarters drunk, are carried home by a fetcher or carrier, for the roads are dangerous and even for men, protection, especially at night, is necessary.

You are in bed this January day, reading the text on mortmaine, which you must be able to vomit forth in June, months from now. The building is quiet. The snow falling outside makes your world even quieter. You are used to this quiet, for it releases the pent up dam of memories of your native city, your family, the people you know and whom you have not seen in ten months. And you realize how great your longing to see them has become, as more and more they press in upon you, all of them, from your native city.

No. 194: Near Nachez, Mississippi. November 6, 1847. [25 days; $825]
You were born in a cabin, about twelve by fifteen feet, no glass in the windows, of course, and a door that was barely that. When it rained, some of the water came through and soaked the few blankets you were given. You are a slave girl, the daughter of a slave woman, coal black and big boned, who worked the fields every day, except Sunday, and who left you to be raised by your seven-year-old sister until you were old enough to work the fields yourself. "There's no lock on the door, but where can you go," they used to say, and "Watch out for the water moccasins. If they get you, you done. Won' hardly dig a hole fo' you when you done." But your mother, you and the others in that cabin, all eighteen of you—stinking, penned up on rainy days, sleeping, breeding, even dreaming sometimes—have stayed together, telling yourselves

stories about the river, singing when you could, when the coughs didn't start going round and people start dying, young and old.

These were your people. You could feel the rhythm in the trees and in the creak of the old shack when the wind was blowing and the rain was coming down, sleeping next to each other to get warm, or dry, and stealing what you could, and sometimes, passing it on to the others—food, liquor, clothes—begging, stealing, growing your own for a little bit more, shuffling around to please some white man's weakness, showing off or playing dumb, all for one purpose, to stay alive, to make living slightly better. And you could do that well, stay alive, as well as could be expected under these times, in this land where you had only yourself and your people to hold you together and sing about, and the storms and the sky and the snakes and the river and the trees and the little hills you walked over in the hot, Mississippi sun. Thank God you were black— you would have been dead by now if you had been white.

You're sixteen and you've learned fast, as everyone has to learn out here, in the darkest hole in the world. First, the white boy, one of the sons of the poor whites who lived nearby and came to visit and look, caught you down under the trees and had you. Then some of his friends came up and had you. You were had by at least a half dozen of them, but after the second one the only way they could have you was to give you food, or jewelry or just cash, which you didn't know what to do with anyway. But you learned.

Now, one of the cousins at the main house is having you. Yes, you worked yourself up, but you know where that will get you. When you're old enough, they'll throw you out "No more use out of this poor filly. Worn out. Throw her on the dust heap and all that. And you know it, too, know more every day about how to get every bit out of them.

Now the nephew is after you. He's taken you into the kitchen, but you don't do much there, just wait till he calls you, and you go in the right way, reluctant, and smart, in a stupidly outward way, to his room, where you've learned to take what you can get while you're smiling stupidly at him. Yes, you learn a lot about these people and their empty, useless lives.

Now you're in his room and he's telling you about his new watch and his trip to New Orleans and describing the city there and asking you if you would want to go there for a while, with him, of course, that weasel who doesn't know a hole when he sees one. And you know exactly what to do.

No. 195: Rabat, Morocco. September 13, 893. [9 days; $575] You are a forty-two year old itinerant carpenter who has traveled throughout the southern Mediterranean coast from Tunis to Tangiers. Your reputation has always been held in high esteem, and you are known as the "carpenter of bones," an expression which has stuck to you because of your large-boned frame, over six feet tall. You look out from this large body through surprisingly small and quiet eyes, the inheritance of your grandfather, a mullah of sorts, who loved the quiet journeys of the hashish pipe and the sounds of good music and poetry, which he sang and recited for hours. Though you could play the ud with some facility, it was among the carpenters you discovered your hands and the beauty of working fine woods.

First, there was a six-month apprenticeship with an instrument maker, but you outgrew him quickly. Then, you met your real teacher, who taught you how to build, houses at first, then fine tracery and cabinets, even to stonework and the designing of fountains. It was the love your father had instilled in you of shade and quiet, of courtyards and the sounds of fountains splashing in the warm air that moved your soul and pleased your teacher.

For five years your labor was light because it was the labor of your love, your love of labor, and though you were praised highly by many, you were quiet about your work, preferring the slow, complete growth to the rapid, pretentious, outward reputation. Such was your master's and your father's way, and such is yours. Allah had given you these hands, and it was his will that you should have such skill and vision.

Unfortunately, your master died—suddenly. Bad food he had eaten killed him. He was forty-eight and light-hearted as a gull over water. And though you inherited his work—you were too good not to be his successor—his enemies, who could not raise themselves against him when he lived, moved against him now, through you. Though you returned their words with calm assurance, their combined strength was too much for you, who had labored only for quality.

And then you made a serious mistake. In a moment of directed anger, you insulted a wealthy, powerful man in Tunis, and there were threats, which your master's enemies were only too happy to encourage. There was no hope but to become an itinerant carpenter. One night you left, with your tools and a small, sturdy mule to carry everything.

In your journeys over the years you have outdistanced them all, those poor, jealous men of Tunis. Your reputation is significant. Everyone knows you and many have seen the work of your hands. There were quiet times you spent, for months even, working for somebody in Algiers, in Oran, in Kasserine, all through that immense land of dates and grain, in the splash of fountains and in earshot of the cry of the muezzin, their profound voices carrying over the stillness of the houses and the densely packed noises of the streets.

Then, slowly, you began to collect and cultivate and seek out the great craftsmen of your trade. You were not disappointed, even when ten years later you returned to your native city and found some of them secretly waiting to greet you. You are now on your way to Rabat, that great city, to work with Ali Ben-Rusha Hazid, to carve some fine doors for a rich man and to spend the wide, expansive evenings at his home and talk and smoke and eat and walk. Nothing could be finer. You have arrived in Rabat and are at the threshold of his dwelling.

No. 196: Liuan to Shucheng. August 3, 762. [4 days; $215] You are a young girl, nine years old who today is taking a walk to Shucheng from your village Liuan for the purposes of shopping in the market in Shucheng with your mother and grandmother, and also visiting your cousins in Shucheng. You are now half way on the road to the market. You will arrive before evening, stay the night and the next day and night with your cousins, then shop, and return home. The mountains are beautiful. You have never traveled them before. You are, of course, looking forward to visiting your cousins.

Dear Past Rentals,

How simple things were then. Now, I get up and must think about many, many things, especially about time. How long does it take me to prepare breakfast? How long to get dressed? How long does it take to wash the dishes? Forty-five minutes after I'm up, I'm out the door and on my way to work. Forty-five minutes—and I think of each thing I do as timed.

And all the objects I must take care of because they can't take care of themselves. The car needs to be tuned up, filled with gas, its oil changed. The refrigerator must be defrosted every two months. We live in a time when time needs to be ordered within us, when everything fits into small boxes called minutes or hours or weeks. What would we do without clocks, schedules, or appointments? I think we would starve. We would lose the knowledge of who we are—that's what I mean by starve.

Therefore, I have yearned for the large period of history in which people did not have clocks, and when they arrived, they arrived, and when they slept, they slept, and when they talked, they did not say, "It is time for me to return to my classes, my work, my wife, my thinking." There was another kind of "time," un-mechanical, that came with the bodies we were born into.

I came into this world screaming. What did I know of time? Gradually I was fitted to this clothing. I learned what it meant to be late. I learned that "coming on time" meant that no one said anything critical of you, and that coming late meant strange looks, withheld greetings, hesitations, an absence of the natural. And all of the time-bound world became a fortress against the other time, the time of the whole world flowing around us.

I wanted the rhythm of work, the rhythm of the body. I wanted to learn, rather than read about learning. I wanted the territory, not the map, the feeling in the body that journeys represent. I wanted my body to know that I had traveled somewhere. I wanted it to tell my mind about how the journey felt, and I didn't want my mind to answer back.

Therefore, I took this short journey, walking all the way, singing and talking and looking on the road from Liuan to Shucheng in China in 762, which in terms of people's conception of time could be 1762 BC. What does it matter? Our time did not begin until recently.

Most of all, it was a ritual journey, an understood activity, buoyed up by everything this young girl knew around her. Yet the excitement of seeing her cousins, the noises and colors of the marketplace, and the shapes of the mountains through which she walked filled her body with true food, a nourishment which made her feel that she and the landscape through which she passed were not separate from each other, that all was a whole and that she was not only who she was but something much larger, fuller, absent of time and schedules and the anxiety to hurry beyond into some created beyond because there was no beyond; there was only here, here at every instant if there were instants.

The idea of the self emerges recently in our history. They say that before the middle of the eighteenth century a sense of self was not entirely known. After about the middle of that century or somewhere around that time, give or take a century, people attempted, through immense effort I believe, to raise this fiction of the self above the world, controlling the world in order to see "themselves" as separate, a created entity, but, unfortunately, ending up like Antaeus, who lost his strength as he became detached from the earth. This act of folly makes us believe that we are detached, that the world is merely something we "create" rather than "integrate" into ourselves. And therefore, we lose respect for both the world and for ourselves. Because of the separation. Because we have created time as the servant of this dislocation.

I have written something about this that I would like to share with you, for it is related to the folly of separation, the illusion, as the writing says, "the grand illusion":

Philosophical Considerations

"I come," he said, "through windows of weeping, with a heart of woe in a week of Wednesdays."

"Think of us," he said. "How are we separate? When we are born, we imitate everything. We need everything. We sleep next to the world, the way light sleeps next to the wall or paint to the building.

"But when we stand on our own two legs, then we tremble, for that erecting denies everything. We tell ourselves we were separate. But we are never separate. We know this. And

even in denial.

"How dare we? Oh, I don't mean it that way (pacing about). I mean what I say—literally. How can we dare this, this separation? It is not in the nature of things. There would be no recognition and the sense of self—an illusion. To travel we take everything with us, at once. Is there another way? No, we are not separate. Separation is the grand illusion, a cosmic assertion, an enormous denial. But necessary. Yes."

But sir, I don't want to know about your assertive lack of assertiveness.

"What smile of light," he said (beginning again) could fall on those eyes, which were truly windows of weeping. Oh, Eden was nothing compared to this."

He lifted the balloon his daughter was holding and like a pillow of air or delicate smoke rings pouring into the absent heart, threw it forward into another future, through the distance of hope.

"To believe you," I said, "would mean lifting everything. But with what lever? There is no lever. It is, if it existed, only an illusion."

"The grand illusion," he replied, noticing the stark drawing of a house on his daughter's notebook. "And yet this folly. This folly."

And so it is with us, this newly created sense of time or rather the time of the machines, more and more particular, more and more exacting. What we have created and given a name creates us in the image we have given it and at the same "time" drives us into smaller and smaller, more and more precise worlds, while the great world which our bodies have known for an immensity lies undiscovered, always redefined and held at bay and therefore feels to us as fearful as death. That is the absence, in the vacuum we have created with our machines, the necessary machines, so we think, that will save us.

Hopefully, the other journey shall restore the world through our action, the delta of the river and not the abstract direction to the sea.

Francis Pace
Age 94. Retired travel guide
Norwich, England

No. 197: Gabon. Near Iguela. September 27, 1449. [3 weeks; $550]
You are a Portuguese sailor who, through your "criminal" actions on board the ship the Tres Marias, has been put ashore on the coast of Gabon as a punishment for your transgressions. You have been given three loaves of bread, some drinking water, and your clothes and allowed to keep your knife and a few minor possessions. It is your third day on the coast of Africa and you have met some people you have traded with before, or rather, people whom your people have traded with. You are almost out of food and water and you have wandered into their village around evening.

You stand looking at each other for a while and then you break into laughter. The laughter goes on, almost uncontrollably, for at least twenty minutes. So powerful is your state of hilarity that you collapse on the ground from it. The moon is coming up over the trees and you point to it and continue laughing, unable to stop. They, too, infected by your gesture, have begun to laugh and cannot stop. Finally there is silence, a kind of awkward silence, since neither you nor the people you have met speak a common language. But there is hope tonight, and you know you will sleep and eat well in this village where you have, in some way unknown to both of you, communicated.

No. 198: Somewhere near Niangara on the Uele River, Zaire. January 3, 1879. [3 hours; $80] You are a twelve-year-old Pygmy boy, now hunting with your small band along the Uele River. These last two months you have hunted monkeys and birds, but occasionally you will go after wild pigs and other, larger animals, that is, when the occasion presents itself. You have watched the men prepare the poisoned arrows with which they will kill or incapacitate the animals they hunt, though you have not been allowed yet to participate in this ritual. This night, after eating the remains of the monkey you killed today, you will sit around the fire or even in the darkness, and sing your songs, all of you together, touching and swaying and singing, each singing his part to the whole chorus of your life in the rich world of the forest which gives you life, the beautiful, wonderful songs which are part of you, songs of the forest, your songs.

> Dear Past Rentals,
> I like to sing. I sing in a chorus but not in a church. We meet once or twice a week and rehearse. We give concerts where we sing everything from fifteenth century masses to gospel music. And we enjoy what we do. Our audience faces us and occasionally, if we get a big enough crowd, it may even surround us on the stage. But there's always the audience and there's always us. The audience's job is to listen.
> Now in other places and times and cultures the audience did not only listen; in fact, it probably participated, danced, sang, and played musical instruments. There were no performers and, as a result, no audiences. Participation was the music.
> What does this division between performer and audience say about us? Perhaps nothing. But perhaps it says that

when it comes to entertainment, we like being passive, letting the experience flow into us, at least most of the time. We are beguiled into believing that we are the critics, that we decide if we do or do not like what we are listening to. Perhaps the music and the experience come through, or perhaps they do not. The fact is that we hire people to do things to us, to act upon us, and we fire them by not coming to listen to them.

But in some cultures there is no hiring and firing, no concept of employment, only a recognition of entrance into the social and the religious world, into the rhythms of things. Culture, then, is not entertainment but ritual integration. How far we have removed ourselves from that participatory world can be seen all around us. How many of us get together and sing just because we like the sounds we make with our own voices? How many of us have grown up from birth singing? How many of us are not embarrassed by bursting into song at a moment's notice or when we feel like singing? I would imagine very few of us, and I would even lay odds that less than one in a thousand people do sing in public, spontaneously.

It didn't used to be this way. I can remember the Italian teenagers on the stoops of the brownstones in Manhattan harmonizing. I can remember people meeting to sing folk songs. I can remember children's games cast in the form of songs. And, of course, the jump rope rhymes and the lore passed down from one child to another, heard from God knows where, are all part of a singing world. This world, like the culture in agri-culture, has disappeared. Today all songs are imitations, in an almost limitless, regressive chamber of echoes. Spontaneity is planned and audiences are manufactured.

The pigmies are a communal people. They have a close sense of kinship, of personal bonding. Communication takes place on an immediate level, person to person. No machines come in the way of that connection. As food is shared, so music is shared. Everyone is a singer, from the youngest child to the oldest grandparent. And there are no tone-deaf singers in this society as there would not be in ours if we grew up listening to and participating in music.

At night they sit around the fire and talk or tell stories and sing. The words are known or improvised and the music allows everyone to enter it. There are no leaders; everyone is a leader. And though there is no pre-conceived music, everyone knows the rhythm, shape and structure of what he sings.

I often wonder what would become of us if we abolished audiences and "sang" our lives. We would certainly hear one another, know one another better. And we would feel a part of a larger life, not be the passive recipient of another's planned assault on our inmost lives. This participatory world would help us to speak (sing?) our minds, say more resonantly what is on our minds, make us far more democratic than we can, at present, imagine ourselves to be, we who think of ourselves as citizens of a democracy, in many ways a sham.

Therefore, people like the pygmies have something for us. They were a bath of cool water after the sweltering heat of a Mississippi summer. And they have led the way for me to be one of the few (and hopefully there will be more) who will sing, spontaneously, in public and without shame.

> Roger Flim
> Age 31. Truck driver
> Denver, Colorado

No. 199: Cologne, Germany. March 10, 1163. [35 minutes; $30] For the last few years you have been engaged with a group of men and women, pious people who have renounced the church as an unholy institution and who claim that they themselves are filled with the holy spirit and can do what they will since, quoting St. Paul, "All things are pure to the pure." Your lover, and the common lover of all the women in your group, is a man named Arnold, who has given you and the others the voice of the holy spirit through his body and who is the most powerful of men in his speech and his feelings for holiness.

It is an understatement that all of you adore him, and when you are close to him, feel that you are filled with the transcendent spirit of God. In feeling this way, you are able to do what you want, allow to emerge from you, like an invisible smoke, a feeling that comes from some deep, spontaneous part of your body. Because you are filled with an enormous sense of freedom, you look upon the church, its monks, priests, institutions, and monasteries, as symbols of rigidity to be cleansed by the healing forces of the free spirit. To this end you live your lives, the lives of the poor weavers of Cologne, half-starved and mostly lice-ridden, filthy in body but filled with an overpowering spirit which causes you to tell others that they are impure and that only you can offer them the salvation (through Arnold) of what they most desire, salvation, but salvation from the church and its followers.

It has been coming for a long time, your martyrdom. You have known it, though you have not known when it would descend upon you. But three weeks ago you were denounced as heretics. The monk Eckbert of Schonau has debated your ideas with you for several days, and you now, after this false and fraudulent process, will be burnt at the stake in a matter of hours. It is the decision of the Holy Inquisition.

In the face of these dreadful trials, you do not feel the fear of losing your earthy life—indeed, you are filled with a greater and greater ecstasy and power of creative love, which shines, even more fully, from your spiritual and bodily lover, Arnold, who has held himself firm and overflowing in his actions and words during these days of trial. You are now bound and led to the stake.

No. 200: Glagow, Poland. April 30, 1788. [3 days; $175] You are now forty-eight, not an old woman, but one approaching old age, though still very much intact. Yours was an arranged marriage to a well-off lumber merchant. You have lived comfortably for thirty years and have two grown children, a girl and a boy, the girl well married and the boy also and working for his father in another city.

For the last nine years you have spent your time at home, arranging the household, directing the servants, and attending meetings of one sort or another, a quiet and increasingly deadly existence, though only recently has this deeply entered your conscience. You are growing old, you are hardening, your children have moved away, your husband has many other interests, and your friends talk of nothing which really effects you.

So now you are drawn back to your childhood, wandering in your mind through the forests of Poland, mentally navigating the small town markets with your mother, singing songs with your friends near the Oder River on summer nights, and remembering the young boys who used to speak to you, you, the shy, young girl with her averted eyes and her long tresses.

And now, one who had loved you then, when you were sixteen, the young "scientist-engineer" as you used to call him, has passed into Glagow. You have seen, talked to, and met him several times for coffee here or there, talked long about everything, his life and yours, his scientific interests, his adventures in Sweden and Norway on the geological surveys. And now you find yourself again falling in love. What is more, his wife is gone—she died several years ago—and he is passing through town and will be here for only a few more weeks. What should you do? He wants you to leave with him. You, also, want to go. But to leave all this? What would your children say? Or do you really care? What to do?

No. 201: Minkovitz, Russia. December 3, 1920. [2 months; $225] You are a ten-year old girl who was born in Minkovitz. Your family and you are Jewish. Your older brother, who several years ago went to live and study in another town, was killed in a pogrom, murdered, along with many others, by fanatical, drunken, anti-Semitic Russians. Your parents, relatively well off, have a hardware store in town. Your father's sister has immigrated to the United States. Two months ago she wrote, asking your mother and you and your older brother to come, as soon as you could. All must be done secretly. The business must be sold, the escape route planned, and the crossing of the border into Romania arranged.

It is December. The river is frozen. It is early morning, hardly light enough to see anything except the ice. You are leaving your home to cross over many rivers, many countries, a big ocean, and much land. You stand by the door, huddled in your coat and warm boots, ready to depart with your parents.

No. 202: Chillan, Chile. November 16, 1817. [2 hours; $40] You have been a shoemaker for forty years and you have seen the Spanish come and go. The one shining moment in your life, as you remember it, is your acquaintance with the great Bernardo O'Higgins, liberator of your country and savior of your land. You did not participate in any of the battles, though you supplied many boots to O'Higgen's soldiers, brave men, all of them. You made shoes for O'Higgens when he was a young boy, and for years after that you continued to make shoes for him, until today, when you proudly presented him with a new pair of boots in honor of his becoming Director of Chile. You are sitting with your friends in front of your home and reminiscing about your acquaintanceship with the great general.

No. 203: Verona, Italy. September 28, 1642. [6 days; $425] You are a lady's maid for a wealthy family in Verona, and still you are not treated well. The food is often bad and the kitchen scraps and leftovers reserved next for the dogs. You sleep in a small room and on a bed that is often infested with lice. You must get up at dawn, make the fire in your mistress's chamber, find the cook and, at the right moment, when you sense that your mistress is awake, enter her room, help her dress, and then bring her the breakfast, a meal which you would be glad to devour.

Your family had not treated you well either. Both your parents were peasants from a small town outside Verona who managed, through hard work, to eke out a living on a small piece of land. You were the bright one in their lives, though your resentment towards them is overwhelming. You are a lady's maid of a high, rich family, and you have identified more with your employers than with your parents. In your anger you think, "How could I have been born to these two crude, simple people? They did not understand me. They have never understood me."

At first you had great hopes, but after three years here, living under conditions only slightly better than those at home, you have become dissatisfied, bitter and conniving. You have begun to steal food from the kitchen. In your mind, your stealing (and you do it out of necessity) is dangerous for your employment but necessary for your existence. You need the food and there is certainly enough. But the pride and stupidity of this family you work for surpasses that of your parents, who were not very educated and had little wealth, if any.

There is one hope in your life. From the little schooling you have gotten, you have managed to acquire more here. There are books in the library—poetry, science, religion, history—subjects that have begun to open your heart and mind, if not your body. You "borrow" the books, returning them as soon as possible. Your mistress certainly does not miss them; to her, books are of little importance. But to you they are a treasure, and with a borrowed candle (or a stolen one) you read.

Your other great pleasure is music. Sometimes, when you accompany your mistress, you may hear the music at the balls she attends, standing against the wall to the room in which she dances, listening as if your ears were your whole body. Long after the music has stopped, it continues inside you, in your'step, your voice, your fingers, which still make lace as they did in your childhood.

Tonight, while you are reading Petrarch's Canzonieri, your father, whom you have not heard from in six months, enters and announces sadly and almost on the point of tears that your mother is very sick. You must come quickly. You put on your torn and shabby coat and leave, knowing that the time has come to see your parents clearly, to find, finally, what you are in them and what they are in you.

Dear Past Rentals,

To be ashamed of your parents, to think that they are nothing, to believe in your great need for them and to despise them because of something not given to you in childhood, some part of you that didn't completely grow up, that yearns to be filled, fulfilled, becomes a terrible burden. Into this endless hole you pour your anger and self-pity and call up nothing but lack. They didn't give me this or that. They didn't hear me when I called to them. They didn't understand me when I spoke, when I needed them. And thus you reduce them to nothing or you raise them in you through your negative poundings. And thus, you, rather than they, suffer, for their suffering is now something beyond you.

So it was with me. Leaving home wrenched me away from a need that I didn't see for years. I thought I had freed myself, that others would complete what my parents could not, others more like myself. But, alas, they were not my parents, they were not the familiar people I had known even down to the gestures, the breathing, the familiar intonation in their speech, even to their touch and smell, known them as all children do more clearly than they had known themselves.

Yes, I found another life. I found friendship, companionship, even love of the kind that requires marriage and children and the solid work that gives dignity and sustains us, providing a purpose to our existence. I have helped some and failed with others. I have eaten my share of dirt and had my portion of triumph. But that old, poorly defined cloud hung over me and never left. And therefore everything I have done has been tinged with a feeling of the incomplete.

Therefore, I now come to your entry. I did not care if I was to enter the body of a young woman, even if she was some family's dishrag. Her problem was my problem, and, I am sure, it has been a problem for many. What was our problem? Simply, our parents were good, ordinary people of average or below average intelligence, and we were not. Somehow, mixed into the genes, the intelligent ones found us. I could read at three. I could do my mathematics at school in one-tenth the time it took the others. I was so bored that I read whole books in the classroom. I argued with the teacher. I created mathematical models of actual events, or so I thought. I learned fifty times as much Spanish as I was taught. And, alone in a field, I noticed the insects, watched the clouds go by, looked at how people walked, talked, ate, even slept. There was too much to learn and my parents couldn't help me.

This young woman was like that, but where I was successful, she was on her way to dying. Fortunately, she had access to a library. Fortunately, her employer never read; the books were there for show. If they had known she had taken a book, they would have fired her, thinking she was stealing it. The idiots! Of course she didn't steal them. How can anyone steal ideas? They are absorbed into our lives and become the lights by which we see, extending our bodies into the darkness and revealing, at the same time, our ignorance.

These idiots for whom she worked were like her parents, a continual reminder of what she had not received from them. It was not hard to see through their pretensions, their simple desires to be loved, obeyed, flattered, looked at with approval. But for her it was all a hollow sham, an opening emptiness which had only one exit, and that was into the library, her one salvation.

But there comes a point, as it happened in my own life, when we must truly understand and forgive our parents for not being what we needed them to be. It is a giving up of something, a recognition of limitations, without which we would destroy ourselves, a giving up of the infant inside us which wants everything immediately and is helpless.

And she did, though she didn't know how she managed. The weight she had been carrying around for so long became too much of a burden for anyone to carry. When she saw here mother lying there in her miserable pile of straw, filthy, in the dim light of the single room she had lived in, when she saw her vacant eyes roving about the room for the image of her daughter and her feeble hands reaching out to touch her through all those years, to hold the now-grown woman who had come out of her womb and whom she had fed and cared for, this young woman, who had despised her mother, who had carried all that weight of anger, suddenly collapsed in front of the woman who had raised her and laying her hand in her mother's hand, said nothing, but looked up, as a child might look up at her parent, and smiled.

That was all that was necessary. Except also to turn her smile up toward her father, toward those simple people who

could not understand her but nevertheless had loved her.
And so my burden was remembered and lightened again,
though it was not so terrible a one as that of this woman's. I
remember the words of Christ on the cross, "Let this cup pass
from me." This bitter liquid we all must drink, the circum-
stances which we are born into and over which we have no
say and must live with and forgive.

> Shiv Shikri
> Age 72. Mathematician
> Calcutta, India

No. 204: Paris, France. August 28, 1572. [2 days; $125] On the 27th
you heard the cries of those inciting you to turn against the Huguenots,
the heretics, the spoilers of the faith, the servants of the anti-Christ,
the murderers of the church, etc. You knew these people, saw them
every day on the street, tidy and clean and not generally poor. They
ran many small businesses and employed a great many people. What
never had felt like envy before rose up in you that day, listening to
those who ordered you to destroy these blasphemers of the faith who
had corrupted the church and the virgin, the mother of God.

For a while you felt the deep pull of conflicting emotions
within you between your experience and something you only
then felt inside, the greed and frustration of your life; for you
were a fishwoman who slept in a small, poor, dark, badly smelling
room with others of her kind, who worked hard every day and
fought for her life, every day of it. A deep, inner protest rose up
inside you. Only until then had the enemy been lacking, and you
thought, "Why couldn't I have seen all along what they were up
to? What blinded me to their power, their secret power?" It
was not true; you knew it was not true. But you wanted it to be
so, to find something within you that allowed the larger angers,
kept so still and secret for so long, to emerge, but not against the

real enemies, the rich and powerful who claimed your life and controlled it. That was too fearful to admit to yourself.

Still there was a question mark in your soul. You had seen them working hard, too, these Protestants, who were generally prosperous and generally righteous. But your body called out; it needed revenge for all the evil that had been forced upon you by great powers so poorly understood. You turned with the crowd, first to set their homes on fire, and after that, as the looting and drinking grew all around you like another fire and you saw them beaten bloody and begging for mercy, a deeper, more fundamental hatred, rose up in you and you began with the others to kill and kill.

How long the killing went on you could only guess, perhaps five or six days, perhaps three—it did not matter. God, so you told yourself, had exacted his punishment. The bodies lay in the street, hundreds, brutally beaten and stripped of their property, their lives. You had also killed, though you could not recall, at first, the faces or the bodies of those whom you had turned upon. Only later, as you sat quietly in your poor room after the violence and before the sun rose, did you begin to remember—the men, the women, the children even—whom you had murdered.

No. 205: London, England. November 29, 1593. [2 hours; $75] You are a cobbler's wife, who manages her household of two rooms above her husband's shop in Chick Lane near Smithfield, a street, because of its filth, popularly known as "Stinking Lane". On rainy days you must be careful to avoid the long patches of mud in the street and the garbage and wastes sometimes thrown out of upstairs windows.

The smell is certainly, awesomely awful—when you care to recognize it—but most of the time you put it out of your mind. For water you go every day to the well fifty yards from your home. The privy is almost as bad as the street itself, and when the weather is too miserable to go to the outdoor one, you must content yourself with the chamber pot, which you empty twice a day. You buy wood from the woodcutter, who comes twice a week. You must be aware that he is coming, or you will miss your two or three day's supply, and there will be no warm food and your husband will grumble and, if he is in a particularly bad mood, strike out at you. (The scar on your left forehead is proof of it.)

But there are people to watch, even in Chick Lane, all kinds of them, the local residents and also the casual travelers, who have increased in number in the last ten or fifteen years. Soldiers from the wars passing through. Beggars by the barrel. (My God, the whole place is thick with them!) Card sharps and dicers and pickpockets or cutpurses. To go out at night alone, especially for a woman, and even for a man, is dangerous. Thieves lurking in the deep shadows would cut your throat as soon as cut your purse. No, you must go home with others from the tavern. And you must avoid the offal in the street, especially at night when it is difficult to see by torchlight. You rise early and go to bed early, curled up with your husband and your two children on the single item of luxury you own, a bed you inherited from your grandmother's brother.

But there is life here, not in the miserable countryside where the plowman talks on and on about his smaller and smaller interests, his usual horses and cows and pigs and the weather for corn and oats and last year's foal. No, you don't want that. You want to be here, in the noise and daytime bustle of people moving and arguing and cozening each other. That's the world for you, and for your husband, the cobbler.   Now, you are making your way to the butcher's shop to buy a small piece of meat for the evening's meal, and you will subsequently spend at least two hours along the way, gathering vegetables, a chicken, if possible, and oil for the lamp, which you use only twice a week. You will listen to the news—which drifts in with the weather, at least two months old—and re-tell the old news, which has been through its rounds at least a dozen times, each time embellished and wrought into a mystery which you cannot help expanding.

Dear Past Rentals,

I don't know. It's all gone. All that excitement of people crowded together, groaning, shrieking, puling, children poking around into everybody's business and adults stopping their work for a moment and gossiping, all that world is gone. Instead, we have the suburbs and the news on TV and artificialized speech that floats through us like some mechanical ghost of language. And because we live in this world and now and then in some other, we have become ghosts ourselves, at least as I see us.

"Let me go back there," I pleaded with my husband, "if only for two hours. I can't stand it here. The neighbors are only forty yards away or only a short walk across the street and yet we don't see them. The neighborhood is deserted in the middle of the day. Everyone has gone away. How did we deserve to live in this place?"

My husband, who is a newspaper columnist for the Frankfurter Algemeiner, perhaps the best paper in Germany, replies softly, "You're right. Of course." And then, as he walks away, mutters, echoing what I have just said to him, "This stinking century...." And thus he has said, "Go, before it's too late, and the whole world is just an empty grid and you and I and the others we used to call human beings have disappeared or become ghosts." That's what he would have said if he had wanted to linger and argue. But he has work to do, and he is off to do it.

I know it was filthy there. You could smell the stink inside the house and in the street; you just had to get used to it. Surprisingly, I've been in neighborhoods which have been noisier, but that's because of the machines and people forced to talk above the sounds of the garbage trucks or the air-planes overhead or the jackhammer down the block. But out there in Stinking Lane, right in the middle of a fired-up London, people's voices wove themselves into what we might call an "aural tapestry," the children's screams of delight, the babies' insistent callings, street hawkers, knife grinders, neighbors calling out to one another across the lane, and the sound of a cart, crammed with firewood, passing through for me with its two day supply. The sounds were both distinct and pleasing, having the same basic pattern but varying at every moment, like water over rocks, infinitely different but always the same.

Then, to descend to the market, where the noise was more intense, human noise or the noise of animals, some being slaughtered in the backs of the stalls and others having been carried piecemeal from the slaughterhouse (or "sham-bles" as it was called), fresh and still hot from the knives which had, only an hour ago, carved up the cow or the pig. Chickens were bought live and killed on the spot, plucked and handed over for a shilling, not much more.

Into this vast confusion (which was no confusion to the good woman I had become) I descended (or perhaps ascend-ed?). I could feel the pulse of life here, people arguing for the sake of, or the joy of, arguing; people carrying great pots of food balanced on their shoulders between the ends of a pole; men pissing in the corners or between buildings or relieving themselves in the public outhouses; infants sucking at the breast in their mother's arms as she carried them, loosely dangling and asleep they were; men at eight in the morning already drunk; men throwing firewood under the great ket-tles of the rending pots; old men and women playing skittles or sitting on a stool, watching the whole pageant; mice and rats scurrying between the legs of the populace, stomped on or beaten with sticks if they could be beaten; card sharps *playing with marked decks for the stupid or the unwary; a whiff of infant shit and then, a second later, it falling at my feet into the horse manure which littered the cobbled streets.*

I made my way to one of many stalls which sold chickens and began to haggle, having known the owner for at least ten years, perhaps longer, and knowing that the price would be the same. But the desire to bargain was irresistible. The chicken was the same as all the chickens I had bought, a poor, underfed, tough bird which had survived the foxes and the abuses of the children and the miserable food it found hunting and pecking in the farmyard. But before I left the chicken merchant, I exchanged some old news about the Papists who, we both felt, littered the streets and should be driven out of England, for had they not attempted to overthrow her majesty our queen, Elizabeth? And were they not plotting again to return a Catholic monarch to the throne and subject us all to the horrors of their inquisition? Never, we both vowed. It would never happen. But we knew we would still have to keep our eyes and ears open, just in case.

As I moved toward the next stall thirty yards from the chicken seller, I stood aside to let an equestrian pass me, a young man, obviously rich (he had a horse and was extremely well dressed) who had pushed his way through the crowd (not easy to do, even with a horse), perhaps having forgotten the way to his tailor or his tavern or wherever he was going. He shouted at everyone in his way to give him some room and even raised his whip to some, his horse splattering its load in the middle of the street. Some cursed him under their breath, others out loud, risking punishment but knowing they would of course escape the constable. One had only to watch out for the spies, who would report you for cursing or swearing at someone as wealthy as this young man.

The oil merchant's wife and I had been companions for years. We grew up together in Stinking Lane and had laughed hard and told stories that made us so taken with laughter we couldn't get off the floor and had nursed each other back to health a dozen times and had, more times than could be counted, talked ourselves silly and gossiped 'till the cows came home.

She was worried. The price of oil was threatening to go up, just a halfpenny a quart but serious enough for these times. The Portuguese had threatened to cut off the sale of their olive oil and the whalers were having a difficult time with hunting and supplies were running low and there was a shortage of fat, and even the tallow for candles would be in short supply.

But half way through her litany of worries, she started to smile, and looking at me straight in the eyes, started to laugh. And pretty soon she was doubled up with laughter, which shook her whole overweight body. She said, after she had got some control over herself, that she "had enough lard on her to supply half of London." Everything she had told me was not true. Business was better than ever and there was no shortage, no threat of the Portuguese and no problem with the whalers.

Then, I told her, in the most serious voice I could muster, that my husband had noticed a spreading crack on the last bit of leather he had bought. He had tried to soak the leather in oil but it did no good. He had cut it for lasts and the lasts split and his leather knife along with it. Then, I told her that he had gone out and gotten drunk and then I winked and she threw an egg at me, hitting me square in the right eye so it ran right down my blouse and onto my dress. She was lifting up another egg when I said, "No, sweet Mary, for the love of our husbands, please. It's a small mercy that doesn't return a joke when it is given him." Her face changed from bewilderment to anger, mock anger that is, and she started cursing me with everything in her vocabulary. "Your father's this and your mother's that and your great uncle had gout from eating his farts and your great aunt had one too many oysters and dreams of a young man in her bed and "your neighbor threw back to your husband his own endearments to her" and so on, for at least ten minutes. Looking at me all the time to see if the gleam in my eye matched the gleam in hers, she went on. It did, of course.

After she had finished, I handed her a bottle for the oil, which she filled and handed back to me. "That will be two pence, hap 'ne," she curtsied, and we both laughed again. "What news of Thursday? Will your husband finish the shoes he is making for the deacon's son, who will be confirmed on Sunday? Or will he waste his time talking, like ourselves?"

"If gossip were money," I said, "we would all be as rich as that cursing gentleman on the horse (pointing in his direction, for he, too, had stopped to gossip and chatter and didn't care where he horse was standing).

And thus I went home and then went home again, to Bremen, to the "impoverished" suburbs where the streets are so clean you could eat off them and where the people do not talk or laugh or gossip or argue or bargain or shop in the midst of a multitude of smells and sounds, where, in short, people feel their bodies and know they are not ghosts.

Maria Schmidt
Age 39. Manufacturer's representative
Bremen, Germany

No. 206: In the mountains west of Chunking, China. April 19, 642. [8 hours; $95] You are a man alone, some call you a hermit, who lives in the wild, empty mountains west of the great city of Chunking. You have lived here for fifteen years, starting when you were twenty-four, through sickness and health, trusting in the spirit and way of the

Tao, and "growing," as you say, "every instant". "Where is my home?" you ask and reply, softly, almost sadly, "There is only the echo of the mountains."

Every day there is the garden to be tended with your hoe, whose handle you have replaced now at least five times. It is the only tool you need, except for your rice bowl and your one knife, sharpened on stones you have found near the river. "The echo of my voice comes back to me through the whole mountain," you say.

They come to visit—the curious, the literati—to paint for a few weeks, "tourists in paradise," and to talk, always to talk, though here are some wise ones, too. You don't need them, these city people, wealthy people, with their servants and their gourmet tastes, though you don't repel them either. They are like the wind and the leaves, a part of your breath. You could not love them more, though love, if you had to think about it, is certainly not the question. There is no question; perhaps there is only the answer. Answer and question—how foolish, unraveling the thread of thought. And when you get to the end, what is there—nothing. Better to listen, walk, be surprised, eat good food and drink mountain water. "My guts are whole and healthy, and you can't tell my feet from the earth," "When you get to your destination, who will greet you?" you say to these travelers, a certain twinkle in your eyes, belching loudly.

Today, the stream nearby loudly pours its water over the rocks, for spring has been here for several weeks and the heavy clothing of winter is put away. You are back to the comfortable sandals you made last year, and you will go where the stream goes, or perhaps where the clouds, the small, delicate ones which are now passing, will go.

No. 207: In a field outside of Le Puy, France. August 6, 1846. [2 hours; $45] The woman you secretly wanted fifteen years ago is back in your town. She was married to a man in Aubenas, who died of scarlet fever. She survived and has come back to live with her mother and father in a house on the edge of the village.

You loved her from a distance when you were fifteen, a certain kind of love, the love of a young boy. But somehow her image all these years has remained with you, through all the other loves you have had, none of them entirely satisfactory. "It's difficult with, it's impossible without," you say, you have said, but now you know. You are thirty and have still not gotten married, though you could have, several times. You realize that her image was there, somewhere, and it prevented you from taking that final, irrevocable step.

More important, however, she is back and is working in town in the small dry goods store her parents own. You have said hello to her a few times. But she has seemed too fallen into her loss to acknowledge you, though you imagine all kinds of things. You have let months pass, seeing her only on occasions when you had to come into town, holding back with an almost impossible will.

But recently you have noticed a change. She seems to be coming out of her state of loss. The last two times you met, she actually smiled at you, not a smile of embarrassment, but a full, sweet, completely open smile, quickly withdrawn, however. Then, she was back to her practical shop work, as had been her way with you. Yet now that she knows why you come, you have begun to see her opening herself more. Suddenly, one day, you see her out in a field, walking, by herself. You feel your heart beating harder. Then, as your body becomes accustomed to this new state, it begins to calm down, and you walk toward her.

No. 208: Czarograd on the Dnieper, Russia. May 28, 1461. [2 months; $1250] You are a wood carver. You make, in the fashion of your city and region, beds, chairs, carved figures, ikons, and other things which you will sell in Constantinople, a long and perilous journey down the

Dnieper River, dragging your boats along the banks to avoid the many cataracts and finally reaching the sea, where you will continue your journey toward that city of cities. There you will trade what you have so laboriously transported and return with treasures, in turn to be traded in Kiev, around the lakes near the Gulf of Bothnia, in Smolensk, in Novgorod, everywhere you are able.

Some of your compatriots have remained in Constantinople, seduced by the charms of that rich city, but you have made the journey four or five times and you are content with your life along the Dnieper, your mother, your God, your homeland, content also with the people you know and have known along the route. You welcome even the dangers, for they are a change from the long, mysterious winters, which hold you tightly in the warmth of your dwellings. You are thirty-three and have two children, two boys, ten and fifteen, who will follow you into your work. Now, one of them, the elder, Boroslav, will accompany you this time to Constantinople, on the long and perilous journey.

The day has come to leave your wife and others. They are crying at the door and will continue to cry until you leave—that is their way. Your son is silent, looking intermittently at the ground and then at the broad, long river down which both of you will journey. The sun, now on the flat earth, has just risen. Your materials are in the boat, along with your companions, and the food you have taken packed tight for the journey. You look back at the city receding in front of your eyes and row downstream, with your son, also, at the oars. You remember the previous journeys and you hope, and pray, for your successes. The river is beautiful. It will be a good day for all of you.

No. 209: Elche, Spain. December 2, 1588. [2 months; $750] You left Elche, the small village south of Alicante, when you were twelve. Your father sent you to Valladolid in the north to be apprenticed to a goldsmith. For twenty years you lived in that northern city, beyond

Madrid. There, you became a respectable goldsmith with ties to the gold, which had poured into Spain from the mines of Potosi in the New World and had made Spain wealthy and made you, too, comfortably well off.

But for the last ten years, the urge to return to the south, to Granada, to Andalucia, to the homeland of your birth, has grown, until it has become an avalanche, sweeping aside everything in your life. You know, the more you think about it, the more you ponder it night after night, that you must return.   O n e night, only ten days ago, you hurriedly packed, told your wife and your wife's grandmother that you had important business, and left. You have been travelling day and night, though the pace seems slower than you could ever imagine it, torture, as the distance slowly shortens between you and Elche, the home of your childhood.

The past comes pouring in, a piece here and a piece there, mingling, like a broken mirror re-united with the landscape around you, now becoming more and more familiar, flooding you with fear. Will it be the same as you remembered? Will everything be there as it was for you in your childhood? Is there ever a return, to the sea of the south, to the olives, the wine, the crowded shade of the white and tiled houses and their narrow streets, and the songs and voices around you, filling you, flooding you with the twelve years of a life that wants to drown you in its caress?

> *Dear Past Rentals,*
>
> *How many of us—removed for decades from our child-hood homes, having moved far off and started anew and settled into another life, have, to say it clearly, left child-hood—have drawn into us that created image of youth we yearn to re-create in order to mold that time of our lives much nearer to our heart's desires? All of us, I would say, or,*

at least, most of us. Thinking back to that childhood which we create according to our desires, we endow it with a feeling of warmth, comfort, and, above all, protection. We know we will be safe in that expanded womb—warm, safe, and protected.

That feeling—we might say, a universal one—goes by the name of nostalgia, a common word in several languages. The world we had entered so rapidly at the explosion of adolescence, with an arrogance that temporarily protected us, wears off after the years pass, and we feel, everywhere, the uncertainty of our daily life, even if we invent explanations, create grand theories, and distribute long, involved prayers as temporary bribes. Then, that created world of our past revives in us, a warm cradle of thought and feeling in which we wrap ourselves against the chaos of the uncertain.

The forces which produced this nostalgia extend further, into some kind of invented historical past. Nostalgia rises in us as "the golden age," the belief that life has degenerated from some perfect time when there was justice, certainty, and above all, a luminous comfort. The Greeks had it and the Romans also, and it emerged fully developed in the Renaissance. Recently, the myth of progress has turned it in the opposite direction, toward the future, where, in the dim distances, it hovers like a dense mirage.

> "Let man be perfected of his ancient ills.
> So say the doctors and the doctrinaire"

—so said the poet and the revolutionary. And so said many in the nineteenth century and some in the twentieth. The golden age this way and that, whether toward the past or the future, forms a part of the feeling we carry within us and which we call nostalgia.

Thus, nostalgia could be called our "created history" or

our created "end of history," for it exists out of time rather than within it. The journey of your man from northern Spain ("1588. Elche, Spain") toward the village of his childhood was a journey powered by nostalgia, which some revolutionaries, fearing that softening of effort, would call "decayed dynamite". Of course, this Spaniard did not find it. But the shock was enough to produce in him a partially defensive revival of that myth, even while he was there, buried alive in his past. Of course, everyone would want this journey, and, hopefully, everyone should visit his childhood, at least once, like a kind of pilgrimage to Mecca. Only then can we see it for what it now is and once was and experience the blending of wish and reality, a feeling that grows within us all the time.

Robert Liu
Age 58. Epidemiologist
Shanghai, China

No. 210: Changan, China. March 22, 123. [14 days; $895] You are a twenty-three year old Hsiungnu tribesman. The Great Wall of China, extended by the emperor Wu-ti, has kept you from the rich cities of the empire, but now again you are ready. You were not as powerful as the imperial forces, but you had one advantage, mobility. With your sturdy steppe horse, your ability to ride even asleep (an ability nurtured from childhood) and armed with a powerful bow, you were a formidable threat. And as the Han empire began to weaken at its extremities and as your need for grazing land and your population increased, you felt even more compelled to attack the rich cities of the other side of that great barrier. Now you are at the gates of Changan, and there will be nothing to stop you. You await the rewards of the wealth which lies inside.

No. 211: Somewhere north of Panama in the Pacific Ocean. 1579.
[4 hours; $90] You are John Bibbons, a sailor who has been at sea for nineteen months with Francis Drake, whom the Spaniards call El Draque. You have sailed across the Atlantic, no easy feat, down through the Caribbean, along the east coast of South America, and through the howling seas of the Tierra del Fuego, where two of the three ships didn't make it, one going down and the other turning back to England, and then up the western coast of South America, to Valparaiso, to continue your scavenging of "the Spanish dogs," whom you all hated, then plundering more gold and silver from the coast, then finally plundering the greatest booty of all, a Spanish galleon, Nuestra Senora de la Concepcion, a little north of the line, eleven tons of silver, 180 pounds of gold, 13 chests of valuable plate, and several more chests filled with jewels. You had boarded the galleon itself— good times these with a captain such as Drake.

And now the seas are calm in the tropical waters off Costa Rica. Now is the time to lie idle, look out at the calm rolling of the small swells, the coast going by so very slowly, and smoke your long pipe, which you have had, thank God, for years. Now is the time to drink with your shipmates the brandy and wine you took off the last ships, good wine, good brandy, and relax, and not think too much about getting back to England. Somehow you will return.

It is mid-afternoon. You are sailing parallel to the Costa Rican coast and sitting next to your shipmate Alan Curtis, listening to stories and telling them also, stories you have told again and again about the voyage and the danger and the glory of the future, cursing the Spanish king and drinking the health of the captain, who has renamed his ship The Golden Hind, getting warm and mellow from the wine and brandy, and staring out at the lush coast slipping by you as the sun falls slowly to your left, the dolphins and needlefish off the bow now leading you northward through the Pacific, the sun shining with its soft, afternoon light on the palm trees lining the shore. Soft. A soft tropical light.

You fall into a long, solitary meditation in which all the events of the last year mingle with one another and the coastline and the dolphins and the waves and the creak of the laden ship bring everything together within you into a warm globe of water. There, in the center, looking out, you sit, breathing the whole of that warm and dreaming coast.

Dear Past Rentals,

A man who dreams, dreams many things, all different at different times in his life. I'm talking mostly of daydreams, but you could also include the deep ones at night. The main thing is the way they move from one picture, one feeling, one situation to another, without any reason but moving. The gaps don't matter. It's only where you are now. If you pasted them all together, you'd have what you'd want to call a montage of daydreaming. But they seem to be bits and pieces, even though something holds them together.

But this guy had two journeys going in him. One was the broken up journey of his daydream. The other was the voyage with Drake, the famous captain knighted by the famous Queen, knighted for bringing her back lots of booty. The sea journey of The Golden Hind we know about, everybody knows about this. But that sailor's other journey was the one I wanted to experience. For me, it's all like walking down the street in a residential district at night and looking into the houses (not house peeping, but just looking as you pass by). It's curiosity. I would have liked to have gone through a lot of people's daydreams, even though they might all be boring, or seem boring. I just don't feel they are. So, as you can see, that's why I choose this sailor entry.

His daydreams for those few hours went all over the place. But they were set up by the mood of the day, the tropical waters off Panama, the quietness of the ship, the Spanish wine and the Spanish brandy and the food he had just eaten. Because they were contented daydreams, they allowed room for "discontent," "pain at a distance," discomfort, like going to watch a horror movie in a comfortable theater.

I think I'm going to give you a frame by frame motion picture of at least a small part of that sailor's daydreams. If I had to give it all, I'd be writing a book. There were too many things going on.

The sound of the water against the ship, a slapping of water against wood. A slight creak in the masts. A door opening and closing somewhere. The shoreline in the distance. Palm trees swaying. The sound of gulls overhead. A door opening in the ocean. A stairway going down, down. Follow it. A large room lit with a thousand candles. People dancing, wearing beautiful clothes. The music from The Three Graces, a tavern in London. A waterfall of rum pouring down one of the walls, which was really a series of tiered rocks. The music stops. The Queen speaks. Her mouth moves, but no words appear. Only silence. The dancers go on, in silence. No music. Dancing to the quiet. The song is "My Lady's Gone to Heaven".

The squawk of a gull, hopping on the wheel, steering the ship, a gull the size of a man, steering the ship toward shore. The speed of the ship increases. Faster and faster. At the speed it will be going when it collides with the shore, it will run up the beach at least fifty feet. Faster. Faster. The wind is blowing. It blows in pieces of long-remembered faces. My mother. My aunt Ellen. The face of the butcher two doors from my room on Benbow Lane. Faces empty of voices, of words. The empty words are blowing the ship closer to shore. They can almost be heard now. Almost.

The rum bottle falls onto the deck. It is empty of rum but filled with a light of many colors. When I look closer, I see the bodies of all the voices trapped inside. They have wings, like the gull that is steering the ship. They wander, slower and

slower, blindly aimlessly, in the small pools of liquid remain-
ing in the bottle. Slower and slower. They are lying down,
prepared for sleep. They are sleeping. The ship has stopped
moving toward the shore. It is turning away. The sound of the
waves. The swaying palm trees. The gentle wind. Faces in the
distant clouds.

I hope that gives you some idea of this guy's mind while
he's half-asleep. You can see there's some unity to it all. The
ship and the ocean are there, and out of it he brings in famil-
iar faces, good times, the Queen, etc. The main thing about it
all, at least all I've told you so far, is the feeling, the touch of
the daydream. I can't really give you that. It would mean
that you were there with me in this man, and for that you'll
have to take the trip yourself. But listen, that's the key to the
whole thing, the touch, the feeling part. He could feel the
music down there in that room under the waves. He could
touch the waves scrolling up on the shore, the way he could
touch his own hair or the rough wood of the railings on the
ship. And he could feel the music of the waves, the music of
the ship accelerating toward the shore. Feeling. Touch. That's
what it was most about. Maybe that's why I like going into
the daydreaming part of it all. Maybe that's why I chose this
sailor. It brings me into my own body and, I might say, into
the "body of the world" and "the body of others," and that's
okay.

Manfred Manx
Age 37. Contractor
Pittsburgh, Pennsylvania

No. 212: Adelaide, South Australia and Queensland. March 5, 1831.
[8 months; $725] You came from Swansea, in Wales, of your own
choice, not having been in any way a transported felon, to Adelaide,

in Australia. And you made the dangerous voyage, four long months from one port to another, rats and poor food following you inside and outside your body, the ports swarming with thieves and the ship swarming with lice.

You made this trip, at eighteen, foolish and excited, for the sake of some woman four years your senior who had promised you—you forgot exactly what she had promised you—her body, money, freedom. You can't remember now, not even what she looked like, though when you arrived she deserted you within three weeks and you never heard of her again. You still don't know why you came.

You have been here for ten years, first in Sydney, then in Melbourne, and finally in Adelaide, as if you were working yourself around the continent. You have begun to wander, getting some money inside you for a while and then going-that's been the story of your life these last ten years. But you're still young, and you feel best when you begin your journeys. For the last few years there were trips up the Darling River northeast of Adelaide, beautiful and wet country, good for the sheep, and there was water there, too, and, at times, the weather was cold.

Now the dry areas are calling, the lake country north of the city, the finder's Range, Lake Ayre, Lake Torrens, Lake Harris, Lake Everard, and beyond Lake Ayre, the rivers that feed it, and beyond the rivers the Simpson Desert and the headwaters of the Diamantina River.

This is where you are going, lured by an unknown reason to a place where there is almost nobody, lured by an illusion to lose yourself in that vast land and to wrest some meaning from it by some sense, some pull in you, larger than the land itself, a voice out of the land and from the land to pull you back to what you always wanted to be, perhaps part of something without the overlays of two thousand years of habitation and the comfort of Swansea and the quiet hills of Wales. Perhaps this is why you have set out on another long journey, with your mules and your guns and your provisions—again toward the unknown.

No. 213: Decatur, Illinois. August 11, 1927. [3 days; $175] You grew up as a street punk in East St. Louis, always a street punk, from the time you were eight, gouging cigarettes and nickels from kids younger and smaller than you, stealing for the fun of it, and when there was someone you didn't like, especially someone who talked back or who was a lot smarter than you and who looked you straight in the eyes, you brought him to a dark alley and kicked him until he begged you to stop, till his blood stained the bricks. Though you were always poor, you hated the rich. Yet at the same time you envied them, wanting to grab what you could get and run. Where, you don't know.

And so the inevitable gang was formed, three of you first, all with the same basic anger, the same feelings of weakness, the same ambivalence toward the rich and powerful—fear and admiration.

You got smarter and worked your way up to being a bank clerk in East St. Louis, for four years, wearing the starched, white collar and the newly polished shoes, six days a week. But how long could you take it at the money they paid you, enough to allow you to walk along the sidewalk on Sundays and notice the rich in their new cars—envy and anger, the story of your life. And the women, who would give you nothing but condescending smiles, never a tumble, which made you more and more angry.

But you stayed on for another year; you watched the comings and goings of money, the locking up of the vault, the bills pouring in, the money changing hands, faster and faster. And you learned to read the faces on the depositors, hardly willing to let go of their small earnings, anxious and nervous around money, money which they might lose by just giving it to you, the bank clerk, who had to account for every penny which crossed his counter.

Then, inevitably, you learned to read the others inside the bank—clerks, supervisors, the vice-president, the guards, everyone, slowly, carefully, quietly, planning everything, reading everything, calming your anger for years, for one explosive few hours of life again after all the embalmed smiles and quiet yes sir's and thank you's you gave out, carefully, like the money you earned—watching, that's what you did, like a dog quietly looking for crumbs in the kitchen.

Then, on August 5, 1919, at eight o'clock in the morning, you entered the bank, as usual, but this time with a gun in your hand, forcing the president to open the safe, where you took out $75,000, all in small bills, pushed the money into a sack, and forced them all into the back room, locking the door behind you as you fled out the alley, around the corner and into the forgotten parts of South St. Louis, to your hole, your tiny room, and back to the life of your childhood.

You waited. You stayed hidden, spending little, planning to leave for South Carolina, where you had a friend waiting for you, then to Boston. You were alive, triumphant, and cursed them all, remembering their faces etched on your memory, every last detail. Now you had it.

But unfortunately you didn't know anyone in Boston nor in North Carolina either. You felt lonely. All your friends and your memories were in South St. Louis, bound up in the neighborhoods you had roamed. You felt you were a kind of king in the pecking order of the town but forced to flee his subjects. Inevitably, you were drawn back, by a force you could not, in all your days, explain, knowing you would be caught—too many people knew you—but you were drawn there nevertheless, the sap of East St. Louis running in your veins.

The third day back someone spotted you. There was a reward. Your picture was everywhere, but you were too busy returning to notice. The jury found you guilty. You were sentenced to twenty years in prison in Decatur. Now you are in a cell with another bank robber, looking out through the bars at the town nearby, not even thinking, only looking, longing for the streets of East

St. Louis, longing to beat up the bank president, the police, the judge, and that whole world you didn't make, you didn't even care about.

No. 214: Florence, Italy. September 14, 1233. [One day; $85] You are a peasant from the countryside around Florence who has, knowingly, sold part of his harvest outside of the jurisdiction of this city and has now been brought before the magistrates to await his punishment, which, he knows, will be severe—the lash, and a heavy fine, which will burden him and his family for years to come.

You stand before them and watch their faces—good, powerful men, jealous of their prerogatives, their city, the laws they have imposed on all men within their confines. You prepare a defense which you know will be of little value, though you need to say something about the needs of your family, your village, and the exacting laws of the florentines, which you consider unjust, though you can do nothing about them, only bend your head, acknowledge their laws, and beg for their mercy.

No. 215: Central Italy. June 3, 499. [3 weeks; $325] You are a member of Theodoric's army, which had maintained hegemony over all the Germanic kingdoms and through which the Roman traditions were perpetuated and maintained. Starting from Florence, you are on your way to Sienna to deliver a message to a subaltern of Theodoric's, but for you the real purpose of this journey is to observe the bright, warm, rich, indeed luscious landscape through which you will pass and to look at the wealth around you, a wealth which you are eager to partake of, though as yet you do not know how you will fulfill your glorious desires.

You give yourself to the journey, your horse well fed and your provisions ample, for now, with the hope of a fine meal in Sienna and a journey which, you know, will open you up to the wealth of these Roman people you so much admire.

No. 216: The Netherlands, The Hague. March 1, 1673. [4 hours; $65]
You were always good at mimicking others. Even from an early age, you caught their voices, their gestures, their walk, and even their silences. And, to increase your talent, you were rewarded. You always performed, sometimes in front of your parents and their friends, at parties, sometimes alone in your room, for yourself, or for your imaginary audiences. All through your childhood, even through your university years, in school and at home, you performed, imitated, and mimicked others. And with practice came a more and more precise observation. People of all kinds—cripples, athletes, street sweepers, garbage collectors, street musicians, clerks—nothing was beyond your observations and talents.

But after college, after your parents were killed in that fatal fire—the fire which swept away your longing to mimic, at least for a few years, after that fire which left you with an emptiness, an unfillable emptiness, an ache, even in the cells, which left an infinite sack to be filled, always filled—you fell from the fortunes you had known, fell farther than you even knew at the time you fell. After a few years you could say of yourself only that you survived, somehow and not with anyone's help. Your friends, your parents' friends had all managed to "disappear," not in the body, of course, but in those subtle meetings with you, able to leave, on the doorstep of your body the hint of distance without the statement of it.

And, of course, you felt their turning away in their fear, their reluctance to attach themselves to someone who they knew could, with such perfect skill, turn himself into them, even to creating the illusion of their double, the one you knew they feared so much and therefore had invariably turned up in their dreams looking just like you.

It was after this period that you decided on total anonymity.

You left Amsterdam—where you had lived for so long, learned so much, known so many people—and moved to The Hague, a place where you were completely unknown, even in so small a country as the Netherlands. There you took two terrible rooms, small rooms whose walls pressed against you until you could not bear them any longer.

You took them, perhaps, so that you could assert your self? Did you have one? What was it? What was the real self? Did you ever have a real self, one you felt secure in summoning? One that sat by your bedside at night, telling you everything was all right, that you in your positive, central place, wherever that might be, were secure, impregnable in your selfhood? You looked for it for a long time, two or three years, living in those small rooms with hardly a table or a candle. There, finally, in an agreement with the voices that surrounded you, you ultimately accepted all the selves you had, the selves you imagined, or created or imitated because, of course, there was no real one yet who said, "Here I am forever."

You were, indeed, the composite of all the people you had ever become. From your youth. From your modeling of others, even of animals and inanimate objects. There must have been something strange in your early childhood, as you reached back for it, remembering. (You could even imitate that self, yourself, that child as you saw him now.) Your parents must have also, like their friends, you thought, turned against you, removed themselves (as you had "re-moved yourself" to The Hague), and you had absorbed that withdrawal, into a distance which allowed you to see others, glue yourself onto their lives, become them, too. You were like a duckling who at birth never got fixated to any one mother, but rather attached himself to everything that came his way, became the entity so deeply, even to the thoughts, the life history, the love and petty poetry or comedy or tragedy of that particular being.

You had finally found this out, and you made a decision, which was the only decision you felt you could make. You would make your fortunes through the only talent at your disposal, one that involved something so deep it could not be explained in words, rather could only be acted out, and then no one would see it, only yourself.

You began with a merchant on the other side of town, someone who would not know you in any way and whom you could keep at a great distance. You bought the clothes he wore, the shoes, the cape, and the lace. Then, you began following this man, learning his speech, listening, inwardly, to the drift of his mind, its rhythm, its silences, its intonations. Wherever he went, you went. You got as close as you could, even into his bedroom. You listened to him on the privy. You listened to him in the shop, talking to customer after customer. In short, you learned the business from him. You could, in fact, have become him.

This first encounter was a great relief, for it brought back that submerged talent, which had been lying dormant for years. You watched and waited, and finally saw your chance. You intercepted a large shipment of money and managed your imitation so well that neither the giver nor the merchant could tell who had made off with it. You were now able to move to better rooms, eat better, dress better, create the costumes of those whose double you became.

And so it went. The disease was incurable. More and more, you became other people, held them up without their knowing it. You became richer. People knew you, yes, but not as your original, only as the person you made them know, who was someone in their heads, projected onto them, though your skill at deceiving them was more a matter of mimicry than of deception.

But now there is a woman you have fallen in love with, your nemesis, a dream, you think, of your downfall. Four months ago she seemed to be looking heavily in the direction of another man. You studied her carefully, and you paid particular attention to the man she was watching. Fortunately, he went away. You didn't find out where until a few weeks ago. But you had arranged a "chance" meeting two months ago, and now you and she are almost on the point of getting married.

However, there is one problem which you cannot sweep away, and it is the problem of your identity. Who are you? How will she "know" you? Who will she "know" you as? And how will you arrange your life? You have been tormented with this dilemma for many weeks and you have resolved to tell her the truth, hoping that she can bear the revelation.

CATALOG INDEX

(asterisk following entry indicates response letter)

50: Prato, Italy (near Florence). 1428 *

51: Hangchow, China. 1377 *

52: Manchester, England. 1877 *

53: Starting from Bario, Kalimantan, Borneo, Indonesia. 1877

54: Oviedo, Asturias, Spain. 283 *

55: Near the present town of Theodore, Queensland. 7005 B.C.

56: Medellin, Colombia. 1936 *

57: Asuncion, Paraguay. 1819 *

58: Maoping, Zhejiang Province, China. 1978 *

59: Haddad, Sudan. 893

60: Chiente, Chekiang Province, China. 1687 *

61: Carupano, Venezuela. 1921

62: Mozambique. 1502

63: Near Belen, Brazil. 1504 * *

64: Kadiri, India. 1697 *

65: Near Wellington, New Zealand. 1698

66: Yedo (Tokyo), Japan. 1750

67: Slightly northwest of the Cape of Good Hope, South Africa. 1504 * *

68: Kurashiki, Japan. 1461 *

69: Burgos, Spain. 1703

70: Buenos Aires, Argentina. 1903

71: Michurinsk, Russia. 1749 *

72: Mienyang, Hupeh Province, China. 1105

73: Suippes, France. 1765 *

74: Near Kas, Turkey. 18,861 B.C. *

75: Kirkuk, Iraq. 1861 *

76: Cuenca, Ecuador. 1889 *

77: Besalampy, Malagasy. 1773 *

78: Wucheng, China. 1231

79: Marsh Harbor, Great Abaco Island, Bahamas. 1841

80: Budapest, Hungary. 1916 *

81: Near Thessaloniki, Greece. 1775 B.C.

82: Porto Velho, Brazil. 548 *

83: Near Arequipa, Peru. 829

84: Somewhere around Waddan, Libya. 27,853 B.C.

85: Wuhu, Anhwei Province, China. 1497

86: Maiduguri, Nigeria.. 1784 *

87: Malatya, Turkey. 1374

88: Chingpien to Chihtan, Kansu Province, China. 548

89: Taegu, Korea. 1501 * †

90: Bucharest, Romania. 1916 *

91: Naples, Italy. 1921

92: Wrightsville Beach, North Carolina. 1881

93: Warsaw, Poland. 1925 * *

94: Brno, Czechoslavakia. 1843

95: Borobudur, Java. 901

96: Bogota, Colombia. 1903 *

97: Harrisburg, Pennsylvania. 1911 *

98: Chicago, Illinois. 1893

99: Rajamundry, India. 1558 *

100: St. Petersberg, Russia. 1841 *

101: Bjorno, Sweden. 847

102: Srem, Poland. 1779 *

103: Chinan, Shantung Province,
China. 1791 *

104: Pontivy, Brittany, France.
1722 *

105: Medellin, Columbia. 1802

106: Heidelberg, Germany. 1822

107: Near Wellington, New Zealand. 1701 *

108: Amersfoort, Netherlands.
1605 *

109: Yedo, Japan. 1747

110: Tomot, Russia (on the Aldan
River). 1834 *

111: Heves, Hungary. 1899

112: Turbat, Pakistan. 775 *

113: Hanchung, China. 831 *

114: Cangombe, Angola. 1631 *

115: Columbia, Pennsylvania.
1846 *

116: 200 miles west of Omdurman,
Sudan. 1903

117: Lerwick, Shetland Island,
England. 1790 * * *

118: Bristol, England. 1919

119: Ploiesti, Romania. 1659

120: Gent, Belgium. 1699

121: Cremona, Italy. 1448 *

122: Cairo, Egypt (Part I). 1372

123: Cairo, Egypt (Part II). 1372

124: Kobe, Japan. 1491 *

125: Livorno, Italy. 1778

126: Yagodharapura (Angkor),
Cambodia. 1241 *

127: Norwitch, England. 1889

128: Hull, England. 1700 *

129: Pontefract, England. 1685 *

130: Halmstad, Sweden. 1629 *

131: Guadalajara, Mexico. 1701

132: Rennes, France. 1705 *

133: Utrecht, Holland. 1618

134: Augsburg, Germany. 1502

135: Venice, Italy. 1499 *

136: Madrid, Spain. 1788

137: Granada, Spain. 1572 *

138: Catania, Sicily, Italy. 1648 *

139: Karnak Egypt. 2134 B.C.

140: Torino, Italy. 1983 *

141: Luxor, Egypt. 1483 B.C.

142: Ur, Chaldea, Iraq. 1875 B.C.

143: Kandi, Benin. 669

144: Somewhere near Moura on
the Branco River, Brazil. 752 *

145: Near the present town of
Burgos, Spain. 15,602 B.C. *

146: Neander Valley, near Dussell-
dorf, Germany. 27,847 B.C. *

147: Southeast of Bandaberg near
the Burnell River, Australia.
1307

148: Bakhtaran, In the Zagros
Mountains. 1225 *

149: Near Cambridge Bay, Victoria
Island, Canada. 1889 *

150: Hyrynsalmi, Finland. 1259

151: Nanyang, Honan, China.
103 B.C. *

152: Arhus, Denmark. 1700 *

153: Greifswald, Germany. 1557 *

154: Satun, Malasia. 335

155: Genoa, Italy. 1116

156: Los Teques, Columbia. 1886 *

157: Adelaide, Australia. 1784

158: Sinop, Turkey. 1708

159: Atlantic Ocean. 1679 *

160: Yermolayevo, Ukraine. 1779 *

161: Alula, Somalia. 1887

162: Bialowieza, Poland. 1921 *

163: Coventry, England. 1731

164: Talsi, Lithuania. 1833 *

165: Galap, Palau. 1025 *

166: Lini, China. 986

167: Pompeii, Italy. 195 B.C.

168: Somewhere near Choyren,
    Mongolia. 1501

169: Malanjoe, Angola. 1927

170: Southern Algeria, Tassili-n-
    Ajjer Plateau. 12,902 B.C.

171: Rome, Italy (The Vatican).
    1281 *

172: Gulkana, Alaska. 1889 *

173: Algiers (in Punic Ikosim: Owl
    or Thorn Island) Algeria.
    278 B.C.

174: Bousso (on the Chari River),
    Chad. 766

175: Tabati village, Cameroon.
    1544 *

176: Changsha, China. 1388 *

177: Calcutta, India. 1757 *

178: Konya, Turkey. 1368

179: Hankow, China. 978 *

180: Kiev, Russia. 1241

181: Crotone, Italy. 1093

182: Pula, Dalmatia, Yugoslavia.
    162

183: Chara, Persia. 327

184: Yorkshire, England. 1605

185: Millerovo, Russia. 1851

186: Wiltshire, England. 1589 *

187: Hsi, Shansi Province, China.
    294 BC

188: Boston, Massachusetts. 1647

189: Saragossa, Spain. 1094

190: Messina, Sicily. 10 B.C. *

191: Shiraz, Iran. 1793

192: Nottingham, England. 1737

193: Leipzig, Germany. 1368

194: Near Nachez, Mississippi.
    1847

195: Rabat, Morocco. 893

196: Liuan to Shucheng. 762 *

197: Gabon, Near Iguela. 1449

198: Somewhere near Niangara.
    on the Uele River, Zaire.
    1879 *

199: Cologne, Germany. 1163

200: Glagow, Poland. 1788

201: Minkovitz, Russia. 1920

202: Chillan, Chile. 1817

203: Verona, Italy. 1642 *

204: Paris, France. 1572

205: London, England. 1593 *

206: In the mountains west of
    Chunking, China. 642

www.ingramcontent.com/pod-product-compliance
Lightning Source LLC
Chambersburg PA
CBHW021212260626
47172CB00002B/394